About

Helen Lacey grew up _____
Green Gables and _Littl_____
childhood classics insp_____
when she was seven yea_____
her horse. She continued to write with the dream of one day being a published author and writing for Mills & Boon is the realisation of that dream. She loves creating stories about cowboys and horses and heroines who get their happily ever after.

USA Today bestselling author **Natalie Anderson** writes emotional contemporary romance full of sparkling banter, sizzling heat and uplifting endings – perfect for readers who love to escape with empowered heroines and arrogant alphas who are too sexy for their own good.

When not writing, you'll find her wrangling her 4 children, 3 cats, 2 goldish and 1 dog... and snuggled in a heap on the sofa with her husband at the end of the day.

Follow her at www.natalie-anderson.com

Liz Fielding was born with itchy feet. She made it to Zambia before her twenty-first birthday and, gathering her own special hero and a couple of children on the way, lived in Botswana, Kenya and Bahrain. Seven of her titles have been nominated for RWA's RITA®; and she has won the Best Traditional Romance in 2000, the British Romance Prize in 2005 and the Best Short Contemporary Romance in 2006.

The Hidden
COLLECTION

Hidden Past

HELEN LACEY

NATALIE ANDERSON

LIZ FIELDING

MILLS & BOON

First Published in Great Britain 2020
By Mills & Boon, an imprint of HarperCollins*Publishers*
1 London Bridge Street, London, SE1 9GF

HIDDEN PAST © 2020 Harlequin Books S.A.

Date with Destiny © 2013 Helen Lacey
The End of Faking It © 2011 Natalie Anderson
For His Eyes Only © 2014 Liz Fielding

ISBN: 978-0-263-28128-6

MIX
Paper from
responsible sources
FSC™ C007454

DATE WITH DESTINY

HELEN LACEY

For Gareth
1966–2009
Forever in my heart

Chapter One

Grace Preston stared down at her bare feet peeking out from the hem of her long dress. Her sister's beach wedding had been romantic and casual—exactly what the bride and groom wanted. But it had left her without shoes and feeling more than a little exposed.

Grace didn't bother to pull up her dress as she walked toward the water's edge. To hell with it—she'd never wear the halter style blue-green chiffon concoction again anyway. The water was cold and she ignored the wet sand clinging to her heels. The moon hung low in the sky, casting a great sliver of light across the ocean. The sound of cresting waves was faintly hypnotic and she relaxed a bit, taking a long swallow from the champagne flute in her hand. Once the glass was empty she quickly refilled it from the bottle she held in the other.

It wasn't like she intended to get drunk. That wasn't her

style. She simply needed to be alone. Away from the cloistering effects of wedding guests and the party.

She's been home for five days and already felt as though it was time to leave.

But I won't.

She had a month. Four weeks to recharge and pull herself together. Not that *she* really believed she needed it. But her boss did. Her therapist did. She had her instructions—go home…go home and spend time with her family. Go home and forget the car crash that had killed a colleague and changed her life.

So, I'm here.

She took another sip, finishing her drink. One glass down. Maybe getting drunk would give her some relief from the heavy band of pressure pressing at her temples.

Relief now, perhaps. But regret in morning.

Grace Preston didn't do hangovers. She did fourteen-hour days and skipped lunches and four-inch heels. Vacations were usually a long weekend in her apartment with a laptop and one eye on the stock market.

And Crystal Point, the small beachside Australian town where she'd been born and raised, was a long way from her office, her apartment, her Jimmy Choos and her life in New York.

She took a few steps and cautiously dipped her toes into the ocean. The sound of music and laughter and clinking crockery faded as she headed farther from the huge tent and the celebration of Evie and Scott's wedding. The stars above seemed particularly bright, like they were mocking her, like they knew all her secrets.

Like they knew she wasn't quite whole and there was a tiny window of emptiness aimed directly in the center of her chest. Maybe it was the happiness radiating from her sister that had Grace thinking things she wouldn't normally think.

With a new husband and a baby on the way, Evie had never looked happier.

While Grace had never been more alone in her life.

The fact her boss knew as much was the reason she was back. She was home to recharge and be with the people who loved her. Not that she was about to admit that to anyone anytime soon. Her family thought she was simply home for the wedding and an extended vacation.

She kicked at the tide with her toes and gasped as cold water splashed up her calf, but then ventured in a little more. When she took a swallow of champagne the bubbles zinged up her nose and down her throat. A couple more glasses, she thought, and she might be on her way to sweet oblivion.

The idea made her laugh and she heard the sound echo and then ripple and somehow quietly disappear into the night as she took another step into the water.

Across from the river mouth, where the waterway met the sea, was Jay's Island. It had been part of the mainland once, but years of sand trenching to allow sugar cane ferries to pass had created a gulf between the two banks. Now it was home to nesting herons and sea turtles. When she was young she'd swum the distance, not put off by the fast current that dragged many swimmers along. But she hadn't done that in a long time.

Despite what some people believed, Grace didn't hate Crystal Point. She just had little in common with the small beachside community that boasted a population of barely eight hundred residents. Not after so many years anyway. Time had a way of creating distance and building walls. Grace simply didn't fit in. She never had.

"Don't think I'm gonna jump in and save you if you fall in and get pulled down by the riptide, *Princess,*" she heard a deep and infuriatingly familiar voice say from behind her.

"I have no intention of ruining a perfectly good suit because you can't hold your liquor."

Grace swiveled in shock at the sudden intrusion and almost toppled over. Clenching her toes into the sand for balance, she moved up the bank to where Cameron Jakowski stood about ten feet away.

She scowled and fought a guilty look at the glass and bottle clutched between her fingers. She absolutely would not rise to his *Princess* jibe.

"What do you want, *Hot Tub?*"

She saw his smile in the moonlight, knew instinctively that his velvet brown eyes would light up, ready for battle with her. They had always called one another names—always worked out new ways to needle each other. *Hot Tub, Princess*—silly names meant to antagonize.

"Just making sure you don't drown."

Grace shrugged her bare shoulders. "I didn't realize you cared."

He came closer. "It's a wedding. I doubt Evie and Scott would want their celebration ruined by your carelessness."

Grace's temper simmered. "I'm not acting the least bit careless," she said through clenched teeth. "And I'm perfectly sober."

He looked at the bottle. "Prove it," he challenged. "Walk a straight line."

Grace bit back a scowl. "I'll do no such thing. You're not on duty now."

He chuckled and Grace forced herself to *not* think about how sexy it sounded. Okay—so he had a great smile and a handsome face and filled out his police officer's uniform as faultlessly as he did the suit he wore. She'd have to be comatose not to notice.

"So, why are you hiding out here anyway?"

Grace moved up the sand. "Who says I'm hiding?"

Cameron hooked a thumb over one shoulder. "The party's that way."

She shrugged. "Maybe I'm not in the mood for a party."

"Nothing's that simple with you."

Grace bristled. "Leave me alone. I don't want to argue with you."

Cameron stepped closer. "Now I know there's definitely something wrong with you. What's eating you tonight?"

"Nothing," she lied. "I'm my usual happy self."

"And now you're lying your shoes off."

Grace tugged at the hem off her dress and exposed her feet. "I'm not wearing shoes," she announced, holding herself upright despite a sudden surge of wooziness.

Of course, he knew that. He was a groomsman and she'd been partnered with him most of the afternoon. He'd already smirked when he'd spotted her bare feet and purple-painted toenails as she'd taken his arm to walk toward the altar.

Because Grace Preston didn't bare anything in public.

And Cameron knew that.

She glared at him some more. "I don't know why the men got to keep their shoes on. Anyway, I'll probably step on a stonefish and that will be the end of me."

Cameron laughed. "So much drama over a pair of missing shoes. Come on, I'll walk you back."

Grace shook her head. "No, thanks—I'll stay here. I've had about all the marital bliss I can stand for one evening."

He was close now and Grace could see the curious expression on his face. "Are you jealous Evie's married?"

Was she? It seemed like everyone was getting married lately and getting their happily-ever-after. First her brother, Noah, had married Callie Jones and now, less than eight months later, Evie was tying the knot with Scott, Callie's younger brother. But no, she wasn't the marrying type.

"Certainly not," she replied quickly and took another sip of

her champagne. "I'm very happy for my sister. I just meant…"
She stopped. There was no way she would explain anything
to Cameron Jakowski. "Nothing. Leave me alone."

He moved toward her again, only this time she didn't step
back. Toe-to-toe, he stood close to eight inches taller than her
and without shoes it was impossible for Grace to stare him
down without tilting her head up.

"And what if you go back into the water and get swept
away by the current?" he inquired. "I don't want that on my
conscience. I'm staying."

Grace shrugged. "Suit yourself," she said as she moved
up the bank some more and headed toward a small cluster of
rocks. She sat on the largest one and refilled her glass. "Want
a shot?" she asked, holding out the bottle.

Cameron followed her steps and took the bottle. "I reckon
you've had about enough of that." He dropped it onto the sand.

Grace watched the champagne seep away. "You're ruining my evening."

"Your evening looked well and truly ruined before you
wandered off down here."

She frowned. "Are you spying on me?"

Cameron laughed. "Hardly—but you did bail on our dance."

"I didn't want to dance," she told him flatly. "With you or
anyone else," she added.

Being partnered with Cameron for the entire celebration
had been more than she could stand. Not only because she
wasn't in any mood to combat his sarcasm or insults, but because the happy smiles and animated chatter of the wedding
party had felt like a cloistering blanket around her shoulders. Since the accident she'd become less adept at handling
crowds. Less inclined to make pointless conversation.

"You know, it wouldn't hurt you to open up a bit."

Grace almost choked on her champagne. Was he reading
her mind? "To you? You're joking, right?"

He shrugged. "Why not?"

"Because you're *you*." She shook her head. "And you and I are like…oil and water."

He stepped closer and thrust his hands in his pockets. "It's a double-edged sword," he said quietly.

Grace stared into her glass. "I have no idea what that's supposed to mean."

"Sure you do," he flipped back. "Admit it, *Princess*—fighting with me gets you all worked up."

Grace wasn't admitting anything. "You're imagining things. Not everything's about you. And stop calling me *Princess*."

"Stop calling me *Hot Tub*."

Gridlock.

As usual.

He didn't move. He stood in front of her, smiling, making Grace so mad she was tempted to toss her remaining drink in his direction. For sixteen years they'd been stuck in this groove—hurling insults, sticking it to one another at every opportunity.

But a lifetime ago it had been different. He was her brother's best friend and because of that relationship she'd known him since she was five years old. She'd liked him back then. He hadn't teased her for her bookish ways as her brother did. By the time she was preparing to leave for boarding school liking him had turned into a crush. But she didn't dare admit it or imagine he felt the same way. She left for school and took her silly dreams with her. Nothing had prepared her for the night of her sixteenth birthday when he'd unexpectedly kissed her for the first time. When school was over she'd returned to Crystal Point to take a break before she headed off to college and in those few months they'd dated one another. Cameron Jakowski had been her first real boyfriend. Her first kiss. The one man she'd never quite been able to forget.

"What's really going on with you, Grace?"

Her back straightened, shoving her into the present. "Spare me your fake concern."

He stepped closer. "It's not fake."

Grace didn't believe him. "Like you care?"

He laughed. "C'mon, Grace—lighten up. You're not in your swanky office now. There's no one to impress by pretending you've got it all together."

Grace stilled. His words hit a raw nerve. Because she'd heard the same ones from the therapist her boss had *insisted* she visit. But Cameron didn't know that. No one knew. The terrible accident and the month afterward where she'd returned to work and pretended none of it had happened, or the way she'd spectacularly unraveled in front of a client. She needed to lie through her teeth—for her own sake. "I always have it together—you know that."

"Do I? I know that you've been hanging around down here for the past hour. I know that you've barely cracked a smile all afternoon, at your own sister's wedding. I know that you're unhappy even if you don't have the courage to admit it."

Grace glared at him, hating she felt so transparent in front of Cameron, hating he could see through her. "And I know that if I admit to anything you'll just use it against me. No, thanks." She got to her feet and stumbled.

He grasped her arm quickly. "Steady," he said as he held her.

Grace tried to pull away but he held her firm. Something uncurled low in her belly, warming her blood. A familiar sensation she experienced whenever he was close. It unnerved her and she fought the feeling. "Let me go."

"You'll fall over."

"So, I'll fall." She was suddenly powerless as one strong arm came around her waist.

"I'd catch you," he said quietly.

Grace frowned. "Let me go...please."

But she wasn't afraid. She'd never feared Cameron. Despite their differences, she'd always trusted him. Grace felt the nearness of him and fought the sudden warmth spreading across her skin. That he could do this to her—make her boil with fury one moment and burn with awareness the next—only added to her resentment and determination to keep as far away from him as possible. He was the only man she'd ever known who'd been able to do that to her. The only man she'd ever thought could see through her, know her and work her out.

"Don't..."

"I'm not doing anything."

"You are. You do. You always do. I just want..." She stopped, stalled and felt herself get dragged into meeting his eyes. She was flustered, uneasy. "I can't..."

"What is it?" he asked softly. "What's going on in that beautiful head of yours?"

Grace's resistance crumbled. The champagne she'd had suddenly freed up her tongue. "I just... I don't belong here," she admitted and pulled herself from his grasp as she stepped backward. "I don't belong anywhere."

Cameron's hands burned from the feel of Grace's skin and he clenched his fists at his sides. The pain in her voice knocked through him, settling behind his ribs in a way that made him think about every feeling he'd had for her—and buried.

"What do you mean?"

She turned away, clutching her arms around herself. "Nothing," she said quietly.

Cameron pushed the heels of his shoes up from sinking in the sand and pressed on. "What do you mean you don't belong?"

Grace twirled around and her long dress billowed around her knees. "Why do you care?"

Why indeed? He shouldn't. Grace was nothing but trouble. A workaholic ice princess who had little time for anyone. *Me included.* He'd found that out the hard way. Beautiful beyond words, smart and independent—and about as warm as an Arctic winter. The perfect antidote for all his fantasies. Wanting her was about as sensible as wanting acid rain.

He shrugged. "Friendly concern."

Her beautiful face looked almost luminescent in the moonlight as she shot him a death stare. "Don't be nice to me," she said quietly, looking suspicious. "We're not friends and I just—"

"We were more than friends," he said and took hold of her hand despite his best intentions to not touch her. "Once."

She stared at their linked hands and this time, she didn't pull away. Cameron's fingertips tingled. He knew that would happen if he touched Grace...expected it...didn't like it one bit but chalked it up to chemistry and tried not to let it mess with his mind. Over the years there had been the odd touch between them, the chance gesture of hands brushing...and every time it was the same. The same vibration rattled inside him, over his skin, through his blood. He knew it wasn't like that for her, of course. Grace was supercool and controlled, with perfectly straight dark hair, immaculate clothes and haunting green eyes—like a mannequin on display. A mere touch wouldn't jangle Grace. But he remembered what it was like to touch her, to kiss her, to hold her in his arms. Those memories were burned into his soul.

As expected, she pulled away. "A lifetime ago."

Her dismissal cut deep. She'd left him without looking

back all those years ago and as much as he wanted to deny it, that rejection still stung. He smiled because he knew it would infuriate her. "So, explain what you meant about not belonging anywhere?"

"No. It was nothing." She shrugged lightly. "And now, if you don't mind, I need to get back to the party."

He didn't believe her for a second. So he pushed. Because he could. Because he wanted to know what was going on inside her beautiful head. "So, has this got anything to do with that suit you've shacked up with?"

Her lips came together. "Erik," she said after a moment. "We broke up a year ago. And we were never *shacked up*. We both kept our own apartments."

She crossed her arms. The movement pushed her breasts upward and Cameron did his best to ignore the swell of cleavage rising up and down with each breath she took. He'd never met the other man, since Grace had kept him under wraps in New York. But Cameron had heard about him from her brother. He was stupidly pleased the suit wasn't in the picture anymore. "You didn't answer the question."

"Because it's a moot point." Grace scowled, but somehow managed to still look beautiful. "And I really don't want to talk to you about my...love life."

Cameron bristled. Did he even think Grace capable of love? "So you loved him?"

"No," she replied swiftly. "I meant...I meant I have no intention of talking to you about him. Now, would you ignore everything I've said and leave me alone?"

Cameron wanted to laugh. "Ignore you? Yeah, right."

Her gaze sharpened. "Ignoring me isn't usually a problem for you. Except of course when you're making fun or insulting me."

"It goes both ways, Grace."

She moved her feet and seemed to come a little closer.

"I guess it does." She dropped her arms. "It only happens with you."

"Do you ever wonder why?"

She raised one perfectly arched brow. "Why would I bother?"

"It might explain one of the great mysteries of the world."

She laughed humorlessly. He could sense her thinking of some kind of cutting retort and wasn't disappointed. "I don't want to rain on your monumental ego, but I really don't have the time to waste wondering about things like that."

"So you never think about it?"

She stilled. "About what?"

"You and me?"

"We were over a long time ago. It was a silly teenage summer romance. I hardly remember."

Her response pushed his buttons. Because he didn't quite believe her. The tension between them had never waned. Every time she returned to Crystal Point, every time they spoke, every time he caught her stare from across a room, the awareness between them was still there. He straightened his shoulders. Down deep, in that place he'd shut off because it stirred up a whole lot of hurt, Cameron remembered what it felt like to want her so much it haunted his dreams. "Maybe you need a reminder."

She faced him with an indignant glare. "And what exactly do you propose?"

"Propose?" He smiled. "Is that what you're after, *Princess*—a proposal? Couldn't you get the suit to the altar?"

Her green eyes flashed. "I have no desire or plans in that regard. I'd think you'd know that better than anyone."

He did. He wasn't likely to forget. They'd started dating when she'd finished high school. She'd come home from boarding school that final time and he'd waited two weeks before asking her out. Three months into their relationship she'd bailed. She wanted a career and a different life…a life that didn't include a small-town police officer. A life that didn't include him or marriage or the possibility of children in the future. She'd made her intentions abundantly clear. Grace Preston wanted a career. And that's *all* she wanted. She'd left Crystal Point for New York without looking back.

Except for now. This Grace was someone new. Someone who didn't seem like she had her usual ice running through her veins. Grace never did vulnerable. And Cameron wanted to know more.

"The corporate life is still giving you everything you need, is it?" he asked, referring to her highly successful job as a finance broker.

"Of course."

"So your little outburst earlier, what was that about?"

Her brows came up. "Are we back on that subject again? It was nothing. Forget it."

"And let you off the hook?" He rocked on his heels. "No chance."

"Haven't you got anything better to do with that mouth of yours than run off with it at me about my life?"

He did. Absolutely. And her words were like a red cape to a bull.

"Did you have something in mind?"

"No, I don't," she said with a caustic smile. "And don't get any ideas."

He laughed at her prickles. Only Grace could make him do that. *Only ever Grace.* "I could kiss you," he teased. "That would shut me up."

She stepped back. "Don't even think about it."

It really was all the challenge he needed and Cameron moved closer. "Grace, you know me better than that."

Her green eyes were alight with fire and defiance. "You're right, I do know you. I know you've got a reputation for nailing anything in a skirt. The last thing I want to be is a notch on your bedpost, Jakowski...so back off."

"You shouldn't believe everything you hear." Cameron placed his hands on her shoulders. She didn't resist. Didn't move. "Kiss me, Grace?"

She shook her head slightly. "No."

The air shifted, creating a swift, uncommonly hot vacuum which somehow seemed to draw them closer. Their bodies brushed and it spiked his blood. He shouldn't want this... shouldn't do this. But everything about Grace Preston took him to another level of awareness. It was almost primitive in its intensity and it made him forget all his good intentions to stay as far away from her as possible.

"Then I'll kiss you."

"I won't kiss you back," she whispered, but he felt her slide a little closer.

Cameron's libido did a wild leap as he moved his arms around her, bringing them together. "Sure you will."

"I won't," she said boldly. "I hate you, remember?"

"You'll get over it," he said smoothly and moved one hand to her nape. For twenty years he'd wanted her like no other woman. For sixteen years he'd been angry at her for breaking his heart.

Grace stared up at him, her green eyes shining and wide in her face.

She looked more beautiful than he'd ever seen her. More desirable. More everything. Without thinking...with nothing but feeling and the need to suddenly possess her, Cameron claimed her lips with his own.

Chapter Two

I will not make out with Cameron Jakowski.

Too late. Grace allowed his mouth to slant over hers and her breath left her sharply.

Maybe just for a moment...

Because he still knew how to kiss. And she hadn't been kissed by Cameron in such a long time....

Her resistance faded and she opened her mouth, inviting him inside. Blood rushed low down in her belly, spiking her temperature upward like a roller coaster moving way too fast. Grace floated along and was quickly caught up in the deep-rooted pleasure which unexpectedly tingled across her skin. The kiss deepened and Grace felt his tongue roll gently around hers. It was so incredibly arousing she couldn't prevent a low moan from escaping deep in her throat.

I should stop this...right now. But she didn't. She just let herself float on a sigh and kissed him back. Her arms moved upward and she curled her fingers into his shoulders. The movement brought their bodies together and Grace melted against him. *Strong and safe.* The words spun around in her head and rocked her to the core. Because she knew she'd only ever felt that way with Cameron. Not with Erik. Not with any man she'd ever been with.

His arms came around her and one hand settled on her hip. And still he kissed her. Grace clung to him as heat charged between them. His touch became firmer and he bunched a handful of her dress in his fist. The tempo between them altered slightly, and the hot surge of desire fanned to life.

He said something against her mouth—her name—something…she wasn't sure. But it fueled the growing need she had to feel his touch. She lifted her leg and wrapped it against him. Her dress rose up and she shuddered when his hand made contact with the soft skin behind her knee. It felt so good to be with him like this, even though some faraway voice told her it was madness. Every part of her came alive when he touched her and she arched her back with a hazy, wanting compliance.

"Grace," he said, leaving her mouth for a moment. He trailed a line of kisses across her cheek and toward the sensitive spot below her ear. "I think it would be a good idea if we stopped…."

Grace turned her head so their lips met again. She didn't want to stop. She only wanted to feel. "No," she whispered into his mouth. "Don't stop."

"You'll hate me tomorrow," he said softly against her craving lips.

"I hate you now…"

She felt his smile against her mouth.

He's right, we have to stop...

Only Cameron's touch was mesmerizing and his kiss had her longing for more. His fingertips burned across her skin in an erotic trail, moving higher, and the blood in her veins boiled over in a powerful surge of narcotic pleasure. She felt his hand on the top of her thigh and she pushed closer. He was obviously as hotly aroused as she was and the notion drove Grace beyond rational thought, beyond reason. His palm curved around her bottom and he drew her hard against his body. Need uncurled low down, liquefying her bones. She groaned as his mouth sought hers again and kissed him back with a hunger that startled her, entwining her tongue with his. She was dazed, on fire, out of control. Grace's knees almost gave way when his fingers traced the edge of her lace panties. *I shouldn't want this. I shouldn't feel this turned on.* But she was so aroused, so completely oblivious to anything other the sudden and unexpected need to be taken to places she suspected he'd effortlessly be able to take her.

But reality intruded and brought her back to earth with a resounding, wrenching thud.

The music resonating from the wedding reception area came to an abrupt halt and the silence was suddenly deafening. "Oh, my God," Grace moaned as she jerked her mouth from his. "My speech!"

Cameron released her. "What?"

Grace staggered back and shoved her dress down her thighs with shaking hands. "I have to give a speech. I'm the maid of honor. I have to get back."

He looked annoyingly calm. "Okay, we'll go back."

"No," Grace said on a rush of breath. "I'm not walking back up there with you. I look like..." She pushed a hand into her hair and was relieved to discover that the up style was still in its right position. But her blood raced, her breath was shallow and she was certain her mouth looked as though it had been well and truly plundered. "I must look like I've been—"

"You have been," he agreed quietly, seeming completely cool and relaxed. "Don't stress, *Princess.* You look fine—as picture-perfect as always."

Grace crossed her arms and glanced toward the reception area. The big white tent stood out like a beacon in the moonlight. She heard someone speaking into a microphone and quickly recognized her father's steady voice. "I need to get back. And don't follow me."

He didn't respond immediately. He just looked at her. Looked *through* her was more the point. Humiliation burned across her skin like an out-of-control brush fire.

This was not supposed to happen. I didn't come home for this. Nothing will stop me from getting my life and career back on track.

He grabbed the bottle and glass from the sand. "Let's go," he said quietly.

Grace considered some kind of cold retort, but failed to find one.

Cameron Jakowski had his hand up my dress.

"All right," she said with a deliberate tilt of her chin and tried not to think about how good his hand had felt. "We won't ever mention this again."

"Sure we will."

Grace lifted her hem fractionally and took a few steps up the sand. "We won't," she said defiantly. "*I* won't. I intend to forget this ever happened."

"Good luck with that."

Grace stomped along the sand, headed for the boat ramp and walked back toward the reception. As she'd suspected, her father's proud speech was in full swing and Grace circumnavigated the huge tent and slipped through an opening behind the wedding table as discreetly as she could.

But Evie's hawkeyed radar caught a glimpse of her immediately and Grace did her best to squash a fresh wave of embarrassment from heating her cheeks. Evie raised both her brows inquiringly and Grace managed a barely decipherable

shake of her head. It didn't help that Cameron chose that moment to make his entrance through the same opening.

Busted...

The look on her sister's face was unmistakable. She knew
Evie would demand answers at some point. That was Evie's
way. Grace steeled herself with a deep breath and took her
conspicuously empty seat at the table. Cameron did the same
a few seats away and she used every inch of effort to not look
at him. Instead, she concentrated her attention on her father's
heartfelt speech.

When it was her turn to say a few words, Grace stood and
took the microphone from her father and softly kissed his
cheek. All the guests clearly waited for her to speak. And
she meant to. Only she made a fatal mistake and glanced at
Cameron. And damn him—he smiled, winked and made her
forget every word she'd planned to say in honor of the bride
and groom.

Nothing came out, only a squeak, a kind of strangled sound
that a distressed cat might make.

And it was pain-in-her-neck, thorn-in-her-side Cameron
Jakowski's fault.

Supercool Grace Preston was at a loss for words. Any
other time Cameron might have been happy about that. But
tonight...not so much. He could still taste her lovely mouth;
still feel the silky texture of her skin against his hands.

One minute they were talking, the next they were kissing
like a couple of horny teenagers. Cameron couldn't remember
the last time he'd felt like that. The last time he'd *done* that.

And he certainly hadn't expected to do it with Miss Icy
Britches.

He'd mostly kept his hands to himself when they were dating. They'd made out plenty of times—but never quite like
what had happened on the beach. She'd wanted to wait to

make love and he'd respected her wishes, although he'd imagined a future together—a wedding, a wedding *night*. Until Grace had informed him of her big plans for a career and a future that didn't include Crystal Point or the small-town police officer who wanted to marry her one day.

But right now, she didn't look like the Grace he'd come to resent. It was easier that way, easier not thinking about her perfectly beautiful face and body. And yet his skin felt tight watching her, waiting for her to speak. She was off balance, askew, and he knew it wasn't the champagne doing damage.

It churned something inside him, thinking he was responsible for the kind of hazy, almost lost look on her face as she stared into the microphone. He smiled again, different this time, without mockery, with only the intent to calm her obviously fractured nerves. She met his gaze and they remained like that for a moment, linked by some invisible thread that had nothing to do with the searing kisses they'd shared, or the years of thinly veiled antagonism that had come to define their relationship. He saw her relax, watched as her jaw loosened and then she began to speak.

"Tonight is a celebration," she said and then swallowed hard, as though the words were difficult to say. "Of love. Of trust. Of the commitment between two people."

She went on to talk about the bride and groom, speaking clearly and concisely as she wished the newlyweds a long and happy life. Cameron wondered if she meant it. He'd never heard her speak about love before. When she was done she returned to her seat and didn't spare him another look.

Dessert was served after that and Cameron pushed the sugary sweet around on his plate. The dancing started again and the woman beside him dug him in the ribs with her elbow, but he was in no mood for that either. He declined her invitation and managed a smile when she scooted off her chair.

Mary-Jayne Preston was a pretty brunette with amazing green eyes—and she was Grace's younger sister.

Grace...

She didn't like him. He didn't like her. But he'd wanted her and loved her most of his adult life. He thought he was over it. Thought he had it under control.

Jackass...

"Why do you look like you want to be somewhere else?"

Cameron turned his head. Noah Preston. His best friend. And Grace's older brother. "You know me and weddings," he replied casually.

The other man ducked into the empty chair beside him. "Are you tempted to take the walk yourself?" Noah asked.

He shrugged to disguise the truth. Because he did want to get married. He wanted a wife and kids and the whole deal. Cameron longed for a family of his own. He was thirty-six years old and had dated a succession of women, none he saw for more than a few months. And none who invaded his deepest dreams like Grace Preston.

He'd built a house designed for a family and lived in it alone. Dated women he knew weren't going to figure permanently in his life. For a long time he'd avoided thinking about marriage and family. Once Grace left Crystal Point he'd pushed his focus into his career as a police officer and tried to forget about her. And their ongoing resentment for one another had fueled that focus. But now he wanted more. More than an empty house when he came home after a long shift at work, more than an empty bed. Or one filled occasionally with someone he barely knew.

He wanted what his parents had. He wanted what his best friend had.

"It's not as bad as you think," Noah said easily. "Actually, it's the smartest move I ever made. You just need to find the right woman."

Noah had married Callie Jones eight months earlier and the stunning, blue-eyed, California horse-riding instructor had transformed his friend's life. His four children had a new mother and Noah had the love of a woman he adored. And with Callie's brother, Scott, now married to Evie, it seemed like everyone around him was getting their happily-ever-after.

Just not me.

It made him think of green eyes. *Grace's eyes.* Noah would have a fit if he knew what he was thinking. Or what he'd been doing with her down by the beach.

"I never said it was bad."

Noah laughed. "I'm sure there's some sweet, easygoing girl out there who—"

"I don't want easygoing," he said swiftly. "Or sweet."

Grace again. Because Grace wasn't either of those things. She was smart and independent and reserved and coolly argumentative and...

And she's the only woman I've ever wanted.

Noah laughed again. "Can't say I blame you. I love my wife's spirit." There was a gleam in his friend's eyes. "Makes life more interesting."

"I'll bet," Cameron said agreeably.

"Were you with Grace earlier?"

Cameron shot a glance at his friend. "For a minute," he said and pushed aside the nagging guilt hitting him between the shoulder blades.

"Something's going on with her," Noah said. "She said she's taking some time off work. But she's not talking about why, not even to Evie or our mother. Maybe breaking up with that attorney has something to do with it."

Cameron remembered what she'd said about the suit and sensed she wasn't all that broken up about it. But what she'd said about not belonging—now that, he was sure, had something to do with her return home. Because it was completely

unlike Grace to say a thing like that. Noah was right—
something *was* going on with her. The Grace he knew didn't
show vulnerability. She was ice-cool and resilient. At eighteen
she'd walked away from him and Crystal Point and moved to
New York and had been there ever since, returning once or
twice a year at the most. That was the Grace Preston he understood. Not the vulnerable one moment, hotter than Hades
the next kind of woman who'd kissed him back like there
was no tomorrow.

Wanting her had made every other woman he'd known
pale by comparison. And now he knew one thing—he either
had to get Grace out of his head for good...or *get* Grace in
his bed and in his life.

She was home, on his turf. Maybe he had a shot. The
way she'd kissed him gave him some optimism. That kind
of response wasn't fake. And he knew Grace. She wouldn't
pretend. Whatever was going on with her, Cameron was determined to find out. She'd resist and fight. She'd make things
impossible. She'd cut him down with icy barbs and indiffer-
ence.

Suddenly that seemed like one hell of an interesting challenge.

Cameron's gaze centered on Grace. She was with Evie,
talking close. His shirt collar got uncomfortably tight and
irritation uncurled in his chest. Because he would bet right
down to his boots that they were talking about him.

"So, what happened?"

Grace tried to escape her sister's viselike grip on her wrist
but failed. Evie was persistent when she wanted something.
She loved her sister and Evie was the one person she could
really talk to. But not about this. Not about Cameron.

"Nothing. We were just talking."

Evie's dramatic brows rose. "Well, I imagine you were doing something with your tongues."

Grace flushed and tacked herself at Evie's side to hide from Cameron's view in case he looked her way. Her sister's seven months pregnant belly was a good shield. "I don't want to talk about it."

Evie chuckled. "Oh, no—you don't get out of it that easy. I want details."

"I won't say what…" Grace's response faded on her lips. "Okay," she admitted. "So we might have…"

"Might have?" Evie interrupted without batting a lash.

"We kissed," she whispered into her sister's ear, feeling about sixteen years old. She certainly wasn't about to admit to anything else. "And that's all I'm saying."

Evie hauled Grace into the corner so they had more privacy. "You kissed Cameron?" she squealed. "Oh, my God! I can't believe it."

Neither can I.

"Well, I mean I *can* believe it," Evie said in a wicked whisper. "Did it bring back a whole lot of memories?"

Of course it did. But she wasn't about to say that. Grace regretted ever telling her sister about the three-month relationship she'd had with Cameron—about the kisses and gentle touches and soft moans as they made out in the front seat of his car. Because it brought back other memories as well—the way she'd left, the way she'd run when she'd sensed he was getting serious. It was so long ago. In a different life. Wanting Cameron now was sheer madness. It was champagne that had made her behave so impulsively. And she hadn't been with a man since forever. No wonder she'd acted like she did. She only hoped no one else saw their conspicuous entrance. The last thing she wanted was the Crystal Point rumor mill churning out theories about what had happened between her and the charming and popular Sergeant Jakowski down by the beach.

Everyone liked Cameron. She knew some of what he did in the community—the volunteer work at the surf club, the time he spent with kids from the Big Brothers Big Sisters program. An all-around good guy. Honest, honorable and socially conscious. Grace knew it about him and had always felt like he was rubbing her nose in the fact. Irrational as it was, he made her feel selfish and, worse...self-absorbed. Like her life was meaningless and superficial. He never said it of course, rarely spoke to her unless to demean her fondness for pricey footwear or call her *Princess* in that infuriating way.

"Can I steal my beautiful bride away for a dance?" Scott Jones approached and took Evie's hand.

"Of course," Grace said and smiled when she saw the glow on her sister's face. Evie had found true love with the handsome, California firefighter. "We were done anyway."

Evie smiled. "We'll talk later," she said and allowed herself to be swept away.

Grace remained where she was and studied the crowd for a moment. The usual suspects were in attendance and a few she'd never met before, mostly friends and colleagues of the groom who'd traveled from Los Angeles. She spotted her younger sister Mary-Jayne, or M.J. as she was affectionately called, dancing closely with Gabe Vitali, the best man and cousin of the groom. She was supposed to have been partnered with the outrageously good-looking American, but M.J. had pleaded they swap groomsmen and Grace agreed, unable to refuse her sister's request.

"They make a cute couple."

Grace froze. Cameron had approached and edged alongside her. She glanced at him and he nodded toward M.J. and Gabe. "I'm no judge."

"And yet you're usually so good at it."

It was a dig, but he was smiling so she let it pass. She wasn't about to have an argument with him in front of so many people. "Did you want something?"

"Just to see how you were doing."

Grace raised both shoulders. "As you can see, I'm perfectly fine."

"Good speech by the way."

"Thank you." She took a deep breath. No thanks to him. "I should get back to—"

He laid one finger against her wrist. "I think we should talk, Grace."

Awareness crept along her skin and she tingled where they touched. "I'd rather not."

"So, where are you staying?"

Grace swiveled on her heels to face him. "At Evie's."

"While she and Scott are on their honeymoon?" His brows came up. "Are they leaving you in charge of the B and B?"

The query in his voice was skeptical. "Don't sound so surprised. I'm not totally inept, you know."

He smiled to expose perfectly straight teeth. "I think it's good of you to help out."

She pulled away from his touch, but Grace couldn't ignore the way he watched her and her body was quickly on high alert.

"So, shall we resume our earlier conversation?" he asked.

Grace stepped back. "Don't push it."

"You know, you look really beautiful when your cage is rattled."

"You're an ass, Jakowski."

"And you're hiding something," he replied. "Whatever it is, Grace, you may as well come clean."

Heat crept up her neck and she hated that he could do that. "*If* there was anything wrong, I certainly wouldn't be sharing it with you."

"Your family is concerned about you. Noah thinks you're nursing a broken heart after breaking up with the suit."

"I'm not."

"I know."

He said the words with such arrogant authority that Grace glared at him. "I wish you wouldn't do that."

"Do what?"

"Act as though you know or care. I'll talk to my brother."

"When?"

Grace's skin burned. "When I'm ready."

"You've been home almost a week, seems to me like you would have had plenty of opportunity to tell your family what's going on."

"Stay out of it," she warned.

"Or what?" He chuckled. He was toying with her. As usual. "Ah, *Princess,* you're about as wound up as a spinning top at the moment."

"No thanks to you," she fired back and crossed her arms.

He smiled again. "By the way, you owe me a dance."

Dancing? After what had happened on the beach she had no intention of falling into his arms again. "You don't have a chance of getting me on the dance floor."

"Things have a way of changing," he said and gently took hold of her elbow. "As we discovered earlier."

The kiss. The touching. The insane desire that had taken hold. Of course he'd remind her about it. "Don't imagine for one minute that we'll be repeating that craziness anytime soon."

"Are you sure about that, Grace?"

She stuck out her chin. "Positive."

"Such confidence," he said in that vague, annoying way of his. "So, about that dance?"

She clung to her resolve. "No."

"I could beg and embarrass you."

Grace refused to react. "You mean embarrass yourself. And surely there are other women here you can try to charm the pants off other than me."

He laughed and she hated that a few people looked in their direction. "Is that what you think I'm doing, Grace? Trying to get your pants off?"

She cast him a sharp look. "Try your best, *Hot Tub.*"

He grinned at her attempt to antagonize. But she knew he would win out. She'd called him the ridiculous name for a decade because he'd installed a huge spa bath at the house he'd built and her brother teased that it was to impress women. She hadn't liked the idea then. And she liked it even less now.

"Are you throwing down the gauntlet, Grace?"

"Not at all." She managed to pull away and put some space between them. "I'm…tired," she said and shook her head. "Too tired to play games."

"Then tell me what's going on with you. If you do I might be inclined to leave you alone."

Exasperated by his persistent badgering, Grace threw up her hands. "So, what do you want to know?"

His gaze narrowed. "Why you've come back for so long this time?"

"Because this is my home."

He clearly didn't believe that for a second. "Last I heard New York was your home, Grace. Crystal Point was the place you couldn't get away from fast enough."

It was a direct hit. She knew what he meant. Her career was the reason she'd left Crystal Point—the reason she'd put an end to their relationship all those years ago. She'd been overwhelmed, crowded, hemmed in…everything she didn't want to be. Leaving had been her salvation. And her career had panned out exactly as she'd dreamed it would. Until the car wreck that had changed her life.

Grace's back stiffened. "You know why I left. I wanted… I wanted…"

"Bright lights, big city."

She stilled. Quiet stretched between them, like brittle elastic. The music seemed to fade and Grace experienced a strange tightening behind her ribs. "It was never that simple."

"Yes, it was, Grace." His voice was velvet-smooth, his expression unreadable. "You knew what you wanted. What you didn't. And who you didn't."

She looked into his eyes. It sounded so black-and-white. But nothing was simple anymore. And she didn't have the courage to admit the truth—that she'd gone to New York to make her parents proud and become everything they'd hoped she would become…or that now she'd come home to save her life.

Chapter Three

On Sunday morning at her sister's bed-and-breakfast, Grace reorganized the upstairs linen cupboard, alphabetized Evie's cookbooks and by eleven o'clock was sitting on the sofa watching a corny movie on a cable channel.

Anything to take her mind off the job she'd left in New York, the empty apartment that had never really felt like a home and the accident that killed her work colleague. An accident that had altered her in so many ways. Before that awful day she'd been in control of her life and future. There were no question marks. No uncertainty. At least none she was prepared to admit. She had known her trajectory. Her plan.

You knew what you wanted. And who you didn't.

Cameron's words rolled around in her head.

Because there had been the sting of truth in those words.

When they'd dated, when he'd said he had serious feelings for her and wanted to talk about their future together, she'd panicked and cut him down immediately. And as she sat in the lotus position on the sofa and stared absently at the television, Grace remembered what she'd said to him in stunning Technicolor.

"I'm just not interested in anything serious. Especially not with a small-town cop. I'm getting out of Crystal Point as soon as I can. There's nothing and no one that could ever hold me here."

Insensitive and cruel. And a pivotal moment in her life. What if she'd said something else to him? What if she'd had the courage to acknowledge her deepest, secret feelings and fears? And if she hadn't left Crystal Point when she did, would she have felt even more trapped in their relationship, perhaps their marriage, had it ever come to that?

Grace sat back on the sofa and uncurled her legs.

Marriage had never figured in her life. Erik, who was as focused on his career as she was, had never mentioned it. Before Erik, she'd had a three-year relationship with Dennis Collier. The handsome and successful orthopedic surgeon had asked her twice to marry him—both times she'd insisted she was happy with the tempo of their relationship. She worked long hours and kept her own apartment. Toward the end they'd go for days without seeing one another. Eventually Dennis had traded her for a third-year resident at the hospital where he worked. Within six months of their breakup she heard he'd married and had a baby on the way.

The news hadn't torn her up. She'd genuinely cared for Dennis—but knew it wasn't the kind of feeling that could sustain her for a lifetime. There were feelings, certainly... but love? Grace wasn't sure she even knew how to be in love. Long ago she'd run from those feelings, terrified they'd trap her, make her less than whole and dilute her ambition. She'd wanted a career. That's what she'd planned for. That's what her parents expected of her. Not marriage. Not babies. Not Crystal Point. That legacy was left to her brother and sisters.

Noah took over running the family business and Evie was the original Earth Mother. While M.J. waltzed through life as a free spirit, making jewelry and saving the world with her causes. She was Grace Preston—smart, successful... *untouchable.*

Her cell rang, interrupting her thoughts, and she grabbed it from the coffee table.

"Hey, *Princess.*"

She bit back a startled gasp and took a deep breath. Strange that Cameron should telephone when her head was full of thoughts of him. "Would you stop calling me that?"

Cameron laughed softly. "I'll do my best. So, how are things?"

"Since last night?" she shot back and ignored the rapid thump of her heart.

He was silent for a moment and Grace could swear he was smiling. "Come down to the surf club this afternoon."

"What?"

"The surf club," he said again. "I want to show you something."

"What kind of something?"

"Something you'll want to see."

Grace colored hotly. The conversation was oddly flirtatious and she was startled by how it made her feel. "I...I don't think so."

"Oh, come on, Grace," he said and laughed. "Live dangerously. You never know—you might like it."

"No."

"You'll miss seeing something great."

Again, more flirting, more...*something.* He was infuriating.

Grace made an unglamorous grunting sound. "Whatever game you're playing, Jakowski, it's not the least bit funny."

"Game?" he said and chuckled. "That's harsh, *Princess*. You need to learn to trust."

He was laughing at her. As always. Her fingers turned white where she gripped the phone. "Jerk!"

She disconnected and wondered why he was the one person who could push her buttons so easily. And then she wondered why she cared that he did.

Her mother came to visit a little later and Grace made some tea and took a spot opposite at the big scrubbed table in the kitchen. Barbara Preston was the übermother. A career teacher, she'd managed to raise four children and work full-time until her retirement a few years earlier.

"So, what's going on, Grace?"

She knew that tone—knew her mother had something to say. "Nothing," she replied and poured the tea.

Her mother made a disbelieving sound and grabbed a mug. "Grace, I know something's up with you. You've been home a week now. And other than at Christmastime every few years, you never stay this long."

Grace looked at her mother. "I'm fine. Just taking a break."

It wasn't exactly a lie. She *was* on a break. A forced break. After the accident, her employer had insisted she see a therapist. Half a dozen visits later the counselor had recommended time off from her hectic job as a finance broker and her life in New York. Grace had resisted until she'd unexpectedly fallen apart one afternoon while meeting a client. Thankfully, the client hadn't been appalled by her unstoppable tears, and instead had called on her secretary, who'd then informed her boss. Another therapy session followed and without any choice but to agree, the week she'd planned to come home for Evie's wedding turned into a month.

"I'm worried about you."

"There's no need," Grace assured her mother. "I was a little burned-out, that's all."

"You're not sick or anything?"

"No," she said quickly. There was no point mentioning the accident. She knew her mother would only worry. "I'm perfectly healthy."

Barbara looked at her and smiled. "Okay, I'll stop smothering. I did think it might have been a man who brought you back home."

In a way it had been. Richard Bennett had been a colleague in the firm where she worked. He was also a devoted husband and father. A forty-nine-year-old man who hadn't deserved his fate.

"There's no man in my life," she said quietly. "And Erik left a long time ago."

"Are you looking for a relationship?"

It was an unexpected question. Her mother never meddled in her love life. And since her family had known of her career ambitions from a young age, her decision to move to New York was never challenged. "You know how I feel about all that."

Barbara sighed and as always, Grace wished she knew how to really connect with her mother. Evie knew how. And Mary-Jayne. They fit in. Grace had always felt like she was watching her family from the outside. Oh, she was loved, she knew that. But being part of things? That was different. She'd never belonged in Crystal Point. New York had embraced her in ways the tiny town never had. Until she'd been forced to abandon that life.

Now she felt as misplaced as she had all those years ago when she'd been sent to boarding school. As a child she'd shown an aptitude for math and music and at twelve had been enrolled into a school that offered a curriculum designed for gifted children. She'd spent six years at that school, coming back only for the holidays. When her high school years were over, Grace had returned to Crystal Point for a few months. It was during that time that she began dating Cameron. Three months later she'd packed her bags and moved to New York.

Sixteen years on and she still didn't know where she fit in.

"Marriage isn't a prison sentence," her mother said gently.

Grace nodded. "I know. But not everyone gets it all. And I'm not the settle down, picket fence type."

"I only want to see you happy."

"I know that, too," Grace replied. "And I am," she said and smiled. Not exactly the truth, but she wasn't about to burden her mother with her problems. She needed to forget. Not dwell.

"Sometimes I think…" Her mother's voice faded for a moment. "I think that you were too young to have left home when you did all those years ago."

"I was strong-willed," Grace said, and managed a smile. "And I wanted to go."

Her mother patted her hand. "I know you did. And your dad and I were so proud of you for having the courage to follow your dreams. And we're still proud, Grace. You always were our shining star."

She'd heard it before. That's why she'd been sent to boarding school while the other Preston children remained in Crystal Point. *Grace is special. Grace is so smart. Grace will have a stellar career in whatever field she chooses.* How often had she heard those words while she was growing up and attending the school? Within six months she'd been pushed up a grade and then spent the following five years as the youngest student in her class. She knew it had cost her parents tens of thousands every year for her tuition. She owed them a lot for giving her the education she'd had. But there were also times when she'd wished she was simply ordinary Grace Preston.

Without the high IQ. Without the pressure to succeed and make good grades.

She'd never told her parent's how she'd felt. There never seemed the right time. To complain would make her ungrateful, undeserving. And once school was over she just wanted to move on from those unhappy years.

When her mother left, Grace changed into designer jeans, high-end mules and a white, immaculately pressed T-shirt. She found a visor hanging on a peg near the back door and positioned it on her head. She needed to walk. To think.

The beach beckoned.

Winter meant fewer swimmers, even though the day was warm and the water temperature would probably be moderate. Grace locked up the private living area upstairs and checked on the single guest who was lazing in the front sunroom. The lone occupant was a gentleman in his sixties who had come to Dunn Inn alone for the first time in ten years, following the death of his wife. Talking with him for a few minutes stretched Grace's emotions and by the time she'd said goodbye and headed outside, her throat was tight and thick. Her nerves were fraught enough and the sad widower somehow pushed her buttons. She took a deep breath and walked across the road. The grassy shoulder led to a long pathway, which ran parallel with the ocean and wound down toward the beach.

Grace followed the trail at a reasonable pace and it took about ten minutes to reach the sandy knolls leading up to the beach. She stalled at the edge of the rise and took a deep breath. The surf club stood to her left.

I didn't come here for this. For him. I'm not going anywhere near that building.

Only…she *was* curious.

Grace took a second, shook her shoulders and walked across the path.

* * *

"There's just no way I can do it!"

Cameron bit back an exasperated sigh as seventeen-year-old Emily Maxwell pulled a pile of books from a battered knapsack. "You knew it was going to be difficult."

"But not impossible," she wailed and dumped the bag at her feet. "I'll never learn this stuff in time."

"You've two weeks before you need to sit that makeup exam, Em," he reminded her.

She rolled her eyes toward the toddler playing on a mat in the corner of the room. "And I've got a two-year-old kid to look after. It ain't gonna happen. It's over."

"How about I ask your grandmother to help with the baby?"

Emily shook her head. "She's got my brothers and sister to take care of. And they're all going out to the farm next week."

Cameron had heard the same story all afternoon. The teenager had been given an opportunity to complete a makeup exam that would go toward her final grade. But she'd talked of giving in to the pressure and Cameron knew he needed to do something to stop her from throwing away her chance at an education. He just didn't know what. Emily was the oldest sister of Dylan. Twelve-year-old Dylan was one of his charges in the Big Brother program sponsored by his station. When Cameron inherited Dylan from the retiring sergeant at the station, he also inherited the teenage mother, her ailing grandmother and two other half siblings. Officially Dylan was his Big Brother charge, but the rest of them were in such dire circumstances, Cameron feared they'd all slip through the cracks and end up separated and in social services. They were a loving family, but down on their luck and needing help.

When Pat Jennings got custody of her grandchildren from her drug-addicted and incarcerated daughter, the town rallied together and raised funds enough for a deposit on a small farm out west. With the house a few months away from being ready for the families' final move, Cameron knew this was Emily's last chance to finish high school. If only she could get past her resistance to study so she could complete the makeup examination. Emily was intelligent, but lacked confidence. She'd missed classes and failed to finish set assignments throughout the year as she juggled single parenthood. It was a heavy load for a girl not yet eighteen.

"You have to find the time to study," he said quietly.

"It's not only the time," she complained bitterly. "The work is just too…well, it's too hard. And I'm not smart enough."

She was. But she clearly didn't believe it.

"I think the best thing at the moment is for you to—"

"Hey, Sarge!" called Dylan as he popped his head around the door. "There's a lady here to see you."

A lady? He looked toward Emily. "Keep studying. I'll be back in a minute and we'll continue this discussion."

"But I—"

"Hit the books," he said and smiled, then turned on his heel.

The second floor of the surf club had recently undergone a complete renovation following a fire four months earlier. Now it was used for Tai Chi classes, the Big Brother program and a couple of other local community events. Today it was a place for Emily to study without interruption while he spent time with Dylan.

Cameron headed down the stairs and came to an abrupt halt when he reached the bottom tread.

Grace.

A jolt hit him behind the ribs. He looked at Dylan, who was hanging off to her left and grinning. "Go and get the fishing gear ready," he instructed and tossed him the keys to his car.

Dylan caught the keys and took off quickly. When he was out of sight Cameron turned his attention to Grace. "Hi."

"Hello."

"You came."

She shrugged a little. "I was walking...I simply happened to... Well, I was nearby and thought I'd come in."

The sensation in his chest amplified. "I'm glad you did." Cameron held out his hand. "Come on up."

She looked at his hand and hesitated. He waited. Grace never acted on impulse. Her actions were always measured. Always in control. She looked immaculate, as usual. Her dark hair was pulled back tightly and caught in a band at her nape. The only anomaly in her seriously fashionable look was the well-worn hot pink visor on her head. She finally took his hand and he instinctively curled his fingers around hers. She didn't resist and followed him up the stairway.

When they reached the landing she withdrew her hand and crossed her arms. "So, what did you want to show me?"

Cameron smiled. "Nothing sinister."

"Not that I'm likely to believe you," she said, raising her perfectly sculpted brows.

He cracked another smile. "Come on, there's someone I'd like you to meet."

Cameron opened the door to one of the two upstairs rooms and beckoned her inside. She tagged after him and he closed the door. Emily looked up from her spot at the desk positioned by the long row of windows. He ushered Grace across the room.

"Emily, this is Grace Preston, a friend of mine."

"Girlfriend?" the teen asked and stood.

"Friend," Grace corrected as she shook Emily's hand. "And I think I just met your brother?"

"Yeah, Dylan," Emily said and laughed. "We look alike."

The toddler in the corner tapped loudly on the plastic drum he was playing with.

"And that's Riley," Cameron explained. "Emily's son."

Grace nodded, frowning a little. He could see her looking at Emily with interest before she glanced at the books on the table. "But it looks as though I'm interrupting you."

"No, you're saving me," Emily replied with a wry grin. "Sergeant Jakowski is a slave driver."

Grace laughed and the sound hit Cameron directly behind the ribs. *Damn.* He wished everything about her didn't affect him like he was a pining schoolboy. "Emily needs to study for a makeup exam in two weeks. This is a quiet place for her to hit the books while Dylan and I go fishing."

"Then I am interrupting you," Grace replied. "I should go."

"No," Cameron said, too quickly. "Stay for a while." He saw her surprised look and fought the color creeping up his neck. But she was here. And he wanted her to stay. "You're handy with the books, right?" he asked and smiled as he pulled out a chair.

Handy with the books was an understatement. Grace was the smartest person he'd ever known. As a child she'd always been top of her class, even before she'd gone to that fancy school. Then she'd headed off to New York to study finance and business. After that he'd heard she'd been headhunted by some of the top brokerage firms in the city.

Grace nodded, clearly still hesitant. "I'm not sure I can—"

"That would be great," Emily said with more enthusiasm than he'd heard from her all afternoon. "I need all the help I can get."

Cameron tapped the back of the chair and spoke. "I'll be back in a little while."

Once Cameron left, Grace sat down. Emily stared at her and grinned.

"So, are you and the Sarge—"

"No," Grace replied quickly and pushed back the heat in

her cheeks. "We're just friends," she said, even if it wasn't exactly true. "We've known one another since we were kids."

And he was the first man I kissed.

Even though she'd developed a silly crush on him when she was twelve, Grace knew she was a "late bloomer" when it had come to boys and sex. While her classmates were pining over pop icons and movie stars, she had her head firmly placed in textbooks or a Jane Austen novel. Being a year younger hadn't helped. She was teased for her bookish ways, her flat chest and seeming lack of interest in any of the boys from the nearby all-male college. By the time her chest arrived she'd already earned the reputation as being stuck-up and closed off from the other girls in her class. And after a while she learned to embrace the isolation from her peers. Making friends lost any appeal and she didn't waste time thinking about boys or romance.

Until the night of her sixteenth birthday.

"That explains why you don't look like his usual type," Emily said and jerked her back to the present. "I mean, they are Gucci jeans you're wearing, right?"

Grace shifted in her seat and took off her visor. She didn't like the idea of Cameron having a *type*. "You know fashion?"

Emily nodded. "I *love* fashion. Not that I can afford anything better than chain-store clothes these days. Riley keeps growing out of his gear quicker than I can buy them. But I would love to have my own store one day. And maybe study design."

Grace pressed her hair back and looked at the textbook on the table. "That's a great ambition. Now, about this makeup exam?"

Emily rolled her eyes. "I've missed a lot of school this year. Nan was helping out with Riley until my half brother and sister came to live with us." The teenager pushed the book toward Grace. "My mother is a screwup. She's in jail.

Her husband died last year. No one knows what happened to *my* dad."

Grace hid her surprise. Teenagers with serious family issues weren't something she had experience dealing with. Unlike Cameron, who she knew spent a lot of time with needy kids like Dylan and Emily. "I'm sorry."

Emily shrugged. "It happens. We're lucky we've got Nan. But she's getting old, you know, and can't do things like she used to. Besides, I have to think about Riley."

Grace glanced at the toddler, still happily playing in the corner. Adolescence, high school exams and a baby? It seemed like a heavy load. "Which is why Cameron wants you to finish high school?"

"Yeah—so I can get a good job or go to college. He's cool, you know…he just nags me a bit sometimes."

Grace smiled. "Well, nagging can be helpful."

Emily laughed. "That's what my nan says. And I guess I know that."

"But?"

The teen shrugged again. "The studying is hard. And I get so tired of being treated differently at school because I've got Riley."

Grace felt the frustration and pain in the girl's voice. She knew firsthand how it felt to be different and then ostracized. "So, how about you show me what you need to study and maybe I can help."

"Are you a teacher?"

"Finance broker."

Emily frowned. "Which means?"

"Which means I'm good with numbers," Grace replied with a wry smile.

She spent the next hour working with Emily. By the time Cameron and Dylan returned, the books were packed away and Riley was asleep in his mother's arms. Emily had asked

Grace to hold the little boy, but she'd resisted. Babies weren't her thing. Making money and math and meetings and work lunches were what she was good at.

Not babies.

Grace didn't have a ticking biological clock. She didn't have some deep-rooted and instinctive yearning to reproduce. She had her career. And it had always been enough.

Being back in Crystal Point wasn't going to change that. Being around Cameron wasn't going to change that either.

"I'll just drop them home," Cameron said as they watched Emily collect her knapsack and haul Riley higher in her arms.

"I should get back to the B and B and—"

"I'll be ten minutes, tops," he said. "Wait here."

Before she had a chance to object, Emily and Dylan waved goodbye and they all disappeared through the doorway. Grace lingered by the desk for a few minutes and got herself all worked up about his high-handed demands. She was just about to head home in protest when her cell rang. It was her boss, Jennifer Mullin-Shaw.

"So, are you relaxing?" Jennifer asked.

Grace was pleased the other woman couldn't see her frown. "Of course."

"And taking the therapist's advice?"

"All of it," Grace assured her. "I'm even watching old movies on cable to relax."

Jennifer laughed and they chatted for a few minutes about mundane things such as the weather and then she gave a brief rundown of her sister's wedding. Minus the part about making out with Cameron on the beach in the moonlight.

"So, you're not dwelling on what happened?"

Grace gripped the phone harder and told a tiny lie. "I haven't thought about the accident at all. I'm feeling…better."

"That's good. I'm pleased you're taking it easy. Give me a call when you're ready to come back to work."

I'm ready now.

But she didn't say it. Instead she ended the call and slipped the cell in her jeans pocket. Her plan to return to the B and B was forgotten when she turned on her heels and discovered Cameron standing in the doorway, arms crossed over his chest, one shoulder propped against the doorjamb.

He looked her over in that slow, infuriating way she was accustomed to. "So, how did it go with Emily?"

She nodded and placed the visor back on her head. "Good. She's a smart girl."

"Yes, she is. Did she tell you about her home life?"

"A little. She told me about her mother and how her two half siblings now live with them and her grandmother."

"Pat took the kids in when her daughter got locked up. Drugs," he explained. "It's been tough for the family. Emily and Dylan's father disappeared years ago and they've lived with their grandmother most of their lives. The father of the two younger kids was killed a few months back. But now they have a chance to start fresh with a new home out near Burdon Creek." He told her how the town had rallied to help the family purchase the small farm.

Grace thought about what he was doing for Emily's family. She tried to think of one selfless thing she done the past year and came up with nothing.

No wonder he thinks I'm shallow. Not that I care one hoot what Cameron Jakowski thinks of me.

"It's good of you to look out for them," she said in a vague way she suspected sounded like some weak attempt to make conversation.

"Someone has to."

Knight in shining armor. Hero cop. All-around good guy. Not the guy for me.

Where did that come from? Grace crossed her arms and

stared out of the window. *Those mindless minutes on the beach the night before, that's where.*

She pulled on her good sense, determined to not think about his arms, his kisses, or anything else to do with the one person who'd managed to get under her skin and make her feel like she was the most self-absorbed woman on the planet. She'd never really cared what Erik thought of her. Or Dennis. Perhaps because she'd always held herself apart and avoided getting too close. But Cameron...he was different. He saw her. Every flaw.

"So, you said you had something to show me?" she asked.

"I did?"

"Mmm-hmm," she replied and tried to dismiss the silly way her pulse raced. But he was hard to ignore in low-rise jeans and a pale blue T-shirt that showed the broadness of his chest and shoulders. And suddenly the air in the room grew hotter, thicker, like a tempting force had swept between them. She'd felt it before and always managed to ignore it. But today she couldn't. He had good looks and charm in bucket loads.

"It's nothing."

She turned her head to glance at him. "Did you get me here under false pretenses?"

"Maybe."

Warmth pushed through her blood. "And now that you have me here, what are your intentions?"

He laughed. "Ah, Grace, you are a confusing and beautiful contradiction."

The compliment part didn't help her determination to not be aware of him. "Then maybe I should leave and put you out of your misery."

"What fun would that be?"

"Who needs fun?" she shot back and managed a tight smile.

"All work and no play, Grace? How's that worked out for you so far?"

"Well enough," she replied.

"Liar," he said softly. "And if I come a little closer you'll be shaking in those three-hundred-dollar shoes of yours."

She drew in a breath. "You really do overstate your charm. If I'm shaking, it's with disbelief that you're so egotistical."

He chuckled and perched his behind on the desk. "You know, Grace, I like you this way...fired up and ready for anything."

Grace raised one brow. "Well, get used to it."

"Don't get me wrong," he said and crossed his arms. "I also like the woman you were last night."

Heat crept up her neck. "Well, don't get too used to *that.*"

He laughed and then just as quickly looked serious. "So, tell me about the accident?" He'd heard that part of her conversation with Jennifer? Damn. *Deny everything.*

"It's nothing."

He shook his head. "I don't believe you. I know there's something wrong with you, Grace. I also know you're too proud, or too stubborn, to say what it is because you think it will give me some kind of ridiculous advantage. Tell me," he insisted as his brown-eyed gaze scanned her face. "What accident were you talking about just now?"

She drew in a breath and the truth felt heavy across her shoulders. Grace closed her eyes for a moment. Images jumbled in her head. Lights flashing, brakes screeching, metal crunching...it was over in a flash of a second. And then there had been an eerie quiet, followed by the sound of her own terrified breath.

And suddenly she wanted to tell him everything.

"I was in a crash," she explained quietly, feeling raw and exposed and more alone than she'd ever dare admit. "I was in a car crash."

Cameron responded quickly. "What? When?"

"A couple of months ago."

"Were you hurt?"

She shrugged. Her scars were emotional, not physical. "I dislocated my shoulder and had a few cuts and abrasions. Nothing serious."

Cameron's gaze was unwavering. "It wasn't just a fender bender, though, was it?"

"No."

"It was a serious crash?"

She shuddered. "Yes."

"And you haven't told your family about it, have you?"

"No."

He pushed himself off the table. "Why not?"

Grace's throat tightened. She hadn't spoken of the accident with anyone other than her boss and her therapist. Her work colleagues had stayed off the topic, even when she'd arrived at the office after taking a week off. They knew she didn't do deep and meaningful discussions. They knew she didn't want to talk about Richard's death. "There was no point."

He shook his head. "No point? They're your *family*. You were hurt, Grace, don't you think they had a right to know?"

The heaviness in her throat increased. "I wasn't hurt badly," she said in a defensive tone. *Not like Richard.* "It wasn't worth making people worry."

He frowned. "People? I'm not talking about random strangers, Grace," he said and grabbed her hand. "I'm talking about your family. Your parents. Your brother and sisters."

She tried to pull away put he held her firm. "You don't understand. I can't be like that. I can't let out every emotion I have. I don't have what it takes to…to…"

"To what?" he encouraged so gently the heat in her throat turned into an all-out burn. "To get close to someone?" he asked.

Grace nodded.

He urged her toward him and she jerked as her body pressed against his. "And yet," he said as he curled one arm around her waist. "You feel close now."

Her emotions heaved. "Please don't...don't tease me."

"I'm not teasing," he said so gently her insides contracted. "I promise. But it might help to talk about it."

Grace didn't want his help. She wanted to run back to the B & B. But she didn't move. And instead, she spoke a truth she hadn't shared with anyone. "Okay...here's the truth. After the crash I had a...meltdown," she admitted. "My boss made me come home. It wasn't my choice. I wanted to work through it in New York. I didn't want to come back here. I didn't want sympathy or pity. I didn't want to feel *anything*."

He looked into her eyes. "Does feeling scare you that much, Grace?"

It scared her. It terrified her. If she let herself really *feel* then she would be exposed...vulnerable. *Weak.* "Yes."

He touched her face. "Then I think you're exactly where you need to be."

In his arms? It was the one place she could never be. She shook her head and pulled away. "Promise me you won't say anything. I don't want my parents to—"

"I promise," he said gently and dropped his arms. "For now."

Chapter Four

Later that afternoon Cameron lingered by the table in his mother's kitchen while she stacked plastic containers into two separate carry bags.

"You know, I can cook for myself," he mentioned, and grinned.

"Me, too," his sister Lauren piped up in agreement.

Irene Jakowski gave a look which said she didn't believe either of them. "Humor me and take this anyway."

Which is exactly what they would do. He inhaled the delicious scent of the cabbage rolls. He did love his mother's *golabki*.

"Not too much, please, *Matka*," Lauren patted her flat stomach and used the Polish word for *mother*, which his parents preferred. "Or I'll end up as big as a house."

"Beef and a little mushroom wrapped in cabbage leaves won't add any pounds," Irene said and raised her brows at her youngest child. "Besides, you're too skinny."

"True," Cameron agreed and winced when Lauren's elbow jabbed him in the ribs.

But he was right. His sister looked too thin. Which wasn't a surprise, considering she'd endured a messy divorce a year earlier. He was pleased she now seemed to be pulling through the worst of it.

"The wedding was just lovely, don't you think?" Irene looked at Cameron as she spoke. He knew where it was going. "Evie made a lovely bride."

He was pretty sure Irene had once hoped he'd hook up with Evie, but he'd never felt that way about her. Grace, on the other hand...his mother knew a little of their failed relationship. It wasn't something he enjoyed mulling over.

"The dress looked fabulous," Lauren chimed in to say. His sister and mother owned a bridal store in Bellandale and he knew they'd fitted Evie for her gown. "I knew the off-the-shoulder design was a good—"

Cameron groaned. "If you two are gonna talk dresses I'm outta here."

His mother chuckled. "I only said she made a lovely bride. But all the Preston girls are quite lovely, aren't they? Even Grace, once you get past her prickles."

"Prickles?" Lauren echoed with a frown. "You mean icy barbs. There's no doubt she's beautiful, but she doesn't exactly bring on the warm fuzzies. Not like Evie and M.J." Lauren grabbed the bag their mother passed her way. "Anyway, enough gossiping, I have to get going."

Lauren hugged them both and was gone within a minute.

"I should get going, too," he said, grabbing his keys from the table.

"Your dad won't be back from golf for another hour," she said and grabbed the kettle. "Feel like staying for coffee?"

He glanced at his watch. "Sure."

"Do you also feel like talking about whatever's on your mind at the moment?"

He had to hand it to his mother—she had the female intuition thing down pat. "Not especially."

"Grace, I suppose?"

He looked up. "What?"

"You're always edgy when she's in town. I saw you talking to her at the wedding so I figured there was some connection to your current mood."

Cameron pulled out a chair and sat down. "You're imagining things. And my mood is fine."

Irene shrugged. "How long is she back for this time?"

"I'm not sure."

"Barbara is worried about her," his mother confided. Barbara Preston was Irene's closest friend. "Know anything?"

Cameron ignored the tightness in his chest. He didn't like lying but wasn't about to get drawn into a conversation about Grace, especially when he'd promised to keep her secrets. "Not a thing."

Irene nodded, gave a wry smile and then switched the subject. "So, you're coming to the reunion this year?"

The Jakowski family reunion was an annual event that had been tradition for more than thirty years. "I'll do my best."

"It will make your father happy if you come."

"I know," he said, but doubted he'd attend. He'd missed four of the past five years and this year was shaping up to be no exception. Because even though Franciszek Jakowski treated him like he was his son in every possible way and he loved the other man dearly, when it came to the huge family gathering, Cameron always felt like a fraud.

His mother had married Franciszek when she was just twenty with a three-year-old on her hip. By the time Lauren arrived a few years later he had already been adopted by Franciszek and he was the only father Cameron knew. His biological father had bailed well before he was born, not prepared for teenage parenthood. Irene never talked about him and Cameron never asked. It was only sometimes that he wondered about him, or when faced with the reunion picnic that he felt like he was there by default. Because Jakowski blood didn't run through his veins. He wasn't really part of the four generations of Polish ancestry that was celebrated by his parents and grandparents and uncle and aunts and countless cousins. He was the biological son of a seventeen-year-old misfit who had disappeared off the radar once his teenage girlfriend discovered she was pregnant.

"Please try," he heard his mother say and it quickly got his thoughts back on track.

He drank some of the coffee she'd placed in front of him and smiled. "I will, *Matka,* I promise."

A few hours later he was sitting on the wide timber deck of his double story, four bedroom, two living rooms, way too big to be practical house, a drink in front of him that he hadn't touched. He'd purchased the half-acre block nine years ago and then designed and built the home, of which he only used about one quarter of the rooms.

It was cold out and he heard the sea crashing against the rocks. In the distance he could see the lights from a vessel in the shipping lane, most likely a tanker on its way to collect cargo from the port south of Bellandale. Locally grown sugar cane was shipped out by the ton and the big ships came by weekly during crushing season.

Cattle bellowed in the distance and the sound was oddly comforting. Living in the most northern end of Crystal Point, he had only one close neighbor—an elderly couple who lived in a small house across from his in the quiet cul-de-sac. Cameron liked the solitude and the view. With hundreds of acres of unspoiled pasture behind and the Pacific Ocean to the front, it was an idyllic location.

The dog at his feet yawned and rolled onto its back and it made him smile a bit. The big, goofy mutt had a way of doing that. But the smile on his face didn't last long. His thoughts were full of Grace.

She'd been in a car crash? She could have died.

Life without Grace in it...

The idea made his bones ache. In just twenty-four hours she'd gotten so deep under his skin he could barely think about anything else. He wanted to call her, hear her voice. He stared at the telephone, then grabbed it and his drink and headed inside. Jed hunkered after him and when Cameron started flicking off lights the dog settled on his big mat by the back door.

Once the house was locked up he took a shower and then dropped into bed. The digital clock on the side table blinked ten-thirty at him. Late enough to sleep, he figured and switched off the lamp before he rolled onto his stomach.

Green eyes haunted him instantly.

He grabbed a pillow and punched it a couple of times.

Green eyes and perfectly straight almost black hair.

Cameron flipped onto his back with a groan, determined to not think about her, and failed miserably. Her unexpected vulnerability distracted him, made him forget she was the world's number one ice princess. He shouldn't want her. But he did.

She made him crazy. Still.

And her kisses were like something from out of this world....

The first time he'd kissed her was on her sixteenth birthday. He'd deliberately arrived late to her party to avoid his growing awareness of her whenever she came near. She was too young. Noah's—his best friend's—sister. And despite the odd time he'd catch her watching him when she thought he wasn't looking, she'd barely give him the time of day. Until that night. A darkened doorway and the heady beat of some old song in the background had shifted her usual reserve. A few minutes alone and the temptation of a birthday kiss and he couldn't help but claim her lips. If it hadn't been for a strict voice in his head telling him she was off-limits for at least a couple more years, they might have done more than share a sweet, unforgettable kiss.

A year and a half later he asked her out for real. By then she'd finished school and he was settled into his career as a second-year officer, had wheels and was saving to buy some land where he'd eventually build a house he hoped she'd one day be proud to live in. He'd had plans, ideas, and every one had included Grace Preston. But three months into their relationship she'd said goodbye and headed to New York.

So what the hell am I thinking? Like I want to be on the receiving end of her rejection again.

Was it just sexual frustration that had him feeling like he did? He flipped back onto his stomach. If he kept thinking about how it felt to kiss her, touch her, stroke her beautiful skin, he'd never get to sleep.

Too late.

Cameron rolled again and stared at the ceiling.

He closed his eyes. A busy week loomed ahead. He had a pile of work on his desk, including a few court appearances. One to give evidence against a repeat DUI offender looking to avoid jail time and Cameron doubted the hard-line magistrate would be lenient. The other two involved breaches of domestic violence orders.

He took a deep breath and tried to relax. But when sleep finally came, his dreams were haunted by bright green eyes...

Because she prided herself on being action oriented, Grace had spent most of the afternoon and evening coming up with ways to pull herself from the uncharacteristic funk that had taken hold of her life.

And one thought kept coming back to her.

Cameron.

If he dared breathe a word to her family she would be completely outed.

And one thing Grace knew for certain—once they knew what had happened to her she would be enveloped in their care and compassion and her fraught nerves would surely fracture. She also knew she didn't have the strength for it. It was easier to stay stoic and in control. Easier to act the role she'd played all her life—the supercool and tough-as-nails Grace who would return to New York without anyone guessing she was broken inside.

All she had to do was make sure Cameron kept his mouth shut.

Grace called him again the following morning and when the call went to voice mail, decided to take more action and see him in person. She took Evie's Honda and drove past his house and since his car wasn't there, figured he was at work. So she headed into town.

The police station was easy to find and she scored a parking spot outside. She'd dressed in a black skirt, matching jacket and collared red shirt. The black knee-high boots and patent bag added to the effect she wanted. All business. All control.

When she reached the reception desk, Grace took a deep breath and spoke to the young woman behind the counter. "I'd like to see Sergeant Jakowski."

"Do you have an appointment?"

"No. But I'd appreciate it if you told him I was here."

One name given, a telephone call and a few minutes wait and she had what she wanted. She took the lift to the second level and when she stepped out into the hall found him waiting.

"This is a surprise."

Grace shrugged as she walked toward him. "I called your cell but you didn't pick up."

"So you decided to start stalking me."

She stilled about five feet from him and waited until two uniformed officers passed before responding. "Yes, you look like you're shaking in your boots."

He smiled. "Speaking of boots," he said and looked her over. "They do the job."

"And what job is that?"

"The job of distracting me enough so you can get your own way."

He liked her boots? "You think I'm that manipulative?" she inquired and stopped in front of him.

Cameron opened a door to his left. "I think you're a woman who wants something."

She did. His silence.

"I just came to talk."

He ushered her into the room and closed the door. "So, talk."

Grace looked at him. He filled out his uniform in a way that got her attention. The pale blue shirt fit him perfectly, highlighting his broad shoulders and lean waist. She quickly ignored her wavering thoughts. "I wanted to know if you'll stand by your promise to keep my private business private."

He came toward the desk and sat on the edge. "I'm not about to be a buffer between you and your family," he said with a kind of irritated disbelief. "They're your *family*, Grace. I don't understand your reluctance to tell them about your accident."

"No, you wouldn't," she shot back. "But it's my decision to make."

He crossed his arms. "It's not hard to let people in."

"Now you sound like my therapist," she said and let out a heavy sigh.

"You're seeing a shrink?"

"Counselor," she corrected and quickly realized she'd said too much. "Because the accident was work-related the company was obliged to supply grief counseling to—"

"Whoa," Cameron held up a hand. "Back up a minute. You're seeing a *grief* counselor. Explain that to me."

Grace's skin prickled. "It's normal in these circumstances."

"What circumstances?"

She drew in a breath, steadying herself. "When someone has died."

He took a second to respond. "Someone died? Who?"

"Richard Bennett," she said quietly and felt the intensity of his stare through to her blood. "A work colleague. We were traveling together at the time of the accident."

"Was anyone else in the car?"

"No," she replied. "Richard was driving. We were on our way to meet with a client. But we crashed. It was no one's fault."

"So he died. And you survived?"

She nodded. Her counselor had explained survivor's guilt several times. She'd brushed it off. Ignored it. "The therapist thought I should come home and be with my family for a while. My boss agreed."

"That sounds like good advice."

Grace shrugged. "But unnecessary. I have a job that I'm good at and a life in New York that suits me. I didn't see the need to change that."

"Obviously the people around you did. What about your friends in New York?"

She shrugged again. There were acquaintances and work colleagues. But friends? None who she was close to. The only person who'd visited her after the accident had been her boss, Jennifer. "You know me."

He looked at her for the longest time before he spoke again.

"I do," he said quietly. "And I know your family. They're kind, good people who care about you."

"Precisely why I don't want to alarm them."

"Nice try. What's the real reason?"

Grace got to her feet. "That is the reason. Does it seem impossible that I don't want to worry them? And it's not like I was seriously hurt. I'm fine. Just fine."

His brows came up and he stood and rocked back a little on his heels. "You're a lot of things, Grace...but I suspect *fine* isn't one of them."

Her annoyance spiked. "You don't know anything about it, so I'd rather you didn't try to psychoanalyze me. All I want is your word that you won't say anything to my family, particularly my parents. I'll tell them when I'm ready, and not before."

"You know, I don't think I quite believe you. You're obviously in denial about an incredibly traumatic experience. The best thing you could do is come clean and talk about it."

What a self-righteous jerk. He knew nothing about what was best for her.

"So you won't keep your word, is that what you're saying?"

He rubbed his chin. "I'm not sure keeping my word would be what's best for you."

She clutched her handbag to her side. "Since it's obvious you don't have the decency to respect my wishes and seem to think you have the right to an opinion about my life, I intend to keep as far away from you as possible while I'm back in Crystal Point." She drew in a deep breath. "Or to put it another way—go to hell, Jakowski!"

Then she was out the door and down the corridor as quickly as her feet could carry her.

Of course, in a town as small as Crystal Point, staying away from Cameron was almost impossible.

When she pulled into the driveway in front of her brother's home that evening and saw Cameron's electric-blue sedan parked there, she immediately considered bailing. But she wouldn't have been able to explain that to Noah. Her brother had dropped by the B and B that afternoon to repair a window lock and had invited her to share dinner with his family. Since she still had one guest to attend to, Grace declined dinner and agreed to a coffee visit instead.

Only she hadn't anticipated seeing the one person she wanted to avoid.

She wondered if he'd wrangled an invitation just to irritate her or dropped in without one. It was her sister-in-law who answered the door and invited her inside.

"We've just finished dinner," Callie said as she closed the door. "But I can get you something if you—"

"Oh, I'm fine," Grace assured her. "I've already eaten."

Her brother and Cameron were in the living room. "Grace," Noah said and came around the sofa. He kissed her cheek. He knew she wasn't the hugging type. "Great to see you. Everything okay?"

"Yes." She glanced at Cameron, who was sitting on the sofa. In jeans and T-shirt he looked relaxed and handsome and possessed such an easygoing manner that when he smiled Grace couldn't help but smile back. *Stay on track.* She rattled the bag she carried. "I brought something for the children, I hope you don't mind?"

Noah grinned. "Not at all. I'll round them up."

Her brother left the room and once Callie disappeared to make coffee, Grace glared at him. "What are you doing here?"

"I was invited," Cameron said, smiling as he looked at the bag she carried. "Gifts are a nice touch. I trust you remember the kids' names?"

She frowned. "I'm not that out of the loop. I am their aunt, you know."

"Nice outfit, by the way," he said of her long denim skirt and pale green sweater.

"Spare me the compliments."

He chuckled. "Very…aunt appropriate."

"Are you suggesting I look like a spinster aunt now?"

He laughed again. "Hardly. There's nothing the least bit spinsterish about you, Grace."

"Other than the fact I'm not married?"

"You've still got time to change that."

Grace shook her head slowly. She didn't want to talk about marriage with him. Because despite the denials she knew would come, being around him made her think, imagine. And those kinds of thoughts were pointless. She had her life—it was set. "Marriage is not in my plans. A husband and kids wouldn't mix with my work."

"And you wouldn't consider giving up your career?"

She placed her handbag by the fireplace and didn't quite have the courage to meet his gaze until she'd inhaled a steadying breath. "My career comes first. I'm not the marriage-and-babies sort. I'll leave that to women like Evie and Callie."

He looked at her oddly. "You don't think a woman can have both?"

She raised her shoulders a little. "I've worked with a few women trying to juggle career and family and they always complained how difficult it was. Better to do one, and do it well, than try to divide the time and become mediocre at both."

"That's a rather dim view of things," he said. "What happens when you fall in love?"

"I won't," she said quickly and tried to breathe through the heat rising up her collarbone. "I mean, I've never felt that. I'm not sure I believe it exists."

"I'm sure your brother and Callie would disagree. And

Evie and Scott. Your parents have had a happy marriage, right? Mine, too."

Grace managed a tight smile. "And yet you've managed to avoid it yourself?"

"But I believe in marriage," he said and rested an arm along the back of the sofa.

"Oh, I thought you were too busy carving notches into your bedpost."

He smiled in that sexy way and Grace harnessed all her resistance. "The fact you've been thinking about my bed leads me to believe there's hope for you yet, *Princess.*"

"I don't know what—"

"Here we are!" Noah said as the kids rushed into the room. The twins, five-year-old Hayley and Matthew, raced toward her, while nine-year-old Jamie trailed behind. Noah's youngest daughter wasn't a child to be held back and she insisted on hugging Grace and then demanded to know what was in the bag. Grace spread the gifts around and made certain Jamie received his while the twins tore at wrapping paper. The books and DVDs were a clear winner. Once they'd said thank-you, the kids quickly disappeared to their rooms.

"Where's Lily?" she asked of Noah's teenage daughter.

"Studying at a friend's," Callie said as she came back into the room carrying a tray.

Grace shook the bag. "I'll leave this for her."

"It's lovely of you to think about the kids like this," Callie said and passed mugs around.

Grace glanced toward Cameron, and then quickly focused her thoughts. Chalk one up for the closed-off aunt. "My pleasure. I don't get to see them often enough."

"We don't see you enough either," Noah said as he took a spot on the other sofa and suggested she sit down.

She made her way around the sofa and sat beside Cameron. He didn't move and his hand rested only an inch from her shoulder. But she could *feel* him. The connection and awareness was like nothing she'd ever experienced. Grace gripped her mug and drank the coffee. Noah watched her, Callie smiled and Cameron's silence was suddenly deafening.

When he finally spoke she jumped a little. "So, Grace was telling me she'll watch the kids for you next Tuesday."

I was?

Noah looked surprised. "Really?"

"I think that would be great," Callie said and squeezed her husband's knee. "Your parents offered—but I know they'd like to be at the awards dinner."

Awards dinner? She looked at Cameron. There was laughter and direct challenge in his eyes. *Damn his sexy hide.* He was deliberately trying to antagonize her. She managed a tight smile. "I'm more than happy to watch them."

"It's only the twins," Callie explained. "Jamie and Lily want to be there to see their dad get his award."

She feigned knowledge, knew that Cameron was laughing to himself and made a point to settle this particular score with him when they were alone. "What time do you want me here?"

"Six o'clock," Noah said.

They chatted for another twenty minutes and she was grateful her brother didn't question her about New York or how long she intended to stay in Crystal Point. Finally, Cameron got up to leave, said goodbye and offered to walk her out.

Once they were by their cars and out of earshot she glared at him. "What was that about?" she demanded. "Has meddling in my life suddenly become an entertaining pastime for you?"

"More of an *interesting* pastime," he corrected with a self-indulgent grin.

"And clearly volunteering me to babysit is your idea of a joke?"

"Well, you did say your therapist suggested you spend time with your family."

She wanted to slug his smug face. Instead, she drew in a steadying breath. "Thank you for your charitable concern. However, I can arrange my own family time without your interference."

He grinned. "Really? And did you know about your brother's award?"

"Of course," she fibbed.

His brow came up. "Well, in case it slipped your mind, it's a community award. And a big deal. Preston Marine offers traineeships for young people with disabilities. The award is recognition of his work helping these kids."

She knew her brother did that, didn't she? Noah had been at the helm of the boat-building business that had been started by her grandfather for over a decade. Her father had retired a couple of years earlier. A niggling shame seared between her shoulder blades. Was she so busy with her own problems she'd forgotten everything about where she came from?

"Of course," she said again and knew he wasn't convinced.

He came a little closer. "On the other hand, if you don't think you're up to the task of watching the kids, I'm sure they could find someone else."

Grace bristled. "No need for that," she assured him and continued to fight the urge to slap his handsome face. "I'm quite confident I'll manage the task."

He laughed out loud. "Well, that's great to hear, *Princess.* Because the price for my silence has just gone up."

Her blood stilled. "What does that mean?"

"Emily needs a tutor for the next two weeks."

A tutor? "I can't possibly—"

"No lessons," he said, cutting her off. "No silence."

Shock leached the color from her face. "That's blackmail."

"Friendly incentive," he said and grinned. "Besides, Emily likes you."

In truth she liked Emily, too, and even though part of her sensed she would be able to help the teenager, Grace wasn't about to be railroaded. "I'm not qualified to do that."

"You're perfectly qualified," he said and moved closer to open her driver's door.

"I won't do it."

"Sure you will. You fight a good fight, Grace," he said with a kind of arrogant overconfidence. "But not good enough. I'll make sure Pat drops Emily off at Dunn Inn around four tomorrow for her lesson. Good night."

He was close enough that for a second she thought he might kiss her. For a second she actually wanted him to.

But he didn't.

She got into the car and drove off and wondered what had happened to the well-ordered, organized life she'd once had. The life that had been about clients and meetings and skipped lunches and business dinners. Not about tutoring teenage girls, babysitting five-year-olds and dreaming about kissing Cameron Jakowski.

And then, she wondered how she was supposed to want that old life back once she returned to New York.

Cameron stayed away from Grace for the following two days. Mostly because he knew it would drive her crazy. Being the rigid control freak she was, he'd bet his boots she'd want to wail at him some more about being pushed into tutoring Emily. So he gave her a couple of days to work with the teenager without him hovering.

He arrived at Dunn Inn late Wednesday afternoon and found Grace in the downstairs kitchen, preparing things for the evening meal. Of course she could cook. There were a couple of unfamiliar vehicles parked in the circular driveway, indicating guests were in residence. Even working over a stove she was immaculate. Black pants and white shirt and a pristine apron he figured probably wouldn't dare crease, made her look formidable and beautiful.

He remained beneath the threshold and watched her work for a moment.

When she finally looked up and let out a small, surprised gasp, he spoke. "How's the tutoring going?"

"I'm holding up my end of the bargain," she replied and placed a lid on a saucepan. "Emily's a smart girl and I think she'll ace the test with a little more studying."

He walked into the room. "I think so, too."

She frowned. "Is her son's father in the picture? I don't want to ask her directly if the subject is off-limits."

Cameron shrugged. "He took off when Riley was born."

She stayed silent for a moment, looking at him. "Is that why you..."

"Is that why I...what?" he prompted. But he knew what she was thinking. His own parentage wasn't exactly a state secret. Barbara Preston had introduced his mother to Franciszek all those years ago, so they were well aware he was adopted by his dad.

"Nothing," she said tightly and pulled a frying pan off an overhead hook.

"Do you think I'm trying to get over my abandonment issues by helping Emily and Riley?"

"I...don't...know," she said and he noticed she looked a little paler than usual. Maybe she wasn't sleeping? Well, she wasn't the only one. "Are you?"

"I never knew my biological father," he said quietly. "So there's no real issue to get past."

One brow rose. "You don't miss what you've never had, you mean?"

"Exactly. And I help kids like Emily and Dylan because

it needs to be done. Otherwise they could fall through the cracks in social services."

She untied the apron. "I don't know how you manage it, but you always make me feel...feel..."

"Feel what?"

"Self-centered," she said and tossed the apron on the bench. "Selfish. Shallow. Superficial."

At least he was making her feel something. That was a start, right? "Success and beauty don't go hand in hand with being superficial."

She stared at him and the mood between them quickly shifted. His attraction to her had a will of its own and air was suddenly charged with awareness. Her hair was pulled back in a tight ponytail and he had the urge to set it free. Memories of kissing her on the beach only a few nights before rushed back and filled his blood. Her icy reserve had slipped and she'd kissed him back passionately. And he wanted to feel that passion again.

"Don't."

Cameron tilted his head. "Don't what?"

"Don't say I'm...you know."

"Beautiful?" He laughed softly. "No point denying the obvious."

"Like it's all I am."

Cameron moved around the counter. "That's not what I said. But I guess it's easier to think the worst of me."

She turned to face him. "Nothing is easy with you."

He reached out and touched her jaw. When she didn't move he rubbed his thumb across her cheek. "Then let's call a truce."

"A truce?"

"Yes," he said and stepped closer. "And let's stop pretending we don't want each other."

Chapter Five

He wants me.

She couldn't remember the last time a man had said that to her.

Or the last time she'd wanted to hear it. Erik's lukewarm attentions hadn't bothered her because she'd felt the same way toward him. And Dennis was no different. But her feelings for Cameron were different. They always had been. They were there, under the surface, waiting to jump up and take hold. For years she'd been safe in New York—away from him and the connection that simmered between them.

She drew in a tight breath. "I don't have casual sex."

"And you think I do?" he asked and dropped his hand.

Grace raised a brow. "We've already had the conversation about your reputation."

"You shouldn't believe all you hear, Grace."

Yes, I should. It was safer to think of him as a woman-izer. Safer to imagine him making love to someone else. But that notion made her insides contract. *Not that I want him to make love to me.* "I've got three weeks, Cameron. And I'm not going to complicate things by...by..."

"Not everything is so black-and-white."

Grace crossed her arms. "What does that mean?"

"It means you can't put every feeling into a neat little package because you're determined to control everything. The truth is we've been dancing around this for years. I'd rather it be out there and on the table."

She pushed back her shoulders. "I wouldn't. We have a deal—and that's all we have. I want your silence and I'll tutor Emily in return."

He blatantly ignored her. "You haven't got anyone staying here after tomorrow, right?"

"Right," she replied suspiciously. "The place is empty until after Scott and Evie return the weekend after next."

"Good. Pat is taking the kids out to the farm in Burdon Creek this weekend. There's still some work to be done on the place before they can make the move permanently, so I thought you might like to help me give them a hand for a couple of days. Plus you'll get a chance to keep tutoring Emily."

No way. "I can't do that."

"Sure you can," he said and smiled. "It'll be good for you."

"I don't—"

"Just think of all that fresh country air," he said with one brow raised. "Wouldn't that be exactly what the doctor ordered?"

Yes, she thought, it probably would be. But it didn't mean she was about to agree. Spending the weekend with Cameron, in any circumstances, was a complication—and temptation—she didn't need.

"No," she said quietly.

He shrugged, infuriating her. "No weekend, no deal."

Grace felt her control slip away. She thought she had everything settled. A month back in Crystal Point and then she'd return to New York—that was the plan. This wasn't. "More blackmail? Forget it. I'm not spending the weekend with you."

"Emily and Riley will be there. And Pat and the kids. There'll be plenty of chaperones, Grace, so you can relax."

She didn't want a chaperone. She didn't want to relax. "I said no."

"No weekend, no deal," he said again. "Unless, of course, you would prefer to tell your family about the car accident which could have killed you and how you didn't care enough to inform them at the time."

Grace glared at him. "You're an ass, Jakowski. I *will* tell them and you'll have no hold over me."

He grabbed the cell phone on the countertop and held it toward her. "Here you go."

She froze. He knew she wouldn't take the phone. He knew she wasn't ready to tell her family what had happened. One word about the accident and she would also have to talk about her therapist, Richard and the whole awful experience. She lingered over another refusal and considered how hurt her parents would be once they found out the truth.

"Okay," she said resignedly. "I'll go with you. To help out and to tutor Emily," she said with emphasis. "And that's all."

He nodded and stepped back. "I'll pick you up Friday morning, eight o'clock."

Then he dropped the phone back on the counter and left.

The next morning Grace went shopping for new jeans and a couple of polo shirts. Bellandale had a few nice boutiques and she couldn't help splurging on a new pair of fire-engine-red heels that simply screamed "pick me." She also purchased a pair of sensible boots. They were the kind she knew people wore in the country, ankle-length with a square block heel. She walked around the B and B at night in them to try to break in the stiff leather and got mean-looking blisters on her toes as a result.

She also kept up her end of the deal and tutored Emily each afternoon.

"So, you're hanging out at the farm this weekend?" the teenager asked as they ended the lesson on Thursday evening.

Grace closed her laptop. "Yes."

Emily grinned. "Ever been on a farm before?"

"When I was young," she replied. "My grandparents had a small fruit farm and I used to visit sometimes." Not often, though. The farm was more Evie's and Noah's thing back then. Most of her vacations from boarding school were spent in Crystal Point. When her grandparents passed away the farm was sold.

Emily packed her books in her satchel. "So," she said with a curious edge. "You and Sarge—there's really nothing going on between you guys?"

"Not a thing," she said quickly and ignored her flaming cheeks. "Make sure you take your books tomorrow—we can continue with this on the weekend."

"I don't get a break?"

"No chance. One more week at this pace and you'll easily pass the exam."

Emily dropped the bag to her feet. "Not that it will do me much good. It's not like I'm going to get a great job or anything."

"It's not?"

The girl shrugged. "I've got a kid, and even with Nan's help it's gonna be hard to do what I really want to do—which is study fashion design. I work at a coffee place three mornings a week when Nan can watch him. But once she moves to the farm I won't have anyone here. It sucks, but I get why she wants to move. Dylan was getting into a lot of trouble before Sarge came along and he's really looking forward to living on the farm."

"What about day care?" Grace suggested, not really having a clue.

She shrugged again. "I can't really afford it. And I don't want to miss out on Riley growing up. But I want to go to design school, too..." She sighed heavily. "I guess it will work itself out."

Grace felt for the girl. "If design school is where you want to go, then it's exactly what you should do." She smiled gently. "You should follow your dreams, Emily."

Like she'd followed the dreams set out before her. But were they her own dreams? New York. A huge apartment. Designer clothes. A successful career. In the midst of trying to prove herself she'd gotten swept up in wanting what had been expected of her. But the truth was, none of it really satisfied her anymore. The money and fancy apartment were part of the facade that had become her life. When she was younger and ambition had burned in her, Grace hadn't noticed how alone she actually was. Perhaps her failed relationships with Dennis and Erik had amplified that feeling. Or maybe it was knowing both Noah and Evie had found their happily-ever-after that made her question what was really important. And now, more than ever, she didn't know where she belonged.

When Cameron arrived to pick her up Friday morning, Grace was waiting outside the bed-and-breakfast, her Gucci luggage at her heels. She pulled at the lapels of her soft leather jacket and ran her hands down her fine-gauge wool trousers as he eased the big, powerful blue car alongside the curb. It was cold and barely eight o'clock.

He got out and flicked open the trunk. Her heart stopped when he moved around the vehicle. Dressed in jeans and a long-sleeved gray Henley shirt, he looked so good she could barely swallow.

"Morning," he said easily.

Grace walked toward the passenger door and tried desperately to ignore her traitorous feelings. "Be careful with my cases," she demanded with a frosty glare.

He laughed. "Not a morning person, *Princess?*"

Grace opened the car and got inside. What was the worst thing that could happen? She might break a nail or get a few blisters? *I can handle that. I can handle anything.*

She took a deep breath and immediately wrinkled her nose. Something didn't smell quite right. When she heard a strange, almost guttural sound she snapped her neck around and found herself staring into a pair of piercing amber eyes and the most unattractive, jowly, drooling face she'd ever seen.

Grace's breath stopped. *Oh, my God!* The dreadful beast licked his chops and saliva leached from his pinkish, puckered mouth. She jerked her head back to the front and closed her eyes, gripping her hands together.

When Cameron got back into the car she spoke through tight lips. "There's something big and horribly smelly in the backseat."

"That's Jed," Cameron said with a laugh. He started the car and the hideous-looking animal woofed.

The sound reverberated in her eardrum like a trombone. "What is it?" she asked, trying not to think about the terrible smell racing up her nose.

"A dog. My dog."

He had a dog. The biggest, ugliest dog he could find by the looks of things. Grace's only recent experience with animals was her neighbor's Himalayan cat she sometimes watched. Noah and Callie had two dogs, but not like the thing in the backseat.

She glanced at him, determined not to look at the beast in the back. "What kind of dog?"

"Dogue de Bordeaux."

It sounded French. The only French dog she'd seen was a poodle. "It smells."

"He's not an *it,*" Cameron corrected as he steered the car in an arc and down The Parade. The road ran the length of the town, a buffer between the narrow parkland and walking track along water's edge and the long row of houses, which ranged from small beach homes to some three-story mansions. "His name is Jed, like I said. And you'll get used to his breath."

"I'd rather not."

Cameron laughed again. "He's a good dog."

"Who needs a breath mint."

"Did you just make a joke, Grace?"

She pushed her handbag to the feet. "Unbelievable, I know. Imagine, me with a sense of humor."

Cameron was imagining a lot of things. Like tugging her perfectly pulled-back hair down for one. There wasn't a tendril out of place. He couldn't see her eyes shielded behind designer sunglasses and wanted to know if they were scorching through him. And the leather jacket fitted like it had been tailored for her. Nothing out of place. Immaculate and beautiful.

She looked at him. "Where exactly are we going?"

"Burdon Creek. It's three hundred and eighteen kilometers west of Bellandale and has a population of one hundred and six. One shop, which is also a gas station, a pub and a post office, and that's about it."

"And the family is happy to settle there?"

"Yes," he replied. "There's a bigger town a few miles up the road where they can get everything they need. It will be good for Dylan. He was a troubled kid when we first met. His father bailed when he was young and his mother had been in and out of drug rehab for years. His two half siblings lived with their father, but he was killed last year in an industrial accident and the kids went back to their mother and Dylan and Emily." Cameron knew how difficult it had been for Dylan to adjust to having his brother and sister living in the small house he shared with his mother, older sister and grandmother. "When his mother was arrested for possession the kids were placed in their grandmother's care. It was her third offense and she got four years' jail time."

"And the children have stayed with their grandmother?"

"Yeah. Pat's a good woman and really wants to give the kids a stable home. But the house she was in only had two small bedrooms. For the past ten months we've been raising money to pull together a deposit so she could buy a home for the kids. A few local businesses came on board and we found the place at Burdon Creek. It needed a bit of work, but most of the structural stuff has been done now. We had contractors volunteer and the past few months they've been traveling back and forth to get the place ready for Pat and the kids."

Grace flipped her sunglasses off and looked at him. "So in between my tutoring Emily what else will we be doing?"

"Painting, moving a bit of furniture, decorating…that sort of thing."

Her perfectly arched brows rose dramatically. "Decorating?"

"I thought you'd be good at it," he said.

"Why?"

He shrugged. "Because you did the decorating for Noah's showroom last year. And you always look like you've stepped off the pages of one of those glossy magazines."

Cameron looked at her and swore he saw a smile tug at the corner of her mouth.

"Is that a compliment?" she asked quietly.

"Absolutely."

"Thank you...I think." The smile grew wider. "But you should know I hired an interior decorator to do my apartment and Noah's showroom. I just supervised."

Cameron grinned. "Looks like you're in charge of moving furniture then."

She laughed delightfully and his insides crunched. It was way too easy being with her like this. He relaxed and pressed a button on the iPod in the center console. Coldplay's unique sound filled the space between them and he wondered for a moment if she'd prefer something else. But she pushed her head back against the headrest, replaced the glasses and closed her eyes. Jed made a weary sound and stretched himself out on the backseat and Cameron headed west.

Grace slept. Not the kind of sleep she got in her bed. This was a deep calm. With the music playing and the soft hum of the motor she was unusually relaxed. Her typical day in a car was driving to and from the office in rush-hour traffic before fighting for a parking space.

She opened her eyes a few times over the following hour or so and watched as the landscape changed. The sugar cane farms were replaced by cattle and pasture and the homes became more infrequent the farther they drove. They didn't speak, which suited her fine and he seemed as content as she was to listen to the music and enjoy the scenery.

The smelly hound in the back didn't stir and she was grateful for that.

Cameron pulled into a roadhouse midmorning, where they refueled and grabbed coffee to go.

"Pat will want to feed us when we arrive," he told her as they walked back to the car. "But if you're hungry we can—"

"I'm fine," she said. "I had a big breakfast." She reached into her handbag and pulled out a small paper bag. "I have muffins for the road."

Cameron grabbed the bag and took a look inside. "You've been holding out on me for the past hour and a half?"

Grace colored. His words smacked of intimacy. And she wondered how she would hold out being with him for the next few days. Because it seemed so incredibly normal to be walking beside him in the morning sunshine.

She shrugged lightly. "I did some baking yesterday. Help yourself."

Cameron took a muffin and ate it in about three bites. "It's good." He unlocked the car and stared at her. He waited until she was in the car before getting in himself. He patted the dog and then wiped his hands on a towel on the backseat. "So, what else can you cook?"

"I just took a Thai cooking class. And I make some mean sushi."

He looked like she'd said rat bait. "Oh. Sushi…I've never tried it."

"It's delicious," she said and clicked her tongue.

His gaze went instantly to her mouth and Grace couldn't stop her lips from pouting ever so slightly. There was something intensely erotic about him looking at her mouth and she felt the sensation right down to the blood in her bones. He turned away before she did, but Grace swore she saw something in his eyes, a kind of raw hunger that turned his irises to a deep chocolate. He cleared his throat and started the engine and she tried not to think about how warm her skin was. Or how much she liked the sensation.

Burdon Creek *was* in the middle of nowhere. It was a quiet, sleepy-looking place that had aura of another time about it. They drove slowly down the one main street and continued past the gas station. The farm was about ten miles from the town center and when they arrived Cameron got out of the car to open the rickety gate.

The house stood at the end of the long gravel driveway. It was old, but she saw where the contractors had worked hard to repair the roof and the large veranda. It needed painting on the outside and the garden was overrun with twisted bougainvillea vine.

There were stables some way from the house and a large machinery shed. A boy in dark overalls was walking across the yard and came over to greet them. It was Dylan, and when they got out Cameron shook his hand.

"I've been feeding the horses," Dylan announced, looking immensely pleased with being in charge of the task.

"The neighbor supplied the kids with a couple of horses for the weekend," Cameron told her as he let the dog out. The big drooling beast made his way around the car and Grace held herself rigid as he pushed against her leg.

"He wants a pat," Dylan told her and came over and rubbed the dog's head. "He always wants pats. Nan said we could get a dog once we get a fence around the house."

"Cam!"

They all turned at the sound of the loud greeting. A sixty-something woman stood on the porch with a walking stick in her hand. She had a mop of frizzy gray hair and a beaming smile. Cameron walked across the yard and hugged the woman close when he reached her. Grace stood still, watching the exchange. She'd never been a hugging sort of person. Even with her family. Of course, it was impossible to avoid it with Evie and M.J., because they were both warm and affectionate, but her parents and Noah seemed to respect her need for personal space.

"Who's this?" the woman asked as both silvery brows rose. "A girl?"

Grace walked across and stood at the bottom of the short stairway. "I'm not really a girl...I'm the decorator."

Cameron laughed and once the introductions were made

Patricia Jennings invited them inside. The house was in various states of repair. Plasterers had been in to replace walls and most of it required painting. There was some furniture scattered throughout certain rooms and the kitchen had received a full renovation.

"Take a seat," Pat invited as they entered the kitchen. "I'll put the coffee on."

Grace sat down while Cameron headed back outside to retrieve their luggage. She placed her handbag on the chair beside her. "Where's Emily?" she asked.

"Putting the baby down for a nap," Pat said and smiled. "I have to say how committed she's become to her studies since you've been helping her. She really wants to finish high school, which isn't an easy task for a young mother. She has had a hard time of it since Riley came along." Pat raised her brows. "I thought of shifting her to a new school but she wanted to stay where she was."

"She's been bullied?"

"A little," Pat replied. "Teenage girls can be cruel."

Grace knew about that firsthand. Her first twelve months at boarding school had been fraught with teasing and isolation. "Are you looking forward to moving here permanently?" she asked, politely making conversation.

Pat turned around, swinging mugs in her hands. "Oh, yes. The kids will love being able to run around and Dylan becomes quite the man of the house when we're here, fixing things and doing chores." Her wrinkled face grew somber. "Maybe he's too grown-up sometimes. We used to be really close. But with the little ones needing me I just don't seem to have the time for him that I used to. I was so worried about Dylan at one stage—but then Cameron came along and he's a changed boy since he's had a man's influence in his life." Her pale blue eyes regarded Grace and she smiled. "Officer Jakowski was a godsend to us. You're a lucky woman."

Grace knew what she meant and quickly set her straight. "Oh, we're not... It's not like that. We're just..."

"Just what?" Pat asked as she poured coffee.

Grace briefly explained how their mothers had been inseparable since they were in their teens, and that Noah was his closest friend. "We've know one another a long time."

Pat nodded, like she suspected there was more to it than that. "It's good of you to come and help us this weekend," she said and brought the coffee to the table. "It's been hard trying to sort through everything, and with the two little ones still missing their daddy I've had my hands full."

Grace couldn't imagine how difficult it had been for the other woman. She looked weary and not in the best of health. But she obviously loved her grandchildren.

"The kids are lucky to have you."

Pat smiled warmly. "I'm the lucky one. When Lynnie..." She stopped for a moment and took a deep breath. "That's my daughter. When she went off the rails this last time I knew I had to do something for the children's sake. Dylan was at such an impressionable age and the younger children needed to be cared for. Their father was killed over a year ago."

"Cameron told me."

Pat tutted. "It was very sad. He's wasn't a bad sort of man. At one time I'd hoped he and Lynnie might have worked things out. But he wasn't prepared to live with an addict. Can't say I blame him." Pat grabbed milk from the refrigerator and placed it on the table. She sat down heavily in a chair and stared at Grace. "You're very beautiful. I can see why Cameron's interested in you."

Grace stopped herself from denying it and put a little sugar in her mug. "It's complicated."

"Life generally is," Pat said agreeably. "I was married for thirty-five years to a good man. When he passed away three years ago I lost the love of my life."

Grace felt a sudden stab of envy. She'd never experienced anything even remotely resembling that. And the look on Pat's face was the same look she saw on Evie's face, and Callie's and her mother's.

True love. When had she become so cynical about it? Her bland relationships with Dennis and Erik hadn't left her brokenhearted. There had been a definite lack of intimacy, both sexual and emotional. She'd lost her virginity to Dennis when she was twenty-two, five months after they'd begun dating. There were no fireworks in the bedroom, though. And in hindsight, very little chemistry between them. Erik had been more sophisticated and more sexually demanding, but that had only created a greater wall between them. Her continued lack of response to him between the sheets had finally made him walk out the door. In some ways she'd been relieved when it had ended.

She remembered the conversation she'd had with Cameron about marriage. It was easy to hide behind the idea that a woman couldn't have it all. And she had told herself she didn't want that time and time again. She had her career and her driving ambition. She wore shoes that probably cost more than the woman sitting opposite her spent on clothes in a year and never let anyone get too close. And that, she realized, was why she'd never felt truly whole. The emptiness had grown bigger as she gotten older, and each year she filled that space with more work, more ambition. She had a half-lived life. But the thought of anything else, anything…more…rattled her to the very foundation of her soul.

"You know, it's the little things that I miss most," Pat said with a soft sigh. "Like how he used to always make that first cup of tea in the morning. Or how he'd mow the lawn and then come inside smelling like cut grass. And we'd play cards every Sunday night." She looked across the table. "There's a lot to be said for the love of a good man."

Grace had no intention of responding to that. Fortunately Dylan and Cameron returned to the kitchen with their luggage and Pat suggested they settle into their rooms. She was surprised to find they weren't going to be in the main house, but in a separate cozy cottage about fifty meters from the mudroom and behind what looked like an old vegetable garden.

Two small children, a boy about four and a girl a couple years older, both with grubby faces and bare feet, raced around to greet them and Pat quickly introduced her other grandchildren, Thomas and Isabel.

"You'll be comfortable here," Pat assured her as they walked across the yard. "This was renovated first, and when we came for weekends we lived here until the house was ready. It used to be a workers' cottage many years ago, when the farm was a working cattle station and before the land was all subdivided."

Grace smiled, walked through the front door and was pleasantly surprised. Although sparsely furnished, it had lovely polished wood floors and high ceilings. It was clean and tidy and inviting.

"You'll have more privacy here than in the house with me and these adorable hellions," she said and gestured to the children zooming up and down the hall making airplane sounds with their arms outstretched.

Pat rounded up the kids and they all left once Grace's bags had been brought into the small hallway, and not before the older woman told them to come back to the main house for lunch in an hour. Once they were gone she turned to find Cameron standing behind her, one shoulder leaning casually against the doorjamb that led into the living room.

So much for chaperones!

"Okay?" he asked.

"It's nice," she replied as she peered into the bedroom off the hall. A large bed filled the room, covered in a crisp white overlay. There was a neat vanity and narrow armoire. She walked across the threshold and turned around. "I'm sure I'll be quite comfortable."

Cameron moved forward and grabbed her bag. "You might want to ditch the leather jacket and change," he suggested as he dropped the luggage into her room. "We'll be painting a little later."

She nodded and cleared her throat. "Um…where are you sleeping?"

He pointed down the hall. "Miles away—so don't fret."

Grace flushed hotly. "I'm hardly fretting."

He smiled and her insides flipped over a little more than usual. He looked good when he smiled, even more handsome. And he had nice hair, she noticed, like the color of beechwood honey. She remembered how it had felt caught between her fingers and the memory made her hands tingle. The small-ness of the room created a sudden intimacy and Grace sensed a shift in the mood between them. She stepped back and collided with the foot of the bed. "Well, I'll just get changed."

"Sure," he said and headed for the door, but suddenly he stopped and turned. "What were you and Pat talking about in the kitchen?"

Love…

"The kids," she replied, and placed her handbag on the vanity. "And the house."

"Was she matchmaking?"

"I set her straight," she replied with a shrug. "I told her exactly how we feel about each other."

He looked at her oddly. "I doubt that," he said and then grabbed his bag and headed off down the hallway.

Grace took about twenty minutes to unpack and change into a pair of gunmetal-gray cargo pants and a long-sleeved navy T-shirt and bright red sneakers. She left her hair pulled back in a low ponytail and took off her watch. The last thing she wanted was paint spattered on her Rolex.

When she was done, she took a tour of the small house. There was one bathroom, the kitchen and dining area and the living room. The furniture looked new and the country-cottage print on the sofa and curtains suited the place. There was also a small fireplace and a thick hearth rug in muted greens.

Emily arrived, books in hand, and announced she would be studying in the kitchen in the main house. They chatted for a couple of minutes before she left to start studying.

"Ready?"

Grace turned on her heels. Cameron stood in the doorway. He'd changed, too. He wore a pair of old jeans that had a hole in one knee and white T-shirt that was splattered in places with various shades of paint. Working clothes, she thought, and then felt ridiculously self-conscious in her immaculate two-hundred-dollar cargo pants.

She swallowed hard. "Sure. Let's go."

Once they were outside he suggested a tour of the farm before they headed to the house for lunch. Grace agreed and followed him toward the old stables. Jed rose from his spot on the porch and ambled behind them. The stables were big and old and smelled musty and she wrinkled her nose when they walked through the wide doorway. She picked up another scent immediately and recognized fresh baled hay. It had a sweetish smell and quickly knocked off the old-barn odor.

Through to the other side of the building was a large paddock. Grace spotted two horses happily munching grass. "It's a lovely spot," she said as she crossed her arms over a fence post.

He turned around and half trapped her against the fence. "Is breathing in this fresh air making you feel all country inside?"

Grace didn't move. To escape she would need to press past him. Maybe touch him. She prepped her sharp tongue. "I'm all city—you know that."

"And yet, you're here."

"I was forced into it."

His eyes darkened to the color of melted chocolate. "I'd never force you into anything."

He stepped back and didn't say another word as he began to walk back toward the house. She felt bad. Of course she knew he wouldn't force her to do anything she didn't want to do. That wasn't his way.

"Cameron?" He stopped walking and waited for her to catch up. "I didn't mean anything by that."

He nodded. "Forget it. We should get back."

Lunch was outrageously delicious and filled with more carbs than Grace usually consumed in a month. Fresh baked bread accompanied roast chicken and gravy and a creamy potato dish that was so scrumptious Grace had two helpings. The kids chatted throughout the meal and the littlest one got potato in his hair.

Grace wasn't sure what she felt sitting with the fractured, yet incredibly loving family. Cameron seemed to fit effortlessly within their little group. It made the world she lived in suddenly seem painfully superficial. On the surface she appeared to have it all—career, success, money.

And yet, for more than the first time lately, she wondered what the worth of it all was? At that moment, she couldn't see or feel anything other than a startling realness during the hour she shared with Pat Jennings and her grandchildren. And the man she'd tried desperately to keep out of her heart for so long, but knew she never had.

Or ever would.

Chapter Six

As Cameron watched Grace his chest tightened. She was laughing at something one of the kids said and looked so incredibly lovely he could barely get air into his lungs. He'd never seen her so naturally unguarded. She was still as picture-perfect as always in her pressed trousers and starched T-shirt and there wasn't a hair out of place. But there was something in her expression he hadn't seen before. She smiled at him, as though she knew he was thinking about her. Did she know it? Was it obvious?

"We should get started on the painting," he said.

Grace nodded and stood. "I'll help clean up the dishes first."

"Nonsense," Pat replied. "Leave the dishes to me. I can manage that even with my bad leg. The painting is too much for these old bones. Off you go. I'll make sure the kids don't disturb you."

Cameron stood and left the room and felt Grace's presence in his wake. He headed for the living room and spotted a pile of drop cloths by the entrance. The room was sparsely furnished and had only a sofa and small coffee table.

"Where do you want me?" she asked.

Cameron turned around. Her words sounded provocative and gave his insides a jolt. He grabbed a couple of the drop cloths and held them out to her. "You can place these over the furniture while I prepare the paint."

"Sure," she said as she took them. The painting gear was on the veranda and he headed outside. He stayed for a while to sort through colors and clear his head. When he returned to the living room Grace was sitting on the edge of the sofa. She stood and waited while he placed the paint and brushes by the door.

"What color are we going for?" she asked as she examined the paint lids for swatches.

"You choose," he replied and lifted off both lids.

She looked at the tins and gestured to the warm beige tint. "That one. And I think we should consider a feature wall." She pointed to the long wall opposite the doorway. "Something darker—maybe the rich toffee. If we add a slipcover over the sofa in the same shade it will pick up the color."

He half smiled, intrigued by the interest she showed. "Anything else?"

She bit down on her lower lip for a moment. "Perhaps a lamp—one of those tall ones for the corner. With a low-watt bulb it will cast some nice shadows around the room. And a plush rug for the spot in front of the fireplace. And maybe a couple of pictures for the walls." She raised her brows with a kind of keen excitement. "You know, Evie has some furniture pieces in a storage shed that she hasn't used for years. I think she'd let them go if she knew they were going to a good home."

Her sudden enthusiasm captivated him and Cameron took a deep breath. "I thought you said you couldn't decorate?"

She looked at him. "I said I'd hired a decorator."

"To do what?'

She smiled. "To do what I asked."

He'd never known a woman so determined to do things her own way. "You'll talk to Evie?"

"Yes. In the meantime let's get started."

Cameron started preparing the paint and Grace grabbed a brush. "Do you want to cut in?" he asked as he poured a small amount of paint into a plastic container.

"Sure." She glanced up at the high ceilings. "I'll need a ladder."

That's not all she needed, he thought, looking at her designer clothing and spotless shoes. "There's one outside, I'll get it."

He took off down the hall, silently cursing the way his insides were jumping all over the place. Being near her was making him nuts. He'd be glad when the painting started so the fumes could drown out the scent of the flowery fragrance she wore, which hit him with the force of a jackhammer every time she moved.

He inhaled a long breath and headed for the cottage.

Grace poked the brush into the paint and examined the color. She'd started cutting in the edges around the doorjamb when Cameron returned. He held something out to her.

"Here," he said. "Wear this."

Grace put down her brush and took the garment. She held the soft chambray shirt in front of her and shook her head in protest. "I couldn't possibly—"

"Wear it," he insisted. "You don't want to ruin your clothes. It's an old shirt."

It was an old shirt. But it was incredibly soft between her

fingertips. She nodded and slipped her arms into the sleeves. It was far too big and she rolled the sleeves up to an accommodating length and did the buttons up, but it was surprisingly comfy.

"Thank you," she said and forced herself to not think about how intimate it seemed to be wearing a piece of his clothing.

Cameron grabbed the roller and paint can. "No problem."

She went to speak again but her mouth remained shut. He smiled slightly and awareness rushed across her skin in an all-consuming wave. The white T-shirt he wore did little to disguise his broad shoulders and muscular arms. And his jeans were so worn and faded they amplified the ranginess of his lean hips and long legs.

Grace struggled to drag her eyes away. Everything about him was wholly masculine and she realized at that moment how naively she'd been denying it to herself for so many years. She'd never been attracted to a man the intense way she was attracted to Cameron.

They worked through the afternoon and by four o'clock she was exhausted. Her palms were pink and puckered from the constant pressure of the brush and her neck ached. But despite her pains, Grace was determined to push past her fatigue. She wouldn't give in. Cameron of course, was like a machine. He worked through the break Pat insisted they have, and because she wasn't giving in to her exhaustion, forced Grace to do the same. She quickly took a couple of massive gulps of icy homemade lemonade Pat had brought in on a tray to avoid looking like she was taking a breather, and climbed back up the ladder.

They had music playing softly in the background and the ugliest dog in world was stretched out beside the sofa, snoring the afternoon away.

"We should finish up soon." He'd stopped painting and

came over to the corner where she was propped up on the ladder. He looked up at her and held out his hand. "Come down."

Grace reached out and grasped his hand. He wrapped his fingers around hers and she felt the contact down to her toes. She stepped down the ladder and when her feet touched the floor her legs were strangely unsteady. She placed the container and brush on top of the small ladder and kept her hand in his.

Cameron looked directly into her eyes. "You have paint on your face."

Any other time Grace would have been immediately self-conscious. She usually hated mess and being untidy. But she was reluctant to break the easy mood that had developed between them over the course of the afternoon. "I guess I should go and wash up," she said quietly.

He grazed his knuckles across her left cheek. "I guess you should. It's water-based paint so you don't need to scrub too hard."

"Okay—well, I'll get going and…" Her words trailed off and she moved to pull away. But he didn't release her. "You still have my hand."

He half smiled. "So I do."

"I'll need it back if I'm to get rid of this paint on my face."

He released her immediately. "I'll clean up the brushes and the rest of the gear."

Grace stepped away and pulled her arms around herself. "Okay." She looked around the room. "We did a good job today." She turned to the exposed fireplace and the lovely pale coffee-colored wall framing it. "And it feels good to *do* something good." She gave a humorless laugh. "But I guess you know that already. You've always been generous with yourself." When he didn't say anything she raised a brow. "That was a compliment, not a dig."

Cameron stared at her. "With our history sometimes it's hard to tell the difference."

He was right and Grace experienced something that felt a lot like shame work its way across her skin. "Looks like our truce is working."

"We've gotten off to a pretty good start. No fights, no insults, for at least…" He checked his watch. "Eight hours."

"I've never liked fighting with you," she admitted. "It was just easier than thinking about…about anything else."

"I know."

She didn't respond and left the room as quickly as she could, making for the kitchen. After spending a few minutes with Emily to see how the studying was going, Grace walked back to the cottage.

A shower topped her list of things to do. Grace collected fresh clothes and toiletries and headed for the bathroom. The claw-foot bathtub was the first thing she saw and she was immediately seduced by the idea of a long soak. She quickly popped in the plug and played around with the water temperature. Once the water flowed she added her favorite Dior scented bath foam and stripped off her clothes.

It took close to ten minutes to fill the tub, but finally she slipped into the bubbly water and stretched out her legs. Grace let out a heavy sigh and her body relaxed instantly. She'd had a long, exhausting day and was physically taxed, but had none of the mental fatigue she often experienced as a result of a fifteen-hour stretch in the office.

She rested her arms along the edge of the tub, closed her eyes and leaned her head back. A simple delight. But it felt better than anything had felt for a long time. When was the last time she'd spent the time to really relax? She couldn't remember. Since the accident she'd become even more wound up, more determined to be in control.

She took a deep breath and slipped a little farther down

into the water. A sound caught her attention but she kept her eyes shut. A creak followed, like a door opening. Had she not closed the door properly? *It's probably just the wind pushing the door open.*

Another creak followed. And another. It was the door. And it *was* opening.

Grace clamped her lids tighter. Surely Cameron wouldn't enter the bathroom? But when she finally found the courage to open her eyes, it wasn't Cameron standing by the bathtub.

It was Jed.

The smelly beast had pushed the door open far enough to invade her privacy and was sitting heavily on his haunches, drooling all over the floor. He made a sound, half growl, half whine.

"Shoo!" she demanded, looking around for her towel. It was on the sink where she'd left it. The smelly dog scooted closer and dropped his chin on the rim of the tub. "Go away."

He whined again and showed off his big teeth.

Grace pushed herself back as far as she could go. *I will not panic.* She heard footsteps in the house and quickly pulled herself together. Cameron was back.

"Hot Tub!" she yelled, knowing the nickname he hated would get his attention.

The footsteps grew louder and she heard a tap on the half-opened door. "Grace?"

"You're dog is drooling in my bathwater—get him out of here."

He laughed.

"It's not funny," she protested. "Please get him out of here so I can finish my bath."

Cameron laughed again. She was taking a bath? He hoped the rainwater tanks could support it. He called Jed to come out. The dog didn't come so he called him again. And again.

Damned dog.

"It's no use," she said shrilly. "He's got one paw up on the tub. If he gets in the water I swear I'll…I'll…"

He tried not to laugh and called the dog again. When Jed didn't respond he said, "So, can I come in?"

She was silent for a moment. "Well, yes…okay."

Cameron took a deep breath and pushed the door back. Sure enough, there was Jed, paw up on the rim of the tub, drool oozing from his mouth, and staring at Grace with what was clearly a serious case of puppy love. "He likes you."

Grace scowled at him and ducked down into the water. "Funny. Get him away from me."

"Come on, Jed," he said firmly. "Let's go."

He walked toward the bathtub and kept his gaze centered firmly on the dog.

I will not look at her.

But Jed had his own ideas and sprang up on his back legs, wagging his tail. Any second now, Cameron thought, and the dog would be in the water with Grace. He lunged for the animal and grabbed his collar. Grace screamed. Jed rose up on his back feet and splashed his front paws into the water. Grace moved against the back of the tub and the foamy water sloshed, exposing her creamy shoulders and the unmistakable swell of her breasts and his breath rushed out with a sharp kick.

I am so not looking at her.

But as the bubbles sloshed and rose her body was silhouetted against the opaque water. A body he'd touched that night on the beach. And suddenly looking at her was all he was good for. He glanced at her face and saw her green eyes shining with a kind of hot awareness.

Sex swirled around the steamy room—potent and powerful.

She used her hands to shield the parts she didn't want him seeing and that just kicked at his libido like an out-of-control sledgehammer. He could imagine sliding the soap across her skin, he could almost feel how smooth and slippery...

"Cameron...I...I..."

Grace's voice, barely a whisper, dragged him from his fantasies.

He pulled the dog back, grabbed his collar and with the animal firmly under control he spun him around and headed out of the room. Cameron shut the door and released Jed instantly. The dog scooted off, leaving a trail of wet paw prints in his wake.

Cameron let out a heavy breath, stood outside the bathroom door and rested his forehead against the jamb.

Idiot...

One glimpse of skin and he was done for. He wanted her so much.

And had two more weeks to do something about it.

Grace pulled herself out of the tub once the door clicked shut and hastily grabbed a towel. She rubbed herself dry and pulled on her clothes with less than her usual care.

Cameron Jakowski saw me naked.

Okay, not completely naked but close enough. Close enough that Grace knew that what she saw in his eyes was raw hunger.

She shoved her feet into flat sandals.

No man has ever looked at me like that.

His gaze had scorched her skin like a lover's touch. He'd looked like he wanted take her into his arms and kiss her passionately—right then, right there.

And the knowledge tapped into something inside her. Grace had never considered herself all that desirable. Erik's complaints about her lack of enthusiasm in the bedroom still echoed in her head. Dennis hadn't been as harsh, but she'd sensed his dissatisfaction with her, especially in the latter months they were together.

But those fleeting moments in the bathroom with Cameron made her feel so sexually charged that every part of her skin tingled. The truth pounded through her like the loud beat of a drum.

She wanted to make love with Cameron.

And she knew, without a doubt, that he wanted it, too.

What had happened between them at Evie's wedding should have knocked the truth into her. But she'd spent a week in a kind of hazy denial. And now, all of a sudden, she knew it, felt it, and could almost taste the reality of it. And it scared her. She feared losing control. Of being vulnerable. Because Cameron could do that to her. He'd always made her feel that way. He'd always had a secret, almost seductive power over her.

Grace checked her hair in the mirror and saw it was doing a faux impression of being straight as it fought for release from its ponytail. She tucked some stray pieces behind her ears and grabbed her toiletry bag before she headed from the room.

She dropped her things off in the bedroom and walked through the house. Jed was in the small living room, spread out in front of the fireplace, his deep snoring sounding as if he needed an inhaler. She grimaced at the sight of his pink-and-fleshy gums and then left him to his nap.

In the kitchen she noticed an aluminum tray on the countertop and immediately popped the lid, inhaling the scent of delicious-looking pasta. Obviously from Pat, Grace found the other woman's consideration heartwarming. The clock on the wall read a quarter past seven and her grumbling stomach figured it was soon time for dinner. She popped the tray in the oven and set it to a low heat.

"Hey."

She pivoted on one heel. "I see Pat prepared dinner for us," she said easily. "I've just starting reheating but it shouldn't take long. I thought I would—"

"Grace?"

She took a breath. He stood in the doorway, arms crossed, seeming like he had something to say but wasn't quite sure how to say it. Still wearing the paint-splattered T-shirt and ridiculously sexy jeans he looked so good her traitorous belly flipped over. "What?"

He shrugged. "About before…I want to apologize."

Grace fiddled with a tea towel to do something with her hands. "It was my fault. I should have made sure the door was shut properly."

"That's not what I meant."

Grace cursed the color she knew rose up over her collar. "Oh, well I—"

"Things have changed between us," he said, cutting her off. He ran a hand through his hair and she watched him without taking a breath. "For years we've been skirting around it, avoiding it, pretending that what happened between us when we were young didn't matter. But it does matter, Grace, and it's stopped us from being anything to each other, if that makes sense. We're not friends, we're not enemies…we're not lovers…we're just stuck somewhere in between."

"I can't—"

"I won't pretend I don't want you, Grace. Not anymore."

She stilled instantly. In another time, another life, she would have shot him down immediately. Because now, despite the voice in her head telling her that her life was about to get way more complicated, she wanted him, too.

Even though she knew it wouldn't be enough. She was going back to New York in two weeks. Starting something with Cameron would be madness. It might be mind-blowing. It might be exactly what she needed to help ease the dreadful grief and guilt that clung to her every pore.

But when she opened her mouth, prudence foolishly disappeared and something else altogether came out. "Is that why I'm here?" she asked. "Because you want to get me into bed?"

He took a moment to respond. "Not...entirely."

She couldn't help but smile. Another man might have denied it. But Cameron was too honest to play games. "If that's the case, then I guess we'll just see what happens."

His brows shot up. "And let nature take its course, you mean?"

She dropped the tea towel on the counter. "In a way. I don't see the point in either of us getting worked up over something that hasn't happened—or might never happen."

He stared at her. "So, it *is* mutual?"

She made a job of looking for plates and cutlery to avoid the question. When she'd unearthed both she turned back around and found Cameron still watching her. "Well," she said with a sigh, "I'm hardly the type of woman who lets just anyone put his...I mean...his hand...up my dress." The heat got her then, flaming her cheeks, and she gripped the plates until her fingers were white.

He didn't say anything for a moment. He looked at her though—that look she'd suddenly come to think of as the sexiest look in history. "Okay, Grace. We'll take things slowly, if that's what you want." He muttered something about taking a shower and turned on his heels, and Grace got back to her task before he'd even left the room.

Cameron took a cold shower and did his best to clear the chaos raging through his thoughts. Of course, it didn't work. And by the time he'd dressed, lingered in his room for what seemed like an eternity, and then finally headed back to the kitchen, Grace was still behind the counter, chopping and dicing vegetables for a salad.

He fed the dog and set the table, trying to ignore how absurdly domestic it seemed, moving around the kitchen together, not speaking, but feeling as though they had been doing it this way for years.

They ate dinner and even opened the bottle of wine Pat had left in the refrigerator. Once their plates were empty and the dishes cleared, they were left at the table, lingering over the remainder of their wine.

She looked different, he thought, then realized it was probably one of the few times he'd seen her without makeup. He liked it. She looked younger and less uptight. She smiled and it ignited something inside him. There'd been a kind of easy camaraderie between them over dinner and he didn't want that to change, but she looked so fetching with her clean face and bright smile, he could hardly think of anything other than hauling her into his arms and kissing her madly.

"You're great with the kids," she said and he got his mind back on track.

"Thank you," he said. "They're easy to like."

"You'll make a good dad."

Cameron's heart suddenly pounded behind his ribs. Could she know that's what he wanted? That he was aching for a family of his own? "One day, I hope so. You know, you're not bad with kids yourself."

She made a scoffing sound. "I'm a train wreck."

"Emily doesn't think so," he said quietly. "She told me you've been patient and understanding, but also firm when she loses concentration."

"Well, she's a good student, despite her lack of confidence. Did you know she wants to go to college?"

He nodded. "She's got ambition."

"Which isn't a bad thing."

"I didn't say it was."

She fingered the stem of her wineglass. "No, you didn't. But..."

"But what?" he prompted.

"You didn't always feel that way."

He pushed back in his chair. "You mean about *your* ambition? I was young and had ideas about the kind of future I wanted. Just like you did, Grace. Only mine were small-town and yours were big-city."

She looked at him. "You were angry."

"I was dumped," he said bluntly. "What did you expect? Roses and violins?"

"I guess not. I didn't deliberately set out to...to hurt you." She drew in a tight breath. "In hindsight I shouldn't have started anything knowing how I felt about wanting a career. But I was young and starry-eyed. Even career girls get swept away sometimes."

His heart pumped. "By what?"

Her shoulders rose fractionally. "By romance, I guess. By that first kiss when I was sixteen. By the way you didn't rush me to sleep with you, even though we were dating for a few months."

"I thought we had..." He stopped, remembering how much he'd wanted her back then. "Time."

She looked into her glass for a moment, and then glanced upward. "Well, for what it's worth—I'm sorry for the way I behaved back then. These past couple of months I've had a lot of time to think. It sounds cliché, but there's something life-altering about facing your own mortality. When the car crashed I had about thirty seconds to consider all the mistakes I've made, all the people I've hurt in one way or another. It was a sobering half minute."

"Apology accepted."

She offered a bittersweet smile and stood, scraping the chair back. "We did have a nice three months, though. Life was way less complicated then. Do you think anyone ever suspected?"

Cameron stood and moved around the small table and took hold of her hands. "My mother figured it out. I'm not sure about anyone else. Noah's never said anything to me."

"I told Evie a long time ago," she confessed. "Did you know you were my first kiss?"

He rubbed her hands with his thumbs. "I kinda guessed."

"Was I that bad?"

"Not at all," he said gently. "But you seemed a little surprised."

"I was," she admitted. "At school I was into books and not boys. It didn't exactly make me Miss Popularity. And you'd never shown any interest...I mean, before that night of my birthday."

He chuckled. "Oh, I was interested. But you were too young and my best friend's sister."

"So what changed that night?"

"Seeing you standing in the doorway," he said and reached up to twirl a lock of her hair. "When I arrived everyone else was by the pool, but you were inside, and alone. You looked beautiful in that little blue dress. Before that I just..." He shrugged and smiled. "I just wanted you to grow up quick so I could kiss you like I'd imagined doing so many times."

He bent his head and kissed her softly. It wasn't like the night on the beach. This kiss was gentler, sweeter somehow. He wasn't sure how long they stood like that—just kissing, just holding the back of her neck tenderly with his one hand while the other lay against her hip. Grace gripped his arms and held on, and he enjoyed the feel of her mouth against his own and the soft slide of her tongue.

When the kiss ended Cameron laid his forehead against her. "Well," he whispered hoarsely. "That seems pretty natural to me. Good night, Grace," he said softly and released her. "Go and get some sleep. I'll lock up."

She rocked on her heels. He knew sleep wasn't what either of them wanted. But he was offering her an out and he knew she'd take it.

She said good-night and walked from the room without saying another word.

Chapter Seven

Cameron didn't sleep more than two hours. With Grace only meters away down the hall he lay awake most of the night and stared at the ceiling. When he'd finally had enough of fighting the sheets he swung out of bed and got dressed. It was just after seven and he could hear Dylan in the yard with his little sister. Cameron looked out of the window and spotted Isabel racing around her brother as he snuck out from the chicken pen clutching a basket in his hands. His sister gave him no peace as he crossed to the house and it made Cameron smile. Lauren had been like that, he remembered fondly. Six years younger, his sister had hung from his every word when they were growing up.

He was still smiling as he left the room, then headed for the kitchen once he'd let Jed outside. Cameron made coffee, drank a cup and was just rinsing off the utensils when he heard a curse. A very loud curse. He stood still and waited. Then it came again.

Grace's voice was unmistakable. But the words coming out of her mouth were unlike any he'd heard from her before. He took off past the living room and headed for the hall. The profanity started again and he stalled outside her bedroom.

"Grace," he said quietly as he tapped on the door. "Are you all right?"

Nothing for a moment, then a clipped, "Yes...fine."

"You sound like you're in—"

"I'm fine, like I said," she insisted. "I'm just having a little trouble with my... I forgot to bring something to this forsaken place, that's all. Can you please leave me alone?"

"Sure," he said, grinning to himself. "I've made coffee."

"Whatever," she mumbled and he heard the frustrated banging from behind the shut door.

Something was up, but he didn't press the issue. He walked back to the kitchen and opened the refrigerator, mulling over the contents. When nothing took his fancy he shut the door and reached for a glass, and then stopped dead in his tracks. Grace stood in the doorway.

And she looked thunderous. "Don't say a word," she warned.

Cameron bit back the urge to smile. "About what?" he asked innocently.

Both her hands snapped up to frame her head. "About this!"

Now he smiled, because he couldn't help himself. Her hair, usually so straight and severe, bounced around her face in a mass of wild curls. Untamed and out of control, she'd never seemed more beautiful in her life. "It looks—"

"I forgot my straightener," she said with a sniff.

"What?"

"Hair straightener," she replied. "My flatiron. And now I have to deal with this *mess*."

He laughed then and she didn't like that one bit. "Your hair looks fine," he assured her. "It looks pretty."

She plucked at a few strands. "It's not pretty. It's not fine," she retorted, then let out a long breath. "You think I'm over-reacting?"

Cameron raised a hand. "Don't accuse me of thinking."

That made her laugh and she clutched her fingers together. "No one has seen me like this since…well, I can't remember the last time."

"You look good," he said and passed her a cup. "Drink up. We've got work to do."

She took the coffee and patted her stomach. He noticed she was wearing his shirt again. He liked that. "I'm hungry. Feed me first."

Cameron's libido did a leap. The mood between them seemed oddly playful and it made him think about fisting a handful of that glorious hair and kissing her neck. "I make a mean batch of scrambled eggs," he said and begrudgingly pushed back the idea of kissing her. "Feel like risking it?"

She nodded, perched on a bar stool and sipped her coffee. "I'm game."

He got what he needed from the refrigerator and began cooking while Grace quietly drank her coffee and stared at the linoleum countertop. She looked like she had something on her mind and he wondered if she'd spent the night staring at the ceiling like he had. After a while she put the cup down and linked her hands together.

"Why did you kiss me last night?"

Cameron stopped whisking eggs and stared at her. His chest tightened. "Because I wanted to. Because you're beautiful." He smiled. "The usual reasons."

"You know I'm leaving in two weeks?"

"Yes."

"And you know I'd never move back?"

Cameron put the eggs aside. "You wouldn't?"

Grace shrugged. "I don't belong in this world, Cameron. I don't belong in *your* world."

"Is that your way of letting me down gently?" he asked, and noticed her green eyes were suddenly luminous as she looked at him. "Even though you're not denying there's an attraction here?"

"But when a relationship is only based on strong physical—"

"Were you in love with the suit?" he asked quickly. "Or the doctor?"

"No."

"Have you ever had an intimate relationship just for the sheer fun of it?"

Her gaze narrowed. "I don't believe in casual sex."

"I'm not talking about something casual, Grace. I'm talking about having a relationship without laying down a whole lot of ground rules."

"I don't do that," she said hotly.

Cameron's brows shot up. "You don't?"

"Okay, maybe I do," she replied. "I like to be in—"

"In control," he said, cutting her off. "Yeah, I get that about you, Grace. But sex shouldn't be about control. It should be fun."

She glared at him. "Just because I take things seriously, that doesn't make me an uptight prig. I know how to have fun. Maybe my relationships with Dennis and Erik weren't all fireworks and passion. And maybe I did insist on separate apartments and avoided having them stay over because I'm too independent about have to be in control of *everything*. Maybe I'm all that and more...but it doesn't mean I'm sex-starved or frustrated or that I'm going to jump into the nearest bed I can find."

If I had any sense I'd forget all about her.

But he was all out of sense when it came to Grace.

"I wasn't suggesting you should," he said and bit back a grin. "Just, to not dismiss the idea entirely."

She shrugged. "I'm not good at relationships. I'm not good with people. With men. I always seem to make them leave." Her hands came to her chest and she held them there. "Do you know that I've only ever trusted three men in my whole life," she said softly and with such rawness his insides constricted. "My father, my brother..." She let out a long sigh. "And you. I know it probably hasn't seemed that way."

"No," he said. "But things often aren't what they seem."

"Like what?" she asked.

"Like the way I've always felt about you, Grace."

The words hung in the room. She didn't say anything else as they sat down for breakfast. They ate the eggs in a kind of forced silence. Grace offered to wash up and he didn't argue as he headed off. He'd said too much. Admitted too much. Her silence was like a swift slap in the face. It was a rejection. Again.

He was accustomed to it.

Don't you ever learn, Jakowski?

He left the room, mumbling something about paintbrushes and getting started on the painting.

By eight-thirty Grace headed for the main house. Pat was in the kitchen and greeted her with a broad smile.

"The kids are in the stable," the older woman explained. "Waiting for kittens to be born. A stray arrived last time we were here and I didn't have the heart to call animal welfare." She looked at Grace. "Did you sleep okay?"

Grace patted down her curls. "Yes, thank you. The cottage is very comfortable."

"But small," Pat said, grinning. "Too small and snug for

one old lady, four kids and a baby. But for you and Cameron—I imagine snug would be good."

Grace's cheeks flamed. "Like I said, we're not—"

"I know what you said," Pat said cheerfully and plopped a tea bag into a cup. "But I also know what I see. Even the bravest man might be afraid of letting his true feelings show," Pat said quietly. "If he believes he's going to get hurt."

Like the way I've always felt about you...

That was just it. He had let his feelings show.

And it terrified her. For years she'd handled his antagonism and sarcasm—that was easy. That she could combat with insults of her own. This was something else. Knowing he had feelings for her, still had feelings for her, made it impossible to keep denying her own feelings...the ones that were madly beating around in her heart.

The back door opened and Dylan entered excitedly. Cameron soon followed. He glanced at Grace and then turned to Pat. "Looks like rain in the distance."

"Rain?" Pat's expression widened. "Wouldn't that be lovely? We need a downpour to fill up the rainwater tanks. What I'd give for something more than the two-minute shower I have every time we're here."

Grace looked at Cameron, instantly mortified when she remembered the luxurious soak in the tub she'd had the afternoon before. She hadn't considered water preservation. She'd only given a thought to herself. His eyes were dark as he watched her, as if he knew her thoughts. Shame raced across her skin. What hadn't he said something to her?

"I'll have one-minute showers from now on," Grace told Pat. "You can use my saved minute for your bathtub."

Pat grinned broadly. "You're a sweet girl, Grace." Her crinkled eyes zoomed in on Cameron. "You shouldn't let this one go in a hurry."

Cameron smiled and leaned against the doorjamb. "I'll see what I can do."

It was a highly inflammatory thing to say and Grace's skin warmed immediately. "We should get started on the painting," she said and avoided the curious look on the older woman's face as she took a step. "I'd like to work with Emily this afternoon."

"The main bedroom needs doing," he said. "We can start there."

She didn't say another word and swiveled on her heels. In the main bedroom seconds later, she saw that Cameron had already moved the furniture to the center of the room and covered it with a drop cloth.

"Grace?"

He was behind her and she turned immediately. "What color today?" she asked, ignoring the thunderous beat of her heart behind her ribs. "Perhaps a pale—"

"Grace," he said again and with more emphasis. "We've got another two days here—so let's not get hung up on what I said earlier, okay?"

She shrugged. "It's forgotten already." She picked up a can of paint and thrust it toward him. "Let's start."

He took the paint and grabbed her hand before she could escape. "There's no need for you to be afraid of me."

"I'm not," she refuted.

"You're shaking."

Was she? Grace looked at her hands. The quiver was undeniable. "Let me go."

"Not until you tell me what's wrong."

"I can't," she said and tried to pull away. "I can't talk to you."

"Grace?"

It was too much. Too much honesty. Too many feelings were emerging and she had no idea how to handle it...or to handle him. She shouldn't have said anything. She should have worked on getting through the next two days without getting involved. But she lay awake for half the night, thinking about him...thinking about his kiss, his touch, and how suddenly it was the one thing she wanted more than anything else.

And it couldn't be.

She wasn't cut out for a relationship with him. She was going home in two weeks. Back to New York and everything familiar.

Grace took the brush and headed for a corner. She turned around and faced him, her back to the wall. "I just want to get through the weekend."

"Is being with me such a hardship?" he asked quietly.

"No," she admitted and looked sideways. "Which is exactly my point." Grace twirled the brush between her fingers. "I'm not going to sleep with you."

He looked tempted to smile. "I don't remember asking you to."

She plucked at the sleeve of the shirt that had become incredibly comfortable against her skin. She had the silly thought she might just keep it after the weekend was over.

"But you said..."

"I said what?" he queried. "That I want you?"

She exhaled. "Yes."

"So, I want you. It doesn't have to mean the end of the world, Grace," he said quietly. "It doesn't have to mean anything."

"Good," she said and pushed back her shoulders. "Because it doesn't." Grace turned on her heels, determined to ignore him and pretended to focus on painting.

Three hours later, and without more than half a dozen words said between them, the room was finished. Lunchtime loomed and Pat stuck her head in the doorway just as Cameron was pulling drop cloths off the bed, and told them to come to the kitchen. Grace ducked past the older woman, muttering something about washing up first and he didn't stop her.

He headed off to do the same once the bedroom was back in order. But he didn't find Grace in the cottage. She was outside with Isabel, examining a low branch on a citrus tree, which was weighed down by its fruit. He stood by the cottage steps and watched the exchange. With her hair down, her jeans spattered with paint and his old shirt hanging loosely off her shoulders she looked so incredibly lovely his chest felt like it would implode. Only Grace could do that to him. Only ever Grace.

Isabel laughed at something Grace said and she pulled a piece of fruit off the tree.

She really is good with kids.

But she didn't want them. That should have sent him running. Because he wanted children. The damnable thing was, he wanted to have them with Grace.

It took ten minutes to clean up, switch T-shirts and head back to the main house. He'd heard Grace come inside and head for the bathroom and left her to wash up as he made his way back to the main house. When he walked into the kitchen he quickly picked up that something was wrong. Pat and Dylan stood opposite one another and both faces were marred with a stricken look.

"What's up?" he asked as the back screen door banged behind him.

"It's Thomas," Pat said quickly, looking ashen. "He's gone missing."

Cameron stepped forward. "Missing? How long ago?"

Dylan shrugged his bony shoulders. "I'm not sure. Could be an hour or more. I thought he was with Isabel in the stable."

"Isabel was the last person to see him?" Cameron asked.
Another shrug. "Dunno."

"Let's ask her, okay?"

Pat called the girl to come into the kitchen. Isabel couldn't remember when she'd last seen her brother and Cameron's instincts surged into overdrive. "We'll look around the house first," he assured Pat. "In all his favorite spots."

Grace entered the room and he told her what was happening.

"I'll help you look," she said and headed directly back out through the mudroom.

Fifteen minutes later, after every possible hiding place had been exhausted around the perimeter of the house, and they called his name repeatedly, Cameron knew they needed to widen the search.

"You head next door," he told Dylan. It was about one mile to the nearest neighbor and Cameron knew the boy would cover the ground quickly. "Grace and I will cut across the back paddock and head east. He can't have gotten too far. You stay here with the girls," he said to a worried Pat. "And call me if he comes back. Also, call the local police station and alert them to what's going on—tell them we're coordinating a search and you'll get back to them within the hour if we need help."

While he gave Dylan instructions he noticed Grace packing a small bag with water and cereal bars she'd found in the pantry. Within minutes they were outside and winding their way past the stables and through the barbed-wire fence.

"Any idea where he might be?" she asked as he held the wire apart while she slipped through.

They both stood and stared at the endless miles of pasture ahead of them. "Just a hunch he'd head this way. He knows not to go near the road because Pat has drummed road safety awareness into all the kids. This way seems logical."

She nodded. "Could he get far ahead of us?"

"Possibly. If he's just walking and not distracted." He raised his hand in an arc. "We'll keep about thirty meters apart. And watch for holes in the ground. I don't want you breaking any bones."

She nodded and walked off, creating space between them. And then they started walking, tracking across the undulating ground, looking for signs, anything that might indicate a little boy had come wandering this way. They were about ten minutes into it when his phone rang. When he finished talking and slipped the phone back into his pocket he noticed Grace had moved toward him a little.

"Who was that?" she asked in a loud voice.

"Fish," he replied.

She frowned. "What does that mean?"

"It was Pat," he explained. "Apparently Isabel remembered Thomas saying he was going to find a fish for the cat. Cats like fish, right?"

"I'm not sure I'm following you."

Cameron pointed toward the horizon. "There are three water holes on this property."

She flipped her sunglasses off her nose. "Do you think he might have—"

"I'm not sure," he said quickly and started walking again. He could see Grace's concern in the narrowing of her features. "Don't worry—he'll be fine."

She nodded. "Okay. Let's pick up the pace."

They did so quickly and thirty minutes later came across a small dam. Cameron checked for footprints and found only those belonging to cattle and the tracks of a lone wallaby.

"Nothing here," he said and trudged back up the side and onto the flat.

"That's a good thing, right?" Grace asked and passed him a bottle of water from the small backpack she'd brought with her. "If he's not here he might be on his way back. Maybe he's home already?"

Cameron forced a smile at her optimism and took the water. "Maybe. Let's keep going, though. The closest neighbor in this direction is about another three kilometers from here."

Five minutes later he heard from Pat again. He told her to call the neighbors and say they were on their way and to contact the police again and keep them updated. His phone crackled and faded as he rang off.

"Reception's gone for the moment," he said to Grace as they headed off again. "From now on we just keep walking and looking."

She nodded and turned away. But not before Cameron saw the fear in her expression. He felt it, too, although he wasn't about to admit that to Grace. They continued their trudge across the undulating landscape and didn't speak, but the tension between them was unmistakable. A shared tension brought on by the building threat that they wouldn't find Thomas—that he was lost, injured or worse.

Cameron spotted the familiar rise of another water hole ahead. A few cattle bellowed in the distance and he saw Grace hesitate on her feet as she walked. He doubted she'd ever been anywhere near a cow. He picked up speed and called the little boy's name. Grace quickly did the same and within seconds they were both jogging. She was faster than he'd imagined, even over the rough terrain. He stayed pace with her and somehow they ended up side by side, moving swiftly across the grass, avoiding stones and dips in the ground. He grabbed her hand and her tight grip seemed to push them harder and faster. Finally they reached the water hole and took long and hard steps up the embankment, sinking slightly in the unsteady clay underfoot.

"Cameron!"

Grace's voice echoed across the water as they both crested the rise. He saw Thomas immediately, on his belly, facedown in the murky water. He was at the water's edge in four strides and pulled the sodden, unconscious little boy into his arms, praying that they'd reached him in time.

Chapter Eight

Grace heard a scream and realized it was her own terrified voice. Cameron trudged up the embankment with Thomas in his arms as she dropped the backpack.

Panic coursed through her blood. She'd felt that panic before. The accident and Richard's death came rushing back into her thoughts. She tried to shake off the memory, tried to act normally, tried to stop her knees from failing.

Take a breath...one...two...

Slow breathing helped whenever she experienced that rush of adrenaline, that same dreaded coldness whispering across her skin. Usually it happened when she was alone at night, or about to drift off to sleep...then the darkness wrapped her up and for a while she was back, trapped in that car, praying... hoping that someone would find her.

"Grace?"

Cameron's voice jerked her back into the present and she quickly pulled herself together as he laid the child on the ground. Thomas looked ghostly pale and she dropped to her knees beside him.

Her voice cracked when she spoke. "Is he breathing?"

Cameron shook his head and rolled the child over to clear water from his airway.

"Try my phone again," he barked and pulled the phone from his pocket as he turned Thomas onto his back again. "The nearest hospital is half an hour away so get an ambulance to meet us at the farm."

Grace grabbed the phone and hit the emergency number. Thankfully, there was a signal and she quickly made the call, ensuring an ambulance was on its way to the house. Time stretched like elastic, and what was seconds seemed like an eternity. She watched, horrified and fascinated as Cameron performed CPR and encouraged the child to breathe in between puffs of lifesaving oxygen. Finally Thomas spluttered and drew in a long gasp of air. She touched the boy's muddy hair soothingly as his breathing steadied. He opened his eyes and croaked out a word she couldn't understand. With instincts she hadn't known she possessed, Grace comforted Thomas and told him it would be all right. Cameron rocked back on his heels and closed his eyes and Grace touched his arm.

"You did it," she said, squeezing a little. "He's okay."

Cameron nodded and let out a long breath. "Let's get him home."

She nodded. "He's cold," she said, touching his pale face. Grace pulled a sweater from the small backpack and quickly threaded Thomas's arms into the sleeves and then took off her own jacket and tucked it around his small body. She rubbed his hands together for moment then looked toward Cameron. "Let's go."

She watched as he lifted the child effortlessly and held him against his chest. He walked back to the house as quickly as

possible, and too emotional to speak, Grace followed. Pat and
the rest of the children were waiting by the fence when they
arrived and she heard Cameron's palpable sigh of relief at
the sight of the ambulance in the driveway. Two medics were
instantly on hand and rushed forward to take Thomas from
Cameron's arms. Within minutes the little boy was wrapped
in a thermal blanket and received the necessary attention
from the officers.

Pat came to Grace's side, tears in her pale eyes. Without
thinking, Grace braced one arm around the older woman's
shoulder and held her tightly. Cameron spoke with the officers as they loaded Thomas into the vehicle.

"You should accompany him," Grace said to Pat. "Cameron will go with you. I'll stay here with Emily and the kids."

Pat nodded as tears welled and fell. "Thank you."

Minutes later Grace watched the ambulance skim down
the gravel road following closely by Cameron's sedan. She
hadn't said anything to him as he'd left. She hadn't needed
to. The realization they could communicate with simply a
look filled her blood, her skin, her very core.

She gathered the children and headed back to the house.
Dylan seemed unusually quiet and she ushered him into the
kitchen with the girls and Jed at their heels and made a quick
meal of ham-and-cheese sandwiches. After they'd eaten Isabel raced off to her bedroom, too young to fully compre-
hend what had happened to their brother, while Emily went
to bathe Riley and put him to bed. Dylan however, lingered
by the sink. Aware that the boy was grappling with his emotions, Grace suggested a makeshift game of cards to help
distract him until he chose to talk about how he was feeling.

It took about thirty minutes.

"Do you think he'll be okay?"

Grace dropped a card onto the table and chose another.
"Of course he will."

"I should have watched out for him." He looked downward. "I wasn't watching. I wanted to muck around with the horses. I didn't want to get stuck watching the kids again. I forgot about him. I forgot and he disappeared. If Nan finds out she'll be really angry."

She heard the panic and pain in Dylan's voice and felt the need to comfort him. "I dropped my little sister on her head once," she admitted and looked at him over her cards. "I was supposed to be looking after her while my mother was outside. We were twirling...but I got dizzy and dropped her."

"You *dropped* your sister?"

"Mmm-hmm."

Dylan's eyes widened. "Did you get into trouble?"

"Big-time," she replied. "For about ten seconds—until my mother realized how upset I was. She knew I didn't mean it. Just like your grandmother will know you didn't mean to forget you were supposed to watch Thomas. It just happened."

He looked instantly relieved. "Do you think so?"

"For sure."

Dylan managed a little smile. "Thanks, Grace—you're the best."

A strange tightness constricted through the middle of her chest and she took a deep breath. When she heard a movement from the doorway she snapped her neck around. Cameron stood at the threshold.

"You're back?"

"Not for long," he said and came into the room. "Pat wants the kids to go to the hospital."

The blood leached from her face. "Is Thomas—"

"He's fine," Cameron assured her, and Dylan, who had jumped up in his chair. "No permanent damage. He's awake and he wants to see Dylan and the girls. I said I'd drive them back into town and they'll stay overnight at a motel. I'll pick them up tomorrow."

"I should get some things together for Isabel and tell Emily," she said as she stood and pushed the chair out. "She'll need to get Riley's booster seat for your car."

"That would be great. Come on, Dylan, let's get you ready." He went to turn, but then halted. "I should be back in a couple of hours."

Grace watched as Dylan scooted from the room and followed Cameron up the hallway. She gathered some fresh clothes for Isabel and then helped her change into jeans and a long-sleeved T-shirt.

Emily took some time gathering Riley's things together and Grace helped pack his baby bag.

"I feel bad," Emily said as she pulled on her jacket. "I've been wrapped up in taking care of Riley and studying. I haven't spent much time hanging out with the rest of the kids."

Grace patted the teenager's arm. "You can only do what you can," she said and picked up the bags. "Come on, your grandmother is waiting for you."

She stayed by the front steps as Cameron organized everyone into his car and packed their small bags into the trunk. He waved goodbye and drove off.

And now I'm alone.

Well, not exactly. Jed had ambled from his spot on the veranda and followed her back inside. Strangely, she didn't mind the company and allowed him to sit by her feet when she returned to the kitchen table. She shuffled the deck of cards and busied herself for a while with a game of solitaire. Once she was done Grace closed up the house and headed back to the cottage. She took a shower and the hot spray eased some of the tension tightening her shoulders. Now conscious of water shortages, she lingered for mere minutes, then changed into sweats and sat on the sofa in front of the television.

And quickly, like a runaway train, it hit her.

Thomas could have died.

For those few terrifying minutes she'd thought he wouldn't make it.

Fear closed her throat over and Grace sucked in some much needed air. She clutched her arms over her chest. Her lids dropped heavily as a familiar chill rushed over her skin. *I'm so cold.* She remembered that feeling. She remembered the fear and the helplessness. She remembered thinking she was going to die. And she remembered Richard's lifeless body, twisted and battered, beside her.

Jed groaned. She glanced at the dog. He pulled himself up, suddenly on alert. Grace quelled the unease narrowing through her blood. She heard a car door shut. Cameron. She got to her feet and rushed to greet him by the front door.

"He's fine," Cameron said as he walked across the threshold.

Grace clutched his arm. "Thank goodness."

"I need to feed the horses and then I'll hit the shower," he said and ran a weary hand through his hair. "Give me half an hour."

Grace released him and watched from the doorway as he walked back outside. The dwindling sun was all but gone when he returned to the cottage and headed for the bathroom. She fed the dog in the small mudroom and remained in the kitchen. Dinner would be pretty hit-or-miss, she realized when she opened the refrigerator. She pulled a couple of cans of soup from the cupboard and popped the contents into a saucepan to heat. Cameron came into the kitchen just as she had finished toasting thick slices of sourdough bread.

"You've been busy," he said as he passed the counter and saw the bread and green salad she'd prepared.

"It's not much," she said, feeling faintly embarrassed.

In low-slung faded jeans, white T-shirt and bare feet, he looked sexy and tempting.

Grace's skin warmed thinking about it and she turned back to her task.

"Do you need some help?" he asked and braced his hands on the edge of the counter.

She glanced sideways and avoided thinking about how his biceps flexed. "I'm good. So you said Thomas was doing well?"

"They want to keep him in for a couple of nights to be sure. But he's awake and talking."

She stopped what she was doing and looked at him. "Thanks to you."

"I wasn't alone," he said and stole a cucumber slice from the salad bowl.

"I didn't do much."

He leaned forward and crossed his arms. "You were there, Grace. You helped me do what needed to be done. You kept him warm," he reminded her. "And you comforted Dylan."

Her eyes widened. "You heard that?"

"About how you dropped Mary-Jayne on the head?" He grinned. "I heard. Explains a lot."

Grace laughed for probably the first time that day. And it felt good. "Poor M.J.," she said and returned to stirring the soup. "I love her dearly, you know."

"I think you have a great capacity for love, Grace," he said quietly. "You just don't show it."

The spoon rattled in the saucepan and she turned fractionally, avoiding his brown eyes. "Too hard."

"To admit you're human?"

She felt his questioning stare in the small confines of the kitchen. "Human? Am I? I've been called a lot of things."

"By me?" he prompted gently. "I guess that's true. We've said a lot of things to one another over the years."

"I deserved it," she said and stirred the soup some more.

"It's not like it isn't the truth. I know what I am. I know what people think of me."

"And what's that?"

"Oh, you know—that I'm a workaholic ice princess. Everyone has their place in a family, I guess. In mine, M.J. is the lovable one," she said. "Evie's the sensible one. And I'm the...smart one."

"And beautiful."

She shrugged and continued to stir.

"And talented in the kitchen. And good with kids." He looked at Jed lolling by the back door. "And dogs."

"Shocked even myself with that one," she said and spooned soup into two bowls. "Who would have thought?"

He grabbed the bread and salad, followed her to the table and sat down.

"I'm not fooled, Grace."

Grace slipped into a chair and looked at him. Really looked. Her heart—the same heart she'd tried hard to wrap in ice for so many years was suddenly pounding behind her ribs—and she was melting. The power he had over her—the power she'd denied because she was terrified of being vulnerable to him, of giving herself, of losing herself...suddenly that power made her want him even more.

She sighed out a breath. "Today I...I thought Thomas was going to die."

"Me, too."

"If he had..." The words caught, lingered, and then disappeared.

"But he didn't. He's safe. And so are you."

She looked up, emotion clogging her throat. Had she truly felt safe since the accident? Almost losing Thomas had brought all those memories back to the surface. And yet, being in the kitchen with Cameron, she somehow didn't have the usual emptiness in her heart.

"I feel safe now."

Cameron stilled. There was something incredibly vulnerable about Grace in that moment. He wanted to race around the counter and haul her into his arms. But resistance lingered. He couldn't be sure what she was feeling. And the idea of rejection suddenly waved like a red flag in front of him.

"I'm glad you feel safe with me."

She shrugged lightly. They ate in silence, but the tension in the room was extreme. Once the food was consumed and the plates taken care of, Cameron made his way to the sofa in the living room. She followed and stood by the fireplace.

"Are you joining me?" he asked and sat down.

She hesitated. The modest lamp in the corner gave enough light to see the wariness in her expression. "I should…go."

"Go where? To bed?" He checked his watch. "A little early for that, don't you think?"

A sigh escaped her lips and he watched her perfectly bowed mouth for a moment. Like everything about her face it was a thing of pure beauty. "I just thought—"

"Safe with me one minute, afraid of me the next. What's really going on with you, Grace?"

"I'm not afraid of you," she replied.

"Then sit down."

She took a few steps and dropped onto the sofa. "Okay, I'm sitting."

"Good," he said. "Now, talk."

She shook her head. "There's nothing to—"

"There is," he said, cutting her off. "I can see it in your eyes."

"Maybe I'm just upset over what happened today. I'm not made of stone, you know. If that little boy had—"

"But he didn't," Cameron said. "And we've already established that you're safe and sound here. So, talk to me," he insisted and rested an arm on the back of the sofa.

"What about?"

"Whatever's on your mind."

"Nothing is," she said and twisted her hands together.

Cameron pushed some more. "You could tell me about the crash and what happened that day."

Her breath caught. "I don't want to talk about it."

"Maybe you don't want to. But I think you need to."

"I have a shrink for that," she said and crossed her arms. "I went to counseling. I talked about *it* in exhausting detail and six sessions later I'm...I'm here."

"Here?"

"Home," she said quickly. "Crystal Point."

"I've never heard you call Crystal Point home before."

She shrugged. "My therapist thought being here would be good for me. I've told you all this already."

There was so much bite in her words Cameron knew she was holding back. "But you didn't say why?"

"I was in a car wreck."

"And your friend died?"

"Richard was a colleague," she said in a whisper. "And again, I've told you what happened. We were driving out to meet with a client and the car ran off the road. Richard died and I survived."

Cameron considered her words. "What happened then?" he asked and shifted to face her.

Her green eyes glittered. "We crashed and were trapped inside. That's the whole story."

Cameron wasn't convinced. "And how long were you trapped inside?"

She looked at him and shook her head. Shutters came up and a second later she stood.

"Grace?"

She shook her head again and headed for the fireplace. Cameron watched, mesmerized and confused, and he quickly pulled together his thoughts. Silence stretched between them, fueling the growing tension in the room. When he finally stood and took a few steps toward her, she was holding her arms tightly around her waist. He said her name again.

"I can't go back there," she said quietly and kept facing away. "I can't go back there with you."

"Back where?"

She shuddered. "To the crash. To that time. I'm trying to forget, not remember. I'm trying to get those days out of my head and—"

"Days?" he asked, cutting off her words. "What do you mean? How long were you in that car, Grace?"

She turned and faced him, eyes shining. She looked lost and he fought the urge to haul her into his arms. "Two days," she whispered.

Cameron stared at her. "You were trapped for two days? You and Richard?"

She nodded faintly. Very faintly. And Cameron's curiosity and instincts surged. Pieces of the puzzle fell into place. He recognized fear and grief in her haunted expression. And he knew that look from the years of police work and of dealing with victims of trauma.

"Richard was dead, wasn't he?"

"I said that already."

Cameron pressed on. "I mean he was dead when the car crashed. And you were alive?"

She took a second. "Yes."

"And there was nothing you could do for him, was there?"

Her lips trembled. "No."

Realization quickly dawned. She'd spent two days trapped inside a wrecked car with a dead man. No sweet wonder she was as closed up as a vault. The walls she'd erected around herself, the shadow of unhappiness in her eyes, her reluctance to let her family know the truth—it made perfect sense. "Grace." He said her name gently. "Has your counselor talked to you about post-traumatic stress disorder?"

She shuddered out a breath. "I'm not crazy."

"Of course you're not," he said and took a step closer. "But when someone has an experience like you've had it's quite normal for—"

"I'm perfectly fine," she said, cutting him off. "And I don't need analysis from your police officer's handbook."

Cameron took hold of her hand and urged her toward him. "Grace, I'm not analyzing you. I just wish you'd told me earlier."

"Why?" she asked, but didn't pull away. "So you can get inside my head and work me out?"

"So I could help you," he said gently.

"I don't need help. I'm not about to fall apart."

"Maybe you should," he suggested. "Maybe falling apart is exactly what you need."

She didn't move for a moment and uncertainty clouded her expression. Cameron remained still and waited. Her eyes filled with tears that slowly spilled over. Her skin looked pale in the lamplight. And she'd never seemed more beautiful. He wanted to soothe her, hold her, kiss her. But he checked himself.

"I can't. I have to fight it. I have to fight…you."

He touched her face. "No, you don't. We're not at war anymore."

"You don't understand—I need to stay strong," she said. "It's all I know."

"There's strength in admitting you're scared, Grace," he assured her and wiped the moisture from her cheek with his thumb. "And there can also be strength in tears. Resisting your grief and fear won't help you move on from the crash. It will only magnify the guilt you feel because you survived."

Grace choked back a sob. *How could he know that?* Months of guilt and anguish pressed between her shoulders. She dropped her head against his chest as his arms came around her.

"I was glad," she admitted as emotion tightened her throat so much she could barely swallow. Grace forced more words out. "I was happy and I shouldn't have been. I didn't have the right to be happy...not when Richard was...was gone."

Cameron stroked her back tenderly. "It would have been relief, Grace. And a perfectly rational reaction."

She shook her head against him. "No. I was *happy,* really happy." She shuddered as fresh tears burned her eyes. "We were trapped inside. I couldn't get out of my seat. Richard was...he was next to me and I knew he wasn't breathing and there was so much blood. But when I knew I was alive and not seriously hurt I started laughing hysterically and I couldn't stop and it—"

"That's not happiness, Grace," he insisted. "It was relief, like I said. You went through a traumatic experience." He grasped her chin, tilted her face and gently kissed her forehead. "You *should* be glad you survived. And thinking that doesn't make you a bad person."

More tears came, hard racking sobs that pushed up from deep inside her. She couldn't stop them. The tighter he held her, the more emotion came to the surface. For months she'd kept it all inside. Even with her therapist she'd held back, afraid to fully let her feelings show. Now, like never before, she felt like telling him everything.

When Cameron led her back to the sofa and sat down she followed and settled beside him. Without a word he turned her toward his chest and rested one hand over her hip, while the other stayed firmly on her shoulder.

"Grace, what happened during those two days, when you were stuck in the car?"

She wiped tears off her cheeks and looked at him. "The client we were to see lived in an isolated place. There was poor phone reception so we didn't know that the client was ill and had actually cancelled the meeting. Because of that, no one knew that we hadn't arrived for our appointment. We weren't reported missing until about thirty-six hours after the crash. It was Richard's wife who reported us missing when he hadn't called her the next day."

"And?" he prompted.

She shuddered. "It was a deserted road and a small animal had rushed out in front of us. Once we crashed, the car flipped onto its side and I couldn't open any of the doors to get out. And I couldn't find my phone so there was no way to contact anyone or call 911. So, I waited and just hoped that wild animals or dehydration wouldn't get me before I was found. And all that time Richard was…" She stopped and swallowed a heavy lump of emotion. "He was strapped in by the seatbelt and I was underneath. I couldn't climb over him. I couldn't do anything. And I kept thinking…why me? Why did I survive? If the car had landed a foot or so over, the passenger side would have hit the tree. But it didn't. It crushed the driver's side and the car rolled and it all happened so fast Richard didn't stand a chance." She sucked in a deep, painful breath. "He was a good man. His family grieved for him so much."

"That's to be expected."

Her shoulders grew heavy. "I know. And I know these things are random and happen and there's no way of controlling it…but still, I can't help wondering. In a split second someone lives and someone dies. There's really no sense to be made."

Cameron touched her hair and her heart contracted at his gentleness. "I think that every time I'm on duty and attend a motor vehicle accident. Your feelings are real, Grace. But if your friend died on impact there's nothing you could have done. It wasn't your fault."

Logically, Grace knew he was right. Her therapist had said it often enough. But the feelings lingered. Fresh tears filled her eyes and she blinked and more truths tumbled out.

"Richard's wife came to see me when I returned to work. She said she was collecting the rest of his things from his office, but I knew that wasn't the only reason." Grace took a long breath. "She stood in the doorway and stared at me... and somehow I knew what she was thinking. She looked around at my office, saw there weren't any photographs on my desk or anything in the room that might indicate that I meant something to someone, and I could feel her resentment. I felt such *guilt* in that moment that I couldn't speak. I couldn't talk about Richard, I couldn't express my sorrow for her loss. He was a man with a loving family and so much to live for, and I was just...I was...*me*—work-obsessed, closed off, friendless."

The truth was raw and painful and her whole body ached, inside and out.

"I don't think I've ever felt as alone as I did in those few minutes," she admitted with a sob. "An hour later I fell apart in front of a client and my boss made me take some leave and see a therapist. My treatment was to come home." She shrugged and didn't bother to wipe the tears from her cheeks this time.

"You don't need validation for surviving the crash, Grace. Not from your family, me or anyone else."

She couldn't pull back the agonized groan that escaped her lips. His insight both scared and soothed her. Her feelings were jumbled and when he moved closer the words she wanted to say somehow disappeared. His mouth hovered near hers. She pushed forward and their lips met, softly, because she wasn't sure she should do it. Part of her longed to kiss him over and over and try to erase the pain and guilt in her heart. And part of her wanted to run. Because she'd run from her feelings for Cameron since she was eighteen years old.

She pulled back and broke the contact of their lips. "I shouldn't have done that."

"I didn't mind."

She sighed heavily. "I know. And that's why I shouldn't have done it. I also shouldn't have told you what happened. It's my problem and—"

He kissed her hotly and the rest of her denials faded. Grace wasn't sure how long the kiss lasted. When he stopped she was breathless.

"Then why did you tell me?" he asked. "If for no other reason than you needed to talk about it to someone."

"Because you—"

"Does my wanting you frighten you that much?"

Her heart stilled. Had she ever really been wanted? By Dennis? By Erik? Had she really wanted them in return? A resounding *no* rang out in her head. She'd only wanted a career. Not love. Not sex. Not a home and family. Just work. And now, she was as vulnerable as she'd ever been, with the one man who could make her forget she had a life waiting for her back in New York.

"I can't," she admitted hollowly. "I just can't. Not with you."

His brown eyes absorbed her as he twirled strands of her hair between his fingers. Finally, he shifted in the seat. "You should get some sleep."

Grace stilled. "I'd like to stay here for a while, if that's okay?"

"Sure," he said and stood. "Good night."

As she watched him walk from the room, Grace knew that as confused and tired as she was, all she really wanted to do was fall into Cameron's strong arms and stay there for the night. And maybe longer.

Chapter Nine

Cameron flipped on his back and stared at the ceiling. Sleep was out of the question. He managed to waste about an hour or so before he got up, pulled on jeans and a T-shirt and padded down the hall.

Grace was asleep on the sofa and he covered her with a knitted blanket hanging over the back of the love seat in the corner. She looked exhausted and he lingered for a moment, considering everything she'd told him. Without her secrets and frosty reserve she seemed achingly vulnerable and it pierced his heart.

He wanted her.

He loved her.

And she was so messed up he should ignore every feeling he had. Because he was going to get his heart smashed. Again. She was leaving in two weeks. She didn't want a relationship with him. She didn't want marriage or kids. She'd spelled it out many times.

Dumb ass.

He longed for the impossible.

She stirred and he quietly left the room and headed for the kitchen. He pulled a glass from the cupboard and filled it with water. *I need to chill out.* Not that he needed any more thinking time. He'd been thinking about Grace all his adult life. She was why he'd never settled, never made a commitment with any of the perfectly lovely women he'd dated.

I just can't. Not with you.

That was plain enough.

It should have worked like a bucket of cold water over his feelings, his longings and his libido.

"Oh—sorry. I didn't realize you were still awake."

He looked up. Grace stood in the doorway.

"Thirsty?" he asked.

She shook her head. "I didn't mean to disturb you."

"That's okay. I couldn't sleep."

She glanced at the clock on the wall which had just ticked past eleven o'clock. "I guess I crashed out for an hour or so."

"You must have needed it," he said and came around the counter.

Grace hesitated by the doorway. "Cameron," she said with a shaky breath. "I wanted to thank you for listening earlier. I've never really talked about the crash or Richard before."

"No problem."

"And about what I said...I meant...I meant that I..."

As her words trailed off he leaned against the counter and shrugged. "You can't force feelings Grace, I get that."

She shook her head. "That's not it."

Cameron's heart surged forward, battering against his chest. "Then what?"

"It's why I left," she said on a breath. "Why I couldn't be what you wanted back then. I knew you were getting seri-

ous and the plans I had didn't include Crystal Point or settling down."

"So you left for New York and didn't look back?"

"Yes," she replied. "And in two weeks I'll be going back
there. You know that, right?"

"Sure."

"So, if anything happened it would—"

"Anything?" he prompted.

Cameron uncrossed his arms and pushed himself off the
counter. As he moved the air between them shifted on some
invisible axis. Hotter somehow, even though it was obviously
cool outside. And thicker, like a gust of something sinfully
seductive had blown into the room.

She sucked in a breath. "I want...I want..."

"You want what?"

Her green eyes glittered. "I want to...*feel*."

Cameron kept his head. As beautiful as she was, as inviting as she was, he needed to be sure of her. "You know,
you've had a pretty harrowing day. And bad days can make
for impulsive decisions."

"I'm never impulsive."

"You were on the beach last weekend," he reminded her.

She shrugged a little. "So, despite what people think, I'm
a normal woman with a normal woman's needs."

"I know you're a woman, Grace," he said quietly. "But
today was hard—not only did Thomas almost die, you talked
about the crash that almost took *your* life. When emotions
come out like that, feelings can get...misdirected." He took
her hand. "The thing is, if you want comfort—I can give you
that. If you want sex—I can give you that, too. But tomorrow, I'll still be me. And you'll still be the same woman who
wanted to get away from Crystal Point."

She moved closer. "Tomorrow isn't tonight. But if you
don't want me I'll understand and—"

"Grace," he said, cutting her off. "Of course I want you." He ran his fingers through his hair. "I'm not made of stone. Do you think I haven't been imagining what it would be like to make love to you every minute of every day?"

She smiled. "Then make love to me. Please."

Cameron blinked twice and wondered if he were dreaming. She looked so beautiful. And startlingly vulnerable. He found some life in his legs and moved across the room.

"You're sure?" he asked.

She nodded.

He gripped her hand and she curled her fingers around his and turned, urging him forward and down the hall to her bedroom.

Once there she released him and stood beside the bed. Cameron's heart hammered. He'd imagined this moment countless times—even when they'd pretended to hate one another. And now he was with her, in her bedroom, standing barely a foot apart.

"But you're not sure about this, are you?" she asked and twisted her fingers together. Grace was nervous.

So am I.

"I'm sure," he replied and took her hand in his. "Only, I'm still me, like I said. I'm still a small-town police officer—and it's what I'll always—"

She reached up and placed two fingers against his mouth, cutting off his words. "I was eighteen and foolish when I said that. Who hasn't said stupid things in their life that they regret?"

She had a point. He regretted many of the things he'd said to Grace over the years. The digs, the antagonism— foolishness to hide behind so he didn't have to face his feelings for her, and the rejection he'd felt. But he wanted her so much. And right at that moment, the risk of getting his heart broken was worth it.

He took her hand and urged her forward, cupping the back of her neck with his other hand. "There's no going back once we do this, Grace."

"I know."

Without another word he drew her close and took her lips in a deep, drugging kiss. She groaned low in her throat and gripped his shoulders, holding on as breath and souls mingled. Kissing Grace was like nothing on earth.

Need for her spiked and his arms tightened around her waist, settling on her hips. Her sweatshirt fell off one shoulder and the bra strap went with it. He trailed kisses down her jaw and neck. The scent of her skin was powerful to his senses and he felt all the blood in his body rush to his groin.

Go easy...go slow.

She said his name and ran her fingers through his hair. Her eagerness spiked his desire. "Take this off," he muttered against her shoulder, tugging lightly at her sweatshirt.

"You first."

Obliging instantly, he released her for a second and pulled his T-shirt over his head and tossed it on the floor. Her palms came to his chest and the touch sent his blood soaring. He kissed her again, hungry for the taste of her. Her mouth opened and she rolled her tongue around his, softly at first, almost tentative and it made him smile.

Grace pulled back, all eyes and swollen lips. "You're laughing?"

"No," he said gently and grasped her chin. "Just thinking how good it feels to be with you like this."

She nodded and stepped back, then grabbed the hem of her sweatshirt and slipped the garment off in one fluid movement. Cameron watched, absorbed by the evocative look in her eyes. The white lace bra pushed her breasts upward and his hands tingled. He wanted to touch her breasts so much he ached. But she was calling the shots at that moment and he didn't mind one bit.

She discarded the top and rested her fingers on the waistband of her sweatpants. It was both excruciating and erotic to watch as she slowly slid the sweats past her hips and over her thighs. They dropped in a puddle at her feet and she pushed them out of the way with her foot. The white lace briefs were quite modest and unbelievably sexy.

She stepped back again and sat on the edge of the bed. When he moved toward her she pushed back farther onto the mattress. Cameron rested a knee on the bed and looked down at her lying against the white quilt. Her dark hair fanned wildly around her face. Her body was curved and toned, her skin smooth. A tiny diamond glittered from her pierced navel and seemed oddly at contrast with the controlled, serious woman he'd always believed her to be.

"You are so beautiful." Cameron moved beside her and grasped her shoulder. "And incredibly sexy," he said as he ran his fingertips down her arm.

"Really?" She took hold of his hand as he curved his palm over one hip. "Cameron," she said, suddenly too serious. "Just so you know…I'm not very good at this."

He stilled. "This?"

"This," she said again, quieter, like she had some terrible secret. "I'm not very responsive. I mean, I like the idea of… making love. But when I'm with someone I sort of shut down. I think there's something wrong with me. I'm only telling you because I don't want you to think it's something you've done. Or didn't do," she added quickly.

A feeling akin to pain pierced his chest. How could she possibly think that? "The suit?" he accused. "He said that? He said there was something wrong with you?"

She nodded. "And before that. Dennis said—"

"How about we don't worry what the suit or the doctor

or anyone else has said to you." He grabbed her hand and brought it to his lips. "Can you feel that?"

She nodded again.

He traced his tongue inside her palm. "And that?"

"Yes," she whispered.

"Do you trust me, Grace?"

Her breath caught in her throat. "I do."

"So, trust me now," he said quietly. "Trust this. Trust *us....*"

He looked into her eyes, saw her agreement and then kissed her. For a while, kissing was enough. She gave her mouth up to him, responding to each slant, every breath and each time he took her bottom lip between his. He threaded his hands through her beautiful hair, loving the way the wild curls got caught between his fingers.

The need to love her right, to pleasure her unselfishly, had never seemed more important. Her hands were on his chest and her soft caress burned through him. He kissed her and reached for the back of her bra, flicking the garment apart. He felt her smile beneath his mouth and then she shifted her shoulders free of the white lace.

He looked at her breasts, wanting nothing more to worship them...and more...worship her. Tonight. Forever. When he cupped one breast and closed his mouth over her nipple he thought he might die a slow, agonizing death. Pleasure and pain ripped through his middle, arrowing downward, making him so hard so quickly, he wondered if he would pass out.

He said her name against the luscious peak and groaned when she pushed toward him. Her hands were in his hair, over his shoulders, his neck, everywhere, like she couldn't get close enough, touch enough, feel enough. He caressed her skin, finding the places she liked. When his fingers reached the band on her briefs she stilled and drew in a sharp breath.

"Relax," he whispered against her mouth. "And trust me."

* * *

Grace looked into his eyes and nodded with a hazy kind of surrender. She did trust him. Completely. More, she realized as he efficiently dispensed with her underwear, than any man she'd ever known. And for the first time in her life, without questioning why, she gave herself up to feel...to really feel... like she'd always longed for in her secret dreams.

His hands were magic over her skin, his mouth hot and demanding, yet also gentle as he coaxed response from her. She gave it willingly and wound her tongue around his as their kisses deepened, touching his chest, his strong, smooth shoulders. And she waited for what she suddenly craved, she waited for his intimate touch. None of her usual apprehension rose up—instead, Grace let go of her insecurities and fell apart in his arms.

He knew how to touch her, knew where, as though he'd been touching her forever, and beyond. While he stroked her, while his skillful fingers drew narcotic pleasure along her every nerve ending, he continued to kiss her mouth. He took her bottom lip between his teeth and suckled gently. When the tempo of her breathing changed he released her mouth and looked down into her face. His eyes were dark, clearly aroused, and she lost all her inhibitions beneath his penetrating stare. Grace spiraled, she flew, her blood fired as every part of her raced toward a shattering climax so intense, so wondrous, she couldn't stop herself from saying his name, over and over.

She came down slowly, breathing in tiny gasps of air, floating on a steady wave of aftershocks. Her eyes burned. No tears, she told herself. Not now.

"See," Cameron said quietly, kissing her jaw, her chin, and the delicate spot below her ear. "Nothing wrong with you at all."

The tears she'd tried to deny suddenly filled her eyes and

she blinked, desperate for him not to see them. Too late. He wiped the moisture from her cheek with his thumb.

So vulnerable, so exposed, Grace felt the rawness deep down to her bones.

"Sorry," she whispered and moved to turn her head away.

Cameron grasped her chin. "For what? Feeling pleasure?" He touched her bottom lip. "Don't ever be sorry for that, Grace."

"For being so emotional," she explained, hot with embarrassment. She was naked and exposed while he remained half-clothed.

"Making love is emotional." He rubbed her lip again. "Or at least, it should be."

He was right. And she wanted it to be that way. She also wanted his clothes off.

Grace moved her hands to the top snap on his jeans. "My turn," she said, pushing past her awkwardness. "Take these off."

It took barely seconds and finally he lay beside her, skin touching skin, arms entwined. In the dim lamplight his tanned body looked bronzed and amazing. Grace touched the soft hair on his chest with her fingernails. She felt his arousal press against her belly.

"Okay?" he asked and traced one finger along her arm.

She nodded and leaned toward him. "Kiss me."

For the next hour he did more than simply kiss her. Cameron kissed and stroked her, using his hands and mouth to drive her toward the pinnacle of pleasure once again. When his tongue dipped in her navel and played around with the tiny piercing she had there, Grace almost bucked off the bed. *Who would have thought...* He groaned low in his throat and offered encouragement when she touched him, kissed him, although there was nothing particularly practiced about her technique.

And then, when Grace thought she could crave nothing else, want nothing more, he passed her the condom he'd placed on the bedside table. She sheathed him quickly, if a little unsteadily, and waited, poised for his possession as he moved over her. He took his weight on his elbows and watched her.

This is it. Some faraway voice spoke to her. *This is what I've been waiting for. This night. This man. This feeling.* And as he entered her slowly, Grace knew a sense of completion she'd never experienced before. He stayed still for a moment and she remained lost in his eyes.

When he moved, Grace moved with him. When he kissed her, she kissed him back. When he smiled against her mouth, she returned the gesture. Two people, somehow fused by more than making love. The pace between them quickened. More need, more urgency, more passion, she thought, from some dreamy place, as her body began the throb with a heady longing once again. She linked her arms around him, holding on, kneading wanting fingers into his back. And finally, when they could take no more, they came together in a white-hot frenzy of release.

When it was over, when the pleasure receded and their breathing returned to something resembling normal, Cameron eased his weight off her and lay at her side.

He grabbed her hand and held it against his chest. "Still okay?"

Grace let out a breath. "Yes."

"No regrets?"

"Not yet," she replied honestly. "Thank you."

"For what?"

"For being so…" Her words trailed as an unusual lethargy seeped across her skin. "So sweet."

"Sweet?" He echoed but she knew he was smiling. "Damned with faint praise."

Grace shifted closer. "It's high praise, actually."

"Okay then." He sat up and swung his legs off the bed. "Back in a minute."

He left the room and Grace stretched her body. She closed her eyes, only to be roused a couple of minutes later when Cameron returned and quickly shuffled her underneath the covers before he got back into the bed.

He reached for her, wrapping her in his arms once he'd flicked off the bedside lamp. "Get some sleep, Grace."

Grace sighed contentedly and pressed herself into his chest, trailing her fingertips up and down his rib cage. She closed her eyes again and listened to the steady rhythm of his heart as she drifted off to sleep.

When she awoke the following morning, Grace was alone. The digital clock on the table read half past seven. She could hear movement around the cottage. A door closed and Jed's familiar whine echoed from the kitchen where he was clearly searching for food.

Footsteps came up the hallway moments later and Cameron rounded the doorway with a cup in his hand.

"Coffee?" he asked as he came into the room.

Grace pulled herself up, conscious to not let the sheet slip past her breasts. Silly, she supposed. He'd seen all of her there was to see. But she couldn't suppress the niggling anxiety that began to knock steadily behind her ribs.

"Lovely," she said as cheerfully as she could. Morning-afters were not her specialty.

But Cameron clearly had no problem with them, she realized when he sat on the edge of the bed and passed her the cup. Lots of practice, no doubt. That thought didn't go down well either. He looked casual and relaxed. He wore the jeans she'd practically ripped off with her teeth the night before and nothing else. The top snap was undone and she stole a glance at the line of soft hair arrowing downward from his belly button. Color rose up her collarbone and she quickly sipped the coffee. "Mmm, good. Thank you."

"I have to go into town this morning to pick up Pat and the kids," he said easily. "If they release Thomas it'll take two trips so I might be gone awhile. But later, we could do something together."

Grace looked at him over the rim of the cup. "Didn't we already?"

He smiled and Grace knew he was remembering how they'd made slow, seductive love again just before dawn broke. "I guess we did."

"What did you have in mind?" she asked, trying to push aside the images in her head and the memory of his kisses. "And does that mean we get the day off today?"

"For sure. You've earned it."

Her eyes popped wide. "I have?"

"For yesterday," he explained, grinning. "And Friday you worked hard. I was thinking we could take the horses out."

"Horses?" Her smile disappeared as she placed the cup on the bedside table. "I don't really do horses."

He shrugged and grinned. "Okay, what would you like to do instead? We could go into town and have lunch if you'd prefer that?"

Her smile returned. He was being very sweet and she decided to make an effort and expand her horizons. "Actually, horseback riding sounds like fun."

He looked skeptical of her sudden turnaround. "You're sure?"

"Positive."

He kissed her soundly. "Great. So, what about breakfast?"

Grace groaned. "Are you always so chipper in the morning?"

Cameron laughed and grabbed her free hand. "Depends what I've been doing the night before."

"Sex puts you in a good mood?"

He rubbed the underside of her wrist. "You put me in a good mood."

They both laughed out loud. "I do not. Most of the time we seem to be working out new ways to insult one another."

"I like this much better," he said and brought her hand to his lips and kissed her knuckles.

"Me, too."

He took a moment to respond. "And if I said I wanted more—would that send you running?"

More what? Sex? "I told you I don't do this casually."

His gaze narrowed. "And I do? Is that your implication?"

"Well, I—"

"Did it feel casual to you, Grace?"

She shook her head. "Not at all."

"Last night I asked you to trust *us,* Grace. Whatever you think of me, you must know I would never make love to you unless it was *real.*"

Did she know that? Is that why her heart hammered so loudly? *I'm afraid.* In the cold light of day, with passion abated and only truth between them, Grace was forced to examine what she knew was her own truth. Somehow, the lines had blurred. The antagonism had gone. The feigned dislike had disappeared. She'd made love with Cameron and had felt love in that moment. From him. From herself.

He smiled and then proceeded to make love to her all over again, wringing the last vestiges of response from her, driving Grace toward some place where only pleasure existed.

Pat and the kids returned midmorning. Thomas was being kept another night at the small community hospital, and according to his grandmother was doing remarkably well.

She remained in the kitchen with the older woman and Emily for a while, sharing tea and talking about the children.

They discussed the upcoming trail ride and Grace did her best to hide her nerves. But Pat wasn't fooled.

"You'll be fine," Pat assured her and tapped her hand. "Cameron won't let anything happen to you."

Grace warmed from head to toe. "I know."

It was well before lunch when Cameron came into the house. She hadn't seen him since he'd picked up Pat and the kids. Instead, he'd been outside tending to the animals with Dylan and doing some minor repairs on the paling fence near the chicken run. She wasn't sure if Pat sensed a change in their relationship. But Grace could feel it with every fiber in her body.

"Are you ready to go?" he asked when he appeared in the doorway.

Grace nodded. "Although I need to get my cap."

Pat moved across the kitchen and grabbed a hat off a peg near the door. "Take this," she offered. "Much better to keep the sun off your face."

Grace took the battered wide-brimmed hat which looked like one her sister-in-law, Callie, often wore. "Er—thanks."

By the time they reached the stables Grace was so nervous her hands were sweating. The horses, both tacked and tied up, seemed huge and ominous.

"The hat," he said, motioning to the object in her hand. "You actually need to put it on."

Grace looked at the hat. It was old and shabby and she had no inclination to put it on her freshly washed hair. In fact, she had become accustomed to her new, all-natural hairstyle. "Oh, I don't think—"

"Wear the hat." He took it from her and plonked it on her head. "I insist."

Grace caught his smile and was just about to playfully protest again when his phone rang. He answered the call and spoke for barely a minute. When he was done he was frowning.

"Something wrong?" she asked.

"Lauren."

His sister. "Is there a problem?"

He shrugged. "Nothing much. Come on, let's get going."

It took a few minutes, but Grace was finally in the saddle. It was one of the Western types, so at least she had a horn to hang on to. And she was pleased the horse appeared to have a calm temperament and good manners.

"I haven't done this for twenty years," she told him.

"You'll be fine," he assured her. "Just follow me."

Clearly an accomplished rider, he reined his mount to the left and headed through an open gate behind the stables and into a wide pasture. It was a picture-perfect late-autumn day. The sky was clear blue, the air crisp and clean. The ground was reasonably flat and grassy with the occasional outcrop of rock and thankfully Grace's horse followed Cameron's. After a few minutes she'd convinced herself to loosen up. And she liked watching him. As with everything he did, he looked relaxed and confident.

"Where did you learn to do this?" she asked as they steadily walked.

"My mother's folks owned a farm out west. I'd go there during school break."

How little she knew about him. A memory clicked in. "They're both gone now?"

"Yeah," he replied. "They died within a few weeks of one another. After fifty years of marriage they couldn't bear to be parted I guess."

It was a romantic notion. Fifty years together—as companions, lovers, friends, parents…what an incredible legacy to leave behind. It softened something inside her and being with Cameron got her thinking. He wanted her like she'd never been wanted before. He'd whispered words against her skin, drawn pleasure from every part of her and given her the confidence to let go of her inhibitions. And now, as she rode with him in the afternoon sunlight, for the first time in her life Grace wondered if she actually could have it all.

Chapter Ten

"So, what did your sister want?" she asked, shifting her mind from images of them making love and imagining happily-ever-afters. Her question sounded impossibly nosy and she was surprised when he answered.

"Giving me a lecture."

Grace immediately tensed. Did his sister know they were together? Was that why Lauren had called her brother? The horse sensed her tension and responded by breaking into a trot. She caught her balance and rose from the saddle every second beat before collecting the reins and easing the gelding back.

Cameron was beside her in a flash. "Are you okay?" he asked and lightly grabbed one of her reins.

"I'm fine." Grace took a breath. "A lecture about what?"

He released the rein. "My mother wants to know if I'm going to the Jakowski family reunion."

Grace had a vague recollection that his entire extended

family got together every year. "Oh, right. It's tradition for you to all meet once a year?"

"Yep."

Grace tilted her hat back. "Well, it should be a good day."

"Maybe."

She pulled back fractionally on the reins. "Isn't it usually?"

He shrugged. "I haven't been for the past few years."

Grace eased the horse to a halt. Cameron took a few more paces to stop and then turned the toffee-colored gelding around. Head to head, the horses nuzzled one another.

She stared at him. "But isn't the day a big deal for your parents? And all your other relatives, like your grandparents and cousins and such?"

"I guess."

Grace took a deep breath. She sensed his energy changing. He didn't want to talk about it. However, she did. "Let's stop for a while," she suggested. "There's a spot over there near those trees. We can tie the horses up."

Without waiting for him she clicked the horse forward and trotted toward the trees. Once they were both dismounted she handed the reins to Cameron and waited for him to securely tether the animals.

She found a rock beneath the shade of a tree and watched as he retrieved two small water bottles from his saddlebag. Once he joined her she spoke.

"Tell me why you don't go. And tell me the truth."

Cameron didn't want to admit to anything. "It's complicated."

She took off her hat and raised her brows. "That sounds like something I'd say. You don't do complicated. So, 'fess up."

He smiled at her words. This was a new Grace. A little playful, even though she regarded him with serious eyes. He liked it a lot. But he wasn't quite ready to admit the truth.

"I'd rather not talk about it."

"Too bad," she shot back.

Cameron sucked in a frustrated breath. "Because it's a *Jakowski* family reunion."

She stared at him. "And?"

"And I'm not a… I'm not really a Jakowski."

It was the first time he'd said the words out loud. In the past he'd been asked the same question and always used excuses like work commitments, or lack of time. But he wouldn't lie to Grace.

And she asked another hard question. "Because you were adopted by Franciszek?"

Relentless, he thought and inhaled. "Yes."

"Do you actually believe he regards you as anything other than his real son?"

He shrugged. "I never said it was rational."

She grabbed his hand and Cameron felt the connection through to his blood. Her nails tapped on his palm. "You were what—three years old when he married your mother? So that's thirty-three years of being your father. Not that I'm an expert on parenting, but I don't imagine he'd be anything other than incredibly proud to call you his son."

He knew she was right…in his head. But the last time he'd attended the family reunion he'd realized he was the only one there not related by blood, aside from respective spouses. The extended Jakowski clan was large and traditionally Polish, where bloodlines and birthright were important. And that blood didn't flow through his veins. It was why he wanted his own family, his own children.

And Grace, he knew, did not.

"Like I said, not rational."

She linked their fingertips. "You know, you don't hold back telling me what I should do—my family not knowing about the accident as an example. So, here's a little of that back at you—you *should* go. Because they're your family and they love you. If that's not enough, then go out of respect for Franciszek, who loved you enough to want to call you his son and give you his name. And out of respect for the man you have become."

Shame hit him squarely between the shoulder blades. She was right. So right. He knew he hurt his parents by not attending. He had a sudden idea. "Would you go with me?"

"Go with you?" she echoed. "Like a…date?"

"Yeah…my date. My friend." *My girlfriend.* He felt about sixteen years old just thinking it.

She managed a wry smile. "I'll…think about it."

When he leaned forward and kissed her it took about five seconds for Grace's brain to kick in. He cupped the back of her neck as she returned the kiss, tasting her lips for the longest time. Finally they pulled apart. She was breathing hard, taking deep puffs into her lungs.

"Let's keep going," he suggested and pushed away the thoughts she had of lying down on the soft grass and making love with him. "The horses will get restless if we stay here."

She nodded, grabbed her hat and stood. Within minutes they were back in the saddle and headed east. They stayed out for a couple of hours, mostly walking through fields that belonged to an adjoining landowner.

When they got back to the farm she left the horse in his care and returned to the cottage.

Grace had blisters on top of blisters. Horseback riding. A great idea—*not*.

She ached all over and as she peeled off her jeans she grimaced at the red and angry blisters formed on the insides of her calves. She figured the ones on her behind would be worse. Just how was she supposed to rub the aloe vera there?

Pat had chopped off a leaf from the overgrown plant by the house when Grace had hobbled from the stables.

"Are you okay?"

Cameron stood in the doorway of her bedroom. His eyes briefly darted to the unmade bed before returning to her face. To his credit he didn't stare at her near-naked bottom half. Her sensible skin-colored briefs disguised little. She pushed the jeans aside with her feet. "Fine."

He nodded and looked like he was doing his best not to smile. "Need any h—"

"Fine," she muttered. "Like I said."

He pulled something from his back pocket and held it out to her. "Balm—for the sore spots," he explained. "Only use a little, it's pretty powerful stuff."

Grace took the tube. "Thanks."

Once he left she sank onto the bed. She needed thinking time.

They were lovers. Did lovers spend an afternoon riding horses, laughing together, enjoying one another's company? Did lovers attend family gatherings like the one he'd asked her to attend with him? Grace was more confused than ever. In the past she'd always been well into a relationship before having sex. Making love before making any kind of commitment. And her history of commitment was one of *noncommitment*.

Their differences seemed suddenly insurmountable. She had a life in New York...Cameron's life was clearly in Crystal Point. She was desperate to regain her edge again, to go back to work and be successful. Cameron wasn't career driven in the same way. She knew he liked being a police officer and was exceptionally good at it—but it didn't define him. And he wanted the kind of woman she could never be.

She showered, hoping to clear her thoughts, and then applied some balm before she changed into gray-and-pink sweats. Her hair seemed to have a life of its own and framed her face in a mass of curls. No makeup. All natural. It felt right in so many ways. And that was the core of her growing dilemma. Her two worlds were clashing. And she didn't know which one would claim her.

"Hungry?" Cameron asked when she walked into the kitchen.

He'd also showered and changed into loose-fitting jeans that sat low on his hips, and a white tank shirt. "Yes. What's on the menu?" she asked as her gaze lingered on his broad shoulders.

He held up a casserole dish. "Just have to heat it up. You could set the table."

She did the task quickly and grabbed sodas from the small refrigerator. As she moved around the room Grace was again struck by how normal it all felt. She couldn't remember ever experiencing such a strong sense of companionship with anyone before.

During dinner and the few hours that followed they talked, laughed and made out for a while on the small sofa. Grace relaxed in his arms as they watched television and sipped coffee. Afterward he took her to bed and made gentle love to her.

They planned to leave midafternoon Monday, which still gave them a couple of hours in the morning for Cameron to continue painting while she spent some study time with Emily. Cameron took Pat to the hospital to collect Thomas at nine o'clock, and while he was gone she and Emily abandoned the books and roped Dylan into helping them with the decorating. By the time Cameron returned she was rinsing out brushes by the back door.

"You're done?" he asked, staring down at her from the top step.

Grace craned her neck around. "I'm done."

"Good job. We'll leave after lunch if that's suits you?"

"Of course. I need to clean up and pack first."

By one o'clock Grace found herself deep in Pat's full arms. The older woman was returning to Crystal Point the following day with Emily and the other children. "Make sure you stay in touch. I know my granddaughter is thriving at her schoolwork with your help." Pat made her promise to stay connected. "It's been wonderful having you."

Grace blinked at the hotness in her eyes. In just days she'd become unexpectedly attached to the harried-looking woman and her grandchildren. "I will," she assured her. "Thank you for having me—I've enjoyed being here."

She said goodbye to the children, lingering with Thomas, who was still a little weak from his ordeal, but assured of a full recovery. She made a date with Emily for a brief lesson on Tuesday afternoon, mindful that she'd agreed to watch Noah's kids that evening. Jed lay on the backseat as Cameron stowed their bags in the trunk and then they were on their way. She watched as the kids waved frantically when they drove off and Grace swallowed the hard lump in her throat.

The return drive took a fraction over three hours. The familiar sight of the Pacific Ocean as Cameron crested the road heading into Crystal Point was unusually comforting to her. He pulled up outside the B and B. Five minutes later her bags were upstairs and they were staring at one another across the small lounge room.

"Everything okay?" Cameron asked perceptively.

Grace nodded. "Of course."

"Scott and Evie will be back next week, right?"

She nodded again. "Monday. I'm looking forward to seeing Evie."

He rubbed his hands together. "Well, I guess I'll talk to you soon."

The mood seemed too casual. Too polite. He wasn't suggesting they continue to see one another. He wasn't suggesting anything. In fact, he looked as though he couldn't get away from her quick enough. "Sure."

He left without another word.

Grace spent over an hour with Emily on Tuesday afternoon. They talked about the previous weekend and Thomas's accident. Emily told her Cameron had visited Pat that morning to check on them. She didn't respond to the information—and didn't admit that she hadn't heard from him at all since he'd dropped her off the day before. Once she was certain the teen had a study plan for the rest of the week, she showered, pulled on jeans, a collared pale blue T-shirt and navy zipped sweater and headed for Noah's house. She was surprised by how happy the kids were to see her, and then remembered the gifts she'd given them last time and was touched when Hayley made her promise to read the book that she said was now her favorite.

It also struck her how nice it was to be an aunt. She'd never really taken the time to get to know her brother's kids. Her trips back to Crystal Point were usually short and infrequent and she always brought work with her. This time was very different. So many new experiences were filling places in her heart—places she was only now prepared to admit were empty. Even the time she spent with Emily had its own reward. The teenager was doing so well with her studies and Grace knew she'd ace her upcoming exam. Thinking she had played a small part in that made her feel good about herself. And genuinely happy for Emily. She'd even made some inquiries about fashion design school for her.

"There's food in the refrigerator. And we shouldn't be too late," Noah told her. Dressed up in a suit her brother looked handsome, and she told him so. "Thanks for doing this."

"My pleasure," she said and straightened his tie. "Have fun."

Callie came into the living room, stopped and stared at her. "You know, your hair looks good like that."

She'd forgotten to straighten her hair that morning. "It's my holiday hair," she said and pushed her curls back. Once she was back in New York, once she was back in her apartment, everything would return to normal.

Then why does this feel normal, too? Why did a weekend with Cameron and Pat and the kids feel like a glove that fit my hand perfectly?

"The twins haven't been in the bath yet," Callie told her. "But they are under strict instructions to behave."

Bath? Right. How hard could it be? She put on a smile. "No problem. Enjoy the night."

"Thanks again," Noah said as he kissed her cheek and then quickly ushered his family outside.

Five minutes later the twins announced they were hungry for dinner and Grace was just about to herd them into the kitchen when the doorbell rang. She told the kids to stay in the living room and went to the front door.

Cameron stood on the threshold. "Hey."

Her stomach flipped over in that way she'd become used to whenever he was near. "What are you doing here?" she asked, letting him into the house.

He shrugged. "I got you into this babysitting gig," he said with a grin. "I thought you'd like some backup."

She couldn't help the smile that tugged at the corners of her mouth. Couldn't help remembering what had happened between them over the weekend. Couldn't help wanting more. Which made it one massive complication.

Grace nodded. "You prepare dinner and I'll get them into the tub."

He gave a lopsided grin. "Good luck."

"What does that mean?"

He chuckled and followed her into the living room. "Don't turn your back."

"My back? I don't under—"

"Uncle Cameron!"

The kids were clearly delighted to see him and when he swung Matthew high in the air the little boy laughed hysterically. Hayley wasn't about to be excluded and clamored for attention. He hauled them both in his arms for a moment and zoomed around the room making *vroom vroom* noises. Grace stood by the doorway. He really was remarkable with children and as she watched him an odd and unfamiliar feeling bunched down low in her belly.

Children had never figured in her life agenda.

Love had never figured either.

She sucked in a breath. *Love.* Impossible. She wasn't about to fall in love. Not in Crystal Point. And not with Cameron. It was just sex. A holiday romance at best. She'd been vulnerable and sought comfort in his arms. Only a fool would think it was more than that. Only a fool would want more.

And only a fool would be mad at him for not calling her for the past thirty-six hours.

"You know where the kitchen is," she said to him and then put on her best serious aunt face. "Come on, you two. Bath time."

They groaned as Cameron set them on their feet and raced around the room for a minute before she was able to usher them down the hallway. By the time she got them into the bath, washed, dried off and changed into pajamas, nearly an hour had passed. The kids had thrown water at her when she tussled with them about washing their hair and Matthew wailed about the soap in his eyes. At the end of it she was wet and short on patience.

"Everything all right in here?" Cameron asked from the doorway of the twins' bedroom.

"Everything's peachy," she lied and finished buttoning Matthew's pajama top. "How's dinner looking?"

"All set," he replied and held out his arms for Hayley. "How do my famous cheese-and-bacon hot dogs sound, kids?"

Her niece raced toward him and climbed up. "Yay, Uncle Cameron."

Good old Uncle Cameron. Grace set her teeth together. The man could obviously do no wrong. She smiled extra sweetly and by the look on his face he knew, damn him, that she was close to tossing a shoe in his direction. "Let's go."

"After you," he said and stepped into the hall so she could pass.

Despite her determination to not like his cooking, she had to admit the hot dogs were the most fabulous she'd ever tasted. They were so good, in fact, she ate two.

Later, once the kids had their fill, Cameron took them off to tuck them into bed with a book for half an hour before they had to go to sleep. It gave Grace a chance to clean up the kitchen and put on a pot of coffee.

He returned twenty minutes later, didn't look the least bit harried and she pushed back a stab of resentment. He did everything with a kind of casual ease she suddenly envied.

"Is it exhausting being good at everything?" she asked when he perched against the counter.

His expression narrowed. "Is that a dig, or a question?"

She poured coffee. "I'm not being snippy."

"Really?" He took the mug she offered. "You know, there's no angle to getting along with people. You just do it."

She raised a brow. "You mean *you* just do it."

"Well, it doesn't help that you've got a Back Off sign stamped on your forehead." He grinned and then drank some coffee. "You've handed things pretty well this past week. You certainly got along with Pat and the kids."

"Strangers aren't as complicated as family or…"

"Lovers?" he suggested when her words trailed off.

Grace looked into her mug. "I was going to say *friends*. But I guess we've changed those boundaries now."

He looked into her eyes. "Friends? I'm not sure we've ever been that, Grace. But we can try...if that's what you want."

The thing was, she wasn't sure what she wanted. They'd crossed a line and she wondered how she'd ever face him when she returned to Crystal Point in the future. What would happen when he married and had children? It's what he wanted. And even though those plans had never figured into her own life, Grace knew it would be painful to see him settled with a wife and children.

Because...

Because her feelings had somehow become muddled. What she wanted had never seemed so unclear. She looked at him and felt his stare through to the blood in her veins.

If only...

If only I was a different kind of woman.

"Grace?"

"Sometimes I wish...I wish things were different."

"Things?" he prompted and placed the mug on the table.

She drew in a shaky breath. "Me. I wish *I* was different."

He stilled. "Why?"

"Because then I wouldn't want to run so far away from you one moment, and run straight toward you the next."

Cameron fought the urge to haul her into his arms. Her admission hit him squarely in the chest. Her behavior confused him. No surprise there, he figured, as women had been confusing men since the dawn of time. He'd spent two days wondering if he'd made the biggest mistake of his life by making love with Grace. Because now he wanted her more than ever.

"I guess you need to decide which one you want to do more."

She stared at her feet. "That's not helping."

"Do you think I'm going to make this easy for you?"

She looked up. "I'd hoped you would."

"Not a chance."

"Even though we both know the odds of this working out are…are…" She stopped and quietly drew in some air. "I live in New York and you live here. And despite this…this attraction between us, I don't want what you want."

Cameron edged toward her. "How do you know what I want?"

"Because I just know," she said on a breath. "You want to settle down and have a family and I've never—"

"Never is a long time, Grace," he said, moving closer as he cut off her words.

She put down her mug and backed up against the counter. "You want me to be blunt? Here it is—I don't want children," she said and he heard the rattle in her voice. "And you do."

"Aren't you jumping the gun a bit, Grace?" he teased. "There's a whole lot of other stuff that comes before having babies."

"I know that it's—"

"Like marriage," he said quietly. "And spending more time together than one weekend."

He watched, fascinated as her cheeks bloomed with color.

"But I thought—"

"You thought what?" he asked, cutting her off. "That I want more from you? You're right, I do. But only if you want to give it. I can't help wondering why you are so determined to *not* have a baby?" he asked and looped a hand around her nape.

She met his gaze. "Because a baby and a career don't mix. And since my career would always come first, that's no way to raise a child. I don't have that built-in *baby* gene like Evie or my mother."

He rubbed her neck softly. "So, never?"

"Never. Like I said."

"Then I guess we're doomed," he said and kissed her.

She sighed against his mouth and moved closer. Cameron gently pushed her back against the counter and cradled her into the crook of his shoulder. She fit so perfectly and was made for his arms, but he held back the words he wanted to say.

She's not ready...

And there was no guarantee she ever would be.

"I'm gonna miss doing that," he said and trailed his mouth to her cheek. "A lot."

She trembled. "I have to go back to New York. I'm not staying here."

"So you said," he whispered against her ear.

"I meant it."

Cameron nuzzled her neck. "But you're here now."

She made a sound, half groan, half sigh. "You're trying to confuse me..."

"I'm not trying to do anything," he said and nibbled her lobe. "Other than make out a little." Cameron found her mouth again and kissed her soundly. "But since I'm on the night shift for the next few days I really have to get going," he said, and pulled back. "I'll see you Saturday, around eleven."

She shook her head. "Saturday?"

"We have a date, remember?"

"A date?"

"The Jakowski family reunion picnic," he said and figured he had to get away from her as quickly as possible. Otherwise he might be tempted to do a whole lot more than kiss her neck. "You said you'd come with me."

Her brows shot up. "I said I'd think about it."

He half smiled. "And?"

"And…it's probably not a good idea," she replied. "It might give the impression that we're…you know, sleeping together."

"We *are* sleeping together."

"Really?" She crossed her arms. "I don't know about you, but I've been sleeping alone this week."

Cameron tried not to laugh. She was mad at him. Good. At least she was feeling *something.* "Missing me, then?" He let the words hang in the air for a moment.

"Not at all."

Her resistance made him ache for her, "Sure you are," he said and grabbed his keys. "I'll see you Saturday, eleven o'clock."

She still looked like she wanted to bail on their plans, but she nodded. "Okay… Saturday."

Then he left.

On Saturday morning Cameron picked Grace up from the B and B. True to his word, he hadn't called her. It hadn't been easy. But he'd done some serious thinking.

She was leaving in a week and he was running out of time. He knew she was fighting it…fighting him. She didn't want babies. She didn't want a relationship. She didn't want to stay in Crystal Point.

And yet, they had an incredible connection. He felt it deep within his bones. It *was* the kind of connection that could last a lifetime…if only she would let it.

Grace wasn't exactly smiling when he pulled up. She got into the car and strapped on the seat belt.

"I thought you might have stood me up," he said.

"A deal is a deal."

"Still mad at me?"

She looked straight ahead. "Jerk."

He laughed. "Well, it promises to be an interesting day.

How are things going with you?" he asked. "Told your folks yet?"

"No," she replied. "But it's you we're here to work on today, remember?"

He remembered. Cameron had a knot in his stomach thinking about it. He would much rather take Grace home and make love to her all afternoon. "I remember."

She frowned and then her mouth was slowly drawn into a smile. "You could have called."

"But we're doomed, remember?"

She shifted in her seat. "I'm here now," she said, reminding him of his words a few days earlier. "And still here for another week."

"Does that mean you'll be wanting my attention?"

"Jerk," she said again and crossed her arms. "I've changed my mind about you. You're as impossible as always."

He grinned. He loved that about her. Loved that she had so much spirit.

When they arrived at the park he spotted his parents' sedan and knew his mother would hyperventilate once she saw him with Grace.

"Everything okay?" Grace asked as he walked around the back of the car.

She smiled and he was quickly bedazzled. "I'm good. Just waiting for my mother to ask what my intentions are."

"And what will you tell her when she does?"

Cameron's hand stilled on the picnic basket he was pulling from the backseat. His three weeks were nearly up and the words he wanted to say remained unspoken. But he knew he needed to get them out soon. He had a plan and he was going to stick to it. He grabbed the basket and closed the door. Grace had insisted they stop at the only organic deli in town and he watched as she organized the bewildered-looking girl behind the counter and pulled together a gourmet hamper.

He gazed at her as she collected a blanket and her bag, and admired how incredible she looked in a skirt, blouse and a bright red button-down sweater. His heart rate rose instantly.

"I'll tell her we've stopped hating one another," he said when she reached him.

"I never hated you," she said and stopped beside him. "Not really."

He touched her hand. It was their first touch in four long days. "No?"

"It was easier than facing the truth." She shrugged. "What can I say. I'm a coward."

Cameron squeezed her fingers. "You survived for two days alone and hurt in that car wreck. One thing you're not, Grace, is a coward."

She gave a brittle laugh. "It was only afterward that I fell apart."

"Which doesn't mean you lack courage."

Her eyes glittered and she pulled her hand away. "Yes, well…we should get going."

The reunion was in full force. About seventy relatives had turned up and tables topped with bright checkered clothes and crockery had been set up beneath a pair of giant trees. Away from the barbecues a group of children played and he spotted his father knee-deep into a game of Twister with a few of his great-nephews.

He saw his mother at one of the tables, sorting through plates and cutlery. She looked up as he approached and he knew the exact moment she realized Grace was at his side. Her surprised stare turned into a genuine wide smile.

She came around the table and hugged him close. "Good to see you here. Your dad will be pleased."

Guilt twinged between his shoulders. It had been four years since he'd shown his face at a Jakowski reunion. "Yeah. I brought—"

"Grace," his mother said, moving from him to take Grace's hand. "Wonderful to have you here with us. You look lovely as always."

"Thank you, Rennie."

All of the Preston siblings called Cameron's mother Rennie, rather than using the more traditional aunt label, which was often given to older, close family friends. "I believe you're looking after the B and B until Evie and Scott return from their honeymoon next week?"

"That's right."

"And Trevor?" Irene asked of Evie's sixteen-year-old son.

"He's staying with his grandparents up north for another week."

Cameron saw his mother's brows go up. "How lovely that they have a grandson to visit them."

He shook his head. "Two minutes."

Irene gave an innocent look. "What?"

"Two minutes before you pull out the no-grandchildren card." He smiled. "You're slipping, Mother."

He could see his mother's mind working in overdrive. Could see her mentally planning weddings and baby showers and happily-ever-afters. He placed the basket on the table and tried to ignore the sudden acceleration of his heartbeat. Because he'd imagined them, too. By the time Lauren sidled up beside him, his mother had ushered Grace toward an adjacent table of relatives and was introducing her to a few of his cousins and their spouses.

His sister pinched his arm. "Just checking that you haven't turned to stone."

He frowned. "What?"

Lauren's brows snapped up. "I couldn't believe my eyes. Of all the women I would ever expect you to be with, she isn't one of them."

Cameron held on to his temper. "She has a name. And I thought you liked the Prestons?"

Lauren shrugged and her blond hair bounced around her face. "I like Evie and Mary-Jayne. And Noah," she said, and then let out a breath. "And Grace, I suppose. Don't mind me. I wallow in self-pity a lot these days. It keeps me company."

"Sorry, kid," he said and rested an arm around her shoulders. "I know you've had it tough."

"That's still no excuse for being mean," Lauren said, then squeezed him back. "Even if I have always thought one look from those green eyes could turn a mortal man to stone."

He grinned. "She's not what you think."

Lauren's eyes glazed over. "People rarely are, I guess. But I thought you hated each other."

"Nope."

Cameron stayed at Lauren's side, but his gaze moved to Grace. As she mingled with his relatives he realized nothing fazed her. The boardroom, his bedroom…a park filled with Jakowskis. She was effortlessly confident, supremely adaptable and worked the crowd as though she had known everyone for years. But he'd seen the other Grace, too—the haunting, vulnerable woman who'd fallen apart in his arms.

"Whoa," Lauren said and tapped his shoulder. "That's a look I haven't seen before." She made a face. "You really do like her?"

"I really do like her."

I love her. And he figured his sister had probably worked that out, too.

Chapter Eleven

Grace allowed herself to be paraded around on Irene's arm. After they'd done the rounds of most of the relatives and spent a few minutes talking with a somewhat breathless Franciszek, they headed back to their table.

"Do I have you to thank for getting Cameron here today?" Irene asked as she pulled lids off plastic containers filled with assortments of cold chicken, potato and green salads and delicious-looking coleslaw.

Grace smiled and pulled a tray of cheese and smoked ham from the basket they'd brought. "He wanted to be here."

"That's sweet," the older woman said. "Although not exactly true. I know my son. But I'm grateful to you for making him see sense." She sighed. "He thinks I don't know why he avoids coming. But I do."

"I'm not—"

"My husband loves him just as much as he loves Lauren." Grace managed a smile. "I think he knows that."

"I hope so. Is Cameron hoping you'll distract me?" Irene asked and smiled. "You might encourage me instead." She paused and then quickly got straight to the point. "Are you dating again?"

Again? So she did know about their past relationship. "Not exactly."

"Sleeping together?"

Grace's skin burned and she dropped her gaze. "Well, I—"

"Your mother is my closest friend, Grace," Irene said quietly. "If you and my son are involved then I'd like to know about it."

"We're...just..." She shrugged helplessly. "I don't know what we are for sure."

Irene tapped her arm. "I know Cameron. And I know you. I hope it works out the way you both want."

But we both want different things.

When they sat down for lunch she was seated between Cameron and his uncle Henryk. Unsurprised to discover Cameron could speak Polish, Grace laughed as she stumbled over the pronunciation of words he tried to teach her. He placed a hand on her thigh under the table and didn't move it for the entire duration of the meal. The awareness between them had been building all morning and so had her need for him. His desire for her made her feel both safe and scared and connected to him in ways that had her heart beating madly.

Later, while Cameron walked off to speak with his father, Grace remained with Irene and Lauren and helped clear away the leftover food. She knew both women were curious about her relationship with Cameron. When Irene wandered back to the car to grab a wicker hamper, Lauren stepped beside her.

"So, you and Cameron, huh?"

Grace placed the lid on a half-eaten tub of pasta salad. "Am I in for an interrogation? If so, I already had one of those from Rennie."

Lauren raised both brows. "You're both of age. You can do what you like."

"But you don't approve?"

"I love my brother," Lauren said quietly. "And I wouldn't want to see him get attached to someone who's not going to hang around."

Like you.

The other woman didn't have to say it. Everyone knew her life was in New York.

Everyone knew she'd never settle for a life in Crystal Point.

"I don't want that either," she said and stacked the tub into a basket.

"I hope so," Lauren said, clearly acting protective of her only sibling. "I know we've never really gotten along. But for Cameron's sake we should probably make an—"

"I'll fold the tablecloths," Grace said, desperate to shut down the conversation. She looked around for Cameron and found he was on his way toward them. She drew in a relieved breath, grabbed the brightly colored cloth from the table and started folding.

He joined them and sidled up beside her. "Everything okay?"

Grace glanced at Lauren, who'd now moved to the other side of the table packing up picnic chairs. "Fine."

"I'll take you home when you're ready."

She glanced at her watch, saw that it was after four and figured there was little point in lingering. She certainly didn't want to answer any more questions from Lauren or Rennie. Grace nodded and he took a few minutes to say goodbye to his family while she finished packing. By the time they were back in the car and on their way to Crystal Point it was half past the hour.

He was quiet and she wondered about his mood. It was hard to tell. Their relationship had changed so much in the past two weeks. The old Cameron she knew and was prepared for. She'd always handled the insults and sarcasm. But now things were different.

When they pulled into the driveway at the B and B the silence between them was deafening. He grabbed the basket from the backseat and headed to the side of the house and toward the door that led to the private living area upstairs. The sensor light flicked on and she pulled out the keys. Once inside, he followed her up the stairs and into the kitchen and adjoining living area.

He placed the basket on the counter before spinning around to face her. He looked tense. Maybe angry.

"Is everything all right?" she asked quietly.

"Sure."

She twisted her hands together. "So, today wasn't too bad."

"You're right, it wasn't." He was unreadable, impenetrable. The only sign that he was feeling anything was the tiny pulse beating in his cheek.

"Would you like coffee?" she asked, desperate for conversation.

He moved across the room and hovered in the doorway. "No, thank you."

Inside the small room the tension between them escalated instantly. He returned her stare, blistering and intense, and so hot it almost burned through to her very soul.

Her breath caught as realization hit. It wasn't anger that held him from her, kept him distant. It was something else. Something she'd only glimpsed once before—the time when she'd been in the bathtub. Since then, every time he'd looked at her, touched her, kissed her, she'd felt his restraint. He'd always handled her gently, as though he sensed her lingering inhibitions. Every touch had been for her –her pleasure, her needs.

This, she thought as her blood pumped with urgent anticipation—this was desire, raw and powerful. This was need generated from long days apart. This was another level, another place, another kind of connection she'd never experienced before.

He wants me.

"Cameron...I—"

"Come here."

She stilled at the sound of his softly spoken command, felt the heat in the room rise up and sweep through to her bones. The only sounds were her heels clicking over the tiled floor as she stepped toward him.

He reached for her, moving one arm around her waist as he drew her close. "I've missed you." His mouth hovered an inch from hers. "So much."

"I've missed you, too."

He fisted a handful of her hair and tilted her head back. When he kissed her, hot and hard and deep, Grace pressed against him. Her blouse got crushed in the onslaught but she didn't care. All she felt was him...his hands, his mouth, his tongue demanding hers. She gave herself up, felt his surging need and matched it. Grace dug her hands into his shoulders as he swiveled around and trapped her against the door frame. She moaned low in her throat, wild with need and an aching hunger for him that boiled her blood. He managed to push her sweater off her shoulders in between kisses and toss it aside. Her blouse gave way beneath his fingers as buttons popped. She didn't care. She wanted his hands on her skin. She wanted him around her, over her, inside her.

Once the blouse was gone her bra was next. Cameron tugged at the straps and pushed them down over her arms. Her breasts rose up to meet his mouth and his hot breath against one nipple, then the other, drove her beyond coherent thought. Her skirt and briefs were quickly dispensed with and Grace gasped as he picked her up rested her against his hips. She wrapped her legs around him and rocked, felt his arousal and rocked again.

She waited while he snapped the top button and zipper on his chinos. Then he was inside her, plunging deep, taking her on a wild ride. Grace wasn't sure where he got the strength to hold her as they moved together, but with one hand braced against the door frame and the other around her hips, he supported both their weights. Pleasure built, skin burned on skin, and when it came she let herself go. Driving, aching, seeking the release she craved, Grace clung to him as they came together in a shattering wave of white-hot bliss.

It seemed an eternity before their breathing returned to normal. When he finally released her and set her on her feet, Grace realized that while she was completely naked, except for her bra settled around her waist, he was still fully clothed. He didn't release her, though. He tucked her head beneath his chin, steadying her with one arm, the other still rested against the door frame.

"Where's your bedroom?" he asked hoarsely after a moment.

Grace motioned down the hall and within a second he lifted her again and held her against his chest. Once in her bedroom he placed her gently by the foot of the big bed. She stayed perfectly still as he discarded his clothes. The lamplight dappled the hard contours of his shoulders and arms and she thought how she'd never seen a more beautiful man in her life. Longing rose up and hit her directly in the solar plexus.

Grace pressed against him. "Cameron..."

"I want to make love to you."

She sighed out a breath. "Isn't that what you just did?"

Cameron grasped her chin and tilted her head back. "That wasn't so much making love as it was my need for you."

"And mine for you," she admitted on a whisper, coloring hotly. "I've never done anything like that before."

He rubbed her cheek. "I'm sorry. I don't usually let that part of my anatomy do my thinking."

Grace bit her bottom lip and smiled. To be desired so completely, so urgently and with so much unabashed passion was highly erotic. For the first time in her life she completely rejoiced in her sexuality. He gifted her immeasurable pleasure and she suddenly longed to return that gift. She wanted him to feel what she felt—complete abandonment, total trust and mind-blowing ecstasy.

She pulled back and linked their fingertips. "Come with me," she urged and led him into the bathroom.

When she flicked on the jets of the double shower spray and pulled him into the open cubicle he raised both brows inquiringly. "What did you have in mind?"

Grace laughed, pushed him gently against the tiled wall and circled her palms over his pectorals. "Whatever I want," she said, kissing a trail from one small budded nipple to the other.

Laughter rumbled in his chest. "Throwing down the gauntlet, Grace?"

She nodded and kissed lower. He was already aroused, already hers to take. "And if I am?"

He raised his arms and braced against the wall. "Whatever you want," he invited softly.

Grace smiled and eagerly took up the challenge. Tenderness and desire transcended through her fingertips, her lips, and her tongue. He offered her moans of encouragement, and when he could take no more, when she felt his control slip, Grace gave him all she could. In that moment she had the power, the potency in her touch to bring him to his knees as release claimed him, and she held him through the pleasure, giving him her strength and the feelings that were in her heart.

* * *

Four hours later Cameron was in the small kitchen making scrambled eggs.

Which look as scrambled as my brain at the moment.

Grace sat on the other side of the counter on a stool, wrapped in a fluffy robe, sipping a glass of wine. With her hair mussed, her eyes a kind of hazy green and her lips the color of cherries, she looked delectable. She smiled at him over the rim of her glass.

"Pleased with yourself, are you?" he asked as he stirred the eggs.

A dreamy look washed over her face. "Hmm?" She shrugged and the robe opened, showing the hint of cleavage.

Cameron did his best to concentrate on the cooking and not her exposed skin. "You know exactly what I mean."

She smiled again, deep and alluring. "It's no secret to you that I've had a fairly repressed sex life." She put down her glass. "Until now."

It was quite the admission. "Why?"

She shrugged again. "Control, I guess. I could close off and only give the parts of myself I was certain wouldn't make me vulnerable."

Cameron pulled the eggs off the heat. "Being vulnerable isn't weakness, Grace."

"I'm starting to realize that."

He came around the counter, grabbed her hands and swiveled the stool ninety degrees. "Can you let go of your control long enough to think about your future?"

His heart pounded as he spoke. He'd had days to plan what he wanted to say to her. But the moment he'd picked her up that morning it confirmed what he wanted to do. What he'd planned to do since they'd returned from Burdon Creek.

"My future?" The tremor in her voice was unmistakable.

"Our future," he said and moved between her legs, pulling her close.

She drew in a long breath and tilted her head. "I don't understand what—"

"Grace," he said as his heart thundered and Cameron took as much air into his lungs as he could. "I've spent the past sixteen years denying what I feel and I—"

"Cameron, I think we should—"

He place two fingertips against her lips. "Let me finish," he said gently. "I have to say this, Grace. I've been working out ways to say this to you for the past week. For a long time I've been pretty casual about how I viewed relationships. I didn't allow myself to get seriously involved with anyone. I kidded myself that I didn't want anything permanent, or any woman to mean more to me than some good times and sex. But that's not really what I want."

She stared at him, unmoving.

"At Evie's wedding everything changed." He touched her cheek and ran a thumb along her jaw. "All those years of fighting and insults and antagonism…it was as though I'd woken up in a reality where none of that stuff existed. And now I want permanent, Grace. And I want it with you," he said, cradling her hips intimately. "These past couple of weeks I've felt an incredible connection with you. Tell me you felt that, too?"

"I did," she whispered. "I do."

His grip tightened. "Then let's not waste that feeling, Grace. A lifetime ago I let you go even though I knew it was the last thing I wanted. And before I had a chance to tell you how I really felt about you." His thumb moved over her cheek and he smiled. He stroked her face one more time before he reached into his pocket and withdrew a small box. "I love you, Grace. Marry me?"

The world tilted on an axis and Grace felt like she was falling. She didn't, though. He was there, in front of her, holding her against him. His brown eyes were dark and rich. He flicked the box open and Grace saw the most perfect ring, a brilliant white diamond surrounded by superbly cut emeralds.

"The green stones are the same color as your eyes," he said and watched her as she continued to stare at the box. When she didn't move he spoke again, slower this time. "But if you don't like it we can change the—"

"I like it," she said quickly and drew in a sharp breath. "I really do." Emotion clogged her throat. And the *yes* she wanted to say so much danced around in her head. "But... Cameron...I...I..."

He pulled back, suddenly pale as he put space between them. "Are you saying no?"

Grace wobbled on the stool and then slid to her feet. "No... Yes... I mean, I'm not saying... I'm just saying—"

"You're saying what?" he asked, cutting her off.

"It's just so unexpected," she said quickly. "So fast..."

"Fast? We've been dodging around this for years. I love you...I'd hoped you loved me back."

Grace pushed back her shoulders and slowly moved across to the living room and sat on the sofa. Cameron remained by the kitchen, a trillion miles away.

"Please, come and sit down," she said and tied the robe tighter.

He nodded, came across the room and sat beside her. Grace took a breath, the longest she could. She wanted to touch him. She wanted to feel the safety of his arms around her. Instead she stared at the jewelry box he still held in his left hand.

"I know how hard that must have been to say," she said quietly. "And if I wasn't leaving next week, things might be different. But I—"

"So we can make them different, can't we?"

Another breath. Another dose of steadying oxygen in her

blood. "How? I have a life in New York. And a career I can't simply discard."

He stayed silent for a moment, absorbing her words. "Okay...you have a career. We'll work around it."

She met his eyes. "How can we do that? Your life is here. My life is there. And we both want different things." Grace grabbed his hand and the jewelry box lay between their palms. They were connected by a ring that part of her desperately wanted, but another part of her knew she couldn't take. "We both know what kind of wife you want, Cameron. One who lives in Crystal Point, for starters. And one who wants to settle down and raise a family with you. That's not me. That won't ever be me." Emotion burned her eyes. "I'm sorry. But I've never pretended to be anything other than who I am. I just can't be that kind of woman."

Despite knowing he was getting exactly what he should have expected, Cameron felt like he'd been punched in the gut. He pulled air into his lungs. "And that's it?"

Her hand moved off his. "I know it's not what you want to hear."

Cameron jumped up and the ring he bought her rolled to his feet. He left it there. "No, it's not."

She looked at the small velvet box and picked it up, holding it for a moment before she placed it on the low glass table in front of her. "My career has always been all I am. And I have to go back and prove to myself that I can do it again. For the first time in months I feel strong enough to do my job properly. Please try to understand."

He did understand. She was rejecting him. Again.

"Ambition above all else?" he asked, pulling a tight rein on his hurt and disappointment.

"Of course not," she replied. "But I've not made any secret of that fact that I intended to go back."

Cameron experienced a strange pain in the middle of his chest. She'd made up her mind. She was leaving. He'd lost her. Again.

"And tonight, Grace? Is it your way of saying goodbye? Chuck in some last-minute hot sex before you pack your bags and leave everything behind?"

"I'm not that—"

"What?" he shot back abruptly, cutting her off. "Cold?"

She looked instantly wounded and Cameron's insides burned with a hollow pain. He didn't want to upset her... not intentionally...but he was angry and disappointed and plain old hurt.

"You think I'm cold?" she asked in a quiet voice. "After everything we've... After tonight and every other time we've been together?"

"Don't confuse sex and love, Grace."

She stood up quickly. "What do you want me to say to you? That I'm torn...of course I am. This is the hardest decision I've ever had to make."

Annoyance began to weave down his spine. "Really? It seems fairly cut-and-dried."

She wrapped her arms around herself. "I didn't lie to you. I didn't make any promises. You know how I feel about marriage and children. I've worked hard to get the career I wanted. And now...now I have to prove that I can do it again without falling apart like I did after the accident." She sucked in a long, heavy breath. "I don't expect you to understand... you've never failed at anything."

I've failed to get your love.

"Of course I have," he said roughly.

"I mean you've never failed to be anything other than yourself," she said tremulously. "Last weekend with Pat and her grandchildren, I really saw you for the first time. I saw that you're funny and charming and incredible with kids and so unbelievably comfortable in your own skin. Wherever you go, you belong."

Cameron stilled. "I'm not sure what that has to do with you turning down my proposal."

"Everything. Nothing. It's just that you know who you are. And I'm a slightly neurotic, overachieving control freak who has never really belonged anywhere except in the life I've made in New York. Whenever I come back here it reminds me of how different I am from everyone else. Most of my life I've felt as though I have been stuck in between worlds."

He knew that about her and his heart lurched. "Then, how about we meet somewhere in the middle?"

She took a shuddering breath. "How can we? In the middle there's an ocean."

"It's just geography, Grace."

"It's more than that," she refuted. "It's about you being an important part of this community. And the kids like Dylan and Emily—they need you. I could never ask you to change or give up being part of that. Just like I can't change what defines me."

Cameron took four steps forward and reached her. He grasped her shoulders and molded the bones beneath his hands. He wanted to kiss sense into her. He wanted to love her until they weren't sure where she began and he ended.

"That's a cop-out, Grace. This isn't about the job or anything other than the fact you're scared to death to really feel something for someone. That's why every relationship you've had has been lukewarm. You chose the doctor and the suit because they didn't threaten your little safe world where you don't have to let yourself be seen for who you really are."

The truth hit Cameron with lightning force.

"I get it now," he said, releasing her. She shuffled back slightly. "I finally get why you came back. It's not about the car crash or your friend's death or because a therapist told you to spend time with your family. You simply don't want anyone to work out that you're not perfect. But now you've regrouped, right? You have your strength back—you've faced what happened in the accident and you want to dive straight back into that life. And by doing that you can once again turn your back on this place and everyone in it."

"I didn't turn my back on Crystal Point," she snapped, emotion bared in her eyes. "I was *sent* away."

He stilled. "What?"

"I was sent away," she whispered this time as she sank back onto the sofa. "To school."

"School? You mean—"

"I mean boarding school," she said, cutting him off. "I mean to a place where I didn't know anyone and where I was put in a class higher than my age because I was considered too smart, too advanced for my normal grade. A class where I was first tormented and then ignored for being younger and smarter…and different. And I'd come home for holidays and my family would all be here—this fabulous tight-knit unit— a unit I wasn't really part of. I was told how lucky I was to be getting such an amazing education. And they were right. I did get the best education possible." Tears glittered on her lids. "But when school was over and I came back I felt so out of place…so distant. That's why I couldn't stay."

The question he'd pondered a thousand times came out. "So it wasn't because of us?"

"No." She shook her head. "It was never about that. In so many ways you were the only reason I wanted to stay." She took a long, steadying breath. "But I knew you were getting serious and I got scared."

"Scared of what?" His insides crunched. "Of falling in love?"

"Of failing to be…more," she admitted unsteadily. "Of not living up to the expectations of my parents, my teachers…

and even myself. I had to live the life that had been planned for me. If I didn't, it meant it would have been a waste to send me to that expensive school. And I couldn't do that to my parents. But when I came back…"

He knew what she meant. "I got in the way?"

She shrugged. "I left quickly because I didn't want to get in any deeper."

His back straightened. "And still don't, clearly."

She held the velvet box in both her hands. "Please don't be like this. We can have tonight…tomorrow…"

"You know," he said quietly, resignedly, "I've pretty much loved you since you were sixteen years old. But I'd just joined the police force and I knew you weren't ready for a relationship. So I waited a couple of years—waited until you were old enough. When you came back from school and we started dating I thought it would lead to a life together. But you told me then that nothing would keep you in Crystal Point— especially not a small-town police officer. So I guess things haven't changed all that much." He took a deep breath and tried to not think about how much he ached inside. "Goodbye, Grace."

Without another word he turned around and walked out of the room. And out of her life.

Chapter Twelve

When Evie and Scott arrived home on Monday, Grace heaved a sigh of relief.

Her flight back to New York was booked and although she was glad to have a few more days to spend with her sister, she also wanted to go home. *And New York is my home.*

She thought Evie looked exhausted and told her so. They sat together in the kitchen, sipping the peach iced tea her sister had begged for.

"I'm fine, honestly," Evie insisted and patted her bulging belly. "Just tired from the trip home. I did nothing but relax and get pampered by my lovely husband while we were away."

"You've popped out," Grace said as she looked at her sister's stomach. "And still a month to go."

"Three weeks," Evie replied. "I wish you were staying until then."

Grace drank some tea. "I have to get back to work. So, tell me about the honeymoon."

Evie grinned. "Everything?"

"Well, not *everything*."

Her sister laughed. "It was romantic in a mostly non-amorous kind of way." Evie rubbed her palms across her abdomen. "What about you? What did you get up to while we were away?"

I made love with Cameron Jakowski. Again and again. Oh, and I got a marriage proposal, too.

"Not much," she lied then explained about babysitting Noah's kids and tutoring Emily.

"Babysitting?" Evie's steeply arched brows rose significantly. "Really?"

"Don't look so surprised."

Evie smiled. "I'm delighted, not surprised. The twins are adorable. Notorious at dinner and bath time, though."

"Mmm…well, I had a little help."

"Help?"

Grace drew in a breath. "Cameron stopped by. He cooked dinner while I was on bath duty."

"Cameron did?" Evie's eyebrows went up again. "And?"

Grace shrugged as the weight of her suddenly complicated life pushed down heavily on her shoulders. "And we had dinner and then he left."

"That's not what I meant. What else has been going on with you two?" her sister asked with way too much intuition. "And don't bother denying it. After what happened at the wedding I wouldn't be surprised if—"

"I slept with him."

Evie's green eyes almost popped out of her head. "Oh—I see. And what else?"

She took a few seconds before she told her sister of the weekend at Burdon Creek, Thomas's accident and briefly mentioned how she and Cameron had become close.

"But why did you agree to go in the first place?" Evie asked.

She wasn't about to admit to Cameron's little bit of blackmail. "To help Emily."

Her sister clearly wasn't convinced. "Another thing I don't understand. Since when have you been a math tutor?"

Grace met her sister's gaze. "She needed help to pass a makeup exam. I'm good with numbers."

"I know that. You're the smartest person I've ever met. But you don't usually get...involved...with what other people are doing."

Now Grace raised a brow. "Is that a nice way of saying I'm a self-absorbed neurotic with little time for anyone other than myself?"

Evie smiled. "Well, I might not put it exactly that way."

"But the gist is the same? Yes, I know what I am. I know what people think."

Evie smiled again and drank some tea. "Well, who cares what others think. I love you for who you are. We all do."

Grace swallowed a thick lump in her throat. Shame and guilt pressed down on her shoulders. She felt like such a coward. She'd returned to Crystal Point and then run from the truth. As she had done over and over. If she was to be with her family and try to heal the disconnect she'd felt most of her life, then she needed to really *be* with them. She needed to let them in and admit she was scared and vulnerable and hurting.

She needed to tell them about the accident.

Cameron was right. Thinking about him brought a deep, hollow pain to her chest. His words resonated in her head over and over.

I love you, Grace. Marry me.

He loved her. It was the first time a man had ever said that to her. And the first time she'd ever wanted to say it back.

"What?"

Evie again, looking way too intuitive. Her sister could be relentless when she wanted to know something. "It's nothing." She took a deep breath. "I'd like to go to our parents' tomorrow night. There's something I need to tell you all."

Then she could go home.

"I hear she's leaving next week."

Cameron sat in the kitchen of his parents' house. His mother stood on the other side of the granite counter, looking at him over the rim of her reading glasses. Irene Jakowski always got straight to the point.

"So I believe."

"And you're letting her go?"

He ignored the jabbing pain at his temple. "Let's not do this."

"I didn't raise a quitter. I raised someone who became the kind of man who goes after what he wants."

Until I got my heart crushed.

"I can't make her feel something she doesn't," he said flatly and stared into the coffee mug in front of him.

Irene tutted impatiently. "If you want her you should fight for her."

"I also can't fight against her ambition," he replied and pushed the mug aside. "She's made it pretty clear what's important in her life."

"Cameron," his mother said, gently this time. "The Grace I saw at the picnic didn't seem too interested in her career. She couldn't keep her eyes off you. You're made for one another—you always were. Besides," Irene's eyes grew wide and she smiled. "I want grandchildren. With Evie's baby coming soon, Barbara will have six little angels and I don't have any. Soon I'll have nothing to talk about with my best friend."

Cameron smiled at his mother's sense of drama. "I didn't realize you were so competitive with Barbara Preston."

"Of course I am," she replied with a laugh. "What else do you think we want to talk about? Kids and grandkids are our staple diet of conversation. At least, it would be if you decided to settle down and supply me with some."

"Maybe you should try your luck with Lauren?"

"Hah," his mother scoffed. "Your sister has convinced herself she's a man-hater after that fiasco with what's-his-name. You, on the other hand, have an opportunity to be with a perfectly lovely girl who just happens to be the daughter of my best friend."

"Since when did you become the president of Grace's fan club?" he asked, trying to diffuse his mother's enthusiasm.

"Since I realized that you're in love with her."

He wasn't about to deny it. Irene Jakowski could see a lie through thick fog. "She's made her choice."

She took a breath. "And when did you become so black-and-white? You negotiate and work through problems every day in your job with those troubled kids you help. You don't give up on them—you don't give up on anyone. What about Dylan? Isn't he another example of keeping faith in what you believe? You wanted to help him and you did. You helped that entire family get back together. Don't the same rules apply in your own life?"

Her point had biting accuracy. "It's not the same thing."

Irene took off her glasses. "Oh, I see…bruised that monumental ego of yours, did she?"

"I don't see what—"

"You're as bad as your father. Did you know he dithered around for months before he asked me out and when I said I had plans he didn't bother to ask me again? I waited three weeks and then I asked him. Then I stood him up just to make a point. He got mad for about two days and then came back groveling. And he proposed marriage three times before I finally accepted him. Good thing, too."

"Is there a point to this?"

"My point," she said slowly, "is that women, even the most complex women, like to be wooed. Chased, pursued…call it whatever you like."

"And if she turns me down again?"

Irene grinned. "Go woo some more."

Cameron laughed for the first time that week. Irene Jakowski always said what she thought. Woo her? But he knew his mother was right. He had quit. Grace had announced her intention and he'd bailed, he'd walked off to lick his wounds in private.

Fat chance of that in this family.

He wanted to see her again. He wanted to hold her again. But he knew Grace…he knew the more he pushed the more she would resist.

"She's going back to New York," he said flatly.

"So, follow her."

Cameron stood and pushed the chair out. "I have to go," he said and grabbed his keys. "Thanks for the coffee." His kissed his mother goodbye and left.

Grace was incredibly touched by the support she got from her family when she told them about the accident, Richard's death and her ensuing breakdown. They sat quietly and listened as she spoke of the two days she was trapped inside the car and the fear that she would die before she was found.

"Why didn't you say something earlier?" It was Noah, her most practical sibling, who spoke.

"At first I was in shock about what had happened. And then…I was embarrassed that I'd fallen apart," she admitted and looked up from her spot on the big sofa. "Anyway, I apologize for shutting everyone out."

"Grace," her mother said and grasped her hand, patting it gently. "Even though you live thousands of miles away, you're still very much a part of this family. If you had called we would have been there for you."

Of course they would have. In her heart she knew that. But the feelings of disconnect she had from when she was sent to boarding school had caused her to close up like a vault. But right now, more than ever before, Grace knew she was loved. Everything Cameron had said was true. Grace could have wept. "I know," she said and managed a tight smile. "And thank you for understanding."

Except when she drove Evie back to the B and B, she couldn't miss the deliberate silence from her sister.

"Okay," Grace said as she pulled into the driveway and turned off the engine. "Say what's on your mind."

"Is there any point?" Evie asked and let out an exasperated breath as she unclipped her seat belt. "I can't quite believe you, Grace. Maybe our parents and Noah and M.J. were too stunned to say anything back at the house—but I'm saying it now—what gave you the right to exclude us so deliberately? You could have been killed. One of us should have been there—heck, we *all* would have been there if you'd only said something. A phone call. Even an email. Would that have been so difficult?"

"No," she replied softly. "You have every right to be angry."

Evie touched her arm. "I'm not angry. I'm…hurt. Don't do it again, Grace. Don't treat us like we don't matter."

Grace was about to apologize again when Evie winced. "What is it?"

"Nothing," her sister assured her and then touched her belly. "Only, I'm thinking the backache I've had today isn't backache."

"What do you—"

"I think I'm going into labor," Evie said on a rush of sharp breath. "You might want to go inside and tell my husband. And also tell him not to forget my bag," she added.

Grace was out of the car with lightning speed.

Sure enough, Evie did go into early labor. Grace stayed at the hospital through the night and was the first person to be told that her sister had given birth to a healthy baby girl.

Evie's husband, Scott, emerged from the birthing room to give her the news.

"They're fine," he said and ran a weary hand though his hair. "The baby is three weeks early, and she's...she's..." He stalled and took a deep breath. "Perfect."

"Congratulations," Grace said and found herself in the middle of a huge bear hug.

She didn't pull away. The old Grace would have balked at hugging anyone, let alone her brother-in-law. But she'd changed. Her prickles were...well, less prickly.

The ice princess had finally begun to thaw.

She left the hospital and headed back to the B and B to shower and change and give the new parents some time with their baby. But that afternoon she returned for a visit with her sister and took only minutes to be persuaded to hold the baby, who had been named Rebecca.

"She's so beautiful, Evie," she said, holding baby Rebecca close. A tiny tuft of dark hair stuck out above the top of her soft pink wrap and Grace touched her head gently.

Evie sighed contentedly and pushed back against the pillows. "I know. I can't believe she's finally here."

"And there were no complications during the birth?"

"Not one. She was eager to come into the world. Although I'd forgotten how tiring the whole thing can be. It's been sixteen years since I had Trevor."

Grace looked at her niece and smiled warmly. "Well, you did great. And Scott?"

"Poor darling." Evie's face lit up. "I sent him home to get some sleep. He's mesmerized by how perfect she is and has been staring at her for most of the day."

"He's a first-time father so I guess that's to be expected." Grace glanced at her sister and smiled. "It's really good to see you so happy."

Evie nodded and adjusted the front of her nightgown. "What about you? Do you truly believe going back to New York will make *you* happy?"

With her emotions bubbling at the surface the last thing Grace wanted to do was break down when Evie was experiencing so much joy. She put on the stiffest face she had. "It's where I live."

"That's not exactly an answer. Is it what you want?"

What I want? Grace didn't know. Holding the baby brought up so many feelings, so many longings. Her womb was doing a whole lot of uncharacteristic backflips and she suddenly found herself doing the unthinkable—actually imagining having Cameron's baby. The very notion brought heat to the back of her eyes.

"I wouldn't be doing it if I didn't think it was for the best."

Evie's mouth twisted. "I know you better than that. What exactly happened between the two of you?" her sister asked. "And don't just tell me you slept with him. There's more, I know it."

Grace touched Rebecca's face and marveled at the softness of her skin. She drew in a shaky breath and told her sister the truth. "He proposed."

Evie's huge green eyes bulged. "Cameron asked you to marry him?"

"Yes."

"And what did you say?"

Grace pushed back the emotion in her throat. "I said I was going back to New York."

"You turned him down?"

"I…guess I did." The pain of the words struck deep and Grace gathered her composure. "We can't have a relationship when we live in different countries, let alone a marriage."

"You could stay," Evie suggested. "Or you could ask him to go with you."

Grace didn't bother to hide her surprise. "His life is here."

"And yours is in New York? Yeah, yeah, I get that. I just don't understand why there can't be a middle road."

"Because…because there just can't. Cameron's life is in Crystal Point—his job, all the work his does with kids… I would never ask him to change who he is."

"And you won't change for him?"

She shrugged.

"Do you really hate Crystal Point that much?" Evie asked.

"I don't hate it," she replied quickly. "I just don't…fit in."

"Look at you," her sister said gently. "You're holding your niece like she is the most precious thing in the world. And for the past two weeks you've been running the B and B, baby-sitting Noah's kids and helping a young girl pass her exams. Does that paint a picture of someone who doesn't *fit in?*" Evie sighed. "You know, love is sometimes about compromise. You do love him, right?"

Grace pushed back tears and looked up, denial hanging on the edge of her tongue.

Evie's gaze narrowed. "Well, even if you won't admit it, I'll bet my boots you do."

Her gaze dropped immediately. "You know I—"

"Don't let anyone know what you're feeling…ever?"

The old Grace would have jumped all over her sister's words. But Evie was so right it hurt through to her bones. "I guess I don't," she admitted, thinking about the small velvet box in her handbag. She'd carried the ring with her since the night he'd asked her to marry him. Sometimes she opened the box to look at it, never quite having the courage to put the ring on her finger—afraid that if she did she would be forever changed.

"Like I said," Evie continued, "compromise. And sometimes one has to give and one has to take. It's not a competition, Grace, I mean to see who has to change the most…it's just the way it is. When Scott moved his life from California to Crystal Point he did it with an open heart. He did it because he *loved* me. And I am grateful for that every single day."

Grace touched the baby's soft hair. "But you had this beautiful girl on the way," she reminded Evie. "That's a big incentive for anyone."

"Love is enough, Grace. You just have to let yourself believe it."

I'm not that brave—I wish I was. Grace snuggled Rebecca against her chest and inhaled the sweet baby smell. She was a wondrous thing and she couldn't get enough of her soft hair and rosebud mouth. All her adult life she'd insisted that children weren't in her future. And now, as she held the newborn infant, Grace experienced a longing so deep and so acute her heart actually ached.

There was a brief knock on the door and Evie invited whoever it was to enter.

Grace almost hyperventilated when the door swung open and Cameron strode across the threshold. He stopped when he saw her and the flowers in his hand dropped to his side. He looked at Grace and then the baby she held in her arms.

The room spun momentarily. Her breath caught, making a sharp sound which echoed around the walls. Grace's heart surged. She hadn't seen him in what seemed like an eternity. In that time she'd experienced every emotion possible—from despair to anger and then a deep wrenching pain. And as he watched her with blistering intensity all of those sensations pulsed through her blood. Time stalled, drawing them both into a moment of acute awareness. With the baby held against her, Grace knew what he was thinking.

This could be our child one day.

A hollow ache rushed through to her bones. Her womb rolled, taunting her with the possibility of what *could* be. Like a speedy camera she saw it all so clearly—the home, the children and the happiness she'd always been afraid to want.

"Hey, Evie," he said, breaking the contact between them as he walked toward her sister, kissed her cheek affectionately and handed her the flowers. "Congratulations on your new addition."

Evie was appropriately grateful and glanced at Grace. United in loyalty, she recognized her sister's questioning look. Grace forced tears back and concentrated on the baby while Cameron and Evie spoke. She couldn't look at him. She was raw. If he said a word to her Grace knew she could break down and cry. And that wasn't an option. Not in front of Evie. And not in front of him.

Dressed in uniform, he'd obviously come straight from work. He looked so attractive and she was struck with images of how she'd often imagined stripping his blues off.

She stiffened when he approached and admired the baby from barely two feet away. The familiarity of him assailed her senses. His hair that she loved running her fingers through. His broad shoulders and arms which had somehow become a safe haven. Everything about Cameron made her want... made her need. She took a steadying breath as she stood.

"Cute kid," he said easily. But Grace wasn't fooled. His shoulders were tight, his jaw rigid. She knew he was hanging by the same thread she was. The temptation to run into his arms became a powerful force and it took all her will to keep a rein on her emotions.

Grace had placed Rebecca in her mobile crib when Evie spoke again.

"Would you like to hold her?" her sister asked Cameron.

His hand immediately rested on the pistol holstered at his hip. "Not while I'm wearing this," he said evenly. "I'll wait until she's home."

Evie nodded. "Well, I think I might take a little walk," she announced suddenly. "I need to stretch my legs. Look after Grace and my angel for a few minutes, will you, Cameron? I'll be back soon."

Grace watched as Evie shuffled off the bed, touched the sleeping baby on the cheek for a moment and then quietly left the room.

"That was subtle," he said once the door closed.

Grace swiveled softly on her heels. "You know Evie."

He raised both brows inquiringly. "You told her about us?" he asked. "I'm surprised."

Grace shrugged and moved across the room to stand near the window. "She's my sister. I tell her things."

He looked instantly skeptical. "You didn't tell her about the accident until yesterday, though, did you?"

"You know about that?"

"Your mother called mine. Mine called me."

Grace shrugged. "Well, everyone knows now, so no more secrets." From the window she spotted a view of the neighboring parklands and tried to concentrate on the scene and not think about how messed up her thoughts were.

Silence stretched like elastic.

"Do you know what I thought when I came into this room and saw you holding the baby?"

She didn't turn. Didn't move. Rebecca's soft breathing was all she heard. And the dreadful silence that grew in decibels with every passing second. She knew exactly what he'd thought. Because she'd thought it, too.

Cameron spoke again. "I thought how beautiful you looked holding the baby. And then I wondered how could I get you to stay? How could I get you to change your mind and give this…give us, a chance?"

Grace turned around and faced him. "You can't."

"I know, Grace," he said, keeping his voice low.

Her heart lurched forward. But she wouldn't break. "I'd like us to still be…friends."

"Friends? You're kidding, right? Since when have we ever really been friends?"

She drew in a shaky breath. "We could try," she whispered.

Cameron stepped toward her. He reached up and touched her cheek. "I don't want to be your friend, Grace. I want to be your lover and your husband and the father of your children. I want you to be the first person I see when I wake up in the morning. I want it all, as scary as that sounds to you. But that's what love is, Grace…having it all, wanting it all."

She nodded, although she wasn't sure how. "Cameron, I—"

"But I know that's not what you want."

Grace closed her eyes. It would be easy to fall under the spell of his gentle touch, his comforting voice. She opened her eyes again when he released her and met his gaze head-on as he stepped back. The growing distance quickly pulled them apart.

"I want…" Her voice cracked. *Like my heart is cracking.* "A part of me…a part of me does want those things." She looked at the baby and experienced a sharp longing so severe she had to grip the edge of the crib for support.

"But?"

She swallowed hard and stared at Rebecca. "But my career—"

"Comes first? Yeah—I got that, Grace."

"No one gets both," she said quietly, suddenly numb.

He didn't say anything. The tension coursing through him was palpable and vibrated around the room. Grace longed to touch him, to reach for his face and hold him between her shaking hands. It had been so long since they'd touched and her skin ached with the need to feel the heat of his body. But she didn't move. Didn't dare ask him to take her in his arms.

What if we never touch again?

"In your world…I guess not," he said quietly.

The door opened and Evie walked back into the room. She hesitated for a moment, clearly sensing the tension in the room, and then plastered on a big smile.

"How's my girl?" she asked cheerfully and walked across to the crib. "Did she miss me?"

Grace pulled her composure together. "She's been a perfect angel." She touched Rebecca's tiny head for a moment before she grabbed her handbag. "I'll head off." She hugged her sister close, hanging on for as long as she could, feeling Evie's innate strength and unquestioning love. "I'll see you soon."

Evie nodded. "Sure."

She didn't look at Cameron. If he saw her eyes, if he were to look deep within her he'd know she was on the brink of a meltdown. She took a gulp of air, said goodbye to her sister and muttered another in his direction and left the room. And she didn't take another breath until she was halfway down the corridor.

Evie Jones's stare made it clear to Cameron that he was in for an earful. He tried to ignore it. "Your daughter is beautiful, Evie," he said and stepped around the mobile crib. "No doubt Scott is—"

"Can I ask you something?" she queried, cutting him off, hands firmly on hips.

He took a second to respond. "Ah—okay."

"Are you really in love with my sister?" she asked bluntly.

He stilled. "Well, I—"

"Because if you are," she said, cutting him off again, "you've a strange way of showing it."

Cameron had always liked Evie. But he wasn't about to get into a conversation about his feelings for her sister. Even if he understood Evie's motives and natural loyalty toward Grace. "She's made her choice."

Evie harrumphed. "Looks like you have, too," she said with bite. "To act like a jerk, I mean."

Why was it that all the women around him seemed to be dishing out insults and advice? First his mother, now Evie. "What did Grace tell you?"

"Enough," Evie replied. "And I know my sister. Better than you do, by the looks of things."

Cameron reined in the irritation weaving up his spine. "I know she wants her career more than...more than anything else."

"Rubbish," Evie scolded, not holding back. "What she wants—what she's always wanted, probably even before she knew it herself—is you."

It was exactly what he wanted to hear. But Cameron wasn't about to get sucked in by Evie's romantic notions. "I know you're trying to help, but—"

"What I'm trying to do," she said, making no attempt to stop interrupting him, "—is understand why you've given up on her so easily."

That got his attention. "And what exactly do you suggest I do, beg her to stay?"

Evie blew out a weary breath and looked at him intently. "If that's what it takes."

Cameron swallowed hard. "I can't do that."

"Even if it means you could lose her forever?"

I've already lost her. It was a ridiculous conversation. "I thought I'd done enough when I asked her to marry me."

"She's scared of...feelings," Evie said with a sigh.

"I know she is," he said and pushed back the pain behind his ribs. "But I can't do any more."

Evie didn't look surprised by his words. "Can't? Or won't?"

"She made her choice."

"I see. So this is about pride?" Evie asked.

Heat rushed through his blood. "It's about knowing when I'm beat."

She'd rejected him again and he wasn't about to go back for another dose. Not now. Not ever.

Chapter Thirteen

New York greeted her with same bright lights and never-ending energy that she remembered.

Grace holed up in her apartment for three days before she pulled herself together, dressed in her best power suit and hightailed it back to her office. Her assistant had a stack of emails, files and interoffice memos waiting for her. There was enough work to keep her busy for the next two months, including weekends.

At least I won't have time to think about anything else.

Or anyone.

Or someone.

She pushed herself all day and when her boss came into her office around four carrying two foam cups of coffee, Grace closed down her laptop and stretched her shoulders.

"So, how was the vacation?" Jennifer Mullin-Shaw asked as she passed her the coffee.

Grace had worked for Shapiro, Cross & Shaw for eight

years. Jennifer had been made partner fifteen years earlier and was the epitome of a committed, successful career woman. For many years Grace had wanted to emulate the other woman. She wanted to be a partner one day. She wanted the money and prestige and to be respected among her peers the way Jennifer was. A couple more years and she knew she'd get there.

"It was fine," she said and drank some coffee.

"And you're feeling better?"

"Fine."

Jennifer, always business, nodded. "So, you're fine? Ready to get back to work?"

Grace pointed to the computer. "I've enough to keep me busy for the next few months."

Jennifer sank into the chair opposite her and looked over the rim of her cup. "There's a spot opening up. Kurt's moving to Chicago. Better salary, bigger office. Interested?"

Grace straightened. Five weeks ago she wouldn't have hesitated to say yes. Five weeks ago she wanted the bigger office and better salary.

Five weeks ago she wasn't prepared to admit she was hopelessly in love with Cameron Jakowski.

"Of course," she said with as much enthusiasm as she could muster.

"It means more high-profile clients," Jennifer said as both brows came up. "Which equates to longer hours and pretty much means you can say goodbye to your personal life. Are you ready for that?"

"Sure."

Jennifer nodded and stood. "Good. I'll talk to Jim and Harris," she said of the two other partners in the firm. "And we'll make it official next week. Congratulations, you've earned this."

Grace got to her feet. "Thank you."

The other woman headed for the door, but turned before she crossed the threshold. "Are you sure you're okay, Grace? You seem distracted."

"I'm fine," she assured her. "Just a little jet-lagged."

"Well, I'm pleased the vacation did the trick for you. It's good to have you back."

As she watched Jennifer disappear her insides were strangely empty.

Grace could barely believe it. A promotion. A new office. She'd arrived at the pinnacle of her chosen profession. It was everything she'd worked toward. *I'm back. I made it.* She should have been jumping through hoops.

Instead, she had a hollow spot in the middle of her chest that seemed to be getting deeper and deeper each day. Five weeks ago she'd returned to Crystal Point, broken and afraid. Miraculously, she'd healed those wounds and made peace with her guilt and fear. Life moved on. *She'd* moved on.

And still the hollowness prevailed, settling behind her ribs, making her remember how she got to be standing alone in her office. And what she'd left behind. In the window Grace caught her own reflection. The black suit, killer heels, perfectly straight hair. All she saw was a stranger, a facsimile of a woman she'd once been.

I have the career I've always wanted. I have the life I've always wanted. It's here, for me to take.

And yet…another life now beckoned. A life she missed. And suddenly she longed to be that woman again. The woman who'd felt like she was really part of her family for the first time. The woman who'd helped Emily ace her makeup exam and who'd spent a crazy weekend with Pat Jennings and her adorable grandchildren. The woman who'd left her hair to create its own curly madness and loped around in paint-stained clothes. And the woman who'd experienced such an acute connection with Cameron she could barely draw breath without remembering how it felt to lie in his arms.

She'd been so determined to not feel anything and to not be derailed, but as she looked out the window, Grace knew she was the world's biggest hypocrite. Because she'd told Emily it *was* possible to have it all. In that last week during their tutoring sessions she'd spouted speeches about having both a career and a family. A career and a personal life.

Do as I say, not as I do.

Memories bombarded her. Bathing the twins. Sharing tea with her mother. Jed loping beside her. Emily looking so proud of her achievements. Holding Evie's baby. And Cameron.

The man I love.

The man she'd always loved. Even at eighteen. Or sixteen, when he'd kissed her for the first time. And through the years where their relationship had been fraught with insults and goading and so much simmering tension.

And he's in love with me, too.

The city below made noises she couldn't hear from the lonely spot in her ivory tower. And as if a great wave of peace had washed over her, Grace knew exactly what she wanted.

She packed the laptop into her case and flung it over her shoulder, grabbed her handbag and jacket and left the room. A few minutes later she tapped on Jennifer's office door and was quickly beckoned inside.

"Grace?" The other woman looked at her bags and jacket. "You're heading off?"

She took a deep breath and a smile curved her mouth. "Actually...I'm going home."

"I can't believe I passed that exam."

Emily's excitement was great to see and Cameron nodded. "I told you that you would."

"I know," she said, and shrugged. "You and Nan both believed I could do it. And Grace."

His back stiffened. It was hard to hear her name. Harder still to not think about her twenty-four hours a day. "Just keep hitting the books and you'll get a good final grade."

"Good enough to go to night school I hope," Emily said cheerfully and bounced Riley on her knee. "Grace made some inquiries for me when she was here."

"She's special, that one," Pat said from her spot at the table and looked directly at him. "But I guess you know that already."

Cameron had dropped Dylan home after the Big Brother meeting and stayed for coffee. He hadn't planned on every part of the conversation being about Grace. "I've organized the moving truck for next Tuesday," he told Emily, ignoring Pat's question as politely as he could.

"Great," the teenager said. "I can't wait to get my own place." She quickly patted her grandmother's hand. "Not that I don't like living here with everyone, because I do. But it will be awesome for Riley to have his own room. And once I get my driver's license I can come and see you all in Burdon Creek every few weeks."

It was a good plan, and one he'd help see through to fruition. They were a strong family, despite the challenges they'd faced, and Cameron knew they'd be okay.

"You know," Pat said and stirred her tea. "I hear New York's quite the place to visit."

He didn't miss the point. "I'm not much for big cities."

No, he was small town. Grace was big city. Oil and water. He should have known better, right? In some ways he knew he'd been waiting for her rejection since that night on the beach. And she hadn't disappointed. His pride took another battering. So he'd bailed.

In every other part of his life, in every other part of himself, Cameron was rational and reasonable. He forgave, he compromised, and he fought for what he believed in. But this was different. Because he'd told Grace he loved her and she hadn't said the same. She hadn't admitted anything. She'd made him hurt and he felt that hurt through to the marrow in his bones. It was excruciating, soul destroying. He was a small-town police officer and that wasn't enough.

His love wasn't enough.

He wasn't enough.

Just like he hadn't been for his father.

Cameron's breath suddenly twisted like a knot in his chest. Damn. There it was—the real reason he'd let her go without a fight. In a way it was the same reason he worked so hard to be a good man...to prove his worth. To override the loss of the father who hadn't wanted him. That's why Grace's rejection when they were young had affected him so deeply. Because he'd felt like he wasn't worthy, like he wasn't enough to have her love. Then resentment and dislike had kicked in and he'd spent the next fifteen years behaving like an incomparable ass.

Until she'd come back and he'd realized that he still loved her, still wanted her, and more. He needed her. Like the air he breathed. Like water he drank. Grace was in his blood, his heart, his soul. And he missed her perfectly beautiful face.

But what could he do? Pat's idea was out of the question. He wasn't about to hightail it to New York to face the blunt force of another rejection—no matter how much he wanted to see her.

Only a crazy man would do that, right?

Grace was back in Crystal Point. It was late Sunday afternoon when she pulled her rental car outside her parent's home. There were several other cars out front, including the familiar sight of Cameron's electric-blue Ford sedan. She knew from Evie that her mother had organized a party to celebrate Rebecca's arrival.

I can do this, she thought as she headed through the front door.

She heard the party coming from the back patio area and made her way down the hall. Grace found her mother in the kitchen and dropped her bag on the counter.

Barbara swiveled around instantly. "Grace!" she exclaimed, quickly looking her over, clearly taking in Grace's disheveled appearance as she came around the counter. "What are you doing here? Are you okay?"

Grace accepted her mother's warm embrace and held on. When she pulled back the other woman's expression was one of deep concern. "I've been so foolish. And so blind."

Barbara frowned slightly. "What do you mean?"

Before she could reply heels clicked over tiles and they both stepped back. Irene Jakowski walked into the kitchen and came to a stunned halt. "Grace...you're here?"

Grace swallowed a lump in her throat. "Yes," she whispered.

Irene smiled warmly. "Good girl."

She managed a smile and her breath came out as a shudder when she looked toward the doors that led outside. "Is... is he..."

Irene nodded and squeezed her arm. "He is."

She took a few steps forward. "Thank you."

Barbara Preston watched her daughter walk outside and turned to her best friend. "What was that all about? What does it mean?"

Irene grinned broadly. "I think it means that one day you and I will probably be sharing grandchildren."

Cameron had walked through the family room and onto the back patio when he heard someone call Grace's name.

Stupid. He heard her name everywhere. On the street. On the television. In his dreams.

But this caught his attention. He stopped in the doorway and looked around.

And there she stood.

Like a vision. A beautiful vision with her hair curling wildly around her face. She wore jeans and an old shirt. *His* shirt he realized after a microsecond. *She's wearing my shirt. She's here and she's wearing my shirt.* His heart almost burst through his chest.

The dozen or so people on the patio all stilled. And stared. She stared back, from one to the next. And then she found him with her gaze. In that moment no one else existed and his mind soared with a hazy kind of hope. He fought the urge to go to her, staying back, head spinning.

She's here.

Cameron's gaze flicked to the group of curious people watching her...taking in her hair and clothes and the faintly expectant expression on her face. She did look different than the Grace they were used to. They were used to the usual perfection of her immaculate clothing and straight hair. Funny, but she always seemed perfect to him. His mind was bombarded with memories—Grace in the morning, her hair spread out on his pillow. A sleepy Grace who couldn't keep her eyes open as they watched television together. Grace coming apart in his arms when they made love.

"Can I...can I talk to you?" she asked hesitantly, looking only at him.

The twenty feet between them suddenly seemed like a huge divide—especially with their respective families watching on the sidelines. Maybe he should have suggested they go inside. But he didn't want to move...he didn't want to shift the incredible contact throbbing between them.

"Okay...talk."

Her eyes widened and glittered. She wouldn't do this in front of her family. Or would she? He tried to be cool and rested one shoulder against the doorjamb and watched as she swallowed hard.

"Here?"

Cameron nodded. "Here."

She glanced at the sea of curious faces watching their exchange and shook her head fractionally. Cameron looked across the patio and saw Evie nodding, almost prompting her sister to continue. He watched and panic rose when she stepped back. She turned on her heels and walked toward the door to the house. His mother was there. As was Barbara Preston.

After a moment she turned again, back to him. Relief pitched in his chest when he saw strength in her eyes.

"You were right," she said quietly and crossed her arms over his paint-splattered shirt. "About me. About everything."

Cameron waited, breathless.

"I *have* always wanted to be perfect," she stressed, looking at him. "But after the accident I was so far from that. I was out of control. I felt weak, like I'd lost my edge. It was as if I'd been cut off at the knees."

"And?" he asked, trying to appear casual even though his insides were jumping all over the place.

"And I came back here to refocus. I had to prove that I could be that person again—the one who was ambitious and strong and successful—because that's who I'd been raised to be. That's what defined me. I knew I had to take back my life and not be afraid, and not feel so wretchedly guilty that I'd survived and someone else had died." She drew in a deep breath. "So, I *did* refocus. Then I went back to New York and got a promotion the very day I returned to work." She drew in another breath, shakier, short. "And it would have been a great job."

Cameron straightened and pushed himself off the door. *"Would have?"*

She nodded. "I quit."

More gasps echoed around the patio. Cameron could barely get his words out. "You quit? Why?"

He saw her lip tremble and watched, both fascinated and agonized as her green eyes filled with tears.

"Because I didn't want to make the biggest mistake of my life." Her voice quivered, almost breaking. "So, I quit, like I said. Which means I'm unemployed." She raised her shoulders and dropped them heavily. "I've decided I'm going to work for myself now. Freelance. I'll get a few clients and who knows…" She blinked at the wetness threatening to fall. "All I know is that I can do that anywhere. I can do that…here."

Cameron harnessed his feelings. They weren't done yet. He had to know more. He had to know how she really felt. "And will that be enough?" *Will I be enough? Will we be enough?*

Grace nodded. "I've been incredibly stupid. And afraid. And dishonest with myself. And with you," she added. "I want things. I want all those things we talked about. I do want my career…but I want everything else, too. I want a home and a family and…and who says a person can't have b-both?" She hiccupped and clasped her arms tightly around herself.

"I guess it depends how much you want them."

She nodded. "I want them badly enough to stand here and make a complete fool out of myself right now."

Cameron bit back a grin. She *was* making a fool of herself. A beautiful, perfectly adorable fool. "And you're doing that because?"

Grace drew in a breath and glanced at the stunned, silent people standing on the edge of the patio. Emotion choked her eyes, her heart and her skin. They were her family and she wasn't being judged as weak or foolish or any of the things she'd always feared.

"Because…" she said shakily and let the tears come, over her lids and down her cheeks. "Because when I'm with you I'm the best version of myself. And I'm…just…so much in love with you."

There it was. Her heart laid out for everyone to see. She ignored the shocked gasps from the sidelines. Ignored everything and everyone except Cameron.

He hadn't moved. But he looked deep into her eyes. Into that place made only for him. Grace tried to smile, hoping to see love and acceptance and forgiveness.

"Say something," she whispered.

He grinned. "You're wearing my shirt."

Grace unhooked her arms and touched the fabric. "It was all I had of you."

"It's not all you have, Grace." He smiled broadly and she saw the love in his expression. "Whatever I am, with every part of who I am…you've always had every bit of my heart."

Relief and love and gratitude flowed through her and she kept crying, but they were happy tears she was proud to show. "So, will you ask me that question again? Because if you do, I'll promise to get the answer right this time."

He laughed softly and looked toward the people staring at them, all stunned by what they had heard. Except Evie, who was smiling the biggest smile and holding her baby against her chest. And Irene Jakowski, who looked at Grace as though she had just hung the moon.

He nodded. "I'm asking."

Grace laughed, happiness radiating through her. "And I'm saying yes."

His smile reached right into her heart. "Then get over here," he beckoned softly.

She took about two seconds before she raced across the patio and flung herself into his arms. For the first time in her life she didn't give a hoot what anyone thought of her. She didn't care that some of her family were now looking at her as though she'd lost her mind. Serious, overachieving, humorless Grace was gone. She didn't want to be *perfect*. She simply wanted to love this incredible man who'd somehow managed to love her too despite her prickly, icy reserve.

He kissed her then, right there, in front of the world, and Grace gave up her heart, her soul, her very self, and kissed him back.

"Am I the only one who didn't know about this?" Grace heard Noah ask in an incredulous voice. She also heard Callie's "no, dear," and smiled beneath the pressure of Cameron's kiss.

Finally they pulled apart. He smiled and gazed down at her. "Let's get out of here," he suggested and grasped her hand. "So I can do this properly."

Grace took a deep breath and vaguely heard him excuse them both. Within less than a minute they were inside the house and he pulled her down onto the sofa in the living room.

"I don't think poor Noah is over the shock," she said, laughing.

Cameron molded her shoulders with his hands and looked into her eyes. "He'll get used to the idea," he assured her. "Once we're married."

"Married?" she echoed dreamily.

He looked panicky all of a sudden. "You did agree to marry me, didn't you?"

She nodded. "Yes. But you'll need this to make it official," she said and pulled the ring he'd offered her weeks ago from her pocket. "It really is beautiful."

"You kept it?"

She nodded. "Of course I did. I've been carrying it with me everywhere."

"Does it fit?" he asked and took the ring from her fingertips.

Grace shrugged. "I'm not sure. I didn't dare try it on. I wanted to…so much."

Cameron smiled deeply and grabbed her left hand. "Where it belongs," he said as he easily slipped the ring onto her finger. "Now and forever, Princess."

Grace's heart did a flip. Hearing him call her Princess was the most wonderful thing she'd ever heard. "I'm so sorry, Cameron. For every time I made you feel like I didn't want this…that I didn't want *us*. I'm sorry for being the foolish girl I was at eighteen who didn't have the sense to see what was right in front her. And I'm sorry for being so self-centered that I—"

"Grace, I—"

"Let me finish," she said and placed a gentle finger against his mouth. She moved her hand to his cheek and held him there. "You are, without a doubt, the most amazing man I have ever known. You're strong and honest and honorable and so incredibly kind. To love you…to be loved by you… is truly humbling."

"That's very sweet, Grace," he said and kissed her softly.

"I'm not sweet at all," she defied as their lips parted. "And you know it. In fact, you probably know me better than anyone."

"I know you're in my heart, Grace. I know I love you more than I ever imagined I could love anyone."

"I love you, too," she said and experienced a swell of love so deep, and so rich, it tore the breath from her throat. "For so long I've been afraid to truly feel anything. I had my career and let that define me…I let that be all that I was. But I was hollow inside." She gripped his hands. "You saved me," she said quietly. "You saved me when I came back and didn't know how tell my family about the accident. You saved me by letting me tutor Emily, which showed me how good it feels to really do something for someone else. And you saved me every time you held me and made me feel less broken. When I think of how close I came to making the wrong choice..." She shuddered.

He brought her hands to his lips and kissed them softly. "You're here now. We're here now. That's all that matters."

"But I—"

"No buts," he insisted and smiled. "Although now is probably a good time to talk about the flight I just booked to New York."

Grace's eyes filled with more tears. "You...you were coming to see me?"

He smiled warmly. "Of course. To see you—or to bring you back—or live there with you. Either way, Grace, being apart from you was never an option."

"But you didn't say anything like that before."

"I'm an idiot," he said flatly. "And too proud to admit I was afraid of rejection. You knew that," he said as he touched her face. "You asked me why I help kids like Dylan and I wasn't honest with you. I don't think I really understood why until the other day. All my life I've felt like I had to somehow make up for my biological father running out on me and my mother, as though in some way it would make the hurt go away." He clutched her hands and his voice broke with emotion as he said the words. "And it stopped me from being truly grateful for the father I have."

"You do have a good father," she assured him.

He kissed her softly. "I know. And, Grace, if you want to go to back to New York, if you want that promotion, then we'll go—together. And if you want to stay in Crystal Point, we'll stay."

Grace closed her eyes for a moment. When she opened them again he was watching her with blistering intensity. "I want to stay," she replied. "I want to marry you and live in your house. I want us to take Jed for long walks along the beach. I want to share our life with our families. I want to be at your side in this community and help kids like Dylan and Emily. And one day soon, I want to have your baby."

He raised a brow. "You want kids? You really do?"

What she wanted had never seemed clearer. "I really do."

He kissed her. Long and sweet and filled with love. "I love you, Grace, so much."

She smiled, remembering what Pat had said to her.

There's a lot to be said about the love of a good man.

Yes, Grace thought as she pressed against him, there certainly was.

* * * * *

THE END OF
FAKING IT

NATALIE ANDERSON

For my awesome daily support structure:
Dave, Mum & Soraya.

You guys helped with the heartache of
this one especially.

Am so happy to be returning the favour now,
Soraya!

CHAPTER ONE

ANOTHER two minutes couldn't possibly matter—late was late and this was too important to leave.

'Come on, Audrey,' Penny muttered softly. 'Let's keep you all healthy, huh?' She scattered the plant food and put the pack back in the top drawer of the filing cabinet. Then she picked up the jug of water.

'What are you doing?'

Her fingers flinched and she whirled at the sound of deep, accusing anger. She saw black clothes, big frame, even bigger frown. Striding towards her was a total stranger. A tall, dark, two hundred per cent testosterone-filled male was in her office, late at night. Not Jed the security guard, but a hard edged predator coming straight for her—fast.

She flung forward, all raw reflex.

He swore as water hit him straight in the eyes. She lunged again, hoping to knock him out with a Pyrex jug to the temple. Only halfway there her arm slammed against something hard, whiplash sent shudders down her shoulder. Painfully strong fingers held her wrist vice-tight. She immediately strained to break free, twisting skin and muscle. He sharply wrenched her wrist. She gasped. Her fingers failed and the jug tipped between them.

The shock of the ice-cold water splashing across her chest suffocated her shriek. She recoiled, but he came forward relentlessly, still death-gripping her wrist. The drawer slammed as she backed up and banged against it.

'Who the hell are you and what are you doing in here?' he demanded, storming further into her personal space.

Shock, pain, fear. She couldn't move other than to blink, trying to see clearly and figure a way to escape.

But he moved closer still. 'What are you doing with the files?' Pure menace.

The cold metal cabinet dug into her back. But he wasn't in the least cold. She could feel his heat even with the slight distance between them. His hand branded her. Her scream couldn't emerge—not with her throat squeezed so tight and her heart not beating at all.

He pushed back his fringe with his free hand, also blinked several times—only his eyes were filled with the water she'd thrown at him, not tears like hers. He actually laughed—not nicely—and his grip tightened even more. 'I didn't think this was going to be that easy.' He looked over her, scorn sharpening every harsh word. 'You're not screwing another cent out of this company.'

Penny gaped. He was insane. Totally insane. 'The security guard will be doing his rounds any minute,' she panted. 'He's armed.'

'With what—chewing gum? The only person going to the police cells tonight is you, honey.'

Yep, totally insane. Unfortunately he was also right about Jed's lack of ammo—the best she could hope for was a heavy torch. And it was a hopeless hope because she'd been lying anyway—Jed didn't do rounds. He sat at his desk. And she was ten floors up, alone with a complete nut-job who was going to…going to…

Jerky breathing filled her ears—as if someone was having an asthma attack. It took long moments to realise it was her. She pressed her free hand to her stomach, but couldn't stop the violent tremors. Her eyes watered more, her muscles quivered. Dimly she heard him swear.

'I'm not going to hurt you,' he said loudly right in her face.

'You already are,' she squeaked.

He instantly let go of her wrist, but he didn't move away. If anything he towered closer, still blocking her exit. But she could breathe again and her brain started sending signals. Then her heart got going, pushing a plan along her veins. All she had to do was escape him somehow and race down to Jed on Reception. She could do that, right? She forced a few more deep breaths as both fight and flight instincts rose and merged, locking her body and brain into survive mode.

'Who are you and what are you doing here?' he asked, a little quieter that time, but still with that peremptory tone, as if he had all the authority.

Which he didn't.

'Answer that yourself,' Penny snapped back.

He glanced down to where the jug lay useless on the floor and, beside her, where the plant's tub sat. 'You're the cleaner?' He looked from her toes back up to her face—slowly. 'You don't look like a cleaner.'

'No, who are *you* and what are *you* doing here?' Now she could see—and almost think—she took stock of him. Tall and dark, yes, but while the jeans and tee were black, they were well fitting—as in designer fitting. And it wasn't as if he was wearing a balaclava. Not exactly hardcore crim kind of clothing. The intensely angry look had vanished, and his face was open and sun-burnished, as if he spent time skiing or sailing. The hard planes of his body, and the strength she felt firsthand, suggested a high degree of fitness too. On his wrist was one of those impressive watches, all masculine and metal with a million little dials and functions most people wouldn't be able to figure out. And now that the water was gone from her eyes she could see his were an amazing blue-green. Clear and shining and vibrant and…were they checking her out?

'I asked you first,' he said softly, putting his hands either side of her to rest on the top of the filing cabinet. His arms made long, strong, bronzed prison bars.

'I'm the PA,' she answered mechanically, most of her attention focused on digesting this new element of his proximity. 'This is my desk.'

'*You're* Penny?' His brows skyrocketed up and he blatantly checked over her outfit again. 'You definitely don't look like any PA Mason would have.'

How did he know her name? And Mason? Her eyes narrowed as the gleam in his grew. Heat radiated out from him, warming her blood and making her skin super-sensitive. No way. She wasn't going to let him look at her like *that*. She sucked up some sarcasm. 'Actually Mason really likes my skirt.'

He angled his head and studied it yet again. 'Is that what that is? I thought it was a belt.' He smiled. Not a scary psycho-killer smile, more one that would make a million hearts flutter and two million legs start to slide apart—like hers suddenly threatened to.

It was that powerful she had to consciously order her

lips not to smile right back at him like some besotted
bimbo. 'It's vintage Levi's.'

'Oh, that explains it. You didn't realise moths had
been at the hem?' His face lit up even more. 'Not that
I'm complaining.'

Okay, the denim mini was teensy weensy, the heels of
her shoes super-high and her curve-clinging champagne-
coloured blouse off the shoulder. Of course she didn't
wear this to work. She was all dressed up for dance-
party pleasure. Yes, she'd dressed in case there was that
other sort of pleasure to be had as well—just because
she hadn't found a playmate in a while, didn't mean she'd
given up all hope. Only now the pretty silk was sop-
ping, plastered to her chest, revealing far more than she'd
ever intended. And she was not, *not*, feeling any kind
of primal response to a random stranger who'd all but
assaulted her. 'Before I scream, who are you?' Not that
there was any need to scream now and she knew it.

'I work here,' he said smoothly.

'I know everyone who works in this building and you
don't.'

He reached into his pocket and then dangled a security
card in her face. She quickly read the name—Carter
Dodds. It didn't enlighten her in the least; she'd never
heard of him. Then she looked at the photo. In it he was
wearing the black tee shirt that he had on now.

Amazingly her brain managed the simple computa-
tion. 'You started today.'

'Officially tomorrow.' He nodded.

'Then why are you here now?' And how? Jed might be
slack on the rounds but he was scrupulous about knowing who was still in the building after hours. And surely

Mason wouldn't have let a new recruit have open access to everything with no one around to supervise?

'I wanted to see what the place was like when it was quiet.'

'Why?' Her suspicions grew more. What did he want to see? There wasn't any money kept on site, but there were files, transactions, account numbers—loads of sensitive investor information worth millions. She glanced past him to Mason's open office door, but could hear no gentle hum of the computer.

'Why are you watering the plants at nine-thirty at night?' he countered.

'I forgot to do it earlier.'

'So you came back specially?' Utter disbelief.

Actually she'd been downstairs swimming in the pool—breaking all the rules because it was after the gym's closing hour. But she wasn't going to drop Jed in it. 'New recruits don't get to grill me.'

'No?'

His smile sharpened, but before he could get another question out she got in one of hers. 'How come you're here alone?'

'Mason wanted to get an early night before we get started tomorrow.'

'He didn't tell me you were starting.'

'Does he tell you everything?'

'Usually.' She lifted her chin in defiance of the calculated look that crossed his face, but he missed it—his focus had dropped to her body again.

'Mason buried his heart with his wife,' he said bluntly. 'You won't get any gold out of him no matter how short your skirt.'

Her mouth fell open. *'What?'*

'You wouldn't be the first pretty girl to bat her eye-lashes at a rich old man.'

What was he suggesting? 'Mason's *eighty*.'

His shrug didn't hide his anger. 'For some women that would make him all the more attractive.'

'Yeah, well, not me. He's like my grandfather.' She screwed up her face.

'You're the one who said he likes your skirt.'

'Only because you couldn't drag your eyes from it.'

'But isn't that why you wear it?'

She paused. He wasn't afraid to challenge direct, was he? Well, nor was she—when she could think. Right now her brain had gone all lame. 'I don't believe you're supposed to be here now.'

'Really? Go ahead and ask your boss. Use my phone.' He pulled it out of his pocket, pressed buttons and handed it to her.

It rang only a couple of times.

'Carter, have you already found something?'

Penny gripped the phone tighter as she absorbed the anxiety in Mason's quick-fire query. 'No, sorry, Mason, it's Penny. Not Carter.' She stuttered when she saw Carter's sudden grin—disarming and devilish. 'Look, I've just bumped into someone in the office.'

'Carter,' Mason said.

'Yes.' Penny winced at the obvious. Had the sinking feeling she was about to wince even more. 'He's given me his phone to call you.'

'Penny, I'm sorry, I should have told you but Carter thought it should wait until he got there.'

Thought what should wait? Why was Carter the one calling shots? What was going on?

'Carter heads up Dodds WD in Melbourne. I asked

him to come to Sydney for a couple of weeks. I need
his help.'

'What for?'

Carter knew he was still standing too close but too bad.
In fact he put both hands back on either side of her.
That way she couldn't readily escape. He was certain she
would, so he made sure she couldn't—by holding a position that was only a few inches away from intimate.

He was having a time shutting up the temptation whispering that he should lose those few inches. He pushed
his hands hard on the cool metal and watched as she
pressed the phone closer to her ear and turned her head
away from him.

The colour ran under her skin like an incoming tide
and Carter couldn't contain his amusement. Mason was
his grandfather's best friend. He'd seen him every few
months all his life and he was on the old boy's speed-dial
to prove it. This was the first time Mason had asked him
for help—and help he would. But just this moment?

Distraction. Capital D.

'Of course.' Penny had turned her head even further
away, clearly hoping he wouldn't hear whatever it was
that Mason was saying.

Carter didn't give a damn what the old guy said right
now. He was too lost in looking at her. She had the biggest, darkest eyes he'd ever seen. They drew him in and
sucked him under—like sparkling pools that turned out
to be dangerously deep, the kind of eyes that you could
stare into endlessly—and he was. Peripherally, bits of
his body were absorbing the detail of hers and the back
of his brain drew rapid conclusions.

A skirt that short, a shirt that sexy, a body that honed, lips that slicked...

This woman knew how attractive she was, and she emphasised all her best assets. Everything about her was polished to pure, sensual perfection. She was no shy, shrinking secretary. She was a siren. And every basic cell in Carter's body wanted to answer her summons. So, so badly.

'Hello?'

She was holding the phone out to him and he'd been too busy gawping to notice. He grabbed it and started talking.

'Hi, Mason, sorry to bother you so late.'

'It doesn't matter. It's great you're onto it so quickly. I can't thank you enough.'

'So Penny's your temp PA?' Carter kept looking at her, still struggling to believe that conservative, eighty-year-old Mason had ever hired such a blatant sex bomb. 'She's working late.'

'She always works late.' Mason sounded pleased. 'She's an angel. I get in every morning and everything is so organised, she makes it a breeze.'

An *angel*? Carter's suspicions sharpened again. Penny wouldn't be the first attractive young woman to turn an older man's head. Carter knew exactly how easy it was for an avaricious, ambitious female to use her beauty to dazzle a fool old enough to know better. He'd watched not one, but two do that to his dad. Despite her outraged reaction, who was to say that wasn't what was happening here? 'How long has she been with you?' He couldn't not ask.

There was a silence. 'Since after the problem started.'

Mason's voice turned arctic. 'I thought I'd made this clear already.'

Yeah. Mason had mentioned his fabulous PA more than once—but not her hotter-than-Venus factor. Not mentioning that didn't seem natural.

'You tell her what's going on,' Mason said sharply. 'I should have already. Carter, she's not who you're looking for.'

Carter stared at the temptation personified before him. Her mouth was as glossy and red ripe as a Morello cherry—and he wanted a taste. That was the real problem. Hell, he was off on a tangent before he'd even started. He owed Mason better than this. 'You're right,' he said brusquely. 'She's not.'

Penny watched him pocket the phone. He didn't seem to be any happier about the situation—offered no laughter or light apology. If anything he looked as angry as he had when he'd first interrogated her. What was he here to do exactly? Mason hadn't elaborated, just told her to help him if he asked her to. They hadn't advertised a new job—she was the one who placed the ads so she'd know. So this was cronyism, some old boys' school network thing. But he was hardly a fresh-faced graduate getting his first contract courtesy of his father. 'You know Mason personally,' she said baldly, annoyed by the fact—annoyed by him—and his attractiveness.

'Have done for years.' He nodded.

Yeah, that was why the job, whatever it was, hadn't been advertised. Mason had probably made something up for him to do. Still smarting from his gold-digger slur, she let her inner bitch out to taunt. 'You don't look like you have to pull favours to get a job.'

'Don't I?' he answered too softly. 'How would you know? Is that what you do?' He leaned closer and whispered low, as if they were intimate. 'What kind of favours do you pull to score a job, Penny?'

Okay, she'd crossed the line a little, but he'd just leapt it. 'What sort of favours do you think I *pull*?' she fired back before thinking.

His eyes flashed, the pupils expanding so fast the piercing colours became the thinnest of circles around the burgeoning black. Riveted, she watched the myriad greens and blues narrow out. He really did have it—perfect symmetry, angular jawbones and hair that just begged to be ruffled and then gripped tight.

The palms of her hands tingled, heated. Only it wasn't just his hair she imagined pulling close, no, now she was pulling on hot, silky hard skin, stroking it faster and faster and—*OMG where had that come from?*

She gulped back the insanity. She couldn't be thinking that. She looked down and clamped her mouth shut, swallowing both literally and mentally, overly aware her breathing had quickened to audible—basically to panting. Again.

Oh, please don't let him know what she'd been thinking. She glanced back up at him. All the blue had gone from his irises leaving nothing but thin rings of green fire around those huge, black pupils. Dusky red tinged his cheekbones. She could relate. Blood was firing all round her body, pinking up all sorts of parts—her face included. But at least he wasn't panting like some dog in heat, which she, unfortunately, was.

He said nothing, she said nothing. But she could see it shimmering in the air between them—razor-sharp attraction. Urges at their most basic. Urges almost uncontrollable.

'There's a problem in the accounts—someone in the company is skimming,' he suddenly said roughly, jerking his head up.

'What?'

'I'm here to check through all the files and find out who and how.'

Someone was stealing? And Carter was here to catch him? Mason had said he headed up some company in Melbourne, so was he some kind of CEO/forensic accountant or something?

Actually that didn't seem to fit. Not when he wore jeans and tousled hair so well. He looked as if he had too much street cred to be a number cruncher.

'The only people who'll know the real reason I'm here are you, Mason and me,' he continued. 'We'll spread it 'round the company that I'm a friend of Mason's who's borrowing an office for a couple of weeks. Which I am.'

The fiery green in his eyes dampened to cold blue serious. The sensual curve of his mouth flattened to a straight, hard line. Penny stared, watching him ice over, as she absorbed that info and the implications.

Then she realised. 'You thought it was *me*?' She basically shrieked, her temperature steaming back up to boiling point. She might be many things, but a thief wasn't one of them. 'I'm the best damn temp in this town. I'm hardworking and honest. How dare you storm in here and throw round your gutter accusations?'

'I know.' His expression went very intense. 'I'm sorry. Mason already told me it couldn't be you.'

He sucked the wind right out of her sails and disarmed

her completely with a sudden flash of that smile. It cracked his icy cover and let the heat ripple once more. But she refused to let her anger slide into attraction. 'You still thought it,' she accused.

'Well, you have to admit it looked…it looked…' His attention wandered—down. 'It looked…'

Her body—despite the freezing wet shirt—was burning. Okay, that attraction was impossible to stop—simplest thing now would be to escape. 'Well, now that you've done your looking,' she said sarcastically, her eyes locked on his, 'are you going to step back and let me past?'

'Not yet,' he said wryly. 'I'm still looking.'

Penny's nerves tightened to one notch the other side of screaming. His lashes lowered and his smile faded. She looked down too. Now her silk shirt was wet it was both skin colour and skin tight and she might as well not be wearing anything. Even worse, she was aching…and horrified to realise it was completely obvious.

'You're cold,' he said softly.

Yeah, completely obvious.

'The water in the jug was from the cooler.'

'So that's the reason…'

All she could do was brazen this out. She tossed her head and met his eyes direct. 'What other reason could there be?'

His lips curved. In his tanned face, his teeth were white and straight and perfect. Actually everything in his face was perfect. And in the dark tee shirt and dark trousers he looked pretty-boy pirate, especially with the slightly too-long hair. The intensity of his scrutiny was devastating and now he'd fixed on one thing—her mouth.

She saw his intention. She felt it in her lips already—
the yearning for touch. But even for her that would be
insane. She didn't like the way her pulse was zigzagging
all over the place. She didn't like the way her body was
so willingly bracing for impact.

'Don't add another insult to the list,' she said, trying
to regain control over both of them. But the words didn't
come out as forcefully as she'd intended. Instead they
whispered on barely a breath—because she could barely
move enough to breathe.

'How can appreciating beauty be an insult?'

Penny's pulse thundered. She was used to confident
men. They were the kind she liked—pretty much bullet
proof. But this was more than just superficial brash-
ness; this was innate, absolute arrogance. He stood even
closer, filling all her senses. Her blood rushed to all her
secret places and left her brain starving of its ability to
operate.

His smile suddenly flashed brighter—like how the
flame flared on a gas hob when you accidentally twisted
the knob the wrong way. His hand lifted and he brushed
her lips with a finger. She shivered.

Shock. She was in shock. That was the problem. That
was why she wasn't resisting....

His expression heated up all the more. 'You okay?'

'Mmm.'

His traversing finger muffled the words she couldn't
speak anyway. She was too busy pressing her lips firmly
together to stop herself from opening up and inviting him
in. But somehow he got that invite anyway because he
lifted his finger and swiftly replaced it with his mouth.

Oh.

It was light. A warm, gentle, coaxing kiss that

promised so much more than it gave. But what it did give was good. He moved closer, not threatening, but with a hint of masculine spice and just enough pressure to make her accept him. To make her want more. Surprised that it wasn't a full-throttle brazen burst of passion, she relaxed. Her eyes automatically closed as her body focused on the exquisite sweetness trickling into her. It had been a long time since she'd felt anything so nice—a subtle magic that melted her resistance, and saw her start to strain for what she knew he was holding at bay.

Her lips parted—she couldn't deny herself. His response came immediate, and powerful. She heard his sound of satisfaction and his hands moved from the steel behind to her soft body. She trembled top to toe as he swiftly shaped her curves, pulling her against him. She had to grab hold of his shoulders or she was going to tumble backwards. The kiss deepened again as she felt the wide, flat planes and hard strength of him. Her neck arched back as he stroked into her mouth. She lifted her hand, sliding her fingers into his thick hair. He showed no mercy then, bending her back all the more as he sought full access, kissing her jaw and neck and back up again to claim her mouth—this time with confident, carnal authority.

She shuddered at the impact, felt him press closer still. Sandwiched between him and the cabinet, she was trapped between forces as unyielding and demanding as each other. Yet she had no desire to escape, not now.

The arrogance of him was breathtaking. But not anywhere as breathtaking as the way he kissed. It was as if he was determined to maximise pleasure for them both and the control she usually held so tight started to slide as her own desire mounted.

He was silk-wrapped steel and she wanted to feel all of him against her, slicing into her. She wanted him. Wanted as she hadn't wanted anyone in a long, long time. Okay, ever. Hungry for his strength and passion, she kissed him back—melting against his body, delving into his mouth with her tongue, so keen to explore more.

And he knew. He lifted his hand from her waist to her breast and, oh, so lightly stroked his fingers across her violently taut nipple.

She felt the touch as if her skin were bare. And it burned too hot.

She jerked back, ripping her mouth free from his. Their eyes met, faces inches apart. A flare of something dangerous kindled in his—different from the earlier fury but just as frightening for Penny. She pushed as far back against the cool metal cabinet as she could, breathing hard. She shook her head, the only method of communication she could manage. While he stood, rock hard, and stared right back at her.

A million half-thoughts murmured in her head—desperate thoughts, forgotten thoughts, *frightening* thoughts.

Carter Dodds wasn't the kind of man to let a woman stay on top—Penny's only acceptable position, metaphorically anyway. He'd just demonstrated he'd always ultimately be the one in charge—his almost pretty-boy packaging disguised a total he-man with all masculine, all dominant virility. He'd made his move that way—lulling her into a sense of sweet security before unleashing his true potency and damn near swamping her reason. She liked sex—enjoyed the chase, the fun of touch, the fleeting closeness. But she never, ever lost control. *She* had to be in charge—*needed* to be the one who was wanted—even if only for that little while. She was very careful with whom she shared her body because she would always walk away. She ensured that a lover understood that. Commitment wasn't something she could ever give. Nor was complete submission. So the sensations now threatening to submerge all her capacity for rational thought were very new. And very unwelcome.

But there was a logical explanation. Less than five minutes ago she'd thought she was being attacked. Her heart hadn't had a chance since to stop its manic stuttering and it was still sending 'escape now' blasts through her blood.

'Well, that was one way to burn off the adrenalin overload.' She totally had to act cool.

'Is that what you were doing?'

'Sure. You know, I was still wired from the fright of you assaulting me in my own office.'

He stepped back, taking his heat with him. But his scrutiny seemed even more intense than ever. 'Oh. So what was it for me?'

She hazarded a simple guess. 'Normal?'

His mouth quirked. 'Not.'

Cool just wasn't happening but she had to scrape her melting body back together. She wasn't afraid of taking fun where it could be found, but there wasn't fun to be had here. Anything that hot eventually had to hurt. And any emotion that intense scared her. In ten minutes with Carter she'd already run the gamut of terror, fury and lust—way too much of the latter. So she turned away from the challenge in his eyes.

'I need to get going. I'm late as it is.' The sooner she got to the bar, the better—she had to burn up the energy zinging round her body like a demented fly trapped in a jar. Fast and free on the dance floor for the next eight hours might do it.

'Hot date?'

'Very.' She lied, happy to slam the brakes on anything between them by invoking her imaginary man friend. She opened up her gym bag; she'd straighten up her appearance and then her insides. But those insides shrieked— she breathed choppily, her heart jack-hammered—so the hairdryer's cacophony was completely wonderful. It muted her clamouring nerves.

Carter took a couple of strides to get himself out of physical range so he could get a grip on the urge to haul her back against him. He didn't know what had got into him. He'd just kissed a complete stranger. A stranger who he'd initially thought was Mason's cheating thief.

He should probably apologise. But how could he be sorry for something so good? Except for a second there she'd looked at him as if he'd struck her, not snogged her. She'd looked shocked and almost hurt, almost vulnerable.

And then she'd blamed that chemistry on adrenalin? Who did she think she was kidding? And now she was apparently late for her *date* and she had her hairdryer blasting. But it wasn't her hair getting the treatment. It was her shirt. She held it out from her body, blowing the warm air over the silk. Then she lifted the nozzle and aimed it down her neckline—what, so she could dry her soft, wet skin? Not helping his raging erection subside any. Nope, that just yanked it even tighter.

A light flickered on her desk. Her mobile. He glanced back up; she was still focused on her shirt. He picked up the mobile to hand it to her, his thumb hit the keypad and, oh, shame, that message from Mel just flicked up on the screen.

Where r u? Kat & Bridge already on d-floor & lookg tragic. Need yr expertise.

Her hot date was with Mel, Kat and Bridge? A bunch of women out on a mission—on a Monday night. That shouldn't amuse him quite as much as it did. He walked up, took the dryer from her hand and pointed it at his wet hair. Immediately he jerked back from the blast of air. 'It's freezing!'

The pink in her cheeks deepened.

'Yeah,' he teased, the sparks arcing between them again. 'I thought you were feeling hot.'

'It's malfunctioning,' she said sulkily.

Carter fiddled with the switch and then aimed the dryer at her like a gun. 'Or maybe it's because you had it turned on cold.'

Boom—even more red blotches peppered her creamy skin. She snatched the appliance back off him and switched it off.

'Here's your phone.' He bit the bullet and handed it over.

She looked at the screen and frowned. 'You read my text?'

'It flashed when I picked it up.' He shrugged almost innocently.

'You didn't need to pick it up.'

'But I like picking up pretty little things.' Even less innocent.

Blacker than black eyes narrowed. 'I'm sure you've had plenty of practice.'

'Well, that does make for perfect performance.' Yep, wickedly sinful now.

'Is that what you think you offer? Perfection?'

He grinned at her tone. She made provocation so irresistible. 'You don't think?'

Her eyes raked him hard and, heaven help him, he loved it. 'I think you could do with some more practice.'

'You're offering?'

She turned away from him, retrieved the jug from the floor and marched to the water cooler to refill it. What, she was literally going to douse the flames again? But, no, she poured the water around the base of the monstrosity that was supposedly an office plant.

'What is it, some kind of triffid?' He reached up to the branches overhanging the cabinet. 'If it grows any more, there won't be room for anyone to work in here.'

'She belongs to Carol and she'll be here when she gets back. All healthy.'

'You think that's really going to happen?' Carter knew Mason's long-time assistant had a cancer battle on her hands. She'd been off for months and Mason was paying her full salary out of his own pocket. Which was why finding the person stealing from him was a priority. He was paying for two PAs. He was a hardworking, generous employer who deserved better than some skunk skimming and putting the entire company in jeopardy.

'Of course she's coming back.' Penny banged the jug back on top of the filing cabinet and finally looked at him directly again. The flames were still there. 'Is someone really stealing from him?'

Carter nodded. 'I think so.'

'But Mason's one of the good guys. He gives so much to charity. He doesn't deserve that.'

'That's why I'm here.'

Her appraisal went rapier sharp. 'Well, you'd better lift your game.'

'Hmm.' He nodded agreeably. 'I was thinking that too.' But the game he meant was the one with her. And he didn't miss the warring desire and antagonism in her expression.

He walked alongside her down the corridor, rode the lift in silent torture. The space between them was too small but he wanted it even smaller—to nothing but skin on skin. Like a tiger, he was ready to pounce. At least his body was; his brain was frantically trying to issue warnings—like he didn't have time for this, like he needed to focus.

The security guard leapt up from his desk to get the door. 'Goodnight, Penny.' His smile widened as he watched her walk across the foyer towards him. That smile faded when he glanced behind her and registered Carter's frown. 'Goodnight, sir.' Suddenly all respectful.

Carter made himself nod and smile.

'Hope Maddie's better when you get home,' Penny said lightly.

'Me too.' The guard's smile spread again. 'See you tomorrow. Not too early, you understand?'

She just laughed as she went through the door.

'Have fun, Penny,' Carter drawled softly as they hit the pavement.

She turned and fluttered him a look one eyelash short of do-me-now. 'Oh, I plan to.'

So she couldn't resist striking the sparks either. And he knew the kind of fun girls like her liked—the eat-men-for-breakfast kind. He smiled, happy to play if she wanted, because experience had made him too tough to chew. She could learn that if she dared.

She walked away, her legs ridiculously long in that sexy strip of a skirt, her balance perfect on the high, narrow heels. Her glossy brown hair cascaded down to her almost too-trim waist. He bet she worked out in the pursuit of perfection. Not that she needed to bother. She nailed it on attitude alone.

Testosterone—and other things—surged again. So did his latent combative nature. That vulnerability he'd seen upstairs when he'd startled her, and again after he'd kissed her? A mirage—she'd been buying time while assessing her position. For Penny the PA knew how to play men—the slayer look she'd just shot him proved it. Mason thought the world of her. The security guy was falling over himself to help her. She'd want to bring Carter to heel like every other man she knew. Yeah, he'd seen her vixen desire for dominance. She thought she could toy with him as some feline would a mouse.

She was so wrong.

But he could hardly wait for her to bring it on.

CHAPTER TWO

PENNY winked at Jed as she walked back into the building just over nine hours later—three of which had been
spent dancing and six sort-of sleeping.

'Too early, Penny.' The security guard covered his
yawn, clearly barely hanging out the last half-hour before
clocking off.

'Too much to do.'

First in for the day, she wanted to get ahead and be
fully functioning by the time Mason showed. Definitely
by the time Carter Dodds rolled in. The super-size black
coffee in her hand would help. But she'd barely got seated
when there was movement in her doorway.

'Thought I'd bring this up before I left.'

Jed walked in—well, from the voice she knew it was
him. His body was completely obscured by the floral
bouquet that was almost too wide to fit through the
door.

'They just arrived,' he puffed.

'Not more?' Penny shrivelled deeper into her seat. She
knew who they were from. Aaron—a spoilt-for-choice
playboy type with several options on the go—the kind of
guy Penny always looked for when she needed some company for a while. Only the spark was missing. Last week

she'd told him no and goodbye—thought she'd made it clear—but the flowers continued to prove otherwise.

'Thanks, Jed,' she said as he offloaded the oversize blooms onto her desk. 'Have a good sleep.'

'Not me who needs it.'

Penny held back her sigh. She'd take the bunch back down to Reception again but she'd wait 'til Jed had gone for the day—he was exhausted after the night shift and had to go home to a sick preschooler. He didn't need to be hauling flowers back and forth for her.

She picked up her phone and hit one of the pre-programmed buttons.

'SpeedFreaks.'

'Hi, Kate,' Penny said. 'I've got a floral delivery please.'

'Penny? Another one?'

'Yeah.' She tried not to sound too negative about it. It was pretty pathetic to be upset by having masses of flowers delivered; most women would be thrilled. But cut flowers didn't make her think of romance and sweethearts, they made her think hospitals and funerals and lives cut way too short. 'Can you pick them up as soon as possible?'

She heard a movement behind her and turned, smiling in anticipation of Mason. But she forgot all about Mason, or smiling, even the flowers. Only one thing filled her feeble mind.

Tall, broad shoulders, dark hair dangerously leaning towards shaggy—she shouldn't be thinking shag anything. But she was. Because his eyes were leaning towards dangerous to match. She half waved with her phone hand to let him know she was occupied. But he didn't go away and she really needed him to because her head wasn't working well with him watching her like that. She pointedly looked past him to the corridor—didn't he know to come back in a few minutes?

No. He just thudded a heavy shoulder against the doorframe, becoming a human door—blocking her exit and anyone else's entry to the room.

And he smiled. Not just dangerous—positively killer.

She tried to look away, honest she did. But that ability had been stolen from her the moment her eyes had met his.

'Can you get them picked up asap?' she asked on auto, her brain fried by Carter's perfectly symmetrical features. Other parts of her body had gone on quick burn too. Thank heavens she still had her jacket on, because her boobs were like twin beacons screaming her interest through her white blouse. Memories of that gentle stroke last night tormented her. 'They'll be at Reception.'

He was even more handsome in the morning light. Even more now she wasn't blinded by fear and her senses weren't heightened by a surge of adrenalin. No, now it was some other hormone rippling through her body making her shiver.

He stared back as if he were mentally undressing her as fast as she was him. There were no black jeans and tee today, it was suit all the way. Dark, so understated it actually stood out, its uniform style showing off the fat-free frame beneath. Penny's heart thundered.

She turned back to her desk, her voice lowering. 'Thanks, Kate.' She wanted off the phone.

'Are you sure you don't want them? Or him?' Kate didn't pick up on Penny's need-to-hang-up vibe. 'He must be loaded to keep sending you these massive bouquets. And he's obviously dead keen.'

Penny winced. Then winced again as she realised Carter would be able to hear Kate too—the phone volume was too loud. She glanced over her shoulder and jumped. He wasn't in the doorway any more. He was about three inches away—at the most.

'No. I'll spell it out in single syllables.' But Penny tensed. She didn't know how more obvious she could be. She'd thought Aaron would be fine with a few dates' fun before saying goodbye. Only they hadn't got anywhere near that far. She figured the over-the-top floral attention was just him not being used to hearing 'no' and now he was determined to make her change her mind for the boy sport of it. But she couldn't be sure. And because she couldn't be completely sure, she couldn't be completely harsh. Not ever again.

'Where do you want them to go?'

'What about the hospice? But send them to the staff-room. Those guys work so hard.'

'Sure.'

Carter had his ultimate weapon loaded again—that smile was amused now, curving his full, sensual mouth. The green-blue eyes were bright and clear, but the clarity itself seemed to be shielding secrets within. Like a mirror they reflected the surface—and blocked access to the depths behind.

She replaced the receiver and turned to face her shameless eavesdropper full on. She ran her hands down the side of her skirt, pretending to smooth it but really trying to get rid of the clammy feeling.

'You don't want to keep them?' He was far too close

in this spacious office—why couldn't he stay on the far side of her desk?

He inspected the behemoth bunch and looked at the card—the millions of miniature red hearts on the cover obviously showed it was a romantic gift. Somehow him knowing that annoyed her all the more. And he already knew she didn't want them, he'd heard the courier conversation.

'I'm allergic,' she lied through a clamped smile. She wanted to get rid of both the flowers and him. How was she supposed to concentrate when her desk was covered with strong-smelling blooms and a man more gorgeous than the latest Calvin Klein model was making the room shrink more with every breath?

His gaze narrowed. 'Really?'

'Sure.' She blinked. 'I need to get these to Reception.' She reached out to pick up the flowers and escape. But in her haste she scraped her finger against one of the green stems, scratching it. 'Damn.' She looked at her skin and watched the fine white scratch flood with red. Then she glared at the bunch. 'I hate them.'

'Let me see.' He sidestepped the flowers and had her wrist in his hand before her brain could even engage.

Her pulse shot into the stratosphere. 'It's fine. A little plaster or a tissue will stop it,' she babbled faster than a Japanese bullet train rode the rail. Every muscle quivered, wanting him to draw her into a closer embrace.

'Suck on it.' His gaze snared hers. 'Or I will if you want.'

For half a second her jaw hung open. Oh, he was every bit as outrageous in the morning as he was at night. And she was dangerously tickled.

'It's fine.' She snatched her hand back, curling her fingers into a fist. 'I need to get these out of here.'

'Hey.' He frowned and reached out again, pushing her wide gold bangle further up her arm. His frown super-sized up as he stared at the skin he'd exposed. 'Did I do that?'

'Oh.' She glanced down at the purple fingerprint bruises circling her wrist. 'Don't worry about it. I bruise easily.'

He looked back to her face, all the erotic spark in his expression stamped out by concern. 'I'm really sorry.'

'Don't be.' She shook her head quickly. 'Like I said, it's nothing.' Honestly, his contrition just made it worse. She *did* bruise easily and his switching to all serious made him all the more gorgeous. And now he was ever so lightly touching each bruise with a single fingertip.

'It's not fine.'

Penny swallowed. With difficulty. Did he have to be so genuine? She needed to get out of there before she did something stupid like puddle at his feet. That gentle stroking was having some kind of weird hypnotic effect, making her want to move even closer. Instead she turned to the flowers.

'I'll take them.' He picked up the massive bunch with just the one hand.

Okay, that was good because he'd be gone and she'd have a few minutes to bang her head and hormones back together. She should be polite and say something. But she didn't think she had a 'thank you' in her this second. The sensations still reverberated, shaking her insides worse than any earthquake could.

'Penny—'

'Mason should be here any minute,' she said quickly to stave off any more of the soft attention.

'No Mason today,' Carter answered. 'He's working from home. He'll have sent you an email.'

She frowned. Mason never worked from home. He might be eighty but he was almost always first in the door every day. 'I'll take what he needs to him there.' Truthfully she wanted to check on him.

'That would be great.'

Their gazes collided again, only this time the underlying awareness was tempered by mutual concern.

'I'll find out who's hurting him,' Carter said, calmly determined.

Penny nodded.

He cared about the old man, that was obvious. Something jerked deep inside her—the first stirrings of respect and a shared goal.

'I'll be back in a minute.' He swept out of the room.

Penny just sank into her chair.

Carter carried the oversize bunch of blooms down to Reception. Taking the stairs rather than the lift used a bit of the energy coiled in his body, but not enough. Like an overflowing dam he needed a runoff to ease some of the pressure.

Penny had got under his skin faster than snake venom got into a mouse's nervous system. He'd thought about her all night instead of getting his head around the company set-up. Seeing her again today had only made it worse. She looked unbelievably different. The clubbing vixen had vanished and in her place was a perfect vision of conservative and capable. An, oh-so-sensible-length skirt simply highlighted slim ankles and sweet curves, a virginal white blouse was covered by a neatly tailored navy jacket. Hell, there'd even been a strand of pearls at her neck. With her shiny black hair swept back into a plait and her even blacker eyes, she'd looked like the epitome of the nineteen-forties secretary. No matter what she wore, she was beautiful.

Ordinarily Carter wasn't averse to mixing business and pleasure. When business took up so much time, it was sometimes the only way he could find room for pleasure. So long as the woman understood the interest was only ever a temporary thing, and that there were no benefits to the arrangement other than the physical. He didn't generally mix it with someone directly subordinate to him, but someone in one of the offshoot companies or satellite offices.

But he shouldn't mess with Penny—not with only a week or two to find the slimeball ripping Mason off. But he didn't think he was going to be able to work without coming to some kind of arrangement with her, because her challenge was enough to smash his concentration completely. Fortunately he figured she was a woman who'd understand the kind of deal he liked, and the short time frame saved them from any possible messiness. He just had to ensure she understood the benefits—and the boundaries.

In the privacy of the stairwell he opened the card still attached to the flowers.

Hoping to see you again tonight—Aaron.

Carter's muscles tightened. Had she seen him last night? Maybe she had had a hot date after meeting up with the women. Had she gone to this Aaron with the taste of Carter still on her? Because he could still taste her—hot, fresh, hungry.

He wasn't in the least surprised to think she'd go to another guy having just blown hot for him; he was well used to women who manipulated, playing one man off against another. His ex had done exactly that—trying to force him into making a commitment by making him jealous. It hadn't worked. And he sure as hell wasn't feeling jealous now. The aggro sharpening his body this minute was because of the threat to Mason. Not Penny.

He stalked out to Reception and put the flowers on the counter. 'I think a courier company is coming to pick these up.'

The receptionist grinned as she looked at them. 'Penny sent them down?' She shook her head. 'That's the third bunch this week. She's mad not to want them.'

The third this week? It was only Tuesday. Yeah, she would like holding the interest of multiple men. His long-held cynicism surged higher—there was no doubt Penny was as greedy and needy as every other woman he'd known.

It was almost an hour before Carter reappeared, a piece of paper in his hand and a frown creasing his brow. 'Penny, I need you to—'

He broke off as her phone started ringing.

She shrugged an apology and answered it. 'Nicholls Finance, Penny speaking.'

'Did you get the flowers?'

'Aaron,' she whispered, inwardly groaning. She darted a look at Carter, then turned away on her chair so he wouldn't see the flush rising in her cheeks. She already knew he was rude enough to stay and listen. Her best option was to end the call asap. 'It really isn't convenient to talk right now—'

'Did you get them?'

'Yes, I'm sorry, I should have called but it's been a busy morning.' And she could hardly let him down without some privacy. 'Can I call you back?'

'The roses reminded me of you. Stunningly beautiful but with some dangerous prickles.'

Yes, she'd encountered one of those real prickles. She shrank more into her chair. 'Look, it was lovely of you but—'

'Dinner tonight. No excuses.'

She breathed in and tried to stay calm. 'That's a nice idea but—'

'I've already made the reservations. It's my only night off this week and I want to spend it all with you.'

'Aaron, I'm sorry but—'

The phone was taken out of her hand.

'Look, mate, don't bother. She has a new boyfriend and she's allergic to flowers. She's already sent them on to the hospice down the road.'

Penny stared as Carter leaned across her desk. She couldn't hear what Aaron said in response— she could hardly process what Carter had just said so complacently.

'Yeah, I know. Save your dough. It isn't going to happen.' Carter hung up the phone and then looked at her coolly. 'So, I was saying I need you to track down some files for me.'

For a moment she was too shocked to fully feel the rising fury. But then it truck-slammed into her. '*What* did you just do?'

Carter met her gaze with inhuman calm. 'Solved your problem. He won't bother you again.'

'How could you do that?'

'Easily. And you should have done it sooner already. Your body language said one thing, your mouth another. You looked like you wanted to hide under your desk for fear he'd appear, but you were brushing him off too gentle. A guy like that doesn't get subtle, Penny. You need the sledgehammer approach.'

'I didn't need you to be the sledgehammer.' She shook her head. 'That was bully behaviour.'

'It was man talking to man,' he argued with an eye-roll for added effect. 'And more honest than the drivel coming out of your mouth.'

'I was handling him,' she said defensively.

'You were *playing* with him.' Now he didn't sound so calm. Now he sounded that little bit nasty.

Her hands shook as she brushed her hair behind her ear. She hadn't been playing with Aaron, she'd been trying to be nice.

'Three bunches of flowers this week already, isn't it, Penny? You're not even honest enough to tell him you don't want *them*, let alone that you don't want *him*.'

Because she didn't want to be rude. She never wanted to hurt anyone. Never. Horrified tears prickled her eyes as she panicked over Aaron's reaction to Carter's heavy-handedness.

'Why are you so upset?' He stepped closer, his eyes narrowing. 'Oh, I get it. You liked to leave him hanging? Was it good for your ego? You like getting all the flowers and attention? You're a tease.'

'I'm not.' She jerked up out of her chair, beyond hurt at the words he'd just used.

'You are,' he argued. 'Why else wouldn't you cut him free sooner?'

'I tried.' She snatched the paper off him and marched

to the filing cabinet, hauling the drawer open with a loud bang.

'That wasn't trying.' He followed and faced her as she rummaged through the files. 'You're not stupid, Penny. You could have flicked him off much sooner.'

'Maybe I'm not as arrogant or as rude as you are.' She slapped files on the top of the steel. 'I don't like trampling on people's feelings.'

'You don't think it's worse to string him along so your ego can be inflated some more?'

'That wasn't what I was doing.' She crossed her arms in front of her chest.

'Oh, don't tell me you really liked him?' He looked stunned. 'Were you just making life hell for him? Playing with him so he'd do anything you ask him to?'

'Of course not!' She clenched her teeth. 'I was trying to make it clear that nothing was going to happen. I thought I had already. But he didn't deserve your kind of in-your-face humiliation.'

'What he doesn't deserve is you screwing him up and spitting him out only when you're sick of chewing him over.'

Breathing hard, she glared at him as fury burned along her veins. 'Wow, you think so highly of me, don't you, Carter?'

His shoulders lifted in a mocking shrug. 'If you really wanted rid of him, you needed to be cruel to be kind.'

'Well, I'm not cruel,' she said painfully. 'I won't ever be.'

He glared right back at her—for what felt like hours. Slowly she became aware of their isolation in the office, the smallness of the space between them. They were just about in exactly the position they'd been in last night.

'How about honest, then, can you manage that?' he asked quietly.

'Not if it's going to really hurt someone,' she muttered. Utterly honest.

'No.' He shook his head. 'That's the coward's way out.'

Well, what would he know about anything? For all his cruel-to-be-kind cliché, she'd bet her last cent he'd never hurt anyone the way she once had.

She blinked back her sudden tears, focused on his eyes instead. Close up now she saw even more colours in them—not just green and blue but shots of gold as well. All of a sudden she was trying really, really hard not to think of that kiss and how incredible she'd felt. Trying really, really hard not to notice how his mouth looked fuller today.

The atmosphere changed completely. It seemed he'd forgotten his anger too. But there was no less emotion in the air—it just transformed and intensified as it swirled around them. Somehow it made her feel even worse than when he'd been so rude on the phone. Somehow she was more afraid. She couldn't move, couldn't speak.

'Do you want me to kiss you again, Penny?' he asked. 'Is that the real problem here?'

That brought her voice back. 'You are so conceited.'

'So you really can't do honesty,' he jibed.

She bent her head and fished for the last few files, needing to find her moxie more than the damn data. He so easily tipped her balance, she needed her defensive sass back. But all she could manage now was the silent treatment.

'So what should that guy have sent you—a big box of Belgian chocolates?' His tone lightened.

'I don't eat chocolate,' she said shortly, not looking up.

'Maybe you should, smooth off some of those sharp edges. Isn't chocolate better than sex?'

'You're obviously not doing it right if the women you know say that.'

He yelped a little laugh. 'Throw out a challenge, why don't you?'

She slammed the file drawer shut.

'And now you're backing away from it again. See, you *are* a tease. You just like having men want you.'

She faced him full on, to put him firmly in his place. Oh, so arrogant Carter Dodds could definitely cope with that—he wasn't exactly crushable. 'You wanting me is not a compliment.'

'You don't think?' He grinned. 'Well, I'm not going to chase after you with a billion flowers or calls. If you want to follow through on this, just let me know.'

'And you'll come running?'

He shook his head. 'I don't run after any woman.'

'Because they all fall at your feet?'

'Much like the men do at yours, darling,' he murmured. 'But I already know how much you want me so maybe I'll make you beg for it.'

'Cold day in hell, Carter.'

'Don't protest too much, you'll only regret it later.'

She held a breath for a sanity-saving moment. 'You always get everything you want?'

'I already have everything I want. Anything extra is purely for fun.' His lips curved so slowly and his eyes twinkled with such a teasing expression she fought hard not to let her lips move in response. They wanted to smile all of their own accord. To mirror the magic in his smile. How could she want to smile when she was mad with him?

Because the fact was, he was honest—and, yes, more honest than her. He might be teasing but he wasn't saying anything that wasn't a bit true.

'Admit it, you love the fun of it.' Both his eyes and voice invited.

'The fun of what?'

'Flirting.'

'Is that what you're doing?'

'That's what *we've* been doing from the moment we saw each other.'

'Oh, please.' This wasn't *flirting*, this was a full-scale, high-impact, brazen sexual hunt. There was nothing subtle about it.

'You can't deny it,' he said. 'You like what you see. I like what I see.'

She dropped her gaze. Yes, that was all it was. A superficial animal attraction—based on instinct and what the eye found beautiful. They were each a pleasing example of the opposite sex with whom to practise procreation.

'That doesn't mean we should do anything about it. You need to concentrate, you've got a job to do here.' And she needed him to give her some breathing space.

'And I'll do it well. Doesn't mean I can't have a few moments of light relief here and there.'

Light relief was all she ever did. But she didn't think Carter would walk as lightly over her as she would him. 'You don't think this is a distraction?'

'I think it's more of a distraction not to give in to it.'

'Oh, right, so really I should be saying yes for Mason's sake.'

He chuckled. 'You should be saying yes because you can't keep saying no—not to this.'

He had the sledgehammer thing down pat.

She'd known many cocky guys. Had heard many lines—hell, she'd even delivered a few herself. But while Carter was confident, she could also tell he meant every word—and not in some deluded way. He really wanted her. And the truth was, she wanted him too—but to a degree too scary. This kind of extreme just couldn't be healthy.

He leaned a little closer and, despite her caution, Penny couldn't help mirroring his movement. She had to part her lips just that tiny fraction—to breathe, right?

He smiled wickedly and lifted his head away again, his eyes dancing with the delight of a devil. He picked up the files she'd thumped on the top of the cabinet. 'I'll see you at the bar later.'

'You're going tonight?' She whirled away to hide the sudden rush of blood to her face. Oh, yeah, all her blood rushed at the thought of him being there.

'Good opportunity to meet and mingle with the staff socially.'

She could hear his smile as he answered. But she frowned, forgetting her feelings about spending social time with him and thinking of Mason instead. 'I can't believe any of them could be stealing.'

'Greed. You never know who has what addiction, what need that'll push them past moral boundaries.'

'But it's not William.' It was the analyst's last day; he was heading overseas to take on the financial markets in Singapore. 'It couldn't be him.'

'I'm checking everyone,' Carter answered, suddenly cool. 'As he's leaving, I'm checking his deals first.'

Penny went straight to the bathroom and spent several minutes touching up her face—pressing powder over her forehead, cheeks and chin with deliberate, dispassionate dabs. She concentrated on her lipstick, not letting her mind think of her mouth as anything other than a colouring-in challenge—certainly not a hungry bundle of nerve endings yearning to feel the pressure of Carter's mouth on hers again.

But then she stared at her surface-repaired reflection. Was he right? Had she been stringing Aaron along? She hated the way Carter had spoken to him but had she been any better? She could have made it clearer—interrupted him and spoken firmly. Only she had that memory, when she'd inflicted so much pain. It was why she was always so careful to establish the ground rules before she entered any kind of affair now. It was why her affairs were so few and far between and super-brief. She had to be careful because she couldn't handle anything more than easy. Anything more than carefree. No pain, just frivolity and superficial pleasure. She enjoyed sex. She didn't have it anywhere near often enough despite her many nights out dancing, preferring to keep safe in all kinds of ways. But this attraction to Carter was the most extreme thing she'd ever experienced.

He'd offered all she wanted—only the physical—no strings, no messiness. There was certainly no fledgling friendship there, not when he obviously thought she was a manipulative tease. She saw how he looked at her, as if she made him as angry as much as she turned him on. Well, she knew exactly how he felt.

But her reaction to him was too strong to be safe. When emotions were out of control, people got hurt. She wasn't hurting anyone or being hurt ever again. That was her one hard-and-fast rule. And this attraction threatened every ounce of control she had—therefore was too dangerous to engage.

But he was absolute temptation.

She shook her head, overruling her warring instincts. He wasn't *that* overwhelming. Her attraction to him was simply a case of it having been too long. Of course she swooned for tall, dark and handsome, any other red-blooded female would too. Except Carter didn't just have those three attributes, he also had a carefree lack of cut to his hair, wicked brilliance in his eyes and the devil in his smile....

Ugh. She turned her back on the mirror and walked out. He was just incredibly over-confident. He probably wouldn't even deliver on the promise he exuded. Because in truth, for Penny, no man delivered.

CHAPTER THREE

'CHAMPAGNE please.' Nine hours of work and thirty lengths of the pool later, Penny had changed into her clubbing gear, heel-tapped her way into the bar and been served ahead of eight people already queued there.

'So you're friends with the bartenders.'

'And the DJs.' She took her glass and turned to face Carter. 'And the bouncers,' she added with just that little bit of emphasis.

His grin flashed. 'Really? I thought you didn't like bullies tossing people out of your life.'

He was dressed in the dark casual again. The edginess suited him better.

She sipped the champagne and pretended she had all the chutzpah she'd ever need. 'There's always the exception, Carter.'

'Oh, that there is.' His brows lifted as he looked over every inch of her second-favourite-ever skirt and then her shirt. 'So this is your hunting ground.' He glanced dispassionately at the dance floor. 'Little loud, isn't it?' He grinned evilly. 'How can you get to know someone properly when you can't hear them talk?'

She sidled another inch along the bar and whispered

in his ear. 'By getting close.' She quickly pulled back when she felt him move.

His hand did lift, but all he did was deposit his glass on the bench behind her. Empty already meant he'd been there awhile and he hadn't had trouble catching the attention of the bar staff either.

Penny searched and spotted her workmates over near their usual corner, some already on the dance floor. Safety in numbers. 'Coming to join the others?'

'If I must.'

She deliberately misunderstood his reluctance. 'You don't like to dance?'

He shrugged.

'You've got no rhythm?' she asked totally overly sweetly.

He took her glass from her and sipped carefully. 'I can hold my own.'

'Really.' She didn't try to hide the dare in her tone.

He turned to face her. There were probably over a hundred and fifty people present, but suddenly there was only him. 'I'm happy to watch for a while first. That's what you want, isn't it? To be watched? That's why you dress like this.' His fingers brushed the hem of her skirt and slipped onto her bare skin.

She took her glass back off him. 'I dress like this because I don't like to get too hot. And so I can move easily.'

'Yeah, real easy.' All innuendo.

Swallowing some sweet fizzing bubbles, she smiled. 'Not jumping to all the wrong conclusions again, are you?'

'No, I'm examining the details and evaluating in a reasoned manner.' His finger traced slowly back and forth over a two-inch stretch of her thigh and, despite the heat of the late summer night and the press of too many people, goose bumps rose.

'Like you did last night?'

'I admit my naturally suspicious instinct overruled my usual close observation. At first.'

'So you admit you were wrong?'

'I already have. And I already apologised. Last night. Stop trying to milk it—we can move on, you know.' He took her glass from her again. 'Or are you too scared to?'

She bit the inside of her lip as he smiled and sipped more of her champagne, intently watching her reaction. He wasn't kidding about the close observation.

'You know we want the same thing.'

'Maybe, maybe not,' she hedged.

'Definitely.'

'All I want right now is to dance.' *With him.* But she had to hold some secrets close.

His grin flared. 'Precisely my point.'

She turned her back on him, positively strutted to where half the others from the office were already getting their groove on. That was one of the things she liked about the company—the really healthy party scene that went with it. They worked hard and played every bit as hard and, despite those thirty lengths already, she still had too much energy to burn. William and some of the other guys joined in and the floor got crowded. Her blood zinged. Yeah, this was what she needed; easy-going freedom and fun.

The music *was* loud—which she liked—the beat both fast and steady. But it wasn't long before she turned her head. Because it wasn't one-way traffic—she wanted to watch him too. She met his stare full on across the floor. For that split second she saw how easily he read her— piercing right into her head to find out exactly what she wanted.

He walked straight towards her.

And, yes, that was exactly what she wanted.

Carter and William were a similar height but Carter drew all attention away from the other man. His aura and his physique commanded it. Broader in the shoulders, bigger, stronger—yes, she was totally going cave-girl, her body instinctively turning towards the male who seemed likely to offer the best protection.

His smile wasn't exactly safe, though. And other instincts were warring with her basic sexual ones—shrieking that getting closer to Carter would be no protection at all. But that look in his eyes mesmerised her again. She couldn't move—like prey frozen in the path of the predator. Not safe at all. But then, at this moment, she didn't want to be.

His hand slid round her back and he pulled her against him, his head descending so quickly she didn't even have a chance to blink. But there was no kiss for her hungry mouth; he was too clever for that. It was the slightest brush on her jaw, so quick and light she wondered if it had just been her desperate imagination. Her breath escaped in a rough sigh of disappointment and then she inhaled—all excitement again as he pulled her that bit tighter to him. Now she was wholly in his arms, her chest pressed to his, his hand wide and strong splaying across her spine, his other lifting to stroke down her plait, tugging at the end of it to tilt her face back up to his.

But she avoided his all-seeing eyes. Turned to look over his shoulder instead. Her workmates' eyes were bugging out. She was definitely breaking a few conventions tonight; she didn't ever dance this close to anyone in the office. But then Carter wasn't officially on the payroll. And in less than a second she didn't care what they were thinking anyway because the impact of his proximity hit her and *she* could no longer think. She couldn't do anything but move with him.

He said nothing, didn't need to, merely moved his hands to guide her where he wanted—natural dancer, natural leader, natural lover. All easy rhythm. And she turned to plasticine just like that.

Chest to breast, hands to shoulder and waist, thigh brushing thigh—but eyes not meeting. The need to deny the madness built in her chest. But he was totally taking advantage of the flickering lights and the crowd of people to crush her closer still. His sledgehammer style—steamrolling over her caution just by being himself.

The feelings intensified. She wasn't comfortably warm any more but unbearably hot. She couldn't breathe either—he always made her so damn breathless, made her heart beat too fast, made her brain go vacant.

She wanted to rest her head on his shoulder for a moment, wanted to escape the crowds and the claustrophobic feeling choking her. She wanted to move slowly with him. Even more she wanted time to stop—to leave her pressed mindlessly against him with no pressure of the past to bear on her.

But that was impossible. And this discomfort was so wrong. Dancing was where she felt the best, the most free. She liked it fast and loud, but now it was only his heartbeat she could hear—strong and regular and relentless—and it scared her. Her own heart thundered, scaring her.

Why was she stumbling, why were her eyes watering, blinded by the flashing lights?

She had to escape. Pushing away from him, she took a deep breath to try to stop from drowning in the sensations. She listened for the beat again. She needed to be alone and unrestricted—alone in the crowd.

She turned, saw William only a couple of feet away. She moved towards him, welcoming the break from Carter. Breathing deeper, more calmly. Yes, she needed recovery time to get her grip back.

William was a handsome guy, easily the best-looking man in the office until Carter had arrived, but there was none of that crazy swimming feeling in her head that she had when dancing with Carter. She had no trouble breathing, or thinking or staying in control of her own body. This made so much more sense.

Manageable.

She breathed deep again and smiled at him. William smiled back. This was better.

Carter stood on the dance floor and watched her spin in some other guy's arms. William. The guy whose work he'd just spent the afternoon cross-checking—and it was all clear. That didn't stop the surge of hatred from rising. Despicable, unwanted, violent.

His fists curled. There was no hope of recovering his calm, not now he'd felt the way she moved against him— all fluid grace and perfect rhythm and soft freedom. All he could think of was her supple body sliding against his as she danced with him intimately. Every muscle ached for the intense release they'd share.

But there she was going from him to another in a heartbeat. Any other woman and he'd roll his eyes and walk away. He made it a rule never to care enough to be bothered by a woman's games. But he had to get out of there before he punched that William guy in the face. And it wasn't even his fault. Penny was the player, not him.

Carter wasn't into violence and the wave of aggression he felt made him even more angry—with himself. He'd punish his own body instead, take it out on the rowing machine or the treadmill or the punchbag that were in the gym down the stairs from his serviced apartment. He'd go there and sweat it out right now.

Raw lust was his problem, and he'd felt nothing like it in his life. So what that she was attractive? There were millions of pretty women in the world—that didn't mean his body had to start acting as if Penny were the only one that could switch him on. It had been a while, that was all, too many hours on the job and not enough off socialising. But maybe seeing her in that half-wet top last night had put some spell on him, because all he could think about was getting her naked. Her and only her.

Well, he'd get over it.

He walked out of the bar, knowing he'd probably just caused a massive stir and a ton of gossip, given he hadn't bothered to speak to any others on the staff. Still, better for them to be gasping over his sex life than his real reason for being there. It provided good distraction in terms of his cover.

But for him, it was an absolute nightmare. Penny's accusation this morning had been on target. She was more than a distraction, she was catastrophic for his concentration, and he couldn't let sexual hunger affect the job he was doing for Mason. He'd commandeered an office on the floor below so he wouldn't even see her during work hours unless it was absolutely necessary, but it wasn't enough. Not when he was hunting her out at night. There was only one way forward—he had to forget her and just get on with the job. She could toy with that other guy. He damn well didn't care.

CHAPTER FOUR

PENNY felt as if she'd overdosed on no-doze. Her heart hammered, she fidgeted. Hyper-alert, she watched every second, hoping he'd hurry up and come say hi. But he didn't. Minutes dragged like decades. Mason had emailed in again to say he'd spend another day working at home. Maybe Carter was with him. Or maybe he was locked in his office down the stairs. She wasn't going to go see. She wasn't going to waste another minute wondering where he was or why he'd done the vanishing act last night. And she certainly wasn't going to regret the fact that he had.

Eventually she went out for a power walk. Fresh air might help her regain her equilibrium and stop her from doing all those things she'd told herself she wasn't going to do.

Twenty minutes later she walked back into the building, even more hot and edgy. As the automatic door slid shut behind her Carter stepped out of the lift. He didn't hesitate when he saw her, just strode straight across the foyer like a man possessed.

'Did you enjoy the rest of your night?' he asked, still ten paces away.

'Yes,' she said brightly. She'd hated it. She'd danced

and danced until she couldn't fake it any more and gone home to stare at the ceiling.

'Really?' Now he looked angry and he lengthened his stride even more.

A rabbit in the headlights, Penny failed to leap out of his path. And all of a sudden he did what she'd wanted him to do less than twelve hours ago—yanked her close—one hand round her waist, his other pulling her plait so she was forced to tilt her head back. Not that he needed to force it, because she melted right into him. For hours in the early morning she'd lain half asleep, dreaming of this. Now she wasn't sure if she was still dreaming—and only by clinging, by putting her palm to that sharp jaw could she be sure that he was real and kissing her hot and rough and right in the middle of Reception.

Her groan caught in her mouth as he plundered. How could she ever say no to this? She was lost to it, utterly lost.

But just as suddenly he pulled away.

'You're still hungry.' His words whispered low and angry.

Stunned, she stared. And by the time she got herself together enough to say something, he'd already gone out of the door behind her.

Her anger hit. What the hell did he think he was doing, carrying on like that in public? Thank heaven no clients had been waiting for appointments. Only the receptionist was there, though that meant everyone in the company would know about it by now—she'd have emailed them already. Not that they'd be surprised after the dirty dancing display last night. Penny ground her teeth. Yes, it was a good thing she was going soon because things were getting more than a little untidy. She marched up the stairs and felt even more hot and furious by the time she got to the top.

Files, she'd sort out the wretched files. She stomped over to the cabinet and slid the drawer open, pointlessly checking all the contents were in the right order. Which they were—but the perfectionist in her just had to be sure.

'Got you some tea to calm your nerves,' Carter said smoothly.

She whirled fast to face him. Stepped so close, so quick, he actually took a step back and deposited the steaming cup on the nearest flat surface—the top of the cabinet. She moved closer still, keeping the scarcest of centimetres between them.

'I don't fool around at work, Carter.' She furiously whispered in his face, using anger to hide both the turmoil raging inside her and the desire he'd roused so effortlessly. 'Don't embarrass me like that again.'

His hands whipped round her, pulling her flush against him. Letting her know how lethally he was turned on. Her nerves shook beneath her skin, her muscles melted—only to reform even tighter and aching to feel his impression.

'You liked it, Penny.' His hand firmly cupped her butt, pulling her yet closer against his thick erection. 'You liked it as much as I did.'

She had and she did nothing to deny it now, did nothing to pull away from the searing embrace. If anything she melted that millimetre more into him. There could be no denying the force of it. She gasped as he thrust his hips harder against her—his expression told her he knew it all. But he was angry too.

'Who was it who ended that kiss, Penny? Who was it who pulled back?' His smile was a snarl. 'If it had been up to you we'd be sweaty and catching our breath right about now. If we'd been alone you'd have let me do anything. And you'd just about be ready to go for round two.'

Her blood beat through her with such force she felt dizzy. 'Well, then, what the hell were you thinking making that move *there*?'

He held still for a moment, and although his body remained rock hard she felt the anger drain away from him. The next second he actually laughed. 'I wasn't thinking. Isn't that obvious?'

Shaking his head ruefully, he looked up above them. 'Here we are again. I'm starting to think this plant is like some kind of magic mistletoe.'

'You always have the urge to kiss me when you're under it?' The urge to flash him a look was irresistible.

'I always have the urge to kiss you, full stop.'

Admittedly he didn't sound that thrilled about it, but even so a spurt of pleasure rippled through her. It was good he wanted her like that. It evened the score. She leaned back against the filing cabinet and looked at him, feeling as if she'd done her warm-up and was ready for the race—excited, a little nervous, full of anticipation.

Carter stepped forward, closing the gap until he was fully pressed against her again. His blue-green gaze devoured her features. She wished he'd just hurry up and kiss her. She put her palm to his jaw again, unable to resist just that small touch.

'Go on, Penny.' Ragged-voiced, he dared her. 'Deal with me.'

Their mouths hovered, barely a millimetre apart, hot

breath mingling with even hotter desire. How could she possibly resist? She opened her mouth that little more.

'Well,' a deep voice sounded. 'Looks like I finally get to meet him.'

Penny leapt a clear foot, or she would have if Carter hadn't had such a grip on her—a grip that suddenly tightened.

'Matt,' she squeaked. Wide-eyed, she stared past Carter at the tall figure standing beside her desk.

'I've heard so much about you but I didn't think I'd get to meet you.' Matt walked closer, his too-intelligent eyes nailing Carter and then flicking to her. 'Penny, you didn't tell us he actually worked with you.'

She was still trying to wriggle out of Carter's grip but he'd tightened it even more to pinch-point. 'Yes,' she managed to say softly but Matt didn't hear her.

'You're him, right?' Matt asked Carter direct. 'The "man" she keeps emailing about—the one who dines and dances and takes her away every weekend.'

Penny wanted the world to open up and suck her under right this second. Because what would Carter think about that lot of detail? What would Matt think when he found out the truth?

She looked into Carter's eyes, saw the blues and greens and ice-cold anger out in equal doses. She pressed against him just that little more, softening herself in the hopes he'd also soften. Okay, she was pleading as she, oh, so slightly nodded her head at him, all but begging with her eyes.

But Carter felt as if he were made of rock as he rubbed one fist across his lips. He seemed to see into her soul with his bleak, penetrating glare. She waited for the axe to fall. Carter wanted her but he didn't think much of her, she knew that. So he wasn't about to come riding to her rescue now.

And Matt, impossibly tall and grown-up Matt, was waiting for an answer.

'Yes,' Carter finally said. 'I'm that man.'

In shocked relief Penny softened against Carter completely, but felt every one of his muscles flinch.

'I'm Matt Fairburn, Penny's brother.' Matt flashed one of his rare smiles and held out his hand.

An infinitesimal hesitation and Carter reached out too. 'Carter Dodds, Penny's man.'

It was a firm handshake, Penny could tell. It went on that half-second too long, as if they were testing each other's muscles and manliness or something. Which was ridiculous, because last time she'd seen Matt he'd still been half-boy, half-man. The intense student too focused and serious for his own good. But now he was…different. Now he was assessing, and judging—just as he wanted to do in his career.

She took the opportunity of their formal introductions to extricate herself from the rock and the hard place she was literally squashed between. Emotionally, she was even more caught.

'What are you doing here, Matt?' She summoned a big smile as she asked, because she had a fictional happy life to live up to.

'Coming to make sure you'll be around to have dinner with me. Has to be tonight because I've got a conference for the next couple of days.'

She hadn't known he was in town. Why hadn't he emailed to tell her? 'Of course I can do dinner,' she said brightly.

'No other plans?' he asked.

'None I can't change.'

Matt's brows lifted. 'What about the man?' He turned to Carter. 'You'll come too, right? I want to grill you. Being the only one in the family to meet you so far, I've got responsibilities to those back home. Namely Mum.'

He spoke casually but Penny understood the under-tone. Her kid brother was checking up on her. She tried to make her muscles relax but her smile felt superglued on. 'Carter has to work tonight. Sorry, Matt. He has a meeting.'

'Actually, honey, that one got cancelled.' Carter tucked a strand of her hair behind her ear as if he had all the rights of such casual intimacy. 'That's what I was coming to tell you only I got…distracted.' He looked from her eyes to her mouth in a blatant sensual stamp and then he turned. 'I'd love to be there, Matt.'

All Penny's internal organs shrank. 'But—'

'You can let me know for sure later,' Matt broke in, his expression impassive. 'I have to see your flat too, Penny. More of Mum's orders.'

'You should have warned me.' Penny laughed. 'I'd have tidied up.'

Matt answered with a quick rare smile again, but Carter wasn't smiling at all.

'I'll walk you out,' Penny said quickly, wanting to take charge of the plans without Carter listening in. She manufactured more brightness as she led him to the lift. 'Why didn't you tell me you were coming sooner? I could have made some plans.'

'Wanted to surprise you.'

Yeah, he was checking up. She hated that he felt he had to do that. Her little brother had had to grow up too soon and he'd got all paternal and protective on her. It was her fault. He should be out there having wild times of his own, not worrying about her or carrying the burden of their parents' worry for her. And that was her fault too. She'd tried to ease it—hence her stupid, overly imaginative emails.

But now she smiled and gave him a hug. 'It's so awesome to see you. I'll text you with details of where to meet, okay?'

'You mean you actually have my number?' Matt asked dryly. 'I wondered.'

Yeah, it was only the occasional email that she sent. She rarely texted, and never talked. It was easier that way. She'd never said she was brave. And she was feeling beyond cowardly now. She went back into the lift and reluctantly pushed the button for the top. Droplets of discomfort sweat slicked her skin yet she felt chilled to the bone.

Carter stood by the windows in Mason's office, looking down at the street scene below. She closed the door behind her and waited.

After a moment that made her nerves stretch past break point, he turned.

'Just how many men have you got on the go, Penny?'

She shook her head. Glad his desk was between her and him. Because he was looking more than a little angry and she needed all four feet of solid wood between them.

'Tell me about him.' Carter's voice lifted. 'He's some sugar daddy you spend the weekends with?'

Her flush deepened. 'No.'

'No?'

Penny swallowed the little pride she had left. 'I made him up.'

Carter blinked. 'Pardon?'

'I made him up. In my emails home, I invented a relationship.'

For the first time she saw Carter at a loss for words— momentarily. His eyes narrowed and he took a couple of steps closer. 'You're telling me this "man" doesn't exist? You don't actually have a real boyfriend.'

'No.'

'And there's no one you're dating, or sleeping with, or friends with benefits or whatever you care to call it.'

She held his gaze. 'I'm not seeing anyone at the moment. No.'

He nodded slowly. 'When were you last seeing someone?'

'It's been a few months.' She was flushed with heat— anger, embarrassment and the burning need for him to believe her. For some stupid reason it was important he understand. 'I don't remember exactly how long.'

'But Aaron doesn't count?'

She lifted her chin and answered pointedly. 'A couple of kisses don't count.'

Carter's jaw went more angular. 'So how many kisses haven't you counted in the last few months?'

Her brows shot up. 'Aaron. Another guy. You.'

'My kisses don't count?' he asked softly.

'Definitely not.'

His devil grin flashed. 'I've figured it out.'

Penny blinked at his suddenly bright demeanour. 'Figured what out?'

'How to tell when you're lying.'

She jerked. 'What? How?'

He shook his head and laughed aloud. 'Not telling because then you'll stop doing it.'

'Stop doing what?' She sighed and gave up, knowing he wasn't about to spill it. Besides, there was something more important to know. 'You do believe me, don't you?'

He went serious again. 'Yeah, I do.'

She was absurdly relieved. She'd been a complete fool with the emails and he knew it, but oddly that didn't matter so long as he believed her when she told the truth.

He walked around his desk, picked up her hand and ran a light finger over the bruises still marking her wrist. 'You know I just said that about coming to dinner tonight to wind you up...make up whatever excuse.' He gave her an ironic glance. 'You've got the experience. Your brother might not know your little giveaway.'

Penny frowned and pulled her hand free.

Dinner with Matt. She'd half forgotten it in her need to clear up the confusion with Carter. But now she thought about it, she was dreading it already—the questions, the search for conversation, all the anxiety... She just didn't want to face it. She'd spent years not facing it.

Actually maybe it would be a good idea to have someone with her. With extra company she could present the happy façade for the night, no problem. And she really was happy. It was just that she'd added an imaginary gorgeous man to give the picture a fully glossy finish. Companionship without complications—she had enough complications inside already. It had been so long since her last real, short-term gorgeous man, she'd invented one.

Now she looked at Carter. Handsome, charming, socially expert Carter.

'I think you should come with me,' she said.

His brows shot up.

'No, I mean it.' She stepped in closer to him. 'Come to dinner. After all, Matt's expecting you now.'

His attention dropped to her body and back up. 'Well, isn't that your problem for misleading him in the first place?'

'But you played up to it. The least you can do is follow through.'

Carter leaned back against the edge of his desk, a small smile tweaking his mouth.

Really, the more Penny thought about it, the better an idea it was. Matt could maybe learn a few things from Carter—social smoothness for one. And Carter would deflect the attention off herself. She didn't know how well she could maintain the façade on her own. Most importantly, the conversation would stay in safe waters. Matt wouldn't drag up the past with Carter present.

'I've seen you talking with the guys who work here... And the girls.' Her gaze narrowed. 'You're good socially.'

Too good actually. Every woman looked at him as if he were the biggest honeypot to hit the town in a decade or forty—and they all wanted a taste.

'Is that a compliment? Because the way you're talking I'm not sure...' He studied her slyly.

She couldn't hold back her smile. He was a charming wretch and he knew it.

'Come to dinner with me,' she leant forward to whisper. 'Be my pretend man.'

Carter's blood was still burning from the horror of

seeing her dance with someone else last night. He wasn't a hypocrite—he didn't expect women to have less experience than him, but the thought of her being in bed with another guy had made his stomach acid boil. The foreign jealousy rotted him from the inside out and he badly needed to ditch it. He'd spent all night awake wondering if she'd taken William home. And despite his vow to forget her, when he'd seen her in Reception this afternoon the urge had hit. He'd had to touch and find out—something, anything—like an animal scenting out a threat. So completely caveman and so unlike his usual carefree style.

And now, now the relief in knowing she hadn't was making him positively giddy, because here he was about to say yes to the most stupid suggestion he'd heard in ages. But he was too intrigued not to. 'Why did you make him up?'

Her gaze dropped. 'I wanted everyone back home to think I'm happy.'

Was she not happy? 'And you have to have a boyfriend to prove that?'

'No,' she said quickly. 'I have a great life—great job, I travel lots. But the man was the icing for them. I know they worry I'm lonely.'

Which she wasn't, of course. She had thousands of adoring suitors. She could have a man every night of the week if she wanted. But it was interesting that she didn't want that. It was interesting that she wanted to kiss *him*.

'So you want me to be the icing?' he croaked. Because if that meant she'd use her tongue on him, he was so happy to oblige.

She tossed her head back. 'It's what we're all supposed

to want, isn't it? Someone who cares, who holds you, who's there for you. Companionship, commitment. Happy ever after. That whole cliché.'

She thought wanting a life partner was a cliché? Hell, where had she been all this time? Because he didn't want a life partner either. He just wanted some uncomplicated fun. 'But that's not what you actually want for yourself?'

He could see the goose bumps on her arms as she recoiled. She really only wanted a lover for a night or two? That was fine by him—although he might have to push for a few nights. 'So what did you tell them about your man?'

'I never named him, always kept everything very vague.'

'How long have you been mentioning him?'

'Only in the last couple of months. They've been putting on the pressure for me to visit home and he was my excuse for saying no. Because we've been doing lots of little trips away.'

She didn't want to visit home? 'How long since you've been back?'

She looked away. 'A few years. I've been travelling a lot.'

But there were thousands of planes crossing the globe daily. She could go to New Zealand for a visit and be back the same day. It was obvious there was more she wasn't saying. Did he really want to know what it was?

Actually he was a little curious. But clearly she didn't want to share and he respected her for that. Better than getting a massive 'emo and drama' dump as his ex had always done. But even so, he couldn't let it go completely.

'I still don't really see why you had to make up a whole relationship,' he said. 'And why you want me with you so badly tonight.'

She froze. Carter's radar screamed louder. She was totally hiding something. And he was only human. So he waited, making her reply by pure expectation.

'The truth is I was one of those fat wallflowers as a teen.' Her head bowed as she mumbled.

Carter gritted his teeth to stop his jaw falling open.

'Overweight, acne, rubbish clothes.' She turned away from him. 'Total pizza face. The worst you can imagine.'

Her self-scathing tone rubbed him raw, making him feel an emotion he couldn't quite define. And he couldn't imagine actually. She had the smoothest skin—not a single scar marked her flawless features—and she was so slim—borderline too thin with a tiny waist and tiny wrists and tiny ankles. But she still had some curves that made his blood thicken.

'I wanted to be a whole new me—fit body, jet-set life, great job, gorgeous guy.'

He sighed and reached out to stop those curves escaping from him altogether. So she wanted to look good with a suitable male accessory. He should *not* be flattered about being a good enough accessory for her. That should *not* be pleasing him the sick way it was. But he couldn't help feeling for her. No wonder she was always so beautifully finished—the taunts of teenage years had obviously gone deep. But didn't everyone have scars from those turbulent times? He sure as hell did—it was thanks to the women in his life then that he'd put the Teflon coating on his heart.

'Okay.' He pulled her close and tried to tease her smile

back. 'What do I get out of it? What are you going to offer me?'

Her lashes lifted and the black pools glittered at him. 'You want me so much you'd sell yourself like some sort of escort?'

He was glad to hear her vixen tongue again and he leaned forward to reward her, whispering so close his lips brushed her ear. 'You have to agree that we kiss like nothing else. I'm very interested to see what it'd be like if we did something more.'

'If you wanted something more then why did you walk out so fast last night?' she breathed back.

'Why did you go dance with someone else?'

'That bothered you?' She leaned away and watched his face as he answered.

'I don't do commitment, Penny,' he said honestly. 'But I do do exclusive. And I do respect.'

She drew in a deep breath. 'Ditto.'

He watched her just as close. No sign of the super-quick double blink that happened when she was doing a Pinocchio. Interesting. 'All right, then, I'll come with you tonight, if you agree to stay well away from any other men in the next week.'

'I guess I can handle that,' she said casually. But he could feel her pulse racing.

'You better be sure.' He grinned as her gaze stayed true.

'I'm not promising anything else.'

'We both know that's not necessary,' he drawled. 'It's already a given.'

'This isn't going to get complicated, Carter.'

He really shouldn't feel that as a challenge. Anyway, he thought things were getting that touch more complicated with every passing second.

CHAPTER FIVE

PENNY hadn't seen Matt in just over a year. She'd been in Tokyo then, slowly working her way back to the South Pacific after her years in Europe.

He'd changed—made that final step from boy to man. And he'd almost caught her out in her web of lies. She knew why he was here—it was the start of even less subtle pressure. Her parents' wedding anniversary was coming up soon and they wanted a big celebration—one at home in New Zealand.

She couldn't possibly attend.

She was hoping to save enough money to fly them to her for a holiday. They could afford it themselves of course, but she wanted it to be a gift from her. She wanted that to be enough because she didn't want to have to go to them. The memories were brought to life there in that big house with their ancient, abundant orchard. The wall of trees linked their home to the property next door—Dan's parents' place.

She tried not to think about it and usually, on a day-to-day level, she succeeded. But Matt arriving out of the blue made everything flash in her head movie-montage style. It was almost seven years ago but sometimes felt as recent as yesterday. The darkness of those last few months at home encroached on her vision. And she remembered the estrangement from her family and friends as she'd got mired in a pit of grief and guilt.

She was out of it now. She was strong, she was happy, she was healthy. But the distance from them was still there—literally, emotionally. She didn't think the bridge could ever be rebuilt. In truth, she didn't want it to be.

And in her mind she saw him—as she always did— the day before he'd died. She swiftly blanked the images, focused on pleating the square piece of memo paper she had in front of her. Her fingers neatly folded and creased, working on a displacement activity designed to restore calm.

Because she hadn't coped with what had happened. It had impacted on the whole family and she'd made it worse. Bereavement had shattered the bonds and only by going away had she been able to recover. She needed them to know she was okay. But she couldn't front up to them and prove it in person. Not there. She didn't think she could ever face that place.

Carter couldn't concentrate on the damn transactions. He kept wondering, wanting to know more. In the end he went upstairs and pulled a chair up next to hers. 'We need to work on our story. For dinner tonight.'

She looked completely blank. She hadn't thought this through that far, had she?

He leaned forward and angled for more information. 'So how did we meet? How long have we been dating?'

She turned towards him, her eyes huge. 'I don't know. Can't you make it up?'

'You trust me to do that?'

Beneath her eyes were blue, bruised shadows. 'Sure.'

He stared, on the one hand stupidly gratified, on the other uneasy. What had happened this afternoon to make her look so hurt and exhausted? He glanced at her desk. It was bare, save a folded paper crane—which was unexpected and frankly intriguing.

'Okay, I'll come up with something,' he said, bitten by a random need to reassure her. 'An elaboration on the truth. We met at work.'

She nodded.

'And there was an instant spark.'

She nodded again.

'We were powerless to fight it.'

Her nod was slower that time.

'And we've been inseparable since,' he muttered.

She gazed into his eyes. Hers were so dark he couldn't tell where her pupils ended and her iris began. Black with longing. Right? He leaned closer, feeling unrestrainable longing himself. He wanted to kiss her. Had to. And never stop until she was right back with him. Right here.

Because the sadness in those deep, secretive eyes was unbearable.

He'd seen the attention she got from other men. He wasn't the only one to notice her combination of hotness and vulnerability. She unleashed both passion and protectiveness with just a look. And if they had any idea how she kissed, she'd need a posse of bodyguards to fight them off. Was it just her attention-grabbing trick? He grimaced ruefully; he didn't think so, because she already had him on a three-inch leash.

'Penny with the perfect plait.' He slipped his fingers

into the tight, glossy braid at the back of her head and massaged gently. 'Relax. I'll be the perfect boyfriend. Attentive, caring, funny...'

Why he was saying that he didn't know. He was supposed to be the perfect investigator. He was supposed to be in his office right now working through all the files and finding the point when the discrepancies occurred. Not planning how he was going to spend the evening pretending to be her lover. But she still looked so anxious and he ached to reassure.

'We can laugh and make small talk. Wow the brother and then leave.' He liked the leaving idea. He liked the idea of dressing up with her, going dancing and then dancing some more in private. Yeah, he was a complete fool.

He dropped his hand and stood—a little test of his own strength. 'Are you going to swim first?' He'd learned that was her routine.

She shook her head. 'No time.'

'You want to go home and change?'

'I've got something here,' she mumbled.

'You always have a party-going outfit with you at work?'

She looked surprised he'd even asked.

He went back to his desk for the last hour but all he did was think about her. She was nervous. Why? He didn't think it was because of him—in fact she was relying on him to carry her through this. So why? What was the big deal about her brother? That prickle of protectiveness surged higher. Why hadn't she been back in such a long time? It clearly was a long time. He couldn't wait to go and get some answers.

* * *

Penny stood under the hot jet in the gym shower until the warmth finally seeped into her skin. Over and over she reminded herself that it was going to be okay because Carter was coming and he'd keep it social.

She met him in Reception. He was back in black and another tee that skimmed his hot frame. Pirate Carter. How little she knew about him. How much she wanted to find out.

'You really don't have a girlfriend?'

'Do you think I'd act like this with you if I did?' His expression shut down. 'I don't cheat, Penny. One on one. I expect the same from you.'

She swallowed. 'But this is just for tonight.'

His grin bounced back. 'Oh, sure, you can think that if it'll make you feel better.' He took her hand as they walked along the street, the summer sun still powerful on their backs.

Penny hated public displays of affection. She hated being touched unless she was in a bed and the instigator or lost in the crowd on a dance floor. But Carter ignored all her unsubtle body language. He wouldn't let her pull her hand back, he measured his stride to match hers, drawing her close enough for her shoulder to brush against his arm as they walked. But she tried once more to slip her fingers out of his.

He stopped walking and jerked on her hand so she stumbled near him. His other hand whipped round her waist and his lips caught hers in a very thorough kiss.

She jerked her head back and glared at him. 'What—?'

'If you keep trying to get out of holding my hand, I'm going to keep kissing you. If you want me to act like your boyfriend, I'm going to act like your boyfriend. That includes lots of touching.'

'No, it doesn't,' she hissed.

'I'm an affectionate lover,' he said smoothly. 'I like to touch.'

'Kissing in public is exclusive, rude behaviour.'

'Passionately snogging for hours in front of everyone would be. So you'd better let me hold your hand, then, hadn't you?'

Otherwise he'd passionately snog her for hours? She so shouldn't be tempted by that. 'Don't tease.'

'Why? Did you think I was here to make this easier for you?'

'Of course that's why you're here,' she said completely honestly. 'Be charming, will you?'

'You think I can be charming?'

'You know you can.'

'Why, Penny—' he ran the backs of his fingers down her cheek '—thanks for the compliment.'

'Stop playing with me,' she begged through gritted teeth. 'Please come and talk nicely to him.'

But as they walked closer the cold feeling returned. Until the only warm bit left of her was the hand clasped inside Carter's.

Already seated at the table, Matt watched them approach—correction, he watched Carter.

'Hi, Matt,' Penny said.

Her brother took his steely gaze off Carter and he looked at her. He almost smiled.

An hour or so into the evening, Carter was wondering why she'd been so insistent about his attendance. And why she'd been so anxious. It didn't seem as though her brother was about to bite. If anything he'd looked fiercely protective when he'd greeted them, as if he'd take a piece out of Carter if he made the wrong move. He'd totally given him the 'Big Brother is watching' look. Which was a bit of a laugh, given he had to be the best part of a decade younger. And then he'd started a less than subtle grilling about Carter's background and prospects. Carter had really felt like laughing then, but Matt's questions were astute and intelligent and in less than two minutes he was on his toes and respecting kid brother for that. And he'd gotten no help at all from the woman he was here to socially save. She'd stared intently as he'd answered. She'd probably learnt more facts about him in those minutes than she had in the past couple of days. He'd like to do the same.

So now he willed time to go by triple speed. It refused—in fact he was sure it slowed just to annoy him all the more. Because he wanted to be alone with her. Alone and in his apartment. But there were the mains to be eaten, and more conversation.

'So what do you do, Matt?' Too bad if he should have known already.

'I'm based in Wellington. I've just finished my law degree.'

'So you're going into your first law job?'

'Matt's going to work as a researcher for the judges at the Supreme Court for the year,' Penny interrupted. 'They take three honours grads. Only the best.' Her pride for him glowed.

'I've deferred the law firm job for the year.' Matt shrugged off the accolades.

So he had his future mapped.

'You want to specialize in criminal law?'

.

'That's right.'

Yeah, that explained the cross-examination he'd just survived. Carter hoped Matt hadn't scoped out the lie right in front of him. Although it wasn't a total lie— Carter did want to be Penny's lover. Just not for ever as 'the man'. He'd settle for just the night. Tonight. Now.

But he forced himself to listen politely as the conversation turned to home and Matt caught her up on the happenings. She was interested, asked a tonne of questions, making him wonder all the more why she hadn't visited in so long. What was so awful about the place when her brother made her laugh about some woman who ran the annual floral festival in their small home town?

'I saw Isabelle the other day.'

It took Carter a moment to register the total silence. The temperature must have dropped too because he could see goose bumps all over Penny's arms again.

'Did you?' she finally answered, her voice more shrill than a rugby coach's whistle. She reached for her water. 'How is she?'

'She's okay.' Matt had stopped eating and was watching her too. 'She's working at the city library.'

Carter had no idea who Isabelle was, but what he did know was that Penny had totally frozen over. Icing over to cover up—what? He tilted his head and looked into her obsidian eyes.

Misery.

Absolute misery.

And she was trying too hard, her smile about to crack. He shot a glance at Matt to see if he'd registered Penny's sudden brittleness.

Yes, he had. He had the same dark eyes as his sister

only now they were even blacker and fiercely focused
on her.

She clung on—just—all smile and another polite question. But the façade was as fragile as fine-spun glass. He
felt the pressing edge of the knife, waiting for it to slice
and shatter.

'You okay?' Her brother ignored her irrelevant question and asked her straight out.

Her lashes lowered and the pretence fell with them.
She didn't look at either of them. Carter slung his arm
across the back of her chair. She needed a moment of
support and that was why he was here. And he wasn't
inhuman; his innards twisted at the sight of her.

'Of course,' Penny answered, so brightly it was like
staring straight into a garish neon light. 'I'm having dessert. Are you?'

She waved the nearest waiter over and ordered the
triple chocolate mousse.

'Excuse me for a moment.' Under cover of the stranger's presence, Matt escaped the underlying tension, shooting a look at Carter as he did.

Penny sat back in her seat after he'd gone and Carter
twisted in his to look at her properly. She was even paler
now and in her lap her fingers visibly shook. Her mouth
parted as if she was working harder to get air into her
lungs. Full lips that he knew were soft and that clung to
his in a way that made his gut crunch with desire.

She looked terrified. Carter knew there was a big part
of this picture that he was missing. But he'd get to that.
All that mattered now was bringing her back—bringing
back the sparkle, the fight and fire, the gleaming promise
that usually filled her.

'Penny?' He slid his arm from the back of her chair to

around her shoulder. Barely any pressure but she turned in to him. Her chin lifted and he saw the stark expression in her eyes.

'You okay?' he muttered as he moved closer. It was pure instinct, the need to protect. To reassure. To make it better.

He couldn't not kiss her.

For a moment she did nothing, as if she was stunned by the touch. But then she kissed him back. Her mouth was so hungry. But then her hunger changed, the tenor of her trembling changed. It wasn't distress any more but need. Her hands clutched his shoulders, pressing him nearer. He wanted to haul her closer still, wanted to curse the fact they were in such a public place.

Her hands tightened round the back of his neck, her fingers curling into his hair. Her breasts pressed against his chest. He wanted to peel her top from her, he wanted to see her as well as feel her. He wanted to touch her all over. He was wearing only a tee shirt and that was too much. He wanted her hands to slide beneath it; he wanted them to slide down his body.

Instead he had to pull back and he had to pull back now.

She didn't move. But her gaze had sharpened, focused. Colour had returned to her cheeks and her lips were redder than they'd been seconds before. She breathed out; he felt the flexing of her shoulders—as if she was shrugging off whatever the burden had been.

Just like that she was back to her perfect image. As if that moment of terror had never happened. As if that shattering kiss hadn't happened.

Carter hadn't felt so rattled in all his life.

There was only one way to deal with it. There was no

going back now. In truth there'd been no going back from the moment he'd laid eyes on her. He'd be her lover for real. He'd see her flushed and on fire and alive. And for someone who'd said kissing in public was rude, exclusive behaviour, she'd been doing pretty well.

Matt noisily returned to his seat and lifted the carafe of water, not meeting Carter's eyes but refilling everyone's glasses as if they all needed cooling down. Carter sure as hell did.

A couple of minutes later Carter was surprised to witness Penny enthusiastically tucking into the chocolate mousse. He'd thought she didn't like chocolate. He thought she worked hard to maintain her figure.

He looked up and saw Matt watching her with wide eyes too. And then Matt looked across at Carter and grinned, the vestige of a wink thrown in. As if he was completely pleased to see his sister putting it away like that.

But because she was so busy dealing with the rich goo, it was down to Carter and Matt to pick up the conversation. Carter darted a suspicious look at Penny. Yeah, she was spinning out the way she was swallowing that stuff—and actually taking the tiniest of forkfuls. In fact he figured she was totally faking her enjoyment of the stuff. Good actress, and calculating minx. But he played along, keeping the conversation safe and saving his questions for later when they were alone.

Only she foiled him.

'Matt can give me a ride home,' she said brightly after Carter had dealt with the bill. 'He wanted to see my flat, remember? And you had to work on those files—you don't want to be too behind tomorrow.'

Carter tried not to bare his teeth as he grinned his way

through acquiescing. He'd been neatly set to the side. But he'd extract a little price of his own.

As Matt went forward to request a taxi Carter pulled her into his arms, so close her body was squashed right up against his. Not as close as he wanted, but it was better than nothing. And as he was staring down the barrel of a night of nothing, he needed a little sweetener. He kissed her, softly, until she opened up for him. Then he slipped his hand up discreetly, quickly rubbing a thumb across her breast. He knew exactly how sensitive she was there. Sure enough he felt her instant spasm, her mouth instinctively parting more on a gasp. But he couldn't take advantage and go deeper. Reluctantly he relinquished his hold on her.

All the wicked thoughts that were tumbling in his head multiplied as he saw her flush and angry sparkle. Yes, it was going to be mind-blowing. But not soon enough.

'Great to meet you, Carter.' Matt walked back from the taxi rank, extending a hand and a bright smile.

So protective little bro wasn't going to throw any punches despite seeing Carter paw his sister? Carter felt smug. He must have the approval, then—on that score at least the night was a success. And he'd claim his reward—tomorrow.

Penny loved her brother but there was only so much she could handle. She yawned and pleaded tiredness. He seemed to understand, getting the taxi to wait while he did a lightning inspection of her flat so he could report back to the parents when he got home.

She stood in her doorway to see him off, thinking she'd got away with the last ten minutes with her nerves intact. Only he turned back, one leg in the taxi already. 'I'm sorry if mentioning Isabelle upset you.'

'Oh, no.' Penny shook her head, swallowing quickly to stop her throat tightening up too much. 'It was so great to see you, Matt. It was a really nice night.'

Aside from that one moment.

'You should come home and visit,' he said, suddenly awkward and emotional. 'You should bring Carter.'

Her throat thickened and tears stung her eyes. Blinking hard, she nodded and stepped back indoors.

Isabelle was Dan's twin and Penny's best friend from age one to seventeen. They'd been closer than sisters. They'd joked about becoming sisters for real when Penny and Dan had gotten together. But then that relationship changed everything—and every other for Penny.

For her, the impact was always there—a weight she carried and could never be relieved of. That was okay, because, as much as she didn't like to think of it, she also never wanted to forget. And her burden was nothing on Isabelle's, or Dan's mother's or his father's.

For so many reasons, Dan's death was the defining moment of her life. The experience and subsequent aftermath were the bases from which she made all her decisions. She wasn't being hurt like that again. More importantly she wasn't hurting anyone else either.

Now she knew life was for living—she would travel, experience and see the world. And always keep her distance.

And that meant distance from Carter too. Especially him.

CHAPTER SIX

'SLEEP well?' Carter stopped by her desk.

'Sure,' Penny lied.

'I didn't either,' he said, eyes twinkling. 'And I blame you for that.'

She didn't rise to his teasing banter. It wasn't entirely because of the memories that had been stirred last night—her instincts had been warning her off Carter from the moment she'd first seen him. She needed to listen to them. He meant danger—not the physical kind, like when she'd thought he was some psycho attacker, but a danger to her head, hormones and heart.

In short, he messed up all her insides.

If she thought she could control it, it would be fine. But she couldn't. Carter wouldn't ever cede dominance and he sought total response. That was fair enough, but it wasn't something she could give.

She wanted to run. That was her usual answer to everything. Only she couldn't. She'd let Mason down if she did and he'd been so good to her and he had troubles enough. He didn't deserve more disloyalty or seeing people flee what could be a sinking ship. If investors got any hint of trouble they might stop the money flow. And in the current economic climate, that was bad news for even the most ancient, venerable financial institution.

So she was stuck here for another month or so. And Carter was only here for a week more. Once he was gone she'd be okay again. She could be strong and stick it out—of course she could.

'What, now I've helped you out with your brother you're ignoring me?' Carter bent and eyeballed her.

'I just think it's better if we keep this on a professional level.'

'Honey, we've never been professional with each other.'

'We're adults, Carter. We can try.' To prove the point, she glanced at him very briefly and offered a tight smile. Then she went straight back to her computer screen.

'Why do women always have to play games?' He sighed. 'Blow hot, blow cold.' The amusement in his voice shouted out his disbelief. 'If I kissed you now, you'd be ten seconds to yes.'

'I'm not playing, Carter,' she said frostily.

He laughed aloud at that.

But she didn't see him again the rest of the day. She worked late, ignoring the lump in her throat and the disappointment that he'd taken her at her word. Slowly the office emptied but she couldn't relax. She really wanted a swim—alone, which meant after hours. It was the only way she could think to ease the aches her muscles had earned from holding her urges in all day.

Jed was on duty tonight so she was in luck. She grabbed her gym bag from her cupboard. She'd log off her computer and collect her purse and jacket later; right now she just wanted to dive into the cool water.

She went via his security station to let him know.

'I shouldn't be that long.' She smiled at the guard. 'Half an hour tops.'

'Sure. I'll lock up in forty, then.'

'Thanks.'

She changed in the small women's room. Kicking the bag under the bench, she took her towel out poolside.

She dived in. The cool water felt fantastic on her hot skin. She stretched out and floated on her back for a while, closing her tired, scratchy eyes. Then she pulled her goggles down and did several lengths. It took longer than usual to get into the rhythm, longer still to try to settle her mind. She was so tired yet she had so much painful energy she didn't quite know what to do with herself—but this wasn't working. Finally she stopped and trod water at the deep end—furthest from the door. Damn it, she'd get dressed and go dancing instead.

She pulled herself up out of the water and turned to reach for her towel. Only someone was there reaching for her instead. Someone who pulled her fast into hot, strong arms. And as she thudded against the wall of masculinity the shrieking fear transformed into sick relief.

'Why do you always have to sneak up on people?' She tried to yell at Carter but it came out like a strangled whisper, her throat all tight with terror.

'Sorry.' His hands smoothed over her shoulders, gently rubbing away her trembles. 'I didn't mean to scare you.' He looked back down at the dim room. 'You're not supposed to be in here.'

'Neither are you,' she snapped. 'Why are you here?'

'Isn't it obvious? I'm looking for you. Why are you here?'

'Isn't it obvious?' She was swimming, for heaven's

sake. She was trying to work him out of her system by exhausting herself.

His grip tightened and he pulled her closer. Her senses were swimming even crazier now. Yeah, the work-him-out hadn't worked.

'You're getting wet.' She put up one last, pathetic defence.

'I don't care.'

'Carter...' she muttered as his mouth descended.

'You don't want me to kiss you?' His lips grazed her temple. 'To touch you? You don't want to touch me?'

Of course she wanted that—she ached to touch him. It was way less than ten seconds to yes.

He laughed, pulling her dripping wet ponytail down the way he liked to, tipping her chin up to meet his mouth. But the laughter died as the kisses deepened and steam rose in its stead.

It was as it had been that first night—a gentle tease to begin with. Until she couldn't resist opening and he immediately went deeper, pushing for more. She lifted her hand and combed her fingers through his silky, thick hair.

His hands slid down her arms, sweeping the droplets from her skin. The hard heat of him burned through his wet shirt. All steel male—with unmistakable purpose.

She managed the first couple of buttons, but he had to do the rest, until she could spread the two halves of cotton and sweep her hands across the hot planes of his chest. Beautiful, hard and hot for her. He saw the look on her face and suddenly tumbled her to the floor, claiming dominance as she'd known he would. The cold tiles were welcome on her burning skin, helping her see straight for one moment of sanity.

'Stop.'

He lifted his head and looked at her.

'You're a player, right, Carter?' she muttered breath-lessly. 'This doesn't mean anything.'

He brushed the back of his fingers along her jaw. 'Not if you don't want it to.'

'Just fun.' She rocked, desire making her body move instinctively against his. All she ever had was just a little fun. Nothing more. This had an elemental undertone of something serious that she wanted to eliminate, but the need to have him was beyond necessity now. That big black hole deep inside her had been ripped open and demanded some good feeling to fill it. Like the good feeling she got when kissing Carter.

And then he did kiss her. She closed her eyes as he moved over her—slowly nibbling across her shoulders, his hands working to peel her tight swimsuit down, ex-posing her breasts. He kissed down her sternum, down to her stomach and then looked back up at what he'd bared. His hands lifted and he cupped her. She shivered at the touch, insanely sensitive there. He rose swiftly, his mouth hot and wide as his tongue swirled around one nipple.

She arched violently, pushing her heels down hard on the cool tiles to get her hips higher—hoping he'd just grip them and surge into her. She wanted it to be powerful and fast. She wanted him to be there now.

But damn him he was slow and toying and touching her all over. His hands slipping into soft parts that she usually held reserved. She tried to guide him back, tried to move her own into dominance—to distract him—but he was focused on his own determined exploration. And it was undoing her completely.

Her whole body broke into a sweat. It was as if she'd

walked into a steam room—suddenly she was so hot, and she couldn't get any of the burning air into her windpipe. She writhed more beneath him, trying to make him move faster—move over her and take her swiftly. She needed it to be finished, because she couldn't cope with heat.

All she wanted was him inside her, riding her, releasing his strength into her. Her mind and body fixated on that one thing—*his* possession, *his* pleasure. Not hers. She got hers from his. That was what she wanted. Not this searing way he was playing with her.

'Carter!' She gasped as his fingers stroked against the strip of her swimsuit between her legs and then slipped beneath the stretchy material. She twisted, suddenly trying to escape him as the strokes grew impossible to bear.

She was drowning, drowning, drowning in the intolerable heat. She couldn't breathe, couldn't think, couldn't control anything. Her fingers dug into his shoulders as the sensations become so strong they scared her.

He lifted his lips from her damp skin. 'Relax.'

How was she supposed to relax? Her toes curled as she flexed every muscle she had, trying to wring the tension from her. But it wouldn't leave her. Instead it worsened.

He sucked her nipple into his mouth and slid a single finger inside. The agony was too complete and she jerked violently—*away* from the source of that frightening intensity. Wrenching herself free from his hold and scooting back on the tiles.

He swore. 'Did I hurt you?' Rising sharply to his knees, his chest heaving, he stared across to where she now sat half a metre away.

She shook her head, breathing hard and shivering as

the sensations still scudded through her. But they were weakening now, becoming manageable.

'Penny?'

'I just needed a second.' Panting, she moved back towards him. Wanting to get the situation under control. She wanted *him* under control. And she knew how—to hold him, kiss him, suck him in deep and squeeze him hard.

Both her mouth and sex were wet with that want. But it was her mouth that wanted first—to lessen his potency. She'd pleasure him enough to make him tolerable for the rest of her, to make him speed up. She wanted him quivering beneath her. She'd be in control again and watch him ride the wave; she wanted to witness the orgasm rippling through him. She wanted to be the source of that pleasure.

Because that was the pleasure in it for her.

Silently Carter watched her crawl back towards him. Still he said nothing as she knelt in front of him. But she felt his ragged breath when she ran her hands down his chest. She spread her palms wide on his thighs, and then she narrowed in on her target. Oh, yes, she loved the size of the erection that greeted her. Her fingers twisted, searching for the zip so she could free him. But all of a sudden he grabbed her hands and stopped her.

She looked up at him. 'Don't you want me to?'

He stared hard into her face—from her mouth to her eyes. 'The setting isn't working for me,' he said. 'We should get out of here.'

She sat back on her heels and swallowed. Suddenly cold. Suddenly aware she was half naked. She wriggled her breasts back into her cold wet swimsuit with absolutely no dignity whatsoever. Not able to look at him again until she was as covered up as she could be, with the towel like a tent around her. By the time she did look across at him he'd fixed his own clothing and was standing waiting for her.

He held out his hand. 'Come on.'

She couldn't refuse his offer of assistance. But as soon as she was on her feet he dropped her hand. He was careful not to walk too close. She was careful not to stare at his strained trousers. She really wished he'd let her do something about that. She really wanted to, wanted *him*, but it had to be her way. Only, as she'd suspected from the first, Carter wasn't one to let that happen.

They got to the door and Carter turned the handle. It didn't move. He twisted it again. Then the other way. It still didn't move.

'It's locked,' Penny said. 'Did you lock it when you came in?'

'No.'

Penny frowned and tried the door herself. Then she looked through the small window to the darkened foyer beyond. 'Jed must have locked it.'

He must have had a quick look in and seen the empty pool—and not seen their entwined bodies in the dark corner at the end of the room. He thought she'd gone so he'd locked it up for the night.

'So we're stuck in here?'

'Looks like it.' She swallowed and drew the damp towel closer around her shoulders.

'We could bang on the door, he'd hear us, right?'

She shook her head. 'He's up one floor and he listens to his iPod.'

Carter rolled his eyes and cursed under his breath.

'Don't make trouble for him,' Penny said quickly. 'I talked him into it. It's my fault really.'

'Why do you come here after hours? Why not when it's open?'

'I like having the pool to myself. It gets really busy before and after work.'

'You don't think it's dangerous?'

'I'm a really strong swimmer. And Jed knows I'm here.'

'He's useless at his job, though, isn't he? He doesn't know I'm in here too.'

'He'd have heard the lift you were in and thought it was me going back up. He probably thinks I left the building while he was down doing the lock-up.'

'Don't try to make excuses for him.'

'He has a young family, he doesn't get much sleep and he needs the job, Carter. Leave him alone.'

'Well, if you really care about him staying in employment then you should stop getting him to break the rules.'

'Okay, fine.'

He sighed and glared back at the deep blue water, and the big still space. Then he looked back at her. 'You can swim in the pool in my apartment complex. It's big and private and hardly anyone swims there.'

'Do you?'

'Yes, but in the morning. You can have it all to yourself at night. And I'll watch.'

'I'm not going to be there at night.'

'Oh, I think you are.' He stepped closer and put his hand on her shoulder. Even through the damp towel she could feel the sizzle. 'You should get dressed.'

She braced for his reaction to this last pearl of info.

'The only way to the changing rooms is through that door.'

'You're kidding,' he snapped, immediately trying the door one more time.

She shook her head.

Carter leaned forward and banged his head on the wood. They couldn't even get to the changing rooms where there might have been a condom machine on the wall. He'd hoped anyway. Because they had no cell phone, no condoms, no couch, no cushions, nothing to cover them in what was going to be a long, cold, frustrating night. He frowned as he felt her shivering beside him.

His clothes were damp and freezing. The whole place was freezing. And all she had on were wet togs and a wet towel. 'What time do they open up in the morning?'

'Six o'clock,' she answered. 'I think the gym attendant gets in around quarter to.'

Just under eight hours away. Eight hours alone with her mostly naked and he couldn't even take advantage of that fact.

'Come on, then, let's try and get comfortable.'

He walked back down to the far end of the pool. Foam flutter boards weren't the softest things in the world, but they were better than cold concrete. He scattered a couple by the wall, gestured for her to take one and he sat on another himself. She cloaked the towel around her and avoided both looking and talking.

Carter tried not to stare at her too obviously while he attempted to work out what had happened when she'd pulled away from him so abruptly. He didn't think he'd hurt her; he'd been being gentle and taking it slow. Well, kind of slow. But it was as if she'd suddenly freaked out—and he'd thought she was so close. She *had* been so close. Right on the brink. Was that the problem? She hadn't wanted to come?

He shook off the idea. So unlikely. Who didn't want to have an orgasm? Maybe he'd touched a too sensitive spot too quickly. Which meant he had to go even more slowly. Which frankly surprised him. It wasn't as if she were some skittish virgin—hell, the way she kissed was so damn hot and welcoming. But when he'd really begun to push for the ultimate? Boom. Was it simply a total withdrawal from a total tease?

Actually he didn't think so. Because her refusal hadn't been total. He didn't think she was playing games—the fact she'd tried to go down on him proved that. But it seemed she didn't want to receive the pleasure herself. Was it some weird control thing? Did she like the power of bringing a man to his knees and begging for her to swallow him whole? Or was she truly that little bit scared?

Wow. She really was a mass of contradictions and complications. And he was beyond intrigued—he was bound to follow through on this with her, he just had to figure out how. His muscles twitched beneath his skin. Patience wasn't one of his virtues. But for Penny Fairburn, he might have to make an exception.

He stretched out his legs and drew in a deep breath to ease the tension still wiring his body. The question now was how to fill in the time. How to tempt her back, how to find out what secrets he needed to unlock her totally. He couldn't make more moves, not in this place, not without warmth, comfort and contraceptive protection. Which left only one thing.

Talk.

'You've always swum?' Lame, but it was a beginning. He couldn't dive straight into all the intense, personal questions that were simmering within him.

'Since I started travelling,' she replied distantly. 'Most places have nice pools somewhere.'

Penny answered his light chat completely uselessly, her brain still barely processing that she was trapped in the pool room all night. With Carter. It was the 'with Carter' bit that really had her reeling. That and the extreme throbbing still going on in some sensitive parts of her body. Staying in control of the next eight hours was going to take serious concentration and she needed to stay in control. The avalanche of sensation he'd triggered in her had taken her by surprise—despite the warning signals she'd had from his earlier kisses.

Too much emotion—even just lust—led to fallout, not fun. She couldn't deal with fallout. Mind you, she might not have to, because he wasn't exactly busting his moves now. In fact he was quite carefully keeping a distance while she grew colder by the second.

He wasn't even looking at her any more. And now the last of the light let in by the high windows was fading so she couldn't hope to read his expression. But he did seem inclined to talk. And she was definitely inclined to ask.

'So your family's in Melbourne.' She'd picked up that nugget at dinner last night.

'Dad is. My mum died when I was fourteen.'

'Oh, I'm sorry.'

'It's okay. Dad's on his third marriage now.'

She clamped her lips to stop her 'oh'.

'He remarried within a year,' Carter continued bluntly.

'Twenty years younger than him, gold-digger. The whole cliché you can imagine, only worse.'

'Oh.' Couldn't stop it that time.

'Eventually he got out of it but went straight into the next marriage. Another much younger woman—Lucinda. They had a baby last year.'

'Really?' That was big.

'Yeah, Nick.'

'You have a baby half-brother,' she processed. 'And you're okay with it?'

'Actually, he's quite a little dude. Why, you don't like kids?'

'It's not that I don't like them...'

He twisted to face her. 'You don't want them?'

'Definitely not,' she answered immediately.

'Not now, or not ever?'

'Ever.'

'Really?' He sounded surprised. 'Me either.' He started to laugh. 'That's what's so great about Nick. He's the new generation Dodds boy to take over from me. No pressure on me to procreate now, Dad's done it.'

'Do you think they'll have more?' Penny couldn't imagine having a sibling she was old enough to be the mother of.

'I don't know. Lucinda probably doesn't want to risk her figure again. She has the new heir now—she has Dad round her little finger as tight as she can.'

'Maybe she loves him.' Penny just had to throw in that possibility because she suspected Carter might have his bitter eyes on.

'She loves his money and status.'

Yeah, bitter. 'Gee, not down on her at all, are you?'

'I've met her type before. The first stepmother—remember?'

'So you're not close to your dad.' She figured his scathing attitude might get in the way of that.

'Actually we are pretty close. He retired from the companies completely a few years ago—mainly to be with her. And part of me hopes their marriage will last because, I think it'd kill him to lose the kid, but it won't. Then he'll undoubtedly find someone else. I try to treat Lucinda with respect. But he knows I don't trust her. He tells me time will take care of that and I guess it will. They'll either break up or last the distance.'

'You don't think it's kind of romantic?'

'I don't believe anything is romantic.'

Ah. Penny sat up and repositioned her towel, her interest totally piqued. 'Who taught you not to?'

Even in the gloom she could see the devilish spark light up his eyes. 'My stepmother's yoga instructor.'

'You're kidding.' She couldn't help but smile. He was so naughty. 'A yoga instructor.' Giggles bubbled then. 'No wonder you won't settle for one woman—she gave you unrealistic expectations.'

'You think she set the bar too high?' he asked, all wickedness.

'A cougar who taught you hot yoga sex? Way too high.' And no wonder he'd shot her through the roof with a mere touch, probably some Tantric trick.

'My stepmother was only eight years older than me,' he pointed out sarcastically. 'And Renee was only six.'

Her name was Renee? Penny maintained her grin, but her teeth gritted. 'But you were how old?'

'Sixteen. What?' His grin broadened. 'Too young?'

'Too young to have your heart broken.'

He laughed. 'That wasn't what happened. It was just sex.'

'Your first time is never just sex,' she said with feeling. 'So what happened?'

'She had a fiancé I didn't know about. She wanted to play around on her man for the power trip. And she wanted to break me in.'

Penny had the distinct impression no woman had ever broken Carter, and none ever would. But he'd definitely been bruised. 'What happens with your first can really leave a mark.' She knew that for a fact.

'You think?' He laughed. 'Renee was just about fun. It was the next one who really tried to do me over.'

'Oh? How old was *she*?'

He chuckled. 'Three months younger than me, honey. She was Head Girl of the school, I was Head Boy. The perfect match—on paper.'

'You were Head Boy?'

He shrugged, looked a bit sheepish. 'Good all-rounder.'

She knew what it took to be appointed the head of one of those elite schools—excellent grades, good sporting or musical achievement, community spirit. The golden boy going with the golden girl. Yeah, she knew all about that. 'So you were King and Queen of the prom. Then what happened?'

'We went to university. She switched to be at the same as me.'

'Oh.' Penny smiled wryly. 'Her first mistake.'

'We were only eighteen, you know? I wasn't looking to settle down.'

She understood that too. And a decade or so later,

Carter still wasn't looking to settle. 'So it turned to custard?'

'She started getting serious about us getting married. Lots of pressure and angst. Eventually she used another guy to try to push me into it.'

'She tried to make you jealous?'

'Yeah, but I don't get jealous. Frankly, I didn't care that much—as bad as that sounds. So it didn't work. I just realised I couldn't trust any of your fair sex.'

He didn't trust women at all. But then who could blame him? His mother had left—okay, she'd died, but it was being left in a sense. His first lover had used him, his first serious girlfriend had tried to manipulate him into something he didn't want…and he'd got ever so slightly bitter.

Well, he didn't need to trust her. He just wanted some fun. In theory he was perfect. Because in theory he posed no threat—he wouldn't ask for anything she didn't want to give.

Except he already had. When he kissed her, his body demanded hers to surrender. Still that step too far for her, but she was so tempted by him she knew she was going to have to figure out a way of working it in a way she could handle.

He was looking at her slyly. 'So what's the deal with your family?'

'What do you mean?' She pulled her legs up tighter and wrapped her arms around her knees. The temperature was really dropping now.

'You haven't been home in years and you take me, a near stranger, to ride shotgun on a dinner with your brother. There's some kind of deal going on.'

'There's no deal,' she said innocently. 'I have a nice family.'

'So what, you're a runaway without a cause?' He looked sceptical. 'There has to be something. Some reason why you don't want to marry or have kids. Not many women don't want that. Most spend half their lives trying to manipulate their way into that situation.'

'You have such a nice impression of women.'

'I call it as I see it. And I like women a lot.'

'You mean you like a lot of women.'

His grin didn't deny it. 'Why limit yourself? And you're the same in that you don't want to settle. Why not? Your parents have an ugly divorce or something?'

'No, they've been married almost thirty years and they're still happy.' Her heart thudded.

'Oh.' Carter looked surprised. 'That's nice.'

'Yeah, they're good together. They're not like you, they fully believe in for-ever happy.'

'So why don't you?'

She fell back on her stock avoidance answer. 'I like my freedom. I like to travel. That's what I do.'

'And you really don't want kids?'

Oh. He'd gone back to that. 'No. I don't want children. Most men who want to marry do. I don't want to disappoint someone. It's easier to be with men who don't want either of those things.'

He looked serious. 'Can you not have kids, Penny?' he asked softly.

'Oh, no,' she said quickly. 'No, it's not that. As far as I'm aware, that's all...fine.' Even in the dim light, she figured her blush was visible. 'I just don't want to bring a kid into this world. It's too cruel.'

He said nothing and eventually she settled back

against the wall, tiredness beginning to pull her down. Age-old tiredness.

'Who's Isabelle?'

'Sorry?' Her tension snapped back.

'You clammed up when Matt mentioned her last night,' Carter said. 'You're clamming up now.'

Penny blew out a strangled breath. 'She's just someone from our home town.' Then she let enough silence pass to point out the obvious—that she wasn't talking any more. She suppressed a shiver and clamped her jaw to stop her teeth chattering. Curled her limbs into an even tighter bunch.

'You're cold.' Carter shuffled closer to where she sat. 'Come on, we have to keep warm.'

That was going to be impossible in this damp fridge. She went more rigid as he came close enough to touch. He sighed and put his arm around her, ignoring her resistance and pulling her down so they were half lying, half propped with their backs against the cold wall.

'Go to sleep,' he said softly, his body gently pressing alongside hers. 'Nothing's going to happen.'

Penny didn't want to wake up, didn't want to move. She was so deliciously warm, even her feet—which were like blocks of ice year round. And a soft wave of even greater warmth was brushing down her arm with gentle regularity.

She wriggled and the warm comfort tightened. The warmth was alive—male arms, bare arms, encircled her. So did bare legs. And against her back? Bare chest.

She jerked up into a sitting position. 'Where are your clothes?'

'You were freezing,' he answered with a lazy stretch.

'So you had to get naked to keep me company?'

'Skin on skin, Penny. It was the best way I could think to warm you up. You wouldn't wake up and I started to think you were getting hypothermic.'

Yeah, right. 'It's the middle of summer.'

'And you're in a basement that's as cold as an icebox,' he pointed out with a total lack of concern. 'You're warmer now, right?'

'Yes.' She was *sizzling*.

'And you're conscious, so it worked.' He pulled her back down to lie against him. 'And you liked it. You burrowed right up against me. You couldn't have got closer.' His arms tightened again. 'No, don't try to wriggle away. I'm feeling cold now. Your turn as caretaker.'

A tremor racked his body, but she could hear his smile. Faker.

She buried her smile in her arm so he couldn't see it. But she didn't try to move away again. Just another five minutes—what harm could that possibly do? He made a fantastic human hot-water bottle.

Then her stomach rumbled.

'You're hungry.'

Then his stomach rumbled too.

'You are too.' She giggled at how loud they gurgled.

'Mmm. We didn't have dinner.' His breath warmed her ear. 'What do you have for breakfast?'

'Fruit, yoghurt and a sprinkle of cinnamon.' Her mouth watered at the thought of it.

'Cinnamon smells good,' he drawled.

'Yeah, so much better than chlorine.' She could feel every inch of him. There were a lot of inches. 'You're in a bad way.' The hard length pressed against the top of her thighs.

'I can live with it.'

'You're sure?'

'Why?' He moved suddenly. 'You offering?'

He rolled above her. She shifted her legs that bit apart to welcome him. Yes, she was offering. Because she knew she couldn't deny herself any more. Desire finally outweighed fear. Some sleep had restored perspective. Besides, given how hard he felt now, she felt confident in her ability to bring him home quickly.

He looked at her closely. She felt his body tense up even more and he smiled, bending forward to close the last inches between them. She closed her eyes, anticipating a full passion blast of a kiss.

Except he merely brushed his lips on her forehead, her cheeks, her nose. So gently, too softly. 'We have the most insane chemistry, Penny.'

She opened her mouth to downplay it.

'No.' He put his fingers across her lips. 'Don't play games. Just be honest. Always be honest with me.'

'Okay.' She could let him have that. 'We have chemistry.' Actually they had more than chemistry. They had some experiences and likes in common. And they also shared no desire for any kind of a relationship.

'And we're going to experiment with it.'

Except there was still that niggling suspicion it might blow up in her face. 'What, like a science project?'

'Pretty much.'

'You weren't kidding about not being romantic.'

'You don't like flowers. You don't like chocolates. You hate romance too,' he teased, pressing even more intimately against her.

'I don't hate diamonds.' She shifted sassily.

He snorted. 'And what would you do if some guy

produced a diamond ring?' He ground his pelvis against hers in a slow circular motion. 'You'd run so fast you'd break the sound barrier.'

She bit her lip to stop her groan of defeat.

'We're going to have an affair,' he told her.

They'd been on this trajectory from the moment they'd laid eyes on each other. All she could do now was try to manage how it went. 'Yes.'

To her surprise the relief hit as she agreed. It was closely followed by excitement. Now she'd admitted it, she wanted it immediately. The sooner she could have, the sooner she could control.

'Tonight.' He levered up and away from her.

She sat up—unconsciously keeping a short distance between them. 'Tonight?'

He grinned at her obvious disappointment. 'No condoms in here.'

Oh. She hadn't thought of that. Thank goodness he had.

'Won't you let me help you out now?' She longed to feel him shaking in her arms. She could stroke him to glory in seconds.

'Will you let me do the same for you?'

She blinked rapidly and ducked his fixed gaze.

'Tonight,' he reiterated, amusement warming his authoritative tone.

She nodded. 'Just a little fun.'

'Can you handle that?' All hint of humour had gone.

Hopefully. If she could stay on top. She looked back into his eyes and waved her independence flag. 'Sure. Can you?'

CHAPTER SEVEN

TWENTY minutes later they heard the door lock click. They hid in the dark corner for another moment and dashed when the coast was clear.

'Get changed quickly,' he whispered.

Giggling in the women's, Penny tossed her skirt and top on straight over her togs, scooped up her bag and was out again in less than a minute. Carter was standing in the little foyer, his shirt water-stained and creased, his jaw dark with stubble. He looked sexier and more dangerous than ever.

He held out his hand. 'Let me take your bag.'

Penny walked quickly. 'I've got it.'

Already people were arriving to use the gym and swim facility and she wanted to get out of there before anyone saw the state she was in.

'No, let me take it,' he insisted, blocking her path.

She frowned but he came even closer, speaking through gritted teeth.

'Look, if you want everyone to see the size of my hard-on, sure, you take it. Otherwise let me just hold it while we get out of here, okay?'

Penny's jaw dropped.

He put a finger under her chin and nudged it closed

again. 'Don't act the innocent. You know exactly what you can do to me. Just like I know what I can do to you.' His gaze imprisoned hers and pierced deep. 'If you'll let me.'

Penny felt as if an adrenalin injection had just been stabbed straight into her heart. The feeling flickered along her veins, molten gold—sweeter than honey yet tart at the same time. Tantalising.

He smiled.

Excitement rippled low in her belly, blocking everything—nerves, memories, fears. All were swallowed in the rising heat. She shook her head but smiled back. Him wanting her felt good. He grabbed her hand and stormed them up the stairs and through Reception.

'Hell, you're not here already, Penny?' Bleary-eyed, Jed looked up from behind his desk.

She shook her head. 'You never saw me.'

'You and I are having a little chat later.' Carter scowled at Jed and held the door for Penny.

He flagged two taxis.

'We can't share?' she asked.

'We get in one of those together now and you know we wouldn't come back. I've got work I have to do.'

Eleven hours later, resentment-filled, she figured he'd done a lot of work. By the time she'd got home, showered, changed and returned to the office, he was already back there and concentrating. He hadn't moved from his chair for hours. She knew because she'd gone into his office a few times—delivering more of the massive numbers of faxes and courier parcels, more wretched files—and he'd ignored her. Hadn't even looked up, lost in a world of figures and transactions and tiny details.

And she hadn't been able to concentrate on a thing—

all jumpy and excited and impatient. Until the tiredness from the little amount of sleep had eaten her nerves and now she was grumpy and ready to stomp home alone because he hadn't even said hello to her all day.

Worst of all, it was only just five o'clock. Theoretically she had another couple of hours to put in first. She glared at her computer screen and banged the buttons on the keyboard.

'So.' He suddenly leant across her desk. 'Your place or mine?'

'So smooth, Carter.' She stabbed through another couple of keystrokes.

'Just answer,' he said roughly, putting his hand over hers. 'I'm barely able to pull together two syllables I'm that strung out.'

She looked at his face and was grateful she was sitting down. No muscles could stay firm against the heat in his eyes. And the grip he had on her now was thrillingly tight. It made her feel a lot better about his distance all day and she dropped any idea of holding out for some grovelling.

'Yours.' She was glad he'd asked. If she went to his it meant she could leave when she needed to, not have to wait for him to decide to go from hers.

'Then let's go.'

'Now?'

The taxi was already waiting and, even better, the trip was short. Her heart drummed faster than a dance-floor anthem and she concentrated on keeping her breathing quiet and even. He still had hold of her hand and as they rode the elevator up to his short-let serviced apartment he finally broke the silence.

'You're tired?'

Actually she was plotting how to handle him. She needed to take charge from the get-go—set the pattern for the evening—and she wanted him on fire as fast as possible.

He must have read her mind because he turned to her the moment he'd closed the door behind them. She melted against him and offered it all, pleased he was so hungry. She wanted him to be uncontrolled, to be in thrall. Passion was powerful and she wanted to succeed in hitting his pleasure high. She moved against him, dancing the way she knew best, her mouth open to his, her fingers working on his buttons—wanting him raw and hot.

But he laughed, low and pure. 'Why are you in such a hurry?'

Because that way she could control it. She shrugged her shoulders and simply smiled, pressing close again.

But he, damn him, suddenly slowed right down. He swept his lips gently across her skin as his fingers so carefully freed buttons. Why was he taking so long to undress her? Hell, they didn't even need to get undressed, he could just push her skirt up and pull her panties to the side—she was ready for him, she would ride hard for him—she badly wanted to feel him come.

Instead his hands drifted south and so did his mouth, gently caressing the skin he'd exposed. Until he was on his knees before her and sliding down the zip of her skirt. She twisted, her discomfort suddenly building, wanting to bring him back up, wanting her hands to be the ones taking the lead. But then his fingers slid higher and she flinched, the pleasure so sharp it was too much, and she couldn't let the sudden rushing feeling swamp her.

Carter had gone completely still. Then he leaned back

and looked up so he could see her face clearly as his hand gently brushed down the front of her thigh. 'I want you to enjoy it.'

'I will enjoy it,' she answered softly. But she knew what he meant. He wanted to hear her scream his name.

He stood, his keen eyes catching the way she wriggled back the tiniest bit from him. He swallowed. 'You don't want me to go down on you?'

She nodded, glad she didn't have to spell it out herself. 'I don't really like that…I…don't feel comfortable.'

He looked thoughtful. 'But you'll go down on me?'

'Oh, yeah, I like that.'

'Well, that's nice.' His devil grin flickered. 'But what turns you on most, Penny?' He watched her steadily.

The heat intensified in her cheeks and she tried to shrug his question off. 'Lots of things…' she mumbled. 'I like…lots of things…'

His head tilted a fraction to the left as he studied her. 'Oh, my…' His arms tightened, his body tensing too as he lanced right through her defences. 'You *fake* it.'

Her mouth opened in horror but the gasp never eventuated. Instead the blush burned all the way down to her toes. She blinked rapidly but she couldn't break away from his all-seeing stare. 'I do enjoy sex,' she said when she got her voice back. 'I like it a lot. It feels good. But… it's…it's just the way I am.'

'You always fake it?' His eyes widened.

'Sometimes it's easier that way.' She licked her lips— not as invitation, but because her mouth had gone Death Valley dry. 'Guys like to feel like they're…'

Carter rubbed his fingers across his forehead.

'It's not going to damage your ego or anything, is it?'

she asked, cringing at his obvious surprise. 'You'd rather I faked it?'

Blunt as she'd been with him before, this was his kind of sledgehammer stuff and she was shaking inside. She was never this honest. But then no one else had ever called her on it either and she was shocked he'd twigged at all, let alone so quickly. The fact was, she did fake it. She had an amazing array of squeals to let the guy think she was there. The Sally chick who met Harry in that movie had nothing on her.

But that didn't mean she didn't enjoy it. She did. She wanted it and she *wanted* Carter. The closeness was enough for her, feeling desired and making someone happy even for a few moments made her feel good too.

His gaze hadn't left hers and surprisingly his smile had gone less devilish, more sweet. 'My ego can handle you,' he said. 'So no faking. Total honesty. Deal?'

'I want to be with you,' she couldn't help reassuring. 'You turn me on, you know you do. But I just don't...'

'Get across the finish line.'

'But I still enjoy the race.'

He actually laughed. 'Don't feel any pressure to perform for me, darling.' He rested his hands lightly on her shoulders. 'We can enjoy each other in our own ways. Let's just see what happens, okay?'

She released the breath that she'd been holding for ever. 'You're sure?' Even for a guy as confident as him she was surprised at his easy understanding.

'Yep.' He nodded. 'I'm sure.'

Carter was trying to stop his head spinning but every thought had just been blown from his brain cells. Wow. He just hadn't seen that coming and honestly he'd just blurted the thought that had occurred so randomly.

For him enjoying sex was so inextricably linked with orgasm it was as if she were talking in a foreign language. He tried to figure it out—was she not physically capable of coming?

Actually he didn't believe that. By the pool he'd felt her shaking in his arms, he'd felt the hunger in her mouth, felt the flood of desire between her legs when he'd touched her there. Physically she'd been all systems go.

But at that point she'd literally leapt out of his arms.

So it was her head that couldn't let go.

Of course, she was a complete control freak. It made sense. That was her job all over—keeping everything in its place and perfect. But at the same time it didn't make sense. The night he'd met her she'd appeared the absolute image of a hedonist. A beautiful young woman out for fun and frolics and seemingly assured of success should she want it. But it seemed she didn't want it—at least not on a level that she couldn't control. Did she pleasure her lovers rather than let them pleasure her? Because that wasn't right. For him sex was all about mutual delight and exploration. Pleasure for both—give *and* take.

Women didn't have total ownership rights on curiosity. Right now it was eating Carter alive. And so was the challenge. How could it not be a challenge? Because this woman could feel it. He could feel *her*—trembling, all hot and aching. He knew how much she wanted him. So how did he help her let go?

He swallowed again. Like anything it came down to the details. She was so sensitive and maybe it scared her. So he was going to have to take it easy.

She was watching him with a worried look. 'I've probably put you off now.'

And the sweetheart looked as if she utterly regretted that.

He grinned. She didn't need to worry—she would get every ounce of what he had to give. 'Not at all.' Oh, hell, no, now he was all the more desperate to strip her and, oh, so slowly warm her up.

But first what they both needed was a little more time. Just a very little. 'You know we haven't eaten,' he said, tucking his shirt back in. 'Come on, I'll make something.'

She looked surprised.

'You hadn't missed dinner?' Now he thought about it, he was starving.

She shook her head. 'Haven't had a chance to think about it.'

Carter smiled inside again. That was because she'd been thinking about him. The key was to get her to *stop* thinking.

He led the way to the kitchen. 'You don't mind a cold dinner?'

Penny was feeling so hot—from embarrassment—that cold sounded wonderful. In fact she'd dive deep into a pool right now if she could. By the time she'd straightened her clothes Carter was pouring the wine—crisp and cool enough to make condensation form on the glass.

He pointed to the stool on the far side of the bench. 'Sit there and talk to me.'

About what? She'd so killed the moment and she was gutted because she did want to have him. Ugh. She should run away, go dancing and forget everything. 'Are you making any progress with figuring out Mason's problem?'

She was reduced to talking work.

All he did was shrug as he pulled a bowl from the fridge. An assortment of salad greens. He deftly sliced tomato, cucumber, feta and tossed the chunks in, adding a few olives from a tin after. Her mouth watered; she loved a summer salad.

He got a pack from the fridge and forked smoked salmon from it onto plates. Then he got a wooden board and from a brown paper bag slid a loaf of round, artisan bread. Her stomach actually rumbled as he sliced into the loaf. He sent her a wicked look.

'Don't tell me you baked the bread,' she teased to cover it.

'Italian bakery down the road.' He winked. 'Looks good, huh?'

It looked divine. In five minutes he'd fixed the most delicious dinner and she was seriously impressed. 'You always eat this healthily?'

'I work long hours, I'm responsible for a lot of people's jobs. I need to keep fit so I can perform one hundred per cent.'

He picked up both plates. 'Come on, we'll go out onto the balcony. You bring the salad.'

He pushed the bifolding doors wide open. The sun was still high and hot but an aerial sail shaded the table and the view of the harbour was incredible. Pity she was too on edge to be able to enjoy it properly.

'How come it's you helping Mason? Not one of your employees?' From all the conference calls and faxes he'd been getting she knew he didn't usually spend his days on a detailed case analysis like this. He was the boss of more than one entity.

'He trusts me.' Carter lifted his shoulders. 'And he's an old friend. And I wanted a break anyway.'

'So this is a holiday for you?'

'It's a nice little change.'

'But you're still in contact with the Melbourne office all the time.'

He shrugged again. 'I'm responsible for a lot.'

'And you love it.'

'Sure. I like my career. I work hard to succeed.'

Yeah, she'd noticed that about him.

The cool wine refreshed and soothed and now she'd begun to eat she realised just how hungry she was. It was only another five minutes and she'd finished.

He looked at her plate and looked pleased. 'Better?'

'Much.'

He went inside and pushed buttons on the iPod dock in the lounge and then came back to the doorway, offering his hand to her. 'Come on, don't you like dancing?'

'To a much faster beat than this.' But she stood anyway.

He smiled as he drew her closer. 'You've got to learn to relax, Penny.'

The slow jazzy music made the mood sultry and they were barely swaying. His shirt was unbuttoned, so was part of hers, so skin touched. This kind of dancing wasn't freeing, it was torture. She was uncomfortably hot again, her breathing jagged. A half-glass of wine couldn't be blamed for her light-headedness, and she'd just eaten so it wasn't low blood-sugar levels either.

It was him. All him.

And she wanted to feel him wild inside her.

She reached up on tiptoe, deliberately brushing her breasts against his chest. His hand moved instantly to hold her hips tight against his.

She sighed deeply. 'Can we just get on with it?'

'So impatient, Penny.' Laughter warmed his voice. 'Come on.'

He danced her down the little hall to the master bedroom. She liked the anonymity of the room—only one step away from a hotel suite. There was nothing personal of him around to make her wonder beyond what she knew already. Burning out the chemistry was all this was. One week and he'd be gone. Another month and she would too.

He pressed a button and thick, heavy curtains closed, giving the room an even more intimate mood. 'You want the lights out?'

'No.' She smiled. 'I like them on.'

He kicked off his shoes and trousers, shrugging off his shirt. She was spellbound by his body. He caught her looking, sent her an equally hot look back. 'You like to be on top, Penny? You'd like to take the lead?'

She did but she hadn't expected him to let her so easily.

He smiled and kissed her, but then moved onto the bed. He lay, his shoulders propped up against the bed head, his legs long in front of him, and looked back at her in challenge. 'Come and get me, then.'

Oh, she would.

She stripped, her eyes not leaving his as she deliberately, slowly shimmied her way out of every single piece of fabric. His expression was unashamedly hot and he openly hungered as she revealed her breasts.

'You on top works for me,' he muttered hoarsely.

She'd been worried he'd get all serious—forgo his pleasure in the pursuit of hers and then they'd both end up unsatisfied. But it seemed he was happy to stretch back and enjoy everything easily. Thank goodness.

As she walked to the bed he reached out to the bedside table and swiped up a condom, quickly rolling it on. So he was ready. Well, so was she.

She knelt onto the bed, meeting his unwavering gaze, and began to crawl up his body. His smile was so naughty, so challenging, so satisfied.

But she'd see him *really* satisfied. She trailed light fingers up his legs as she moved, bent forward and pressed little kisses, little licks. Nothing but tiny touches designed to torment—his thighs, his hips, his abs, his nipples. She'd get to his erection soon—when he begged.

His breath hissed. 'Are you afraid to kiss me?'

She knelt up and smiled. No. She wasn't afraid of that. She moved up the last few inches and pressed her mouth to his—and felt him smile.

His hands settled on her hips, pulling her to sit on him, his erection only inches from her wet heat. How the man could kiss. Slow and then firm, his lips nipping and then his tongue sliding. He turned it into an art form. He turned it intense.

She shifted, wanting to move right onto him, wanting to tease him some more. But he took her hands in his and imprisoned them beside her hips—so she couldn't touch or move. Then he went right back to kissing her. Just kissing. As if they were young teens on a marathon make-out session.

She was getting desperate now—to touch more, feel more—because his kisses were driving her crazy, building the need inside her. Every one seemed to go deeper. Every one increased her temperature another notch. Every one made her kiss back with the same increasing passion—until it was at an all-new level. She closed her eyes, breathless, yearning for the finish.

Finally he kissed down the side of her neck—just a little. She shivered at the first development of touch.

'Cold?' he murmured against her.

She shook her head a fraction. She was anything but cold.

She was completely naked, so was he, but he didn't move to take her or let her slide down on him. His erection rubbed against the front of her mound, teasing exquisitely.

She wanted to diffuse his power and have him in thrall to her—just for the moments that they'd cling together. That was how she always liked it—to be close, to be held. Intimacy beyond that was too much for her to bear. But Carter didn't seem inclined to settle for anything less than absolute intimacy. Her eyes smarted; she shouldn't have admitted anything to him. She shifted again, eager to move things on more.

'We've got all night, honey,' he muttered between more searing kisses. 'I'm not going to explode if I don't come in the next ten seconds.'

Yeah, but she was afraid she was going to go *insane*—this was too intense.

She rose above him, escaping his grip, demanding they move forward. She glanced down at the broad, flat expanse of his chest and the ridges of his washboard stomach. He was remarkably fit. And before he could stop her she gripped the base of his erection and slid down on him hard and fast.

His abs went even tighter and she felt his quick-drawn breath, but his expression remained calm.

She smiled because he felt so good. So damn good. And she could make him feel even better. She circled, clenching her muscles at the same time, and watched his reaction—the glistening sheen of sweat, the dilation of his eyes. Yes, now she was back in control.

Sort of.

She moved, increasingly faster, increasingly desperate. She searched for that look—the harsh mask of rigid control that tightened a man's expression just before he lost it completely. But Carter stayed relaxed, gazing up at her, his hands trailing up and down the sides of her body, letting her set the pace while still teasing her so lightly.

But the thing was, she was tiring, every time she slid up and down his shaft she felt more sensitised—every stroke hammered at her control. Just looking at him made her senses swim, so feeling him like this had her dizzy. Her breathing fractured. She was unable to keep the swamping sensations at bay, and her head tipped back, her eyes closing. Every inch of her skin felt raw, and at that vulnerable moment Carter slid his hand to her breast.

She gasped, bending forward in an involuntary movement. He caught the back of her head, fingers tangling in her hair, pulling her further forward to meet him. He kissed her again, deep and erotic, while with his other hand his fingers and thumb still circled her screamingly sensitive nipple.

She groaned into his mouth, mostly wanting him to stop—and yet not. And he didn't. Instead he lifted up closer so his body was in a crunch position, his abs pure steel. He wouldn't free her from his kiss, from his caresses, from the powerful thrusts up into her. Slow, regular, his fingers mirrored the rhythm as they moved to scrape right across the tip of her breast. And she wanted to run, she wanted a break—to slow for a second so she could recover some sense.

But the relentless friction of him against her, inside her and the kisses all combined to bring her to a level of sensation she couldn't escape. Devastating. She groaned again, desperate—alarms were ringing but nerves were singing at the same time.

He nibbled on her lips, upping the pressure from every angle, the hand at her breast sliding down hard against her belly to below—to that point just above where their bodies were joined.

She couldn't think any more now. She couldn't move. Too overwhelmed to be able to do anything but be guided by him and that was too much, too scary. But his hands clutched and controlled. He filled her body and all of her senses—all around her, inside her—holding her more tightly than she'd ever been held. And suddenly she realised—she couldn't fall because he'd caught her so close and sure. She was all safe—and free. In the prison of his embrace, she could be free.

And now the heat was delicious. Delirious with it, she danced in the flames—and had no desire to escape any more. For the escape was right here in this moment as she moved with him. Groaning, she sank deeper into the kiss, her body yielding, letting him in that last bit more—she could do nothing except absorb all of him as he relentlessly drove into her.

She was so hot, so incredibly hot and wild and free. It was as if a river had burst inside—a lava flow of sensation and heated bliss. On and on he pushed her along it—intensifying the heat and ride to a point where the waves of fire rushed upon her. Her eyes opened for a second and she broke the seal of the kiss as her breath, heart and mind stopped. There was no scream, no cry, just a catch of breath as her muscles clamped and then violently convulsed.

She shuddered, releasing hard on him with an incoherent moan, her hands clawing, so out of control. She was intensely vulnerable and yet utterly safe in the cocoon he made for her.

She went lax, totally his to mould. And he did, hauling her closer still, his grip even firmer, both hands across her back, pulling her so from top to toe she was flush against his hot damp skin. He frantically ground up for a few more beats and in her mouth their moans sounded like magic.

Reality was on some other planet and she was protected from the harshness of it because she was floating in a pool of paradise set at the perfect temperature.

She'd never been out of her mind before but all her reason had been totally submerged. Now she kept her eyes closed as she glided on that warm tide of completion. Every muscle in her body had gone on strike anyway. She couldn't talk, couldn't open her eyes, would never move again.

He lay a few inches away alongside her, having eased her onto the sheets a while ago. She didn't know how long—time was something she couldn't hope to figure out.

His fingers loosely clasped her wrist and that small connection was just enough. Anything more would be too much, but it seemed he understood that. It seemed he understood a lot.

But he wasn't gloating, wasn't lying on his back and beating his chest like a victorious he-man. And he

had every right to do that if he wanted. She wouldn't
even mind if he did, she couldn't, because she was
so completely relaxed. Actually, she was absolutely
exhausted.

But that was okay, because she didn't want to think,
to talk, to see. In this moment, she just wanted to be.

Carter really wanted to pull her close, but he suspected
she might be feeling super-sensitive right now and he
didn't want to overload her system—or freak her out
emotionally. Taking it easy was the only way to go. So
he fought the instinct to cradle; instead he watched her
quietly, waiting for some sign of life. For her conscious
reaction.

He already knew her unconscious one. He had his
fingers loose on her wrist. He could feel her pulse tripping every bit as fast as his own.

She couldn't fake that.

Sparks of satisfaction fired in his chest and her sudden
smile blew them to full-on flames. Because that smile
was full of warmth.

'Wow.' Her voice hardly sounded, but he read her
lips.

'Yeah.' He couldn't resist—reached out with his spare
hand to stroke her hair.

His arms ached even more to hold her. Usually he
hated post-coital cuddles—because usually he was too
hot and sweaty. And he was damn hot and sweaty now.
But he wanted to hold her, to keep the connection open
between them. Having her collapse in his arms like that
had filled him with the most pure pleasure of his life.
He didn't care about his own orgasm after that—only in
that instant it had hit and wiped him out.

But now he watched her eyes as the thoughts trickled back into her brain and she was too tired to hide the vulnerability as they darkened.

'I should go.'

He rolled onto his side, towards her, his muscles complaining at the movement. 'I'm only in town for another week. Don't think you're spending a minute of it alone.'

'You didn't say that earlier.' Her dark eyes darkened even more. 'I don't sleep well in a strange bed.'

'You slept okay with me by the pool last night.'

She had nothing to say to that. So he pressed home a point designed to lighten the scene.

'It'll make it easier to be near you at work knowing I'll have you with me all night.'

'Oh, you're back to that argument, are you?' She gave him the smile he'd been seeking.

'Yeah.' He chuckled. 'You'll just have to lie back and think of the company.'

'But I really should—'

'Have you honestly got the energy to get up, get dressed and get out of here right now?' he asked.

Silence for a second, then a very soft answer. 'No.'

'Then shut up and go to sleep.'

Her smile was drowsy and compliant and he switched off the light while he had the advantage. In the darkness he listened as her breathing regulated. He was shattered himself, but he couldn't stop thinking about the experience he'd just barely survived. Yeah, the most challenging moment of his life. He'd been holding back from firing from the moment he'd seen her naked, let alone finally been buried inside her.

She'd been out to claim him—she'd been all tease,

NATALIE ANDERSON 123

all sensual siren, twisting him hard to force his release, not hers. Now he knew why she liked the light on. She watched him as they moved—noting his reactions and adjusting her movements accordingly. Thinking too much—and all about him. On the one hand she was working out what he liked, and that was great. But not to the extent that she wasn't getting lost in the moment. She was too focused to be feeling it. Like her work, she was determined to be perfect at it. The best. Most guys would lie back and let her, loving it.

And, oh, he had loved it. She'd driven him insane with want for her. But he'd wanted more than that. He'd wanted her to surrender to the exceptional. He'd wanted her to realise and accept this *was* exceptional. And holding back long enough for her to become overwhelmed by their magic had almost broken him. Now he wanted an hour or so to pass quickly so he could recover even a bit of his energy. Because, although he was utterly drained, he couldn't wait to do it all again.

Asleep by the pool last night, she'd curled into his embrace so easily, as if it were the most natural thing in the world. As if it were home. And honestly, he'd enjoyed it. He'd thought that was because they'd both been cold. But he wasn't cold now and he wanted to sleep like that with her in this big, comfortable bed. So he flicked another switch—the air conditioner—cooling the room enough for them to need a light sheet for cover. And for her to want a warm body to curve into.

CHAPTER EIGHT

YAWNING, Penny opened the fridge, her eyes widening when she clocked the contents. 'I wouldn't have picked you to be so into yoghurt.'

'I'm not.' He reached past her for the milk. 'But you said you like it, only I didn't know which sort so I got one of everything.'

He wasn't kidding. There was an entire shelf crammed full of yoghurt cartons.

'I've got cinnamon and there's a ton of fruit in the bowl,' he added. 'Although I got tinned as well, just in case.'

When had he gotten all that exactly? She'd only told him her breakfast choices yesterday by the pool—he must have gotten them in before getting back to work after they'd finally escaped the place. That was efficient. And it deserved a reward.

She leaned closer to where he stood at the bench. 'What do you like for breakfast?'

He swept his arm around her waist and planted a kiss on her smiling mouth. 'You, sunny side up.'

Yeah, she liked that too. She'd woken swaddled in his arms again and the runny honey, so-relaxed-she-could-hardly-stand feeling was still with her. 'You need something more to sustain you.'

'Toast. Eggs. Fruit. Cereal. Breakfast's a big deal for me, especially on the weekend.' His brows pulled together. 'You know I have to work through.'

'I'd figured that already.' She smiled.

'But I have to have your assistance.' Both hands on her waist now, he hoisted her up to sit on the bench.

'Well, Mason did instruct me to do whatever you needed me to do,' she said, giving him a less than demure look from under her lashes.

'Excellent.' His hands wandered more freely. 'Then you're staying right here.'

It was two hours later that Carter sighed and slid out of the bed they'd tumbled back into. 'Come on, we have to go to the office for a few hours.'

Her cherry lips pouted irresistibly.

'I'll get you a coffee from the café on the way,' he said to sweeten the deal.

But it felt like hours later and Carter was sprawled back on the bed still waiting—fully dressed and ready to go. Penny could shower for all eternity, testing his patience even more than when he had sex with her. But then she made up for it by dressing in front of him. She was super quick then and he wouldn't have minded if she'd taken longer...so he avidly watched her every movement. He'd never have guessed that her perfect appearance would take only minutes to achieve. Her well-practised fingers twisted her hair into a plait. He reached across and undid it—earning a filthy look—but it was worth it to watch her weave it again. She had the most beautiful long neck and shoulders.

He drove the rental car he'd picked up at the airport

and ignored 'til now, detouring to her flat on the way so she could pick up some clothes. He insisted on enough for the week and to his immense satisfaction she didn't argue. He glanced round her shoebox while she expertly packed a small case. He looked at the few tiny knick-knacks she'd gathered on her travels. It seemed everything was small enough to fit into a couple of suitcases. Hell, the whole apartment could fit in a suitcase. It didn't surprise him that she lived alone, but he was disappointed not to discover anything much more about her from her few possessions. An ebook reader lay on the arm of the sofa. His fingers itched to flip it open so he could check out the titles she'd loaded.

After he'd stowed her bag in the boot, they stopped at the café just down from the office. He didn't want to take away, gave the excuse that he didn't want to face all those files again just yet, but really he just wanted to relax and hang with her some more. It was peaceful. They split the papers and he skimmed headlines, glancing at her as she concentrated on the articles that really caught her interest—in the international affairs section mostly. He asked and she talked through the list of places she'd lived in. He refused to believe her so she proved it by telling him who was prime minister or president in every one of those countries. Mind you, she could have made a couple of them up and he wouldn't have known. But she spoke bits of a billion languages and was totally animated when she talked about the highlights of each place.

It was almost another two hours and another coffee before they moved on. He picked up the little paper crane she'd made out of the receipt and pocketed it before she noticed.

In the office he had to force himself to pay attention.

But every few minutes his mind slipped to the sensual. He'd woken her through the night, warming her up again. He'd let her set the pace—initially—forcing his patience to extremes so she got so involved there was no pulling back, getting her used to letting go. She was starting to get a little faster already—turning easily into his arms, trusting him with her body. But not quite enough.

He wanted to please her all kinds of ways. He wanted her to trust him to do anything—and for her to enjoy it. She still tried to give more than she took, which was as wonderful as it was difficult. But he was determined to get her to the point of just lying back and letting him make love to her. Of becoming the pure hedonist he knew she could be.

As he had less than a week, he had to go for the intensive approach. Not that he had a problem with that either. He was having a ball thinking hard about ways to tease her into total submission. The trick was taking his time over the stimulation. Not too much, too soon. And maybe he needed to take her where she was at ease the most—on the dance floor or in the water. He liked the water idea. She spent hours in the shower. Uh-huh, he had some serious shower fantasies going.

Back at his apartment that night he cooked a stir-fry as fast as possible so he could focus on her. They hit a bar and club for a while but before long went home and continued their own dance party. She wouldn't let him put the jazz back on, instead she let him in on her favourite radio station—some Czech thing she listened to over the Internet. He'd never have imagined that having sex with Euro-techno blaring in the background would be such an amazing experience.

* * *

Early Sunday, Penny walked with him down to the craft and produce market that burst into being this time each week in the local primary school grounds.

Carter swung the bag. 'Free-range eggs and fresh strawberries—I'm happy.'

She was happy too, but not for those two reasons.

'There are some amazing markets in Melbourne,' he said. 'You ever been there?'

She shook her head.

'You've been to all these other capitals of culture and not Melbourne?' He looked disapproving.

She hadn't gotten there yet and she wouldn't ever live there now. When this week was over she didn't want to see him again. He would become the perfect memory. That was all this could ever be.

To stop suddenly melancholic thoughts sweeping in, she paid more attention to the products on display— organic honey, bespoke tailoring, spices, sausages, pottery, glass, jewellery... She lingered over them, tasting the samples, touching the smoothness of the craftsmanship.

'Perfect for Nick,' Carter called from a couple of stalls away. He waved a bright-coloured, hand-crafted wooden jigsaw puzzle at her. 'Help him learn his numbers.'

'But he's how old?' she teased, walking over to join him.

'Eight months,' Carter answered, unabashed. 'It's never too soon to start working on numbers. He's got to be groomed to take over the business.'

'Thus speaks the accountant.' Had he been groomed from birth too? 'Look.' She pointed out another puzzle that had six circles, the parts cut like pizzas. 'Get him that and he can get to grips with fractions before he's one.' She held it up as if it was the best invention ever.

'Oh, good idea.' Carter took it off her.

'You're not serious.'

Actually it appeared he was.

She shook her head. 'What about this one—this is much more cool.' Like a globe, a fanciful underwater scene with sharks and whales, seahorse, octopus, glitter and fake pearls.

He screwed up his nose. 'Bit girly, isn't it?' Then he shot her a look and winked. 'Okay, that's three.' He gathered them together and then glanced at her, a sheepish smile softening his face to irresistibly boyish. 'Am I going over the top?'

'No.'

'You're right.' Carter reached into his wallet and handed money to the stallholder. 'He's going to love them.'

Penny couldn't help but wonder what Nick looked like—was he a mini-Carter? Did he have his big brother's amazing multi-coloured eyes? She hoped so. She'd love a baby with big blue-green eyes and a cheeky smile. She'd sit her on her knee and pull faces to make her giggle.

Oh, hell, here she was so swamped by warm fuzzies from all the fabulous sex, she was having fantasies about what their babies would look like. She was pathetic.

She never wanted to have children. And Carter most certainly didn't want any.

What he wanted was a week's fling, nothing more. Nor did she. And that was all this was. Okay, so he'd made her feel everything she'd never before felt. But now she'd learned to let go, she would with other lovers, right?

She closed her eyes against the sudden sting of tears and her uncontrollable spasm of revulsion.

She didn't want another man ever to touch her. She only wanted Carter. And she wanted him again now—already addicted to the highs he gave. She felt so good with him. Except that was all this really was—he was the ultimate good-time guy, filled with fun and sun and laughter. He looked carefree in his casual clothes, his red tee shirt as cheerful as his demeanour.

She didn't want him to be so free and easy. It wasn't fair. She wanted him to want her with the same kind of underlying desperation she felt for him. The desperation she was trying to bury deep and deny.

But she had the compelling urge to push him into a glorious loss of control. Because even though she knew they shared the most amazing sex, it was she who lost it first. He always hung on until she was truly satisfied. And while he was the only lover ever to have been able to do that for her, part of her didn't like it. It made her feel like the weaker link. She knew that didn't really matter—this wasn't going past the one week. She wished she could shatter him just once.

But she was the one falling apart.

She tugged on his hand and turned to face him. 'Kiss me.'

Carter looked at her. He could feel the tremors running under her skin. What had happened in the last sixty seconds to make her so edgy?

'I thought you didn't like lust in public?' he teased to joke a smile out of her.

'Just kiss me,' she said.

And how could any man resist a sultry command like that? Carter pulled hard on her hair so her head tilted back. He kissed down the column of her exposed throat. With his other hand he pushed her pelvis, grinding it into his.

He stepped back pulling her into the shadows behind a row of stalls. Truthfully he didn't do public displays much—and certainly not of unbridled lust like this. But the moment he touched her he was lost. Uncaring about what anyone thought, he just had to hold her closer and let the glory wash through him.

'You are amazing.' Breathing hard and deep, she looked at him, her black eyes shining. Suddenly she smiled. 'You make me feel so good.'

His skin prickled. Okay, that was nice because he did aim to please, but it wasn't just the kissing that made him feel good. Fact was, he felt good every moment he spent with her.

After the market it was back to the office for a long afternoon that Penny struggled through every second of. Baby images kept popping in her head. Cute Carter-as-a-kid imaginings. So stupid.

When they finally returned to his apartment he went fussing in the kitchen, so Penny swam in the pool—needing twenty minutes alone to sort out her head. But a zillion lengths didn't really help so she went back up-stairs. Something smelt good and Carter was busy on his computer. She didn't think he even noticed when she walked past on her way to shower. So much for the revitalising benefits of exercise—all she felt was even more tired and emotional. She wanted to fall into his arms again and let him take her to paradise. She wanted him to hold her and never let go.

It was the sex. Her weak woman's body wanted to

wrap around his and absorb his strength. But he was mentally miles away in an office in Melbourne controlling his companies. So she could control merely herself, couldn't she? She flicked on the lights in the big bathroom and twisted the shower on. She stood under the streaming jet and let the water pummel the tension in her shoulders.

'Is it okay if I join you?' His erection pointed to the sky, already condom sheathed.

Her bones dissolved, she leant against the wall, wanting to cling to him and just hang on for the ride. His face lit up, his low laugh rumbled and he flashed a victorious smile.

She closed her eyes because his all-male beauty was too much to witness. But when she opened them again, everything was still black. The room was totally dark.

'Carter?' she asked quickly. 'What happened?'

'Bulb must have blown.' He stepped into the wet space with her.

She slid her palms all over his chest, loving it as the water made him slick. It was like discovering him all over again only by touch this time, not sight. Somehow it seemed more intimate, more intense. He pulled her close and kissed her. Oh, she loved those kisses. She loved the way he twisted her hair into a rope and wound it against his wrist—pulling it back, exposing her throat to his hot mouth. And then he went lower.

She gasped and pressed back against the cool wet tiles as he licked down her torso. His hands cupped her breasts, lifting them first to the water, and then to his tongue. She shuddered, the sensations excruciatingly sublime.

In the velvety darkness all she could do was soak up

his caresses and listen to the falling water. As he gently, rhythmically tugged on each nipple with his lips, her knees gave out. He grasped her waist, easing her to the floor and following, kept doing those, oh, so wickedly delicious things with his tongue and hands.

Blind to everything but sensation, she groaned and his kisses went even lower. She reached, finding his broad shoulders with her hands and sweeping across them, loving the smooth hot skin and the hot water raining on them.

She arched up, unable to stop her response to the wide, wet touches, hardly aware of who she was any more. His hand splayed on her lower back, pushing her closer to his hungry mouth. The other he used to test her, torment her, tease her. Just one finger at first, smoothly entering her slick heat. She gasped, but his tongue kept stroking, and then she was blind to everything except how it felt. She moved uncontrollably, rocking to meet him. Panting, she shuddered as he plunged deeper, and withdrew only to return with more. She was so sensitive to the way he toyed with her, and in the dark, wet heat all she could do was *feel*. Her fingers, thighs, sex pulsed and gripped as all she felt was pure lightning-bright pleasure. The orgasm knifed through her—ripping her to exquisitely satisfied shreds. She totally lost her mind.

His muscles bunched and rippled beneath her clutching hands. Displaying a scary kind of strength, he scooped her up again and flattened her against the wet wall. His hands cupped her, spreading her so he could thrust straight in. She wound her legs around his waist and had no hope of controlling anything. Not her instinctive rhythm, her screams, her next orgasm. Not when he held her and kissed her and claimed her so completely.

The water ran down them as they leaned together, taking for ever for their breath to ease.

'Are you okay?' he finally spoke. 'That wasn't too uncomfortable?'

She mock-punched his arm. 'Carter.'

He started to laugh. And then she laughed too.

'You sure you didn't mind?' His laugh became a groan as he carefully curved his hands around her hips.

How could she mind that? 'Give me half an hour and then do it again, will you?'

'You don't need half an hour.' He swung her into his arms and carried her back to his bed. And made love to every inch of her all over again.

Monday morning she couldn't move. Wouldn't. Point blank refused to let the weekend be over. She screwed her eyes shut when he appeared by the bed dressed in one of his killer suits. 'Don't ask me to get up yet. Please.'

She just wanted to snuggle in the sheets and enjoy absolute physical abandonment. He was perfect. He was playful. He wasn't ever going to ask anything more of her. And now he was fresh from the shower.

All she could let herself think about was this. She buried herself in his sensuality, blinding herself to everything else that was so attractive about him. Ignoring the ways in which they were so compatible.

But the humour she couldn't avoid—not when he brought it into bed with them.

He tugged the sheet from her body; she stretched and squealed with the pleasure-pain of well-worn muscles. She really didn't want to get up yet. But then he unzipped his trousers. Delighted, she scrunched a little deeper into the mattress.

'Oh, my,' she murmured as he straddled her. 'You want me to set a personal record or something?'

'Well, it's like anything—the more practice you have, the better you get.'

'Then hurry up and practise with me.' Oh, she was so into it now—utterly free in the physical play with him.

His brows lifted.

'Come on,' she begged. 'You'll have me hit orgasm just from thinking about it soon.' Just from thinking about *him*.

'You're complaining?'

'No,' she giggled as he nuzzled down her stomach like a playful lion.

Suddenly he stopped and looked up her body into her eyes. 'Seriously, though, you're not too sore?'

She arched, brazenly lifting her hips to him. 'Don't you dare stop!'

Monday sucked. Monday meant other people were in the office—meaning he couldn't go and kiss her freely. So Carter locked himself in his office and ploughed on with the tedious task of hunting for tiny financial irregularities. He didn't move from his desk for hours—just to prove to himself that he could concentrate for that long. Because all he really wanted to do was hang out by Penny's desk and talk to her. He wanted to spend every minute with her, resenting the job he had to do, even though it was because of the job that he'd met her in the first place.

Tuesday sucked just as much—another night had gone and the ones remaining felt too few. Stupid. Because he'd achieved his aim—she was wholly his and he had the rest of the week to indulge and that should totally be enough.

And now he'd just found the needle in the haystack. He carefully pulled it out to inspect it—drawing with it the thread that could unravel the whole company. Once he'd followed the poison all the way to the source, and gathered the documentation, his job was done.

Success all round.

He could go back to his own business, in another city, and get on with it. So he didn't need to feel this rubbish.

Wednesday he was even more grumpy, the evidence was almost complete, but Penny was out and he wanted her to hurry up and get back so they could go to lunch. He went up to her office to see if she was back. There was someone there, but it wasn't Penny. It was her brother.

'Hi, Matt.' Carter held out his hand. 'Penny's not here. She's taken some stuff to Mason. She shouldn't be more than another half-hour.'

'Oh.' The younger man shifted on his feet. 'I can't wait. I have to get to the airport.'

'She'll be sorry she missed you.' Man, her family was awful at communication. This past fortnight he'd been away, Carter and his dad had Skyped a couple of times, and he'd been sent the latest picture of Nick looking cute. There were no excuses in the technology age. But Matt looked so disappointed, Carter felt bad for him. 'I'll walk out with you.' He led him back to the lift. 'Conference was good?'

'Yeah.' Matt smiled but looked distracted.

'You want a taxi called?' Carter blinked as they got out in the broad sunshine.

Matt didn't answer, still looked both disappointed

and distracted. 'You'll take care of her, won't you?' he suddenly said. 'She needs lots of support. She's been cut off for so long.'

Yeah, that was pretty obvious. Carter waited. Because Matt looked as if he had something on his mind he wanted to share. And it didn't look like happy thoughts.

'She hasn't been back home since she went away. Not once. That's seven years.' Matt stared across the street. 'Mum and Dad are desperate for her to. Maybe she'd come with you.'

'I'll talk to her about it.' That and a few other things. Carter wanted to know so much more. Like everything.

'I know I shouldn't have mentioned Isabelle. But I wanted to see what would happen.'

Carter knew he was in murky waters without any floatation device, so he just nodded and waited. Fortunately Matt soon filled the gap.

'I saw you taking care of that.'

Carter faked a small smile. He supposed kissing her was one way of taking care. Pretty basic but it had been effective at the time.

'I didn't think she was ever going to get over Dan and get that close to another guy,' Matt continued. 'When she started mentioning you in emails I couldn't believe it. For a while I thought she might have been making you up. But you're real. And I can see how it is between you.'

Carter's brain processed even faster than its usual warp-factor speed. Dan? Who the hell was Dan? Hadn't they been talking about someone called Isabelle?

'She looks better. She looks fitter than she did when I saw her in Tokyo last year,' Matt added. 'You're obviously good for her.'

Anger flared in Carter's chest. What did it matter if she looked fit? Maybe this was why she didn't want to see her family—were they too obsessed with a perfect image? Who cared if she put on a few extra pounds or didn't swim her lengths so religiously? He sure as hell didn't. He just liked her laughing. So he answered roughly. 'She likes my cooking.'

'After he died she never used to eat with us.' Matt shook his head. 'Those last months it was like she wasn't there. She didn't want to be. She got so skinny you could see every vertebra in her spine. Every rib. Every bloody bone.'

The bottom fell out of Carter's world completely. He couldn't speak at all now. He stared at Matt, replaying the words, reading the tension etched on the younger guy's face.

'But she seems really happy now.' Matt cleared his throat and kept staring hard at some building over the road. 'I want her to stay that way.'

Was that why Matt had looked so pleased to see her eating that chocolate mousse? Because Penny had once been so sad she'd starved herself sick? Tension tightened every muscle. Carter folded his arms across his chest to hide his fists.

'She's not going to move again, is she? She's settled, with you, right?'

Carter's brain was still rushing and he didn't know how he could possibly reply to that.

'Because it's coming up to moving time for her but she's not going to now, right?' Matt turned sharply to look at him.

Carter put his hand on Matt's shoulder—to shut him

up as much as anything. 'Don't worry.' He avoided answering the question directly. 'I'll take care of her.'

'Yeah,' Matt croaked. 'Thanks for caring about her.'

Matt was avoiding his eyes again now and Carter was glad because he wouldn't have been able to hide his total confusion.

'I better get going.'

Carter fumbled in his pocket and pulled out a business card. 'Stay in touch.'

Matt handed him his too. Carter pocketed it and got back into the building as fast as he could. Then he took the stairs—slowly.

Dan. Who the hell was Dan?

Some guy who had died. And Matt hadn't thought Penny would get close to another guy again. Penny, who hadn't been home since…

Seven years ago she'd have been seventeen or eighteen. It didn't take much to work it out. While he'd yet to figure Isabelle's place in the picture, the essentials were obvious.

Dan must have been Penny's first love—and hadn't she once said the first left a real mark? That it was never just sex? Carter felt sick, hated thinking that Penny had suffered something bad.

He'd never felt that kind of heartbreak. He'd been betrayed—but that had meant more burnt pride than a seriously minced-up heart. And since then he hadn't let another woman close enough to inflict any serious damage. But to love someone so deeply and lose them, especially at such a young age? Yeah, that changed people. That really hurt people.

And weirdly, right now, Carter felt hurt she'd held back

that information from him. Which was dumb, because it wasn't as if they'd set out for anything more meaningful than some fun.

But he knew how bereavement could affect people. Hadn't he seen it in his dad? His parents had been soul mates, so happy until the cancer stole his mum away decades too soon. And his father hadn't coped—couldn't bear to be alone—walking from one wrong relationship to the next. Searching, searching, searching for the same bliss. And every time failing because nothing could live up to that ideal.

For the first time he felt a modicum of sympathy for his father's subsequent wives. Imagine always knowing they came in second. They could never compete with that golden memory. But Lucinda was trying, wasn't she? Giving Carter's dad the one thing he'd wanted so badly— more family. And sticking with him now for years longer than Carter had ever thought she would—providing the sense of home and security that had been gone so long. Carter's respect for her proliferated just like that.

Then his attention lurched back to Penny. Questions just kept coming faster and faster, falling over themselves and piling into a heap of confusion in his head. He wanted to know everything. He wanted to understand it all.

But he didn't want to have to ask her—to hear her prevaricate, or dismiss, or, worse, lie. He wanted her to tell him the truth. He wanted her to trust him enough to do that. The hurt feeling in his chest deepened. Somehow he didn't think that was going to happen in a hurry.

He knew it was wrong. But he was a details man and he'd get as many as he could, however he could, because he was low on advantage points. In the office he opened the filing cabinet and pulled her personnel file. Her being a temp, there wasn't much—just a copy of her CV, security clearance and the references from the agency. Brilliant ones. But it was the CV that he focused on. The list of jobs was almost a mile long. And so were the towns. She'd been serious about her travelling. She'd moved at almost exactly the same time each year. Britain, Spain, Czech Republic, Greece, Japan, Australia.

The regularity with which she'd moved made his blood run cold. Never more than a year in the one town. He looked on the front of the file that recorded the date she'd started at Nicholls—seven months already. But she'd worked at another temp job in the city for four months before that. So her year in Sydney was almost up. When that time ticked over would she move to another place? If so, where? There seemed to be no pattern to the destinations. She just moved, running away—from something big.

Had her heart been that broken? His own thudded painfully because there was someone in her past whose death had cut her up so badly. Who'd put her off relationships—so far for life. She acted as if she wanted fun but she could hardly let herself have it—not really. She wasn't the brazen huntress he'd first thought. Not selfish or self-centred. Certainly not any kind of free spirit. She worked conscientiously—and she cared. She was a generous giver who struggled to accept the same when it was offered in return. And hadn't he seen it those few times—the vulnerability and loneliness in her eyes?

She was hiding from something even she couldn't admit to.

He flicked through the CV again and another little fact caught him. She'd been Head Girl at her school? He half laughed. No wonder she'd been interested when he'd mentioned he was Head Boy. And she'd said nothing, secretive wench. He looked closer. Her grades were stellar. Really stellar. He frowned—why hadn't she gone to university? She would have had her pick of colleges and courses with grades like those. But she'd gone overseas as soon as school had finished and she hadn't been back. She must have been devastated. And for all the party-girl, clubbing life she lived now, she obviously still was.

His upset deepened. He hated that she covered up so much. He liked her. He wanted to know she was okay. He wanted to be her friend. He actually wanted *more*.

Well. That was new.

He'd never met a woman who held back her emotions the way she did. Okay, he'd freed her from one aspect of that control. Maybe he could cut her loose from another? Even if he suspected it was going to hurt him to try. Could he bear to know the extent to which she'd loved that guy?

Pathetic as it was, he was jealous. She'd cared so much for Dan she'd been devastated. Carter wanted her to care about him instead.

But how could he ever compete with the perfect first love? He winced even as he thought that thought. He didn't have to. He didn't want her so totally like that— did he? Did he really want to be the one and only, the number one man in her life?

No. Surely not.

But in a scarily short amount of time she'd become important to him. Her happiness had become important to him. And he wanted her to trust him enough to talk. Sure she'd opened up sexually—but it was the only way she'd opened up. And in some ways it was another shield in itself. Just a fling—it was the defence he'd used for years himself, even with Penny to begin with. And hadn't it turned around to bite him now? He'd never been in a situation so confusing, so complicated. An adulterous older woman and a manipulative girlfriend seeking an engagement ring had nothing on Penny and her inability to share. Hell, she must have such fear.

His anger deepened because he wanted her to be over it and feel free to fall in love again. Preferably with him.

In the evening at his apartment she was the same smiling flirt, teasing him, talking it up—the banter that, while fun, didn't go deep. He had to bite the inside of his lips, bursting inside to ask her what had happened. Desperate to know where her heart was at now. But he wanted her to offer it, not to have to force it.

She let him lie between her legs, all warm and impishly malleable, smiling at him delightfully. It wasn't enough.

He kissed her tenderly. As if she were one of the fragile flowers she said she didn't like.

'Don't.' She frowned and swept her hands across his back. He knew she was trying to hurry him.

'Don't what?'

'Be so nice.'

He carefully studied her. 'You think you don't deserve someone being nice to you?'

She just closed her eyes.

And then he didn't even pretend to let her take the lead. He dominated. Intensely focused on making love to her. It was about more than just giving her pleasure, but about bringing her closer to him any way he could.

Afterwards he lay holding her sealed to him, refusing

to let her wriggle even an inch away, telling her more about his work in Melbourne. Stupid stories about his youth. Trying to grow the connection between them. To build trust. Blindly hoping she might talk back.

But all she did was listen.

CHAPTER NINE

CARTER took a taxi to Mason. He had the files; the job was done. In theory, after this meeting, he was free to fly out. But he couldn't bring himself to book a ticket.

The old man had aged more in the last week than he had in the last ten years. Guilt squeezed Carter—he should have been to see him sooner. But Penny had been making daily visits with paperwork and sundry items. Even so.

'I've got the information you need.' He dragged out a smile and put the small packet of printouts on the dining table. 'It's all there. Once spotted, the pattern is pretty obvious.'

'I knew I could rely on you.' Mason sank heavily into his favourite chair.

'Get in your auditors. It won't take much to sort it out.'

'He'll have to be prosecuted.'

'Yes.' Carter nodded. 'But I think the impact will be minimal because we caught him.' He tried to put the best spin on it. 'And quickly too. If anything the investors should be impressed at the efficiency of your system checks.'

'It was instinct, Carter.' Mason shook his head. 'Just a feeling.'

'Well, you've always had good instincts, Mason.'

'And now my instinct is telling me I've failed.'

'In what way?' Surprised, Carter nearly spilt the coffee he was pouring.

'That company is my life.' Mason stared past him to the big painting on the wall. 'And in the current climate it could have been swept away so quickly if this had got out of hand. It makes me wonder what's going to be left after I'm gone. It'll probably be bought out, the name will go. It'll be finished.'

Carter inhaled deeply. Mason had long been his mentor. He'd admired the dedication, the drive, the single-minded chase for success. And there had been huge success. 'You've already built an amazing legacy, Mason.'

Mason lifted his arms. 'What is there? A house? A few paintings that will be auctioned off? Where are the memories? Where's the warmth?'

The unease in Carter's chest grew. Mason's wife had died early on in their marriage—before they'd had time to have kids. And Mason had buried his heart alongside her. As far as Carter was aware there hadn't been another woman—totally unlike his father. Until now Carter had always respected Mason more for that. But now he wasn't so sure—not when he was confronted with Mason's obvious regrets. And loneliness. Another lonely person. 'You've given so much to charity, Mason. You've helped so many people.'

'Who have their own lives and families.' Mason sighed. 'I shouldn't have been such a coward. I should have tried to meet someone else. But I just worked instead.'

'And you've done great work. You've employed lots of people, you helped lots of people.' That was a massive achievement.

But personally fulfilling? Yes and no.

'How's Nick?' Mason asked.

Carter's grin flashed before he even thought. 'He's a little dude.'

'Your father is a braver man than me. I regret not having a family. I regret devoting all my life to accumu-lating paper.'

'Hey.' Carter leaned forward and put his hand on Mason's arm. 'You have me.'

Mason said nothing for a bit, just stirred the milk in his coffee. Then he set the teaspoon to the side. 'Is everything else at the office okay?'

'Penny has it all under control.'

'Told you she was an angel.'

Carter winced through a deep sip of the burning-hot coffee. 'Yeah.'

A broken angel.

He sat back in his chair and settled in for the after-noon. He'd hang with Mason. He needed the time out to think.

Penny had been desperate for Carter to return from Mason's—he'd gone to hand over what tricks he'd found but he'd been gone for hours and, being a complete Carter addict, she was antsy with unfulfilled need. Resenting the waste of the precious few minutes she had left. Finally he showed up, just as she was about to pack up and go to her own flat and cry.

So she went to his apartment instead. She had no shame, no thought of saying no. They only had a night or two left, and she wanted every possible moment with him. Because she wasn't thinking of anything beyond the present moment. She couldn't let herself.

He was unusually quiet as they walked into the apartment building. Maybe it hadn't gone well.

'Was Mason okay?' She finally broke the silence.

His shoulders jerked dismissively. 'Pleased with getting the result.'

Okay. He didn't just look moody, he sounded it too. Once inside, he tossed the key on the table and turned to look at her.

Wow. She walked over to him—obeying the summons. She tiptoed up and kissed his jaw. Did he want her to take the lead this time?

It seemed so. She kissed him full on the mouth—teasing his lips with her teeth and tongue. His eyes closed and she heard his tortured groan. It thrilled her—maybe this was her chance to make him shatter. Was he tired and needy and impatient? The thought excited her completely because she ached for him to want her so badly he lost all his finesse. Quickly she fought to free him from his clothes. Oh, yes, he wanted her—she could feel the heat burning through him. But his hands lifted and caught hers, stopping her from stroking him.

'Matt called by the office yesterday.' He all but shouted in her ear.

She pulled back to look at him. 'He did?'

'Passing by on his way to the airport.'

'Oh.' She was sorry she'd missed him. She had to do better at staying in touch. She'd text him later.

'We had a little chat.'

'Did you?' Little goose bumps rose on her skin—because Carter's expression had gone scarily stony.

'He said you're looking better than when he saw you in Tokyo. And way better than you did years ago.'

She blanched at the bitter tone in his voice.

'You've put weight on, Penny. Not taken it off.'

'Oh, don't, Carter.' She turned away from him.

'What, speak the truth?' He laughed roughly. 'Penny, what on earth is going on?'

'Nothing.'

'You lied to me. You said you were overweight as a teenager. But you weren't, you were a walking skeleton.'

'Does this really matter?'

'Yes, it does.'

'Why?'

'You've been using me this whole time to get off. To hide from whatever nightmares it is that you have.'

And what was so wrong with that? It wasn't as if he'd been offering anything more. 'I thought the whole point of this was for us to get off.'

'Yeah, well, if it's only orgasms you want, Penny, get yourself a vibrator.'

Oh, that made her mad. She turned back, found him less than an inch away—so ran her hand down his chest.

He jerked back. 'I'm not interested in being your sex toy.'

'Really?' She reached forward and cupped his erection. 'Maybe you'd better tell your penis that.'

'I can control it.' He stepped away. 'If you want to get off, why not go find someone else? Any of those analysts in the office will stand for you. Hell, you could have all of them at once if you want.'

She flinched. She didn't want another lover. None. Ever.

'I'm not interested in being your man whore,' he snarled. 'I actually have more self-respect than that.'

'What are you interested in, then?' she said, stung to anger by his sudden rejection. 'You were the one looking at me like that.'

'Like what?'

'You know what,' she snapped. 'All simmering sex.'

He just laughed—bitterly.

That pissed her off even more. She pushed back into his space. 'You were stripping me with your eyes and you know it.'

'And you were loving it.'

'So what the hell do you want?' Why was he going septic on her when they wanted the same thing?

'I want the *real* thing—if you even know what that is. Because maybe you've been faking all along? You said yourself you usually do. How would I know? You're so damn good at lying and holding back.'

She gaped for a stunned second. 'You think I was faking?' Now she was furious. And really hurt. She'd never felt like that with anyone, never let anyone...not like that.

He filled the room, his arms crossed, watching her with that wide bright gaze that revealed nothing but seemed to be searching through all her internal baggage.

'I *wasn't* faking.' Jerk. As if that kind of reaction happened every other day? She wouldn't have practically moved in with him and be making an idiot of herself lying back and letting him do anything, if she didn't feel as if it were something out of this world. And she wouldn't be so completely miserable about it being the end of the week if she hadn't been more than moved by him—in so many more ways than sexual. And she really didn't want to be getting upset about it this instant. But her eyes were stinging. Angrily she tried to push past him.

But his arms became iron bars that caught and brought her close against his body. 'I know you weren't.' He sighed. 'I'm sorry.'

'What is your problem?' she mumbled, completely confused now.

His hands smoothed down her back. His hardness softened her.

'I want to know where I stand with you,' he said. The gentle words stirred her hair.

'What do you mean?' She tilted her head back to read his expression and swallowed to settle her tense nerves. 'There's nowhere to stand. We're having a fling.'

'Not enough.'

Her heart thudded—beating caution now, rather than anger.

His gaze unwavering, he told her. 'I want more.'

How more? What more? Anything more was impossible. Tomorrow was Friday. They were almost at farewell point.

As his gaze locked hers the safe feeling she'd had all week started to slip. Why was he messing with the boundaries?

'You're leaving here…' Her breathing shortened. 'Like on Saturday. This was just for—'

'Fun,' he finished for her. 'Yeah, roger that. But we can still be friends, can't we?'

Friends? She didn't have that many of those. Plenty of acquaintances. But not very many friends. And what did friends mean—did he want this to go beyond the week? Because she couldn't do that—she had to keep this sealed in its short space of time. She *had* to keep those emotions sealed. She tried to step back but his hands tightened. She broke eye contact. 'I don't think we need to complicate this, Carter.'

'Talking won't make it complicated.'

He wanted to talk? About what?

'Can't you let me into your life just a little bit, Penny?'

'Will you put some clothes back on?' She couldn't think with him like this.

'Why?' he answered coolly. 'I'm not afraid to get naked with you, Penny. I'm willing to bare all.'

'Don't be ridiculous, Carter. This is a one-week fling.' She pushed away from him—and he let her. 'You don't want to talk any more than I do. Why waste that precious time?'

'When we could be rooting like rabbits?'

'You like it that way. It's what you've wanted from me from the moment we met.' She turned on him, hiding her fear with aggression. 'You're not interested in me opening up to you in any way other than physical.'

'Not true.'

'Totally true. As far are you're concerned all women are manipulative, conniving cows who're trying to trap men into marriage.'

'Many of the women I've met are.'

'Well, I'm not like them.'

'And that's one thing we will agree on.'

She blinked. Then shook her head. This conversation was going surreal. Why was her ultimate playboy going serious? 'Trust me, you don't want to get to know anything more about me, Carter.'

'Yes I do.'

Why? What had happened to turn him into Mr Sensitive? She wanted him back as Mr Sophisticated—and never-let-a-woman-stick smooth. 'You know, from the moment we met you thought the worst of me,' she provoked. 'I was a thief, I was "pulling favours" to get a good job...'

He actually coloured. 'I didn't really mean—'

'It must be so hard for you to swallow the fact that your thief is the most conservative *man* in the damn building.'

'Yeah, we both know I was wrong. I leapt to a couple of conclusions. You're nothing like what I first thought.'

She turned away from him. 'What if the truth was worse?'

'How worse?' He sounded surprised.

Way, way worse. But she shook her head and dodged it. 'You're as much of a commitment-phobe as I am. Can't we just have some fun, Carter? We've only got a night or two left.'

So many of the women in Carter's life had been total drama queens—living their lives from one big scene to the next, which they maximised as if they were the stars of their own reality TV shows.

Penny wasn't into big scenes at all, even though it appeared her life had had its share of real drama. She'd pared it down, trying to live as simply as possible—at least in terms of her relationships. Getting by on the bare minimum.

But she couldn't deny all of her needs all the time. She needed to be needed—hence her determination to be indispensable in any job she took on. She needed to care for someone—that came out in the way she tended to Mason. She needed physical contact—that came out in the way she sought Carter's body. But he wanted her to want more from him. More than just sex—even though that had been all he'd offered initially, now he wanted her to want it all. He'd always walked from any woman who wanted too much, so wasn't it ironic that, now he wanted to give it all, the woman in question was determined *not* to want it?

Perfectly happy in the past to provide nothing but pleasure, now he wanted to keep her fridge stocked, to make her salmon and salad, to watch her swim every night. He wanted her company, her quiet smiles, her interesting conversation, her compassion. He wanted his kitchen tinged with the scent of cinnamon. He wanted to travel the world with her, explore it the way she did—immersing in a different culture for a while, exploring the arts and politics and being interested. And damn it, there was even that newfound soft secret part of him that wanted to hold her, and to see her holding a tiny, sweet body. The thought of a baby with black-brown eyes and full cream skin made his arms ache.

He wanted everything with her. And he wanted her to have everything. She needed it and he yearned to give it to her—to make her smiles shadow free. To give her some kind of home. He, who'd been happy for so long in his inner-city apartment, was now thinking about a place with a private tennis court and swimming pool and space to play with her.

But he was in trouble. Because although she'd opened her body to him, he had a lot of work ahead of him to get anywhere near her heart.

Carter wasn't used to wanting things he might not be able to achieve. Carter wasn't used to failure. And the threat of failure made Carter angry.

He'd wanted her to tell him about Dan herself but she wasn't going to. The resulting frustration flared out of control. In desperation he wielded a sword, hoping to pierce through her armour to let whatever it was that festered deep inside her free, so she could heal.

He kissed her—hard, passionate and at great length. She wanted it. He could feel her shaking for it. And she thought she'd won—that she'd shut him up. At that moment he pulled back and hit her with it fast. So she'd be unprepared and unable to hide an honest response.

'I know about Dan.'

Her eyes went huge. Shimmering pits of inky black-ness. 'What?'

'I know about Dan,' he repeated and then followed up fast. His need to communicate almost making him stumble. 'I know you loved him. I know how much you loved him. I know your grief literally ate you up.'

'What?' Penny couldn't feel her body, and her thoughts were spinning. What had Carter just said?

'I know how hurt you are.'

'You don't know anything.' She walked out of his arms as a ghost walked through walls. No resistance, not feeling anything. She didn't know who he'd been talking to but it was obvious he hadn't got even half the story.

'You can't let losing him stop you from ever loving

anyone again,' Carter said passionately. 'You can't be lonely like this.'

'I'm not lonely.'

'You're crippled with loneliness. You're screaming for affection but you're too scared to admit it.'

She stared at him, utter horror rising in every cell. This couldn't be happening, he just couldn't be going there. He couldn't be asking her about that.

'Please tell me about it,' he asked. 'Let me help you.'

She couldn't bear to see the concern in his eyes. The compassion. The sincerity. He really didn't know anything.

Sick to her stomach, she turned away, pulling the halves of her blouse back together.

'Damn it, don't hide from me.' His volume upped. 'You promised to be honest with me, remember?'

'You really want honesty?' She swung back, stabbing the question.

He paused, his eyes widening in surprise.

She puffed out angrily. He had no idea he'd just taken the scab off the pus-filled hole in her soul. And spilling the poison would spoil their last days together. But there was no avoiding it, he'd pushed over a line she never let anyone past and one look at him told her he wasn't going to let it go.

'It wasn't grief killing my appetite, it was guilt.' The raw, ugly truth choked and burned her throat. 'I didn't love him. That's the whole point.'

Carter froze. Her breathing sped up even more. She hated him for what he was asking her to do. Thinking on this, remembering, speaking of it... It had been so long but it still crucified her heart. She tried to say it simply, quickly. So then she could go. Because then Carter would want her to.

'Dan was my best friend's twin.'

She could see him processing—quickly.

'Isabelle.'

She nodded and pushed on. 'We were neighbours. Born the same year, grew up together. Like triplets, you know? But when we were sixteen, Dan and I…grew close.' She ran her tongue across dry lips. 'It just happened. It was so easy. We were just kids…'

But there was no excusing what she'd done. She closed her eyes; she didn't want to see Carter's reaction. Her breathing quickened more; she couldn't seem to get enough air into her lungs to stop the spinning.

'Everything changed that last year at school. I changed. Isabelle changed.' Penny shook her head, trying to clear it. 'Dan didn't change—at least, not in the same direction.' She sighed. 'We were together a year or so, but I was bored. I had plans and they were different from his.'

Icy sweat slithered across her skin, her blood beat just as cold.

'He didn't want us to break up. He cried. I hadn't seen him cry in years. And do you know what I did?'

Beneath her closed lids, the tears stung. 'I giggled. I actually laughed at him.'

Looking back, it had been the reaction of a silly young girl taken by surprise by his extreme reaction. She hadn't realised he hadn't seen the end of them coming—that she'd shocked him. But she was the one who hadn't seen the most important signs of all—his distance, his depression, his desperation.

She flashed her eyes open and stared hard at Carter,

pushing through the last bit. 'Our orchard ran between our houses and was lined with these big tall trees.'

Her heart thundered as the memory took over her mind completely. 'He was more upset than I realised. The next morning when I got up I looked out the window. And he…and he…'

She couldn't finish. Couldn't express the horror of the shadow in the half-light that she'd seen from her bedroom. She felt the fear as she'd run down the stairs, the damp of the dew on her bare feet as she'd run, slipping, seeing the ladder lying on the grass.

Carter muttered something. She didn't hear what but all of a sudden his arms were around her as her lungs heaved. And this time she heard his horrible realisation.

'You found him.'

Hanging.

Penny raised her hands, trying to hide from the memory. The scream ripped out from the depths of her pain. She twisted, to run, but his arms tightened even more. His whole body pinned her back and pulled her down to the ground.

Her scream became a wail—a long cry of agony that she'd held for so long. The expression of a pain that never seemed to lessen—that just lay buried for days, weeks, months, years until something lifted the veil and let it out.

And now it reverberated around the room—the anguish piercing through walls, smashing through bones. Until Carter absorbed it, pulling her closer still, pressing her face into his chest. His hands smoothing down her hair and over her back as she sobbed.

She hated it. Hated him for making her say it. Hated remembering. Hated the guilt. Hated Dan for doing it.

Hated herself for not stopping him.

And for not being able to stop her meltdown now. She cried and cried and cried while Carter steadily rocked her. She hadn't been held like this in so, so long. Hadn't let anyone—but she couldn't pull away from him now.

She'd broken.

He bent his head, resting it on hers as he kept swaying them both gently even as her shudders began to ease. He said nothing—something she appreciated because there really was nothing to say. It had happened. It was a part of her. Nothing could make it better.

Nothing could make it go away. It would never be okay.

Finally she stilled. She closed her eyes and drew on the last drops of strength that she knew she had—for she was a survivor.

But in order to survive, she had to be alone.

She pushed out of his arms. She didn't want to look at him, her eyes hurt enough already.

'Talk to me,' he said softly.

'Why?' What was the point? She wiped her cheeks with the back of her hand, shaking her head as she did. 'You didn't sign up for this, Carter. You're going away. You don't want baggage and I come with a tonne. A million tonnes.'

Finally she glanced at him. He looked pale. She wasn't surprised. It was a hell of a lot to dump on anyone. And the last thing Carter wanted was complication—he'd made that more than clear right from the start.

And, yeah, he wasn't looking at her any more. All the pretence had gone. All the play had gone. He'd wanted her naked? Well, now she was stripped bare and what was left wasn't pretty.

Anger filled the void that the agony had drained. Why had he forced it? Why pry where he had no right to pry? This was a one-week fling, supposed to be fun, and he'd wrenched open her most private hell.

And for what? Where was the 'fun' to come from this?

'Penny…'

'Don't.' She didn't want his pity. She didn't want him thinking he had to be super-nice to her now because she had problems in her past.

'I want you to talk to me. I want to help you.'

She wasn't a cot-case who needed kid gloves and sympathy. That was second best to what she really wanted.

'No, you don't,' she struck out. 'You think you're so grown-up and mature with your sophisticated little flings. All so charming and satisfying. But you don't want to handle anything really grown up. You don't want emotional responsibility.'

'Penny—'

'And I don't want anything more from you either.' Her fury mounted, and she lied to cover the gaping hole inside. Her biggest lie ever. Desperately she wanted forgiveness and understanding and someone to love her despite all her mistakes.

For Carter to love her.

But he wanted to be her *friend*. And she couldn't accept that because there was that stupid, desperate part of her that wanted to crawl back in his arms and beg him to hold her, to want her, to love her. She couldn't do that to herself. The end hurt enough already and he'd feel awkward enough about easing away from her now. She had to escape to save him from her humiliation. Tears streamed again so she moved fast. Scrabbling to her feet, she literally sprinted.

'Penny!'

She heard a thud and a curse. But she kept running. Running was the only right answer.

For hours she walked the streets, trying to pull herself together.

Putting the memories back into the box was something she was used to. But putting away her feelings for Carter was harder. They were new and fragile and painful. Yeah, she strode out faster, she was as selfish as she'd been as a teen—wanting only what she wanted. Wanting everything for herself.

But she wasn't going to get it.

Determinedly she thought back over what she'd eaten that day. Not enough. She made herself buy a sandwich from a twenty-four-hour garage. Chewed every bite and swallowed even though it clogged her throat. She grabbed a bottle of juice and washed the lumps of bread down. She wasn't going to get sick again. She wasn't going to let heartbreak destroy her body or her mind. She'd get through this—after all, she'd gotten through worse.

She'd stay strong. She'd rebuild her life. She'd done it before and she'd do it again. Only the thought made her aches deepen. Always alone. She was tired of doing it alone. But she always would be alone—because she didn't deserve anything more.

She didn't deserve someone like Carter. Funny, intelligent, gorgeous Carter who could have any woman on a plate and who frankly liked the smorgasbord approach. Her eyes watered and it hurt because they were still sore from her earlier howling. Pathetic. What she needed was to pull herself together and move on. For there was no way she'd stay any longer in Sydney now. Her skin had been burnt from her body—leaving her raw and bloody and too hurt to bear any salt. And, with the memory of a few days of happiness it would hold for ever, Sydney was all salt.

CHAPTER TEN

CARTER was furious. And desperate. Penny had jumped up so fast, and he'd followed only to trip, having totally forgotten that his damn trousers were still round his ankles. In the three seconds it had taken to yank them back up, she'd vanished.

He went to her flat. She wasn't there.

He went to her work. She wasn't there.

He went to her favourite club. She wasn't there.

He went to every open-late café in the neighbourhood, and the neighbourhoods beyond. And then back to the beginning again.

She still wasn't anywhere.

He searched all damn night. But he couldn't find her. Nor could he think of what to say or do when he did. He was beside himself. So upset for her and mad with his stupidity. Hadn't he always said it—the details, it was always in the details.

He hadn't realised the absolute horror of the detail.

Poor Dan. Poor Penny. Poor everyone in their families.

How did anyone get over that? What could he say that could possibly make it better for her? There was nothing. He felt so useless. Right now he *was* useless.

No wonder she'd been worried about how he'd spoken to Aaron-the-flowers-man. No wonder she skated through life with only the occasional fling with a confident player. She was terrified of intimacy. And he didn't blame her.

And she was right, he hadn't signed up for this. He hated this kind of complication, hadn't ever wanted such soul-eating turmoil. He liked fun, uncomplicated. Not needy.

But it was too late. Way, way too late.

He had too much invested already. Like his whole heart.

And despite the way she constantly uprooted her life, she couldn't stop her real nature and needs emerging. She was the one who knew all about the security guard's family, she was the one running round mothering Mason. She couldn't stop herself caring about people. She couldn't stop forming relationships to some degree. But she couldn't accept anywhere near as well as she could give.

Yet surely, surely in her heart she wanted to. That perfect boyfriend she'd described in her emails wasn't the ideal she thought her family would want, it was her own secret ideal.

Yeah, it was there—all in the details. That was her projecting the innermost fantasy that she was too scared to ever try to make real. Well, he could make her laugh. He'd dine and dance with her and take her away on little trips every weekend. He'd be there for her. Always there. Companionship. Commitment. For ever and happy.

Yeah, maybe there wasn't anything he could *say* to make it better. But there was something he could do. He could offer her security. The emotional security and commitment he'd sworn never to offer anyone. For her possible happiness he'd cross all his boundaries. She needed security more than he needed freedom.

Anyway, he wasn't free any more. He was all hers.

He just had to get her to accept it. As he'd got her to accept taking physical pleasure from him, he'd help her accept the love she deserved.

Somehow. He just didn't know how the hell how.

As he drove round and round the streets he rifled through his pockets to find Matt's number. He didn't care about calling New Zealand at such an insane hour. He needed all the details he could get to win this one.

Penny rang Mason's doorbell, so glad he was having another day at home and she didn't have to go into the office. He opened the door and greeted her with a big smile. She tried so hard to return it but knew she failed. Nervously she followed him through to the lounge. But her fast-thumping heart seized when she saw someone was already sitting in there. Someone dishevelled in black jeans and tee with shaggy hair, stubble and hollow, burning eyes.

'Don't mind Carter.' Mason grinned, apparently oblivious to the tortured undercurrents. 'Is that for me?' He nodded at the envelope in her hand.

Penny couldn't take her eyes off Carter, but he had his eyes on the envelope.

She handed it to Mason, amazed she hadn't dropped it. It took only a moment for him to read it. Miserably, guiltily, she waited.

The stark disappointment in Mason's expression was nothing on the barren look of Carter's.

'I'm really sorry, Mason,' she choked out the inadequate apology.

'That's okay, Penny. I'm sure you have your reasons.'

He left the sentence open—not quite a question, but the hint of inquiry was there. She couldn't answer him. She didn't even blush—her blood was frozen.

'Well, you'll stay and have some tea?' Mason asked, now looking concerned.

'I'm sorry,' she said mechanically. 'I really have to go.'

'Right now?' Mason frowned.

'That's okay.' Carter stood, lightly touching Mason's shoulder as he walked past him. 'I'll walk you out, Penny.'

'You don't have to do this, you know,' he launched in as soon as the front door closed behind them. 'I'm leaving later. You can stay and carry on like normal.'

'It's got nothing to do with you,' she lied, devastated to hear he'd made his plans out of there. Even though she knew he would have.

His lips compressed. 'You're happy here, Penny.'

No, she'd been deluding herself. Pretending everything was fine. But he'd come along and ripped away the mirage and shown her just how unfulfilled she really was. It was all a sham.

So she'd go somewhere new and start over. Maybe try to stay there longer, work a little harder on settling. Because now she knew her current way of doing things wasn't really working. It was just a façade.

She knew she'd never forget what had happened between them, but she couldn't stay in Sydney and be faced with a daily reminder of how close she'd been to bliss. 'It's time for me to move on anyway.'

'So you're quitting? You're just going to run away?' Carter's composure started to crack. 'What about Mason? What about the company? You're just going to up and leave him in the lurch?'

'I'm just a temp, Carter.'

'You're not and you know you're not,' he said sharply. 'That old guy in there thinks the world of you. Jed thinks the world of you. All the guys think the world of you. I—' He broke off. 'Damn it, Penny. These people want you in their lives.'

'Give them a week and they'll have moved on.'

'While you'll be stuck in the same hell you've been in the last seven years.' He shook his head. 'You can't let what Dan did ruin the rest of your life.'

She wasn't going to. But she knew what she could and couldn't handle and she couldn't handle the responsibility of close relationships. It scared her too much. And it wasn't just what Dan had done—it was what she'd done.

'It was just as much me, Carter,' she said with painful, angry honesty. 'I was a spoilt, immature bitch who shredded his world. I was horrible to him.'

'He was high, Penny. You know they found drugs in his system. He was struggling with school, with sporting pressure, feeling left behind by your success. He had depression. You didn't know that at the time.'

Oh, he'd got the whole story now. He must have talked to Matt. And even though she knew those things were true, she still felt responsible—certain her actions had been the last straw for Dan's fragile state. 'But I should have known, shouldn't I? If I'd cared. Instead I lost patience. I told him he needed to man up. I was insensitive and selfish.' She admitted it all. 'It was my fault.'

'No.' Carter put heavy hands on her shoulders. 'You didn't kill him. That was a decision he made when he was out of his mind on pot and booze. He was sick.'

'And I should have helped him. Or found someone to help him. I should have told someone about the break-up.'

'There were many factors at play. What happened with you was only one of them.'

If only she'd told someone how badly Dan had reacted. If only she'd told Isabelle that he was really upset and to watch him. But she'd been too selfish to even think of it. She'd gone home feeling free—because he'd become a drain on her. But he'd gone home and decided which way to kill himself.

Even now, her self-centredness horrified her.

'Don't shut everybody out, Penny. Don't let two lives be ruined by one tragic teenage mistake.'

'I'm not shutting everybody out.' She tried to shrug him off. 'I like traveling, Carter. I'm happy.'

'Like hell you are.' His hands tightened.

'I want to go someplace new.' Doggedly she stuck to her line. It was her only option.

He drew breath, seeming to size her up. 'Okay, then I've got an option for you. Move to Melbourne. Move in with me.'

It was good he still had his hands on her—if it weren't for those digging fingertips, she might have fallen over. 'What?'

'Move to Melbourne with me.'

He couldn't possibly be serious. What on earth was he thinking?

'Penny, I've spent the last twelve hours out of my mind with worry for you. I don't want more of that.'

And there was her answer. He wasn't thinking. It was pity and responsibility he was feeling—and exhaustion. Not a real desire to be with her. He didn't love her. She couldn't possibly believe he did.

'I didn't mean to make you worry,' she said quietly. It was the last thing she'd wanted to do to him. That was the problem with her family too. She'd made them worry so much. That was why she tried to email home the breezy-life-is-easy vibe.

Only clearly she'd failed at that because Carter had been talking to Matt. And they'd conspired together to sort her out somehow. But she wasn't going to let compassion trick Carter into thinking he wanted to be with her. That was worse than anything his ex had deliberately tried to manipulate.

'I don't need you to rescue me, Carter,' she said softly.

'That's not what I'm trying to do.'

'Isn't it?'

'I want us to be together.'

'Well—' she took a deep breath '—I don't.'

'I know you're lying.' He leaned close. 'You want me to prove it to you?'

She stepped back. No, she did not want that. She couldn't bear it if he kissed her right now. She'd be ripped apart.

His smile flattened. 'What are you going to do, put us all on your occasional email list and send details of your fictional life?' His anger suddenly blew. 'The minute you feel yourself putting down roots, you wrench yourself away again. It's emotional suicide.'

She struck out—shoving him hard.

How dared he? How *dared* he say that to her?

'It *is*, Penny.' He squared up to her again. 'You're too scared to live a whole life.'

Her only defence was offence. 'And you're living a whole one?'

'I want to. I want you.'

'No, you don't.' He felt some stupid honourable responsibility.

'So you just quit? Is that the lesson you learned from Dan—to give up?'

'Don't.' She took another step back from him. 'Just don't. You can't ever understand what it was like.'

'Maybe not, but I can try—I would if you'd let me. Damn it, Penny, I don't want to just have fun any more. I want to be happy. I want you to be happy. I want everything. And I want it with you.' His words tumbled. 'We could do so much together. We could do great things.'

The urge to ask was irresistible. 'Like what?'

'Like have a family.'

She caught her breath in a quick gasp, blinking rapidly as she shook her head. But he knew, didn't he? He'd seen her flash of longing.

His fleeting smile twisted. 'You just told me you were selfish back then. But don't you think you're being selfish now? Denying not just yourself, but me too?'

'The last thing I need is more guilt, Carter.'

'No, I'm strong, Penny,' he answered roughly. 'You can throw your worst at me and I'll survive. You'll survive too. I know you've found yourself a way to survive. But you're too afraid to live.'

Her eyes burned, her throat burned, her heart burned.

'Are you brave enough to fight for what you really want?' Somehow he'd got right back in front of her, whispering, tempting. So beautiful that she couldn't do anything but stare.

And then her heart tore.

For there was no point to this—what she wanted she didn't deserve. And the person she wanted deserved so much more than what she could give him.

'I don't want to hurt anyone the way I hurt him,' she breathed.

'No, *you* don't want to be hurt. And that's okay. I won't hurt you.' His eyes shone that brilliant green-blue—clearer than a mountain stream. 'I'm offering everything I have. Everything I never wanted to give is yours—you just have to take it.'

'I can't.'

'Why not?'

Because she'd never believe that he really meant this. And he was wrong about how strong she was. She wouldn't survive it when he realised the huge mistake he'd made.

'I just can't.'

Carter stood on the path and watched her walk further and further away. Slowly ripping his heart out with every step. He hadn't meant to lay it all out like that—not when he was angry and she was angry. He knew she'd need time. But she'd blindsided him with the speed of her resignation and intention to run. And her rejection. It hurt. So he'd thrown all his chips down, gambled everything—too much, too soon. And he'd blown it.

CHAPTER ELEVEN

PICK a destination. Any destination. Anywhere had to be better than here.

Penny stared at the departures board but the only place her eyes seemed willing to see was Melbourne.

Melbourne, Melbourne, Melbourne.

She could go to Perth—lots of sun in Perth. But there was art and champion sport in Melbourne. How about Darwin or Alice Springs—maybe a punishing climate was what she deserved. But Melbourne had a superb café culture and fabulous shopping.

She slumped into the nearest seat.

Carter would be flying out there soon. If he hadn't already.

Yeah, that was the draw. Melbourne had Carter.

She really ought to go to the international terminal and go halfway round the globe. Instead she sat in the chair, tears falling. Not sobbing, just steady tears that leaked from her eyes and dribbled down her cheeks and onto her top. People were looking sideways but she didn't care. It was normal for people to cry at airports. Okay, so maybe it wasn't quite so normal to sit for over an hour staring at the destination board with only a small suitcase and not having bought a ticket yet. Not having even chosen where to go, let alone what to do once she got there.

She regretted the decision. But it was the only decision she'd been able to make and it had hurt. So much. There was no going back. She could never go back. She could never have what her heart wanted the most.

But it whispered. It constantly whispered—beating hope.

He'd said she was strong. She wasn't at all. He'd been more right when he'd said she was afraid. That was totally true. She hadn't laid herself on the line. And he had. What if he'd really meant it? Could she honestly live the rest of her life always wondering what if? And even if he hadn't meant it, even if he might change his mind, wasn't it time for her to be honest about her own emotions anyway?

He deserved her honesty. It was the one thing he'd asked from her but she'd lied to him at the most crucial moment and that was so unfair. Even to the last she'd held back. He'd been right. She did torpedo her relationships when people got too close. She was a huge coward.

No more. Even if nothing else happened, she needed to prove to herself that she could be more than that. She needed to express her feelings openly. It was beyond time she faced up to them. To her family. To everything.

Carter had shown her how beautifully her body could work if she let go, maybe his other gift was to help her grow true courage.

She went up to the counter. It took less than three minutes to purchase a ticket. The departure lounge wasn't far. She sat and waited for the boarding call. Beyond that she couldn't think.

Finally the call was made. She reached down to pick

up her pack, about to stand to join the queuing passengers. But right by her pack was a pair of big black boots, topped by black jeans. Someone was standing in front of her.

She looked up at the tall figure with the hair so tousled it stood on end, the creased tee and jeans, the unnaturally bright blue-green eyes.

'I've been sitting in that café over there,' he said. 'Watching, waiting, wanting to know what you were going to do. Where you were going to go. I've had four long blacks. It's been almost two hours.' He sat in the seat next to hers. 'So, where are you going?'

Surely he knew already—they'd just announced the flight. Emotion swelled inside her, becoming so huge she had to let it out. It was bigger than her, and she was only hurting herself more by trying to deny or control it or hide it. She held up the boarding pass for him to read: *Melbourne.*

As he stared at the card the colour washed out of his face, leaving him as pale as he'd been the night before. Then he looked at her again, she stared back. Her eyes filled with tears but she couldn't blink, couldn't break the contact with him. Wordlessly wanting him to know, to believe beyond any doubt just how much he meant to her.

Abruptly he turned, facing the window. The plane waited out on the runway, the luggage carts were driven warp speed by the baggage handlers. And with her fingers she squeezed her ragged tissue into a tighter and tighter ball.

She heard him clear his throat but still he said nothing. Her doubts returned—had she just freaked him out? Was he regretting what he'd said earlier already?

But then he held out his hand. The simple gesture seemed to offer so much. She drew a sharp, shuddering breath and put her hand on his.

He guided her to stand beside him. With his other hand he scooped up the handle of her case, wheeling it behind them—away from the flight queue.

She couldn't really see where they were going, the tears still fell too fast. And she kept her head down, unsure if she could believe this was actually happening or if she'd gone delusional.

'The great thing about airports is that they have hotels very close by.' He sounded raspy. He matched his pace to hers—slow—but kept them moving steadily. 'You need a shower and a rest, Penny. You look beat. And I need...' He stopped and closed his eyes for a moment. Then he took a deep breath and began walking again. 'We'll fly tomorrow.'

They went out of the doors and straight into a taxi.

'How did you find me?' she asked once Carter had instructed the driver.

'Been stalking you all day.' His hand tightened.

'Why did you wait so long?'

His expression twisted. 'I thought you were going to go somewhere else. I sat there and waited. It was torture. Every minute I expected you to just get up and go to the counter and buy a ticket who knew where. But then you did and you went to that departure lounge and I had to see if you were really going to do it.'

'It was the only place I could go.'

He was silent a long moment. 'Why did it take you so long to realise?'

'Because I was scared.'

'Of what?'

'My feelings for you.' Her whisper could hardly be heard. 'Your feelings for me.'

He turned his head sharply, but the taxi stopped, interrupting them. But it took only a few minutes to book into the hotel, another couple to ride the lift and then be in privacy.

She walked into the middle of the room—needing to say her piece before passion overtook her mind. 'I don't want you to feel like you have to rescue me, Carter. I don't want your pity.'

'I have no intention of rescuing you. I want to rescue myself.'

That startled her. 'From what?'

'From a life of meaningless flings.' He shrugged and looked sheepish. 'In fact there wouldn't be any more flings anyway. I don't want to sleep with another woman ever. Only you. So, you see, you have to rescue me from a life of celibacy and terminal boredom.'

'Carter—'

'I'm not the person I was a couple of weeks ago,' he said quickly. 'I believe in you like I've never believed in another woman. I trust you like I've never trusted another woman. You make me want to love and be with just one woman.'

She swallowed. Yeah, she still couldn't quite believe that. 'I'm hardly exciting. I'm not flashy or amazingly talented or anything. I'm just a temp PA.'

He walked nearer. 'You want to know what you are, Penny?' He reached up to tuck her hair behind her ear. 'You're warm, you're funny. You're competitive, you definitely have your ball-breaker moments. Sometimes you're misguided but you're passionate in everything you do. You have such heart. You can't hide it. And I want it.'

But it was still a very scared heart.

'You'll like Melbourne,' he said. 'We can find a house. My apartment is nice but we need more space and our own private pool and a deck big enough to dance on so you can have raves at home.' He winked. 'It takes a couple of weeks to organise the licence but we'll get married as soon as it's possible.'

She shook her head, had to interrupt the fantasy at that point. 'Carter, that's crazy talk. We've only known each other a week.'

'Nearly two,' he corrected.

'Yeah, and I've been on my best behaviour.'

Laughter burst from him—just a brief shout. She gave his shoulder a little push, but inside the fear was resurging. This was happening too fast—he'd changed his mind too fast; he might change it back again just as quick.

'I'm serious. You can't go making a decision like this so quickly. I'm a cow. I get moody. I get itchy feet.'

'Okay.' He gripped her just above the elbows and pulled her close. 'Here's the deal. You move to Melbourne and move in with me. I'm making my claim public and I'm proud to. Give us six months to settle, and then I'm asking you again. I guarantee we'll be even happier by then. There'll be no answer but yes.'

'Six months is still too soon.' It was still lust-fuelled infatuation territory—for him anyway. For her, well, her heart had long been lost to him already.

'It isn't. You know it isn't. You can trust me. There's nothing about you that's going to put me off. I already know you're not perfect, Penny. No one is. But we can both be better people together.'

She couldn't move, too scared to blink in case she was dreaming this. Was she really this close to having everything? Still the shadows in her heart made her doubt.

'Six months to the day, sweetheart,' he said firmly. 'And I'll tell you what else.' His hands firmed up too. 'I'm taking you home. You take my hand and we go to your parents' anniversary party Matt told me about. And you show me that tree. We'll face it together, and maybe we'll plant something under it. A bulb or something so every spring a new flower will grow and then it'll die and then another will grow. You like to leave the flowers to grow, right? But we'll grow too—we'll get on with life together. And maybe in a year or two we'll grow a family together.'

Penny pressed her curled hands to her chest, unable to say anything, unable to blink the searing tears away.

'I know you're scared.' He gently cupped her face. 'But I'll be with you and I won't let you down.'

She pressed her cheek into his palm. 'I don't want to let you down either.'

'You won't. Give us the time. You know this is right. You know how happy we're going to be. We already are. You just have to let it happen.'

'You have the details all worked out.'

'I do.' His gaze dropped for a moment. 'You once promised me honesty. Will you give me it now?'

'Yes.' That was the least she could give him.

He paused, seeming to consider his words. 'Do you really...want me?'

Her eyeballs ached, her temples, her throat and all the way down her middle right to her toes—every cell in her system screamed its agony. 'Oh, yes,' she cried. 'It hurts so much.'

'It doesn't have to hurt, sweetheart.' His arms crushed her tight. 'It doesn't have to.'

He lifted his head so he held her gaze, seeing right into her. And she should have been afraid. For a second the panic swept up in a wave inside her because he saw it all. How deep her longing went. But then he kissed her.

And then, for the first time, his patience left him.

'I need to be with you,' he groaned. 'I need to feel you.'

Now she saw his vulnerability. Saw just how much her leaving would have hurt him. How much he'd been hiding from her—or more that she'd been too blinded by fear to be able to see. How much he wanted her, and wanted to care for her.

He whipped off his top, undid hers too. His hands shook and fumbled to unzip her skirt and slide it off. His breathing roughened, his hands roughened.

So she helped and soon she was naked and he was naked and warming her. He didn't kiss her all over, didn't tease or torment her with his fingers or tongue. He just held her close and kissed her as if there was nothing else on earth he'd ever want to do, as if he needed her more than anything.

She loved the weight of him on her. The way he held her hair hard so he could kiss her. The way he ground his body and soul into her. He moved—all power and passion and pure frantic force. He held—truly, tenderly, tightly held her as he poured his want and need and love as deeply into her as he could. And she clung, feeling the sublime beauty between them, so awed that they could make such magic together. And then there was no room for thought. She was reduced to absolute essence—pure emotion.

'I'm sorry,' he panted. 'I just couldn't hold back.'

She turned towards him and smiled.

He lifted his head slightly from the pillow, his eyebrows shooting up. 'No way.'

She nodded.

'You're not just saying that?'

'I'll never fake it with you. Never have. Never will.' She gazed at him. 'I loved it. I loved feeling how desperate you were to touch me.'

'I've been desperate to touch you since the minute we met.' It wasn't a teasing comment, but honest vulnerability.

She snuggled closer, so content she thought she might burst. And the fantasy he'd painted for her rose in her head.

'You really want children?' she wondered aloud—her heart still stuttered over that step too far into the realm of paradise.

'Can't have Nick acting all spoilt like he's an only child. He needs a nephew or niece to give him a run for it,' he joked. But the next second he went totally sober again. 'I never thought I wanted them. Or marriage. You know that. But it took meeting the one woman who's so right for me to make me realise just how much I do want those things. The problem before was that I hadn't met you. Now I have. So now I know.'

The most incredible feeling of peace descended on Penny—as if he'd soothed every inch of her, inside and out. With utter serenity and certainty, her faith blossomed in the strong man beside her. In herself. In what they already shared and could yet share if she let them.

She shifted position, curling even closer and resting her head on his chest.

'Your heart is beating so fast.' She swept her hand across his skin, feeling the strong thudding beneath. 'Must be all that coffee.'

Carter let out a helpless grunt of laughter. 'No. It's you. All you.'

He slid his hand down her arm, down the slim wrist, until his palm pressed over hers. He bent his fingers and felt her mirror the action, locking their hands together.

'I love you,' she finally whispered. 'I love you so much. I want to live with you at my side.'

'Then that's where I'll be.' Carter trembled. Having never before in his life trembled, he trembled now as he felt her absolute acceptance of him. And of every ounce of love he had to offer.

Their future had just been born.

CHAPTER TWELVE

Five and a half months later.

PENNY sat glued to her laptop, trying to fritter away the last hour before Carter got home. Thank heavens that in New Zealand Matt was still at work and she could instant message him.

Have you asked that cute bookstore girl out for a date yet?

Working up the courage. Concentrate on your own love life.

Working up the courage here too.

Why are you scared? He'll love it. He loves you. He put up with Mum and Dad fawning for an entire week for you. Case proven.

Still scared. OK, excited too. Very excited.

Bordering on TMI.

Ha-ha. Wish it was over already.

'Where are you?'

Penny jumped as Carter called out downstairs. She hadn't even heard the door. A stupidly happy giggle bubbled out, even though her heart started thudding so fast it threatened to dance right out of her chest.

Have to go. He's here.

She slammed her laptop shut and raced down the stairs to meet her so very real man. Nervous as she was, she couldn't stop her smiles, lifting her face to kiss him. He was earlier than she'd asked him to be. But then he always gave her more than she asked for. And she loved him for that.

'So why do you need me home from work so early?'

'An adventure,' she said, her mouth cabin-bread dry. 'I'm driving,' she said. 'You just sit back and enjoy the ride.'

He followed her out to his car. 'A mystery tour?'

'Yes.' She bit her lip but still couldn't stop smiling. It was that or cry with the nerves.

He'd been right, of course, that day in the airport hotel. Everything had got better. They'd visited her parents, she'd gotten to know his dad and his wife and little Nick. They saw Mason regularly and his company had weathered the skimming scandal no problem. Even the sex between them continued to blossom—she'd never have thought that could possibly improve. But it had. She'd fallen in love with Melbourne too. She temped— short-term contracts—refusing to work for Carter, claiming she needed to maintain an element of independence. Something she knew he wasn't entirely happy about. But he had absolutely no cause to worry.

She, on the other hand, was still nervous.

She drove the route she'd been along a million times already. The last fifty times she'd rehearsed this moment in her head. But the reality wasn't anything like she'd imagined. Every cell was so aware and on edge it was as if she had acute vision and hearing and a heart still beating way too fast.

But in a good way. She wanted it to be so good.

It was the very end of winter, so the garden was at its most dormant phase. But still so very beautiful—private, tranquil and spacious. She walked slightly ahead of him, hoping he didn't mind the dropping temperature of the late afternoon. She showed him the lawn, pointed out the pathways and the water features of the by-appointment-only private grounds that had been built by an older couple—wonderfully mad visionaries whom Penny had gotten to know and adore.

'In six months it'll be summer and there'll be so much colour.' She gestured wide around her. 'Flowers every-where.' She turned back to face him. 'I won't need a bouquet because we'll be in the midst of one.'

'A bouquet?' A half-step behind, he didn't take his eyes off her.

'Yes…' She swallowed. 'I wanted to know if…' She took a breath. 'Will you marry me? Here? Then?'

He didn't move.

Nor did she.

It was one of those moments that took for ever but where the anticipation was a painful, heart-stopping pleasure. A moment she'd treasure the rest of her life. Because as she watched, the smile stole into his blue and green and gold eyes. It spread to his mouth. And his whole face filled with that rakish, irresistible charm.

'Yes.'

She simply fell into his wide open arms, struggled to get her own around him so she could hold on tighter than ever, kissing him with every particle of passion she had.

Eons later, she managed another breathless question. 'You don't mind I beat you to it?'

'I like it most when you beat me to it.'

She giggled and pressed her hot face into his neck as she whispered, 'I wanted to ask you. I wanted to offer you everything I have.'

Because he'd already given his all to her and she knew it and she wanted to be an equal match for him.

He tugged her hair so she looked back up at him.

'I'm honoured you asked,' he said, intensely sincere. 'I know what you're saying.'

That she truly believed in him, in them and finally in herself.

'I want you to understand how happy I am.' She smiled softly through a trickling tear.

'I do.' He smiled back. 'And nothing would make me happier than to be your husband. We're a really good team, Penny.'

Her smile spread. 'You do realise this means more time with my parents.'

'More time with my step-mother,' he countered.

'You know she's lovely.'

'Just as you know your parents are lovely. And so is Matt.'

She nodded vigorously and they both laughed.

The difference in her life was so dramatic—full of family, full of fun—real, every day and every night joy. It was because of her anchor—the strongest, most loving man. And the most shameless.

Because now he swept her back into his arms and took control of the situation. 'I'm so glad we've got you over your dislike of public displays.'

But there was no one around to watch him pick her up and carry her out of the chill wind, into the glass building that housed the exotic plants in the cold season. And there, under the bowers of some giant green monstrosity of a plant, they made sweet, perfect, sizzling love.

FOR HIS EYES ONLY

LIZ FIELDING

With thanks to Kate Hardy and Caroline Anderson for their never-failing belief. And to Gail McCurry Waldrep for the fudge frosting.

CHAPTER ONE

'WHAT'S GOT MILES's knickers in a twist?' Natasha Gordon poured herself half a cup of coffee. Her first appointment had been at eight and she'd been on the run ever since. She had to grab any opportunity to top up her caffeine level. 'I was on my way to a viewing at the St John's Wood flat when I got a message to drop everything and come straight back here.'

Janine, Morgan and Black's receptionist and always the first with any rumour, lifted her slender cashmere-clad shoulders in a don't-ask-me shrug. 'If that's what he said, you'd better not keep him waiting,' she said, but, shrug notwithstanding, the ghost of an I-know-something-you-don't smile tugged at lips on which the lipstick was always perfectly applied.

Tash abandoned the untouched coffee and headed for the stairs, taking them two at a time. Miles Morgan, senior partner of Morgan and Black, first port of call for the wealthy flooding into London from all corners of the world to snap up high-end real estate, had been dropping heavy hints for weeks that the vacant 'associate' position was hers.

Damn right. She'd worked her socks off for the last three years and had earned that position with hard work and long hours and Janine, who liked everyone to know how 'in' she was with the boss, had casually let slip the news on Friday afternoon that he would be spending the weekend in the country with the semi-retired 'Black' to discuss the future of the firm.

'Down, pulse, down,' she muttered, pausing outside his office to scoop up a wayward handful of hair and anchor it in place with great-grandma's silver clip.

She always started out the day looking like a career woman on the up, but haring about London all morning had left her more than a little dishevelled and things had begun to unravel. Her hair, her make-up, her shirt.

She tucked in her shirt and was checking the top button when the door opened.

'Janine! Is she here yet?' Miles shouted before he realised she was standing in front him. 'Where the hell have you been?'

'I had a viewing at the Chelsea house first thing,' she said, used to his short fuse. 'They played it very close to their chests, but the wife's eyes were lit up like the Blackpool illuminations. I guarantee they'll make an offer before the end of the day.'

The prospect of a high five-figure commission would normally be enough to change his mood but he merely grunted and the sparkle of anticipation went flat. Whatever Janine had been smiling about, it wasn't the prospect of the office party Miles would throw to celebrate the appointment of the new associate.

'It's been non-stop since then,' she added, and it wasn't going to ease up this side of six. 'Is this urgent, Miles? I'm showing Glencora Jarrett the St John's Wood apartment in half an hour and the traffic is solid.'

'You can forget that. I've sent Toby.'

'Toby?' Her occasionally significant other had been on a rugby tour in Australia and wasn't due home until the end of the month. She shook her head. It wasn't important, but Lady Glen... 'No, she specifically asked—'

'For you. I know, but a viewing isn't a social engagement,' he cut in before she could remind him that Lady Glencora was desperately nervous and would not go into an unoccupied apartment with a male negotiator.

'But—'

'Forget Her Ladyship,' he said, thrusting the latest edition of the *Country Chronicle* into her hands. 'Take a look at this.'

The magazine was open at the full-page advertisement for Hadley Chase, a historic country house that had just come on the market.

'Oh, that came out really well...' A low mist, caught by the rising sun, had lent the house a golden, soft-focus enchantment that hid its many shortcomings. Well worth the effort of getting up at the crack of dawn and driving into the depths of Berkshire on the one day in the week that she could have had a lie-in. 'The phone will be ringing off the hook,' she said, offering it back to him.

'Read on,' he said, not taking it.

'I know what it says, Miles. I wrote it.' The once grand house was suffering from age and neglect and she'd focused on the beauty and convenience of the location to tempt potential buyers to come and take a look. 'You approved it,' she reminded him.

'I didn't approve this.'

She frowned. Irritable might be his default mode but, even for Miles, this seemed excessive. Had some ghastly mistake slipped past them both? It happened, but this was an expensive full-page colour ad, and she'd gone over the proof with a fine-tooth comb. Confident that nothing could have gone wrong, she read out her carefully composed copy.

'"A substantial seventeenth-century manor house in a sought-after location on the Berkshire Downs within easy reach of motorway links to London, the Midlands and the West. That's the good news. The bad news..."' She faltered. Bad news? What the...?

'Don't stop now.'

The words were spoken with a clear, crisp, don't-argue-with-me certainty, but not by her boss, and she spun around as the owner of the voice rose from the high-backed leather armchair set in front of Miles Morgan's desk and turned to face her.

Her first impression was of darkness. Dark hair, dark clothes, dark eyes in a mesmerising face that missed beauty by a hair's breadth, although a smile might have done the business.

The second was of strength. There was no bulk, but his shoulders were wide beneath a crumpled linen jacket so old that the black had faded to grey, his abdomen slate-flat under a T-shirt that hung loosely over narrow hips.

His hand was resting on the back of the chair, long calloused fingers curled over the leather. They were the kind of fingers that she could imagine doing unspeakable things to her. Was imagining…

She looked up and met eyes that seemed to penetrate every crevice, every pore, and a hot blush, beginning somewhere low in her belly, spread like wildfire in every direction—

'Natasha!'

Miles's sharp interjection jolted her back to the page but it was a moment before she could catch her breath, gather her wits and focus on the words dancing in front of her.

…the bad news is the wet rot, woodworm, crumbling plasterwork and leaking roof. The vendor would no doubt have preferred to demolish the house and re-develop the land, but it's a Grade II listed building in the heart of the Green Belt so he's stuffed. There is a fine oak Tudor staircase but, bearing in mind the earlier reference to wet rot and woodworm, an early viewing is advised if you want to see the upper floors.

Her heart still pounding with the shock of a sexual attraction so powerful that she was trembling, she had to read it twice before it sank in. And when it did her pulse was still in a sorry state.

'I don't understand,' she said. Then, realising how feeble that sounded, 'How did this happen?'

'How, indeed?'

Her question had been directed at Miles, but the response came from Mr Tall, Dark and Deadly. Who *was* he?

'Hadley,' he said, apparently reading her mind. Or maybe she'd asked the question out loud. She needed to get a grip. She needed an ice bath...

She cleared her throat. 'Hadley?' His name still emerged as if spoken by a surprised frog, but that wasn't simply because all her blood had apparently drained from her brain to the more excitable parts of her anatomy. The house was unoccupied and the sale was being handled by the estate's executors and, since no one had mentioned a real-life, flesh-and-blood Hadley, she'd assumed the line had run dry.

'Darius Hadley,' he elaborated, clearly picking up on her doubt.

In her career she'd worked with everyone, from young first-time buyers scraping together a deposit, to billionaires investing in London apartments and town houses costing millions. She knew that appearances could be deceptive but Darius Hadley did not have the look of a man whose family had been living in the Chase since the seventeenth century, when a grateful Charles II had given the estate to one James Hadley, a rich merchant who'd funded him in exile.

With the glint of a single gold earring amongst the mass of black curls tumbling over his collar, the crumpled linen jacket faded from black to grey, jeans worn threadbare at the knees, he looked more like a gypsy, or a pirate. Perhaps that was where the Hadley fortune had come from—plundering the Spanish Main with the likes of Drake. Or, with the legacy now in the hands of a man bearing the name of a Persian king, it was possible that his ancestors had chosen to travel east overland, to trade in silk and spices.

This man certainly had the arrogance to go with his name but, unlike his forebears, it seemed that he had no interest in settling down to live the life of a country gentleman. Not that she blamed him for that.

Hadley Chase, with roses growing over its timbered Tudor heart, might look romantic in the misty haze of an early summer sunrise, but it was going to take a lot of time and a very deep purse to bring it up to modern expectations in plumbing, heating and weatherproofing. There was nothing romantic about nineteen-fifties plumbing and, from the neglected state of both house and grounds, it was evident that the fortune needed to maintain it was long gone.

On the bright side, even in these cash-strapped days, there were any number of sheikhs, pop stars and Russian oligarchs looking for the privacy of a country estate no more than a helicopter hop from the centre of London and she was looking forward to adding the Chase to her portfolio of sales in the very near future. She had big plans for the commission.

Miles cleared his throat and she belatedly stuck out her hand.

'Natasha Gordon. How d'you do, Mr Hadley?'

'I've been stuffed, mounted and hung out to dry,' he replied. 'How do you think I feel?' he demanded, ignoring her hand.

'Angry.' He had every right to be angry. Hell, she was furious with whoever had meddled with her carefully worded description and they would feel the wrath of her tongue when she found out who it was, but that would have to wait. Right now she had to get a grip of her hormones, be totally professional and reassure him that this wasn't the disaster it appeared. 'I don't know what happened here, Mr Hadley, but I promise you it's just a minor setback.'

'A minor setback?' Glittering eyes—forget charcoal, they were jet—skewered her to the floor and Tash felt the heat rise up her neck and flood her cheeks. She was blushing. He'd made her blush with just a look. That was outrageous... 'A *minor* setback?' he repeated, with the very slightest emphasis on 'minor'.

His self-control was impressive.

Okaaay... She unpeeled her tongue from the roof of her mouth, snatched in a little oxygen to get her brain started and said, 'Serious purchasers understand that there will be problems with this type of property, Mr Hadley.'

'They expect to be able to view the upper floors without endangering their lives,' he pointed out. He hadn't raised his voice; he didn't have to. He'd made his point with a quiet, razor-edged precision that made Miles's full-blown irritation look like a toddler tantrum.

'Natasha!' Miles prompted, more sharply this time. 'Have you got something to say to Mr Hadley?'

'What?' She dragged her gaze from the seductive curve of Darius Hadley's lower lip and fixed it somewhere around his prominent Adam's apple, which only sent her mind off on another, even more disturbing direction involving extremities.

Do not look at his feet!

'Oh, um, yes...' She'd tried desperately to get her brain in gear, recall the notes she'd made, as she stared at scuffed work boots, jeans smeared with what looked like dry grey mud and clinging to powerful thighs. He'd obviously dropped whatever he was doing and come straight to the office when he'd seen the ad. Did he work on a building site? 'Actually,' she said, 'there's more than one set of stairs so it isn't a problem.'

'And that's your professional opinion?'

'Not that I recall there being anything wrong with the main staircase that a thorough seeing to with a vacuum cleaner wouldn't fix,' she added hurriedly when Miles sounded as if he might be choking. Come on, Tash...this is what you do. 'I did advise the solicitor handling the sale that they should get in a cleaning contractor to give the place a good bottoming.'

A muscle tightened in his jaw. 'And what was their response to that?'

'They said they'd get the caretaker to give it a once-over.'

Some property owners did nothing to help themselves, but this probably wasn't the moment to say so.

'So it's just the woodworm, rot and missing lead flashing on the roof that a potential buyer has to worry about?' Darius Hadley raised his dark brows a fraction of a millimetre and every cell in her body followed as if he'd jerked a string.

Amongst a jangle of mixed messages—her head urging her to take a step back, every other part of her wanting to reach out and touch—she just about managed to stand her ground.

'Actually,' she said, 'according to the paperwork, the woodworm was treated years ago.' Something he would have known if he'd taken the slightest interest in the house he'd apparently inherited. 'I think you'll find that it's the cobwebs that will have women running screaming—'

Behind Hadley's back, Miles made a sharp mouth-zipped gesture. 'Mr Hadley isn't looking for excuses. What he's waiting for,' he said, 'what he's *entitled* to, is an explanation and an apology.'

She frowned. Surely Miles had already covered that ground? She assumed she'd been called in to discuss a plan of action.

'Don't bother; I've heard enough,' Hadley said before

she could get in a word. 'You'll be hearing from my lawyer, Morgan.'

'Lawyer?' What use was a lawyer going to be? 'No, really—'

Darius Hadley cut off her protest with a look that froze her in mid-sentence and seemed to go on for an eternity. Lethal eyes, a nose bred for looking down, a mouth made for sin... Finally, satisfied that he'd silenced her, his eyes seemed to shimmer, soften, warm to smoky charcoal and then, as she took half a step towards him, he nodded at Miles and walked out of the office, leaving the room ringing with his presence. Leaving her weak to the bone.

She put out a hand to grasp the back of the chair he'd been sitting in. It was still warm from his touch and the heat seemed to travel up her arm and spread through her limbs, creating little sparks throughout her body, igniting all the erogenous zones she was familiar with and quite a few that were entirely new.

Phew. Double phewy-phew...

'He's a bit tense, isn't he?' she said shakily. A sleek, dark Dobermann to Toby's big, soft Labrador puppy—to be approached with caution rather than a hug. But the rewards if you won his trust...

Forget it! A man like that wasn't a keeper. All you could hope for was to catch his attention for a moment. But what a moment—

'With good reason,' Miles said, interrupting a chain of thought that was going nowhere. Dark, brooding types had never been even close to the top of her list of appealing male stereotypes. Far too high-maintenance. *Rude* dark, brooding types had never figured.

A barrage of hoots from the street below distracted her, but there was no escape there. Apparently oblivious to the traffic, Darius Hadley was crossing the street and several people stopped to watch him stride down the road in the direction of Sloane Square. Most of them were women.

It wasn't just her, then.

Without warning he stopped, swung round and looked up at the window where she was standing as if he'd known she'd be there. And she forgot to breathe.

'Natasha!'

She jumped, blinked and when she looked again he'd gone and for a moment she was afraid that he was coming back. Hoped that he was coming back, but a moment later he reappeared further along the street and she turned her back on the window before he felt her eyes boring into the back of his head and turned again to catch her looking.

'Have you spoken to the *Chronicle*?' she asked; anything to distract herself.

'The first thing I did when Mr Hadley's solicitor contacted me early this morning was to call the *Chronicle*'s advertising manager.' Miles walked across to his desk and removed a sheet of paper from a file and handed it to her. 'He sent this over from his office. Hadley hasn't seen it yet but it's only a matter of time before his lawyer contacts them.'

It was a photocopied proof of the ad for Hadley Chase— exactly as she'd read it out—complete with a tick next to the 'approved' box and her signature scrawled across the bottom.

'No, Miles. This is wrong.' She looked up. 'This isn't what I signed.'

'But you did write that,' he insisted.

'One or two of the phrases sound vaguely familiar,' she admitted.

She sometimes wrote a mock advertisement describing a property in the worst possible light when she thought it would help the vendor to see the property through the eyes of a potential buyer. The grubby carpet in the hall, the children's finger marks on the doors, the tired kitchen. Stuff that wouldn't cost much to fix, but would make all the difference to the prospects of a sale.

'Oh, come on, Tash. It sounds exactly like one of your specials.'

'My "specials" have the advantage of being accurate. And helpful.'

'So you would have mentioned the leaking roof?'

'Absolutely. Damaged ceilings and pools of water are about as off-putting as it gets,' she said, hating that she was on the defensive when she hadn't done anything wrong.

'What about the stairs?'

'I'm sure they'd be lovely if you could see them for the dust and dead leaves that blew in through a broken window.' The house had been empty since the last occupant had been moved to a nursing home when Alzheimer's had left him a danger to himself a couple of years ago. 'The caretaker is worse than useless. I had to find some card and fill the gap myself but it's just a temporary solution. The first serious gust of wind will blow it out. And, frankly, if I were Darius Hadley I'd put a boot up the backside of the estate executor because he's no help.' He didn't reply. 'Come on, Miles. You know I didn't send this to the *Chronicle*.'

'Are you sure about that? Really? We all know that you've been putting in long hours. What time was your first viewing this morning?'

'Eight, but—'

'What time did you finish last night?' He didn't wait for her to answer but consulted a printout of her diary, no doubt supplied by Janine. No wonder she'd been smiling. This was much more fun than an office party. Gossip city...

'Your last viewing was at nine-thirty so you were home at what? Eleven? Eleven-thirty?'

It had been after midnight. Buyers couldn't always fit into a tidy nine-till-five slot. Far from complaining about the extra hours she put in, that they all put in—with the exception of Toby, who never allowed anything to interfere with rugby training, took time off whenever he felt like it and got away with murder because his great-aunt was married to Peter Black—Miles expected it.

'They flew from the States to view that apartment. I could hardly tell them that I finished at five-thirty,' she pointed out. They'd come a long way and wanted to see every detail and she wasn't about to rush them.

'No one can keep up that pace for long without something suffering,' he replied, not even bothering to ask if they were likely to make an offer. 'It seems obvious to me that you attached the wrong document when you emailed your copy to the *Chronicle*.'

'No—'

'I blame myself.' He shook his head. 'I've pushed you too hard. I should have seen it coming.'

Seen *what* coming?

'I didn't attach the wrong anything,' she declared, fizzing with indignation, her pulse still racing but with anger now rather than anticipation. How dared anyone tamper with her carefully composed ad? 'And even if I had made a mistake, don't you think I'd have noticed it when the proof came back?'

'If you'd actually had time to look at it.'

'I made time,' she declared. 'I checked every word. And what the hell was the *Chronicle* thinking? Why didn't someone on the advertising desk query it?'

'They did.' He glanced at the ad. 'They called this office on the twentieth. Unsurprisingly, they made a note for their records.'

'Okay, so which idiot did they speak to?'

He handed her the page so that she could see for herself. 'An idiot by the name of Natasha Gordon.'

'No!'

'According to the advertising manager, you assured them that it was the latest trend, harking back fifty years to an estate agent famous for the outrageous honesty of his advertisements.' His tone, all calm reason, raised the small hairs on the back of her neck. Irritable, she could handle. This was just plain scary. 'Clearly, you were angry with the executors for not taking your advice.'

'If they didn't have the cash, they didn't have the cash, although I imagine their fees are safely in the bank. Believe me, if I'd been aping the legendary Roy Brooks, I'd have made a far better job of it than this,' she said, working hard to sound calm even while her pulse was going through the roof. 'There was plenty to work with. No one from the *Chronicle* talked to me.' Calm, cool, professional...

'So what are you saying? That the advertising manager of the *Chronicle* is lying? Or that someone pretended to be you? Come on, Tash, who would do that?' he asked. 'What would anyone have to gain?'

She swallowed. Put like that, it did sound crazy.

'You are right about one thing, though,' he continued. 'The phone has been ringing off the hook—' her sigh of relief came seconds too soon '—but not with people desperate to view Hadley Chase. They are all gossip columnists and the editors of property pages wanting a comment.'

She frowned. 'Already? The magazine has been on the shelves for less than two hours.'

'You know what they say about bad news.' He took the ad from her and tossed it onto his desk. 'In this instance I imagine it was given a head start by someone working at the *Chronicle* tipping them off.'

'I suppose. How did Darius Hadley hear about it?'

'I imagine the estate executors received the same phone calls.'

She shook her head, letting the problem of how this had happened go for the moment and concentrating instead on how to fix it. 'The one thing I do know is that there's no such thing as bad publicity. I meant what I said to Mr Hadley. Handled right...'

'For heaven's sake, Tash, you've made both the firm and Mr Hadley into a laughing stock. There is no way to handle this "right"! He's withdrawn the house from the market and, on top of the considerable expenses we've already incurred, we're not only facing a hefty claim for damages from Hadley but irreparable damage to the Morgan and Black name.'

'All of which will go away if we find a buyer quickly,' she insisted, 'and it's going to be all over the weekend property pages.'

'I'm glad you realise the extent of the problem.'

'No...' She'd run a Google search when Hadley Chase had been placed in their hands for sale. There was nothing like a little gossip, a bit of scandal to garner a few column inches in one of the weekend property supplements. Unfortunately, despite her speculation on the source of their wealth, the Hadleys had either been incredibly discreet or dull beyond imagining. She'd assumed the latter; if James Hadley had been an entertaining companion, his money would have earned him a lot more than a smallish estate in the country. He'd have been given a title and a place at Charles II's court.

Darius Hadley had blown that theory right out of the water.

Forget his clothes. With his cavalier curls, his earring, the edge of something dangerous that clung to him like a shadow, he would have been right at home there. Her fingers twitched as she imagined what it would be like to run her fingers through those silky black curls, over his flat abs.

She curled them into her palms, shook off the image— this wasn't about Darius Hadley; it was about his house.

'Come on, Miles,' she said. 'You couldn't buy this kind of publicity. The house is in a fabulous location and buyers with this kind of money aren't going to be put off by problems you'll find in any property of that age.' Well, not much. 'I'll make some calls, talk to a few people.' Apparently speaking to a brick wall, she threw up her hands. 'Damn it, I'll go down to Hadley Chase and take a broom to the place myself!'

'You'll do nothing, talk to no one,' he snapped.

'But if I can find a buyer quickly—'

'Stop! Stop right there.' Having shocked her into silence, he continued. 'This is what is going to happen. I've booked you into the Fairview Clinic—'

'The *Fairview*?' A clinic famous for taking care of celebrities with drug and drink problems?

'We'll issue a statement saying that you're suffering from stress and will be having a week or two of complete rest under medical supervision.'

'No.' Sickness, hospitals—she'd had her fill of them as a child and nothing would induce her to spend a minute in one without a very good reason.

'The firm's medical plan will cover it,' he said, no doubt meaning to reassure her.

'No, Miles.'

'While you're recovering,' he continued, his voice hardening, 'you can consider your future.'

'Consider my future?' Her future was stepping up to an associate's office, not being hidden away like some soap star with an alcohol problem until the dust cleared. 'You've got to be kidding, Miles. This has to be a practical joke that's got out of hand. There's a juvenile element in the front office that needs a firm—'

'What I need,' he said, each word given equal weight, 'is for you to cooperate.'

He wasn't listening, she realised. Didn't want to hear what she had to say. Miles wasn't interested in how this had happened, only in protecting his firm's reputation. He needed a scapegoat, a fall guy, and it was her signature on the ad.

That was why he'd summoned her back to the office— to show the sacrifice to Darius Hadley. Unsurprisingly, he hadn't been impressed. He didn't want the head of some apparently witless woman who stammered and blushed when he looked at her. He was going for damages so Miles was instituting Plan B—protecting the firm's reputation by destroying hers.

She was in trouble.

'I've spoken to Peter Black and he's discussed the situation with our lawyers. We're all agreed that this is the best solution,' Miles continued, as if it was a done deal.

'Already?'

'There was no time to waste.'

'Even so… What kind of lawyer would countenance such a lie?'

'What lie?' he enquired blandly. 'Burnout happens to the best of us.'

Burnout? She was barely simmering, but the lawyers— covering all eventualities—probably had the press statement drafted and ready to go. She would be described as a 'highly valued member of staff'…blah-de-blah-de-blah… who, due to work-related stress, had suffered a 'regrettable' breakdown. All carefully calculated to give the impression that she'd been found gibbering into her keyboard.

It would, of course, end with everyone wishing her a speedy return to health. Miles was clearly waiting for her to do the decent thing and take cover in the Fairview so that he could tell them to issue it. The clinic's reputation for keeping their patients safe from the lenses of the paparazzi, safe from the intrusion of the press, was legendary.

Suddenly she wasn't arguing with him over the best way to recover the situation, but clinging to the rim of the basin by her fingernails as her career was being flushed down the toilet.

'This is wrong,' she protested, well aware that the decision had already been made, that nothing she said would change that. 'I didn't do this.'

'I'm doing my best to handle a public relations nightmare that you've created, Natasha.' His voice was flat, his face devoid of expression. 'It's in your own best interests to cooperate.'

'It's in yours,' she retaliated. 'I'll be unemployable. Unless, of course, you're saying that I'll be welcomed back with open arms after my rest cure? That my promotion to associate, the one you've been dangling in front of me for months, is merely on hold until I've recovered?'

'I have to think of the firm. The rest of the staff,' he said with a heavy sigh created to signal his disappointment with her. 'Please don't be difficult about this.'

'Or what?' she asked.

'Tash... Please. Why won't you admit that you made a mistake? That you're fallible...sick; everyone—maybe even Mr Hadley—will sympathise with you, with us.'

He was actually admitting it!

'I didn't do this,' she repeated but, even to her own ears, she was beginning to sound like the little girl who, despite the frosting around her mouth, had refused to own up to eating two of the cupcakes her mother had made for a charity coffee morning.

'I'm sorry, Natasha, but if you refuse to cooperate we'll have no choice but to dismiss you without notice for bring-

ing the firm into disrepute.' He took refuge behind his
desk before he added, 'If you force us to do that we will,
of course, have no option but to counter-sue you for malicious damage.'

Deep, deep trouble.

'I'm not sick,' she replied, doing her best to keep her
voice steady, fighting down the scream of outrage that
was beginning to build low in her belly. 'As for the suit
for damages, I doubt either you or Mr Hadley would get
very far with a jury. While the advertisement may not have
been what he signed up for —' she was being thrown to
the wolves, used as a scapegoat for something she hadn't
done and she had nothing to lose '—it's the plain unvar-
nished truth.'

'Apart from the woodworm and the stairs,' he reminded
her stonily.

'Are you prepared to gamble on that?' she demanded.
'Who knows what's under all that dirt?'

She didn't wait for a response. Once your boss had offered you a choice between loony and legal action, any
meaningful dialogue was at an end.

CHAPTER TWO

HOW DARED HE? How bloody dared he even suggest she might be suffering from stress, burnout? Damn it, Miles had to know this was all a crock of manure.

Tash, despite her stand-up defiance, was shaking as she left Miles Morgan's office and she headed for the cloakroom. There was no way she could go downstairs and face Janine, who'd obviously known exactly what was coming, until she had pulled herself together.

She jabbed pins in her hair, applied a bright don't-care-won't-care coating of lipstick and some mental stiffeners to her legs before she attempted the stairs she'd run up with such optimism only a few minutes earlier.

She'd been ten minutes, no more, but Janine was waiting with a cardboard box containing the contents of her desk drawers.

'Everything's there,' she said, not the slightest bit embarrassed. On the contrary, the smirk was very firmly in place. They'd never been friends but, while she'd never given Janine a second thought outside the office, it was possible that Janine—behind the faux sweetness and the professional smile and ignoring the hours she put in, her lack of a social life—had resented her bonuses. 'It's mostly rubbish.'

She didn't bother to answer. She could see for herself that the contents of her desk drawers had been tipped into the box without the slightest care.

Janine was right; it was mostly rubbish, apart from a spare pair of tights, the pencil case that one of her brothers had given her and the mug she used for her pens. She picked it up and headed for the door.

'Wait! Miles said…'

In her opinion, Miles had said more than enough but, keeping her expression impassive, she turned, waited.

'He asked me to take your keys.'

Of course he had. He wouldn't want her coming back when the office was closed to prove what havoc she could really cause, given sufficient provocation. Fortunately for him, her reputation was more important to her than petty revenge.

She put down the box, took out her key ring, removed the key to the back door of the office and handed it over without a word.

'And your car keys,' she said.

Until that moment none of this had seemed real, but the BMW convertible had been the reward Miles had dangled in front of his staff for anyone reaching a year-end sales target that he had believed impossible. She'd made it with a week to spare and it was her pride and joy as well as the envy of every other negotiator in the firm. Could someone have done this to her just to get…?

She stopped. That way really did lie madness.

No doubt Miles would use those spectacular sales figures to back up his claim of 'burnout', suggesting she'd driven herself to achieve the impossible and prove that she was better than anyone else. *So very sad…*

He might even manage to squeeze out a tear.

All he'd have to do was think of the damages he'd have to pay Darius Hadley.

Taking pride in the fact that her fingers weren't shaking—it was just the rest of her, apparently—she removed the silver Tiffany key ring Toby had bought her for Christ-

mas from her car keys and dropped it in her pocket, but
she held on to the keys. 'I'll clear my stuff out of the back.'

'I'll come with you,' Janine said, following her to the
door. 'I need to make sure it's locked up safely.'

She wasn't trusted to hand over the keys? Or did the
wretched woman think she'd drive off in it? Add car theft
to her crimes? Oh, wait. She was supposed to be crazy...

'Actually, you'll need to do more than that. I'm parked
in a twenty-minute zone and it'll need moving before—
Oh, too late...'

She startled the traffic warden slapping a ticket on
the windscreen with a smile before clicking the lock and
tossing the keys to Janine as if she didn't give a fig. She
wouldn't give her the pleasure of telling everyone how she'd
crumpled, broken down. It was just a car. She'd have it back
in no time. Just as soon as Miles stopped panicking and
started thinking straight.

She emptied the glovebox, gathered her wellington
boots, the ancient waxed jacket she'd bought in a charity
shop and her umbrella and added them to the box, then
reached for her laptop bag.

'I'll take that.'

'My laptop?' She finally turned to look at Janine. 'Did
Miles ask you to take it?'

'He's got a lot on his mind,' she replied with a little toss
of her head. In other words, no.

'True, and when I find out who's responsible for this
mess he won't be the only one. In the meantime,' she said,
hooking the strap over her shoulder and patting the soft
leather case that held her precious MacBook Pro, 'if he
should ask for it, I suggest you remind him that I bought it
out of my January bonus.'

Janine, caught out, flushed bright pink but it was a short-
lived triumph.

'There's a taxi waiting to take you to the Fairview,' she said, turning on her heel and heading back to the office.

Tash glanced at the black cab, idling at the kerb. Even loaded as she was, the temptation to stalk off in the direction of the nearest Underground station was strong, but there was no one apart from the traffic warden to witness the gesture so she climbed aboard and gave him her address.

The driver looked back. 'I was booked for the Fairview.'

'I have to go home first,' she said, straight-faced. 'I'm going to need a nightie and toothbrush.'

Darius strode the length of the King's Road, fury and the need to put distance between himself and Natasha Gordon driving his feet towards the Underground.

A minor setback? A house that she'd made unsellable, and a seven-figure tax bill on a house he couldn't live in—what would merit serious bother in her eyes?

Cornflower-blue, with hair that looked as if she'd just tumbled out of bed and a figure that was all curves. Sexy as hell, which was where his thoughts were taking him.

Once on the train, he took out the small sketchbook he carried with him and did what he had always done when he wanted to block out the world. He drew what he saw. Not the interior of the train, the woman sitting opposite him, the baby sleeping on her lap, but what was in his head.

Dark, angry images that had been stirred up by a house he'd never wanted to set foot in again but just refused to let go. But that wasn't what appeared on the page. His hand, ignoring his head, was drawing Natasha Gordon. Her eyes, startled wide as he'd confronted her. The way her brow had arched like the wing of a kestrel hovering over a hedgerow, waiting for an unsuspecting vole to make a move. The curve of hair drooping from an antique silver clasp, the tiny crease at the corner of her mouth that had appeared when she'd offered him a smile along with her hand. It was as if her image had burned itself into his brain, every detail pinpoint-sharp. The blush heating her cheeks, a fine chain about her neck that disappeared between invitingly generous breasts. Her long legs.

Was he imagining them?

He couldn't remember looking at her legs and yet he'd drawn her shoes—black suede, dangerously high heels, a sexy little ankle strap...

He did not fight it, but drew obsessively, continuously, as if by putting her on paper he could clear his mind, rid himself of what had happened in that moment when he'd stood up and turned to face her. When he'd looked back, knowing that she'd be there at the window. Wishing he'd taken her with him when he'd left. When he'd hovered for a dangerous moment on the point of turning back...

Wouldn't Morgan have loved that?

He stopped drawing and just let his mind's eye see her, imagining how he'd paint her, sculpt her and when, finally, he looked up, he'd gone way past his stop.

Tash sat back in the cab as the driver pulled away from the kerb, did a U-turn and joined the queue of traffic backed up along the King's Road.

A little more than twenty minutes—just long enough to get a parking ticket—that was all it had taken to reduce her from top-selling negotiator at one of the most prestigious estate agencies in London, to unemployable.

'It's a beautiful house, Darius.' Patsy, having dropped off some paperwork and made them both a cup of tea, had discovered the *Chronicle* in the waste bin when she'd discarded the teabags. 'Lots of room. You could make a studio in one of the buildings,' she said with a head jerk that took in the concrete walls and floor still stained with oil from its previous incarnation as a motor repair shop. 'Why don't you just move in? Ask me nicely and I might even come and keep house for you.'

'You and whose army?' He glanced at the photograph of the sprawling house, its Tudor core having been added to over the centuries by ancestors with varying degrees of taste. At least someone had done their job right, taking time to find the perfect spot to show the Chase at its best. The half-timbering, a mass of roses hiding a multitude of sins. A little to the right of a cedar tree that had been planted to commemorate the coronation of Queen Victoria.

The perfect spot at the perfect time on the perfect day when a golden mist rising from the river had lent the place an ethereal quality that took him back to school holidays and early-morning fishing trips with his grandfather. Took him back to an enchanted world seen through the innocent eyes of a child.

'It's got at least twenty rooms,' he said, returning to the armature on which he was building his interpretation of a racehorse flying over a fence. 'That's not including the kitchen, scullery, pantries and the freezing attics where the poor sods who kept the place running in the old days were housed.' Plus half a dozen cottages, at present occupied by former employees of the estate whom he could never evict, and a boat house that was well past its best twenty years ago.

She put the magazine on his workbench where he could see it, opened a packet of biscuits and, when he shook his head, helped herself to one. 'So what are you going to do?'

'Wring that wretched girl's neck?' he offered, and tried not to think about his hand curled around her nape. How her skin would feel against his palm, the scent of vanilla that he couldn't lose… 'Subject closed.'

He picked up the *Chronicle* and tossed it back in the bin.

'It said in the paper that she'd had some kind of a break-down,' Patsy protested.

A widow, she worked as a freelance 'Girl Friday' for several local businesses, fitting them in around the needs of her ten-year-old son. She kept his books and his paperwork in order, the fridge stocked with fresh milk, cold beer, and his life organised. The downside was that, like an old time travelling minstrel, she delivered neighbourhood gossip, adding to the story with each stop she made. He had no doubt that Hadley Chase had featured heavily in her story arc this week and her audience were no doubt eagerly awaiting the next instalment.

'Please tell me you don't believe everything you read in the newspapers,' he said as, concentration gone, he gave up on the horse and drank the tea he hadn't asked for.

'Of course I don't,' she declared, 'but the implication was that she had a history of instability. They wouldn't lie about something like that.' She took another biscuit, clearly in no hurry to be anywhere else.

'No? She was in full control of her faculties when I saw her,' he said. 'I suspect the breakdown story is Morgan and Black's attempt to focus the blame on her and lessen the impact on their business.' Lessen the damages.

'That's shocking. She should sue.'

'She hasn't bothered to deny it,' he said.

'Maybe her lawyer has advised her not to say anything. What's she like? You didn't say you'd met her.'

'Believe me,' he said, 'I'm doing my best to forget.' Forget his body's slamming response at the sight of her. The siren call of a sensually pleasing body that had been made to wrap around a man. A mouth made for pleasure. The feeling of control slipping away from him.

Precious little chance of that when his hands itched to capture the liquid blue of eyes that had sucked the breath out of him, sent the blood rushing south, nailing him to the spot. A look that eluded his every attempt to recreate it.

It was just as well she was safely out of reach in the Fairview, playing along with Morgan's game in the hopes of hanging on to her job. Asking her to sit for him was a distraction he could not afford. And would certainly not endear him to his lawyers.

'I wonder if it was anorexia?' she pondered. 'In the past.' Patsy, generous in both character and build, took another biscuit.

'No way.' He shook his head as he recalled that delicious moment when, as Natasha Gordon had offered him her hand, the top button of her blouse had surrendered to the strain, parting to reveal the kind of cleavage any red-blooded male would willingly dive into. 'Natasha Gordon has all the abundant charms of a milkmaid.'

'A milkmaid?'

Patsy's grandparents had immigrated to Britain in the nineteen-fifties and she'd lived her entire life in the inner city. It was likely that the closest she'd ever come to a cow was in a children's picture book.

'Big blue eyes, a mass of fair hair and skin like an old-fashioned rose.' There was one that scrambled over the rear courtyard at the Chase. He had no idea what it was called, but it had creamy petals blushed with pink that were bursting out of a calyx not designed to contain such bounty. 'Believe me, this is not a woman who lives on lettuce.'

'Oh...' She gave him an old-fashioned look. 'And did this milkmaid apologise with a pretty curtsy?' she asked, confirming her familiarity with the genre.

'She didn't appear to have read the script.' No apology, no excuses... 'She suggested that the advertisement was little more than a minor setback.'

'Really? You're quite sure the poor woman is not cracking up?'

'As sure as I can be without a doctor's note.' But there was a distinct possibility that he was.

Milkmaids, roses…

Forget wheeling her in to apologise. If it was possible to be any more cynical, he'd have said they were hoping that she might use her charms, her lack of control over her buttons, to distract him from taking legal action.

He shouldn't even be thinking about how far she might go to achieve that objective. Or how happy he would be to lie back and let her try.

'Dad's really worried about you, Tash. You've been working so hard and all this stress…well…you know…' Her mother never actually said what she was thinking out loud. 'He thinks you should come home for a while so that we can look after you.'

Tash sighed. She'd known that whatever she said, they'd half believe the newspaper story, convinced that they had been right all along. That she would be safer at home. No matter how much she told herself that they were wrong, it was hard to resist that kind of worry.

'Mum, I'm fine.'

'Tom thinks a break would do you good. We've booked the house down in Cornwall for the half-term holiday.' So far, so what she'd expected. Her dad the worrier, her brother the doctor prescribing a week at the seaside and her mother trying to please everyone. 'You know how you always loved it there and you haven't seen the children for ages. You won't believe how they've grown.'

Twenty-five and on holiday with her family. Building sandcastles for her nieces during the day and playing Scrabble or Monopoly in the evening. How appealing was that?

'I saw them at Easter,' she said. 'Send me a postcard.'

'Darling…'

'It's all smoke and mirrors, Mum. I'm fit as a flea.'

'Are you sure? Are you taking the vitamins I sent you?'

'I never miss,' she said, rolling her eyes in exasperation. She understood, really, but anyone would think she was still five years old and fighting for her life instead of a successful career woman. This was just a hiccup.

'Are you eating properly?'

'All the food groups.'

When the taxi had delivered her to her door, she'd gone straight to the freezer and dug out a tub of strawberry cheesecake ice cream. While she'd eaten it, she pulled up the file on her laptop so that if, in a worst case scenario, it came to an unfair dismissal tribunal she had a paper trail to demonstrate exactly what she'd done. Except that there it all was, word for word, on the screen. Exactly as printed. Which made no sense.

The proof copy she'd seen, approved and put in her out tray had been the one she'd actually written, not the one that was printed.

Either she really was going mad or someone had gone out of their way to do this to her. Not just changing the original copy, fiddling with the proof and intercepting the phone call from the *Chronicle*, but getting into her laptop to change what she'd written so that she had no proof that she'd ever written anything else.

Okay, a forensic search would pull up the original, but there would be no way to prove that she hadn't changed it herself because whoever had done this had logged in using her password.

Which meant there was only one person in the frame.

The man who hadn't let her know he was back a week early from a six-week rugby tour. The man who hadn't come rushing round with pizza, Chianti and chocolate the minute he heard the news. Who hadn't called, texted, emailed even, to ask how she was.

The man who was now occupying the upstairs office that should, by rights, be hers.

Her colleague with benefits: Toby Denton.

She wouldn't have thought the six-foot-three blond rugby-playing hunk—who'd never made a secret of the fact that he saw work as a tedious interruption to his life and whose only ambition was to play the sport professionally—had the brains to engineer her downfall with such cunning.

His cluelessness, off the rugby field, had been a major part of his appeal. When there was any rescuing to be done—which was often when it came to work—she was the one tossing him the lifebelt. Like giving him her laptop password so that he could check the office diary for an early-morning appointment when, typically, he'd forgotten where he was supposed to be.

The announcement of his appointment as associate partner had appeared on the company website the day after she'd been walked to the door with her belongings in a cardboard box. Photographs of the champagne celebration had appeared on the blog a day later. It was great PR and she'd have applauded if it hadn't been her career they were interring.

'Tash?' her mother asked anxiously. 'Are you baking?'

'Baking? No...' Then, in sheer desperation, 'Got to go. Call waiting. Have a lovely time in Cornwall.'

Call waiting... She wished, she thought, glancing along the work surface at the ginger, lemon drizzle and passion cakes lined up alongside a Sacher Torte, waiting for the ganache she was making.

She *had* been baking. She'd used every bowl she possessed, every cake tin. They were piled up in the sink and on the draining board, along with a heap of eggshells and empty sugar, flour and butter wrappers and a fine haze of icing sugar hung in the air, coating every surface, including her.

It was her displacement activity. Some people played endless computer games, or went for a run, or ironed when they needed to let their brain freewheel. She beat butter and sugar and eggs into creamy peaks.

Unfortunately, her mind was ignoring the no-job, no-career problem. Instead it kept running Darius Hadley on a loop. That moment when he'd turned and looked at her in Miles Morgan's office, his face all dark shadows, his eyes burning into her. His hands. The glint of gold beneath dark curls. The air stirring as he'd walked past her, leaving the scent of something earthy behind.

That moment when he'd stopped in the street and looked back and she'd known that if he'd lifted a hand to her she would have gone to him. Worse, had wanted him to lift a hand...

Her skin glowed just thinking about that look. Not just her skin.

Madness.

Her skin was sticky, her eyes gritty; she had no job and no one was going to call. Not Miles. Not any of the agencies that had tried to tempt her away from him. Last week she was the negotiator everyone wanted on their team, but now she was damaged goods.

If she was going to rescue her career, this was going to have to be a show rather than tell scenario. She would have to demonstrate to the world that she was still the best there was. Her brain hadn't been dodging the problem; it had been showing her the answer.

Darius Hadley.

She was going to have to find a buyer for Hadley Chase.

A week ago that had been a challenge, but she'd had the contacts, people who would pick up the phone when she called, listen to her when she told them she had exactly the house they were looking for because she didn't lie, didn't waste their time. Matching houses with the right buyers was a passion with her. People trusted her. Or they had.

Now the word on the street was that she'd lost it. She was on her own with nothing to offer except her wits, her knowledge of the market and the kind of motivation that would move mountains if she could persuade Darius Hadley to give her a chance.

She was going to have to face him: this man who'd turned her into a blushing, jelly-boned cliché with no more than a look.

In the normal course of events it wouldn't have been more than a momentary wobble. It had been made clear to her by the estate's executor that the vendor wanted nothing to do with the actual sale of his house and if he'd let her just get on with it she would never have seen him again. Apparently her luck had hit the deck on all fronts that morning.

At the time she hadn't given the reason why Darius Hadley was keeping his distance any thought—it had taken all her concentration not to melt into a puddle at his feet—but the more she'd thought about him, the more she understood how it must hurt to be the Hadley to let the house go. To lose four centuries of his family history.

If there was no cash to go with the property, he would have no choice—death meant taxes—but it was easy to see why he'd been furious with them, with *her*, for messing up and forcing him to confront the situation head-on. Maybe, though, now he'd had time to calm down, he'd be glad of someone offering to help.

Selling a country estate was an expensive business. Printing, advertising, travel, and she doubted that, in these cash-strapped days, he'd be inundated with estate agents eager to invest in a house that had been publicly declared a money pit.

Hopefully she'd be all he'd got. And he, collywobbles notwithstanding, was almost certainly her only hope.

Fortunately she had all the details of Hadley Chase on her laptop.

What she didn't have were the contact details for Darius Hadley.

She'd had no success when she'd searched Hadley Chase on Google hoping for some family gossip to get the property page editors salivating. She assumed it would have thrown up anything newsworthy about Darius Hadley, but she typed his name into the search engine anyway.

A whole load of links came up, including images, and she clicked on the only one of him. It had been taken, ironically, from one of those high society functions featured in the *Country Chronicle* and the caption read: 'Award-winning sculptor Darius Hadley at the Serpentine Gallery...'

He was a sculptor? Well, that would explain the steel toecaps, the grey smears on his jeans. That earthy scent had been clay...

His tie was loose, his collar open and he'd been caught unawares, laughing at something or someone out of the picture and she was right. A smile was all it took to lift the shadows. He still had the look of the devil, but one who was having a good day, and she reached out and touched the screen, her fingertips against his mouth.

'Oh...' she breathed. 'Collywollydoodah...'

CHAPTER THREE

THE NARROW COBBLED backstreet was a jumble of buildings that had been endlessly converted and added to over the centuries. All Tash had was the street name, but she had been confident that a prize-winning sculptor's studio would be easy enough to find.

She was wrong.

She'd reached a dead end and found no sign, no indication that art of any kind happened behind any of the doors but as she turned she found herself face-to-face with a woman who was regarding her through narrowed eyes.

'Can I help you?' she asked.

'I hope so… I'm looking for Darius Hadley. I was told his studio was in this street,' she prompted.

The woman gave her a long, thoughtful look, taking in the grey business suit that she kept for meetings with the property managers of billionaires; she had hoped it would cut down on the inexplicable electricity that had sparked between them in Miles's office. A spark that had sizzled even when he was outside on the pavement looking up at her.

Okay, maybe she should have worn a pair of sensible, low-heeled shoes, added horn-rimmed spectacles to make herself look *seriously* serious. Hell, she *was* serious, never more so—this was her career on the line—but there was only so far she could stretch the illusion. As for her favourite red heels, she'd needed them to give her a little extra

height, some of the bounce that had been knocked clean
out of her. Besides, Darius Hadley wouldn't be fooled by
a pair of faux specs. Not for a minute.

She'd experienced the power of eyes that would see right
through any games, any pretence and knew that she would
have to be absolutely straight with him.

No problem. Straight was what she did and she had it
all worked out. The look, the poise, what she was going to
say. She was going to be totally professional, which was
all very fine in theory but first she had to find him. She'd
called in a big favour to get his address but now she was
beginning to wonder if she'd been sold a fake.

The woman, her inspection completed, asked, 'Is Darius expecting you?'

'He'll want to see me,' she said, fingers mentally crossed.
'Do you know him?'

'Sure,' she said, a slow smile lighting up her face. 'I
know everyone. Even you, Natasha Gordon.'

Tash, still dragging her chin back into place, followed
the woman back down the street towards a pair of wide,
rusty old garage doors over which a sign suggested someone called Mike would repair your car while you waited.
She produced a large bunch of keys and let herself in
through the personnel door.

'Darius?' she called, leaving the door open. Tash, grabbing her chance, stepped in after her. 'How are you feeling
about the milkmaid today?'

Milkmaid?

There was a discouraging grunt from somewhere above
her head. 'Not now, Patsy.'

She looked up. Darius Hadley was standing on a tall
stepladder, thumbing clay onto the leaping figure of a horse.

'Do you still want to wring her neck?' Patsy persisted.

'Nothing has changed since last week,' he replied, leaning back a little to check what he'd done, 'but, to put your

mind at rest, that damned house has given me enough trouble without adding grievous bodily harm to the list.'

'So it would be safe to let her in?'

Now she had his attention.

'Let her…' He swung around and her heart leapt. He was so high… 'She's *here*?'

'She doesn't have a milking stool, or one of those things they wear across the shoulders with a pail at each end, but other than that she fits the description. Abundantly,' she added with a broad smile. 'Of course it helped that you've been drawing her on any bit of paper that comes to hand for the last few days.'

'Patsy…'

'I found her wandering up and down the street looking for your studio. Your name on the door would be a real help,' she said, apparently not the least bit intimidated by the growl.

'That would only encourage visitors. People who interrupt me while I'm working,' he said, looking over Patsy's head to where she was hovering just inside the doorway.

Maybe it was just the sunlight streaming in through the skylight above him, but today his eyes were molten slate, scorching her skin, melting the starch in her shirt, reducing her knees to fudge frosting.

It wasn't just his eyes. Everything about him was hot: the faded, clay-smeared jeans hugging his thighs, midnight-black hair curling into his neck, long, ropey muscles in his forearms. And those hands…

She had tried to convince herself that she'd imagined the electricity, the fizz, the crackle… There had been a shock factor when she'd seen him in Miles's office, but he'd been in her head for days and not just because he was her only chance to get back to work.

She'd been dreaming about those hands. How they'd feel on her body, the drag of hard calluses against tender skin…

'I know I'm the last person on earth you want to talk to, Mr Hadley,' she said quickly before he could tell her to get lost, 'but if you can spare me ten minutes, I've got a proposition for you.'

'Proposition?'

The word hung in the air.

Darius looked down at the shadowy hourglass shape of Natasha Gordon, backlit by sunlight streaming in over the city rooftops.

It was just a word. Morgan couldn't possibly be using her as a sweetener. But then again, maybe it was her idea...

'If you could spare me ten minutes?' From above her he could see straight down the opening of her blouse, the way her luscious breasts were squished together as she raised her hand to shield her eyes from the light pouring in from the skylights. 'Maybe we could sit down,' she suggested, lifting her other hand a little to show him a glossy white cakebox, dangling from a ribbon. 'I've brought cake. It's home-made. I'll even make the tea.'

He picked up a damp cloth and wiped his hands, giving himself a moment to still his rampaging libido. He should send her packing but how often did a man receive a proposition from a sexy woman bearing cake? And now she was here he'd be able to capture the look that had eluded him, draw her out of his head.

'I hope you or your mother can cook,' he said and Patsy nodded, apparently satisfied that it would be safe to leave him alone with her, and left them to it.

'Would I come bearing anything less than perfection?' she asked.

Not this woman, he thought. She'd pulled out all the stops... 'How did you find me?'

'Does it matter?' she asked, the wide space between her brows crumpled in a tiny frown that didn't fool him for a moment. Not many people knew where he worked. She'd had to work hard to locate him.

'Humour me,' he suggested, taking a step down the ladder, and she caught her breath, muscles tensed, barely stopping herself from taking a step back. She was nowhere near as cool as she looked. Which made two of them.

'I did what anyone would do. Ran an Internet search,' she said quickly, 'and there you were. Darius Hadley, award-winning sculptor, presently working on a prestigious commission to create a life-size bronze of one of the greatest racehorses of all time.' Lots of details so he'd forget the question. He was familiar with the technique. His grandfather had been a past master at diverting him whenever he'd asked awkward questions. 'There was a photograph,' she added.

'Of me?' He took another step down. She swallowed, but this time stood her ground.

'Of the horse. It was in the *Racing Times*. Photographs of you are scarce. You don't even have a website.' She made it sound like an accusation.

'I seem to manage.'

'Yes…'

She turned away, giving them both a break as she looked around at the dozens of photographs taken from every angle of the horse—galloping, jumping, standing—that he'd pinned to the walls. She paused briefly at the anatomical drawings of the skeleton, the muscles, the blood vessels and then looked up at his interpretation of the animal gathered to leap a jump.

'If I'd known who you were when the house came on the market,' she said at last, 'I could have used the information to get some editorial interest. Racehorse owners are among the richest men in the world and Hadley Chase is close to one of the country's major racehorse training centres.'

'You managed an excessive number of column inches

without any help from me,' he said, 'but that's who, not where,' he said, refusing to be sidetracked.

A rueful smile made it to a mouth that was a little too big for beauty, tugging it upwards. 'The where *was* more difficult. And the address was only half the story. If it hadn't been for Patsy I'd still be looking for you.'

'So?' he insisted.

'I'm sorry, Mr Hadley. An estate agent never reveals her sources.'

'A journalist?' No, the piece in the newspaper had not been kind. Reading between the lines, anyone would be forgiven for assuming her 'collapse' had been the result of a coke-fuelled drive for success. Something in her past... Journalists would not be flavour of the month. 'An art dealer?' he suggested. Who would be vulnerable to those big blue eyes and a loose top button? No... Who had moved recently? 'Freddie Glover threw a house-warming party a few months back,' he said.

She neither confirmed nor denied it and, satisfied, he let it rest.

'If you've come to apologise...' She seemed bright enough so he left her to fill in the blank.

'I was sure Miles would have performed the ritual grovel but I could go through the motions if you insist,' she offered.

A little movement of her hand, underlining the offer, sent a barely discernible shimmer through her body—a shimmer that found an answering echo deep in his groin. Yes...

She waited briefly, but he was too busy catching his own breath to answer.

'I'm sorry about what happened, obviously, but that's not the reason I'm here.'

'Why are you here?' he demanded. He hated being this out of control around a woman. Could not make himself send her away. 'For heaven's sake, come in and close the door if you're staying. I won't eat you...'

She didn't look entirely convinced, but she closed the door, took a breath and then walked towards him with the kind of mesmerisingly slow, hip-swaying walk that had gone out of style fifty years ago. Around the same time as her hourglass figure.

No longer backlit from the street, the light pouring in from the skylights overhead lit her up like a spotlight and he could see that she'd made an attempt to disguise its lushness beneath a neat grey suit. Or maybe not. The skirt clung to her thighs and stopped a hand's breadth short of serious, leaving a yard of leg on display, always supposing he'd got past the deep vee of her shirt. She really should try a size larger if she was serious.

As for her hair, she'd fastened it in a sleek twist that rested against the nape of her neck; it was a classically provocative style and his fingers, severely provoked, itched to pull the pins and send it tumbling around her face and shoulders.

She'd stopped a teasing arm's width from the ladder, looking up at him. Near enough for the honeyed scent of warm skin, something lemony, spicy, chocolatey to reach him but, maybe sensing the danger, not quite close enough to touch. Clearly her instincts were better honed than his because every beat of his pulse urged him to reach for her, pull her close enough to feel what she was doing to him...

Forget the cake. Eating her, one luscious mouthful at a time, was the only thing on his mind.

'Well?' he snapped. Angry with her for disturbing him. No one was allowed to disturb him while he was working. Angry with himself for wanting to be disturbed. For the triumphant *Yes!* racketing through him at her unexpected appearance, despite the certainty that this was some devious scheme of Morgan's—sending in the sex bomb to persuade him to drop his claim for damages.

Tash ran her tongue over her teeth in an attempt to get some spit so that she could answer him. Lay out her offer like the professional she was.

She was used to meeting powerful men and women but she was having a tough job remembering why she was in Darius Hadley's studio. The concrete floor and walls made the space cold after the sun outside, but a trickle of sweat was running down between her breasts and an age-old instinct was telling her to shrug off her jacket, let her hair down, reach out and run her fingers up his denim-clad thigh, perched, tantalisingly, at eye level.

'What do you want, Natasha Gordon?'

She looked up and saw her feelings echoed in Darius Hadley's shadowed features and for a moment it could have gone either way.

She was saved by the crash of a pigeon landing on the skylight, startling them both out of the danger zone.

'I don't want anything from you, Mr Hadley,' she said quickly. Could this be any more difficult? Bad enough that he thought she'd sabotaged the sale of his house without acting like a sex-starved nymphomaniac. 'On the contrary. I'm going to do you a favour. I'm going to sell your house for you.'

'Miss Gordon...'

'I know.' She held up her hand in a gesture of surrender. 'Why would you trust me? After the debacle with your ad,' she added, and then wished she hadn't. Having found him, got through the door a darn sight more easily than she'd expected and survived that first intense encounter, reminding him why he should throw her out was not her brightest move.

'Is there any hope that you're not going to tell me?' he asked.

Phew... 'Not a chance.' She slipped the strap of her laptop bag from her shoulder and let it drop at her feet, anchoring herself in his space. Then she placed the glossy white cakebox on his workbench alongside his neatly laid-out tools—most of which appeared to be lethal weapons. Most, but not all. She picked up a long curved rib bone.

'That belonged to the last person who annoyed me,' he said, finally stepping off the ladder.

'Really?' Apparently there was a sense of humour lurking beneath that scowl. Promising...

'What did he do?' she asked, looking up at the sculpture rearing above her, heart swelling within its ribcage as the horse leapt some unseen obstacle. From what she'd seen of his work on the Net, it appeared that visceral was something of a theme. 'Did he throw you? Is this you getting your own back?'

'Anyone can make a pretty image.' He took the bone from her, replaced it on the bench. 'I want to show what's behind the power, the movement. Bones, sinews, heart.'

'The engine rather than the chassis.' Eager to avoid close eye contact, she walked around the beast, examining it from every angle, before looking across at Darius Hadley from the safety of the far side. 'That's what you do, isn't it? Show us the inside of things.'

'That's what's real, what's important.'

'I saw your installation outside Tate Modern. The house.' That had been stripped back to the bones, too.

'You've done your homework,' he said.

'I was just walking past. I didn't realise it was yours until I looked you up online. I thought it was...bleak.'

'Everyone's a critic.'

'No... It was beautiful. It's just...well, there were no people and without them a house is simply a frame.'

'Perhaps that was the point,' he suggested.

'Was it?' He didn't answer and she looked back up at the horse. 'This is…big.'

'I'll cast a smaller version for a limited edition.'

'Just the thing for the mantelpiece,' she said flippantly. Then wished she hadn't. His work was more important than that. 'I'm sorry; that was a stupid thing to say. I'm a bit nervous.'

'I'm not surprised. Does Miles Morgan really think he can buy me off with a glimpse of your cleavage and a slice of cake?'

'What?' She checked her top button but it was still in place. Just. She'd worn her roomiest shirt but working ten, fourteen hours a day didn't leave much time for exercise, or a carefully thought-out diet. And she'd moved less and eaten more in the last week than was good for anyone; it was definitely time to get out of the kitchen and back to work. 'Miles didn't send me. As for the cleavage…' She lifted her shoulders in a little shrug that she hoped would give the impression that she was utterly relaxed. She was good at that. The most important thing she'd learned about selling houses was to create an image. Set the stage, create an initial impact that would grab the viewer's attention then hold it. This time she was selling herself… 'I've been on a baking binge and eating too much of my own cooking.'

'And now you want to share.'

'I thought something sweet might help to break the ice.'

Ice?

There was no ice as she bent forward to tug on the gauzy bow that exactly matched the shade of her lipstick, her nails; only heat zinging through his veins, making the blood pump thickly in his ears.

He'd been drawing her obsessively for a week, trying to get her out of his head, but while the two-dimensional image had been recognisable it lacked the warmth, the sparkle of the original.

Right now all he wanted to do was peel away her clothes, expose those rich creamy curves to the play of sunlight and shade.

He wanted to draw her from every angle, stripping away layer after layer until he could see her core. Until he could see what she was thinking, what she was feeling; transmute that into a three-dimensional image exposing the heart of the woman within.

He wanted a lot more than that.

'What have you got?' he asked.

'I wasn't sure which you'd like so I brought a selection,' she said, looking at him. For a moment the air seemed to crackle and then she was looking down at the box, her eyes hidden by silky lashes. 'There's lemon drizzle, chocolate, coffee, sticky ginger and, um, passion cake.'

The scent of vanilla rose enticingly from the box, taking him straight back to his childhood—that sweet moment when he'd been allowed to lick the remains of the mixture from the spoon; when he'd sunk his teeth into a cake still warm from the oven.

He was no longer a boy but he resisted one temptation only to look up and find himself confronted by the reach-out-and-touch-me lure of warm breasts.

Was this how it had been for his father? An obsessive urge to possess one woman wiping everything from his mind. One woman becoming his entire world.

Stick to the cake...

'You weren't kidding when you said you'd been on a baking binge, Miss Gordon,' he said, taking the first piece his fingers touched, anything to distract him. 'Did the Fairview recommend it as occupational therapy?'

'Tash, please. Everyone calls me Tash.'

'I prefer Natasha,' he said, sucking the icing from his thumb, and she blushed. Not the swift suffusion of heat that rose to her face in that moment when they'd confronted one another in Morgan's office and seen how it would be if they ever let their guard down, but a real girlish blush.

'Nobody calls me that,' she said. 'Only my mother. When I've done something to exasperate her.'

'That would be your mother and me, then.'

'Point taken.' The corner of her mouth tilted upwards in a wry sketch at a smile. 'I'd be annoyed with me if I were you. I'm pretty annoyed myself, to be honest. It wasn't much fun having to phone my parents and warn them that they and their neighbours and everyone they knew would be reading about my breakdown in the evening paper. Warn them that they'd probably have reporters ringing them at home, knocking on the door. Which they did, by the way.'

'No comment.'

The smile deepened to reveal a small crease in her cheek. She'd once had a dimple...

'It's not true, by the way. About the Fairview. In case you were in any doubt. Just so that we're on the same page here, Miles Morgan and I parted company less than fifteen minutes after you left the office.'

'He fired you?' He should have waited. Gone back. Followed his gut instinct to grab her hand and take her with him... 'I'm not big on employment law but I'm fairly sure he can't have it both ways. He can't dismiss you when you're on sick leave.'

'You're probably right,' she admitted, 'but I refused to cooperate with his plan to have my sanity publicly questioned and hide away in the Fairview in the cause of saving the firm's reputation.'

'I saw the paper.'

'Everyone saw the paper,' she said. 'I'm supposedly giving my brain a rest in the Fairview while I consider my future.'

'You didn't deny it,' he pointed out.

'Like that would have helped.' She clutched at her throat

with both hands. *'I'm not mad. It wasn't me. I was framed!'* she croaked out, rolling her eyes, feigning madness.

He was expected to laugh, but it was taking all his concentration just to breathe because she'd forgotten not to look at him. And then she remembered and he could see that it wasn't just him. They were both struggling with the zing of lightning that arced between them.

'Since Plan B was a threat to sue me for malicious damage…' Her voice was thick, her pupils huge against the shot-silk blue; what would she do if he reached out and took her hand and held it against his zip, if he sucked her lower lip into his mouth? '…I didn't think there was much point in hanging around.'

He turned away, crossed to the kettle, picking it up to make sure there was some water in it before switching it on. Any distraction from the thoughts racketing through his head. The same thoughts that had driven him from Morgan's office amplified a hundred times.

He had no problem with lust at first sight. Uncomplicated, life's-too-short sex that gave everyone a good time and didn't screw with your head. This was complicated with knobs on. He should never have let her stay.

He could not have sent her away…

'It's a bit like denying Hadley Chase is riddled with woodworm,' he said, tossing teabags into a couple of mugs, making an effort to bring the conversation back to the house—as effective as any cold shower. 'Once it's in print, who's going to believe you?'

'Exactly… Not that it is,' she said, as eager as him to get back to business, apparently. 'Riddled with woodworm. The house has been neglected in recent years, the roof needs some work, but the structure is sound and the advertisement did get people talking about the house,' she stressed earnestly, as if that were something to be welcomed. 'My photograph was reprinted in all the weekend property supplements.'

'Your photograph?' He waved her towards the ancient sofa that he sometimes slept on when he'd worked late and he was too tired to stagger the hundred yards home. 'Didn't Morgan employ a professional?'

'Oh, yes, and he did his best with the interior, but it was raining on the day he was there so, despite his best efforts with Photoshop, his exteriors weren't doing the house any favours,' she said, sinking into the low saggy cushions. 'We were running out of time so, when the weather changed at the weekend, I grabbed the chance to dash down the motorway early on Sunday and take some myself.'

'You've got a good eye.'

'Oh, I took hundreds of pictures. That one just leapt out at me.'

It was more than that, he thought, getting out the milk, keeping his hands busy. She'd taken the trouble to go back in her own time. Given it one hundred per cent... 'It's a pity the property pages didn't just stick to the photograph.'

'That was never going to happen. It was too good a story to pass up on and it was a fabulous PR opportunity. If Miles hadn't panicked...' She paused, as if something was bothering her.

'What? What would you have done?'

'Oh... Well, first I'd have got in a firm of cleaners at the firm's expense. Then I'd have invited the property editors to lunch at the Hadley Arms and, once I'd got them gagging at the perfect picture postcard village, I'd have driven them up to the house, slowly enough so that they could appreciate the view, that first glimpse as the house appears.'

'And then?'

'Well, obviously,' she said, 'I'd have got you an offer within the week.'

Her smile was bright and as brittle as spun sugar. He

wanted the real thing. Not just mouth and teeth, but those eyes lit up, glowing...

'Despite the dodgy staircase and the leaking roof?' he pressed.

She tutted but it earned him a hint of what her smile could be. 'It hasn't rained all week.'

'This hot spell can't last.'

'No, which is why we need to get cracking. Hadley Chase has so much *potential*,' she continued. 'I hadn't realised the extent of the outbuildings until I went down by myself. The stables, the dairy and how many houses have got a brewery, for heaven's sake?'

'It was standard for big houses back in the day, when drinking small beer was safer than water. It hasn't been used in my lifetime. Nor has the dairy.'

'Maybe not, but they're ripe for conversion into workshops, holiday accommodation, offices. Miles isn't usually so slow...' She let it go, a tiny frown buckling the smooth skin between her brows. 'My mistake.'

'Surely it was his?'

'It's a little more complicated than that.'

She propped her elbow on the arm of the sofa, chin on hand, giving him another flash of her assets. By way of distraction, he picked up the cakebox and offered it to her.

'You do still want to sell the house?' she said as she leaned forward and did an eeny-meeny-miny-mo over the cakes with a dark red fingernail before choosing one.

Some distraction.

'I assumed you'd been sent by Morgan to persuade me to drop my suit,' he said, helping himself to another look straight down the front of her shirt. She was wearing one of those lace traffic-accident bras and all the blood in his brain went south.

She looked up when he didn't say any more. 'Do you still think that?'

Thinking? Who was thinking... He shook his head. 'No. You're pitching for the business.'

She looked up, no smile now, just determination. 'This isn't business, it's personal. What you do about Morgan and Black is your own affair, but my expertise won't cost you a penny.' She gave another of those little shrugs and, as she recrossed her legs, he switched from imperial to metric. A metre...

It had to be deliberate, but he didn't care.

'Of course, if you'd rather sit back and wait a year or two for the fuss to die down...?' she offered before biting into a small square of lemon drizzle cake, her teeth sinking into the softness of the sponge. White teeth, rose petal lips...

Forget the inner woman, he wanted to draw her naked, wanted to mould that luscious body in clay, learn the shape with his hands and then recreate it. Wanted to taste the tip of her tongue as it sought out the sugar clinging to her lip...

'You *might* be lucky,' she said, cucumber-cool, apparently unaware of the effect she was having or of the turmoil raging within him. 'It might be a big news week in the property business and they won't dredge up the story all over again. Reprint the original advertisement.' She finished the tiny square of cake, sucked the stickiness off a fingertip. It was deliberate and he discovered that he didn't care. Just as long as she went on doing it. 'I'll leave you to imagine how likely that is.'

'You seem to forget, Natasha, that I've seen your expertise at first hand.'

'What you've seen, Mr Hadley, is me being stitched up by a man who wanted the promotion I'd worked my socks off for without the bother of putting in the hours.' A fine rim of sugar, missed by her tongue, glistened on her upper lip.

'Darius,' he said, aware that a film of sweat had broken

out above his own lip. Whatever it was she was doing, it was working. 'Only my accountant calls me Mr Hadley.'

He expected her to come back with *your accountant and me*. Instead, she said, 'I'm sorry, Darius. When I said it was a bit more complicated than you thought, I meant really *complicated*.' She looked up, her eyes intent and just a touch desperate. 'The mess-up with the advertisement wasn't a mistake.'

'Not a mistake?'

'Not a mistake,' she repeated, 'but *I* was the target. You were just collateral damage.'

CHAPTER FOUR

'COLLATERAL…?' DARIUS REPEATED, rerunning what she'd said through his head. 'Are you saying this was all about some internal power play at Morgan and Black? That it was deliberate?'

'I really am sorry,' she repeated.

'Not half as sorry as I am.' Or Miles Morgan would be if it was true. 'Did he get it? Your promotion?'

A sigh of relief rippled through her. 'My promotion, my car and, as the icing on the cake, my reputation down the drain.'

The desperation had been fear, he realised. She'd been afraid that he would laugh out loud or call her a liar. The truth of the matter was that he didn't know what to think. It seemed preposterous and yet he'd already half convinced himself that she hadn't messed up the ad. Apparently Freddie Glover wasn't the only one susceptible to a pair of blue eyes and a great pair of—

'The kettle seems to have boiled. Shall I make the tea?' she asked.

'You did volunteer.' Tea was the furthest thing from his mind, but it gave them both a moment and, besides, he wanted to watch her move. The lift of her head, the unfolding of her legs, the muscles in a long shapely calf as she fought the clutches of the sofa. 'Why did he want to destroy your reputation?' he asked, reaching on automatic for his sketch pad, a pencil, working swiftly to capture the image. The lines of her neck, her shoulders as she clicked the kettle back on. Her back and legs as she bent to open the fridge. 'Wasn't your promotion enough?'

'There was no other way of being certain I'd be history,' she said, concentrating on opening a carton of milk. 'I'm really good at my job.'

After an initial wobble when she'd looked as if she wanted to tear his clothes off, Natasha Gordon was doing a very good job of presenting herself as a woman totally in control of her emotions but her eyes betrayed her. A pulse was visible at her throat and if he slid his hand inside the open invitation of her shirt, laid his palm against her breast, he knew he would feel her heart pounding with rage.

The pencil he was holding snapped…

'So are you looking for revenge?' he asked.

'I have my revenge,' she said, losing patience with the carton and jabbing the end of a spoon into the seal as if stabbing whoever had done this to her through the heart. Milk shot over the sleeve of her jacket and, embarrassed, she laughed. 'Okay, maybe I do have issues, but Miles Morgan was panicked into grabbing the first answer that presented itself. No doubt with a little prompting from…' Catching herself, she slipped off the jacket and used a piece of kitchen paper to mop the milk from her sleeve.

'From?'

Right at that moment he didn't much care about the who or the why, he simply wanted to keep her looking like that, and the stub of his pencil continued to work as she shook her head and a wisp of hair escaped the prim little knot, floating for a moment before settling against her cheek.

She frowned. 'I can't be sure. It all happened so fast… Someone had it all worked out in advance and knew exactly which buttons to press.' She pulled a face. 'There's nothing like a champagne celebration to show the world that it's business as usual.'

'Does this someone have a name? I'm sure my lawyer would like to know.'

'No doubt, but I'm not here to help you bring them down,' she said. Nevertheless, the tiny frown persisted. She wanted answers, too.

'So you do want your job back,' he pushed.

'That's not going to happen.'

'You won't work for the man who took your job?'

She shrugged, managed a smile of sorts. 'Never say never. Who knows how desperate I'll get…? How do you like your tea?' she asked, glancing across at him. 'Weak, medium, stand up your spoon…' She stopped. 'Are you drawing me?'

'Yes. Do you mind?'

'I'm not sure.'

'I'll stop if you insist,' he said. 'And strong. Dash of milk. No sugar. You think Morgan will regret it?' he asked, dragging his gaze from his contemplation of her long upper lip just long enough to commit it to paper. 'Grabbing the easy option?'

'Who knows? Toby's bright enough, but he's never allowed work to interfere with his weekends on the rugby field. He's always put that first. To be honest, I never thought he was that interested in property sales and management. I had the impression that his family had pushed him into the day job.'

Toby. He logged the name to look up later. 'I'm surprised he got the job at all if that's his attitude.'

'His great-aunt is married to Peter Black.'

'Oh.'

'He's just turned twenty-three,' she said thoughtfully. 'Maybe he's realised he's not going to get a professional contract.'

'He lost his dream so stole yours? It demonstrates a ruthless streak. That's vital in business, or so I'm told.'

'It's a trait he kept well hidden. I still find it hard to believe…' She shrugged, letting whatever it was she found hard to believe go. 'Lazy and ruthless is a bad combination, Darius. Would you want him at your back in a crisis? More to the point, would you want to work for a man who'd thrown you to the wolves without a proper hearing? Without any kind of investigation? Forget Toby Denton. He might have my promotion, but it'll always be second best as far as he's concerned. It's Miles I can't forgive. It'll be a cold day in hell before I work for him again.'

'Never say never,' he reminded her and got a reprise of the smile for his pains.

'Maybe if he offered me a full partnership,' she said, 'which is undoubtedly his version of a cold day in hell at the moment.'

'Okay, I get it. It's not going to happen, but if you don't want revenge,' he asked, 'and you don't want your job back, what do you want?'

Natasha's shoulders dropped a fraction. Darius knew that he'd asked the right question, but didn't know whether to kick himself or cheer as her lips softened into the smile he'd asked for. The one that reached her eyes.

His body was divided on the issue; his brain was definitely up for the kicking while the rest of him was responding like a Labrador puppy offered a biscuit.

While he distracted himself by capturing her mouth on paper, Natasha cupped her hands around her warm mug, leaned her hip against the arm of the sofa, making herself at home.

'A week ago I could have walked into any real estate agency in London and been offered a job,' she said. 'Since I've become available, my phone has remained ominously silent.'

'Are you surprised?'

'No, and I haven't embarrassed anyone by reminding them of their generous offers.'

'I'm sure they're all extremely grateful for your tact,' he said, unable to resist a smile of his own. Forget the allure of a body made for sin, he was beginning to like Natasha Gordon. She'd just had the feet knocked out from under her but she'd come up fighting.

'I don't imagine they've given me a second thought. I'm history, Darius. I'll have to restore my hard-earned reputation before anyone will give me the time of day.' She paused, evidently hoping he'd chip in at this point. He drew the line of her jaw. Firm, determined... 'The only way I can do that is by selling Hadley Chase,' she said, offering him the opportunity to help her out.

'Then you really are in trouble.'

'That makes two of us,' she said, taking a sip of her tea. 'I admit that it will require a certain amount of ingenuity and imagination to pull it off, but who has a bigger incentive?' She looked sideways at him, blinking as she caught him staring at her, but this time she didn't look away. 'Who would work harder to find you a buyer?' she asked. 'And for nothing?' she added as a final incentive.

'For nothing? You'll be drummed out of the estate agents guild,' he warned.

Her lips twitched into another of those little smiles. Parts of him twitched involuntarily in response. His head didn't have a chance.

'Believe me, it's a once-in-a-lifetime offer. What have you got to lose?' Energy, excitement at the challenge poured off her in an almost physical wave. 'We're a match made in heaven.'

He shook his head, afraid that he'd already lost it. He shouldn't even be having the conversation. The lawyers would have a fit.

'An estate agent no one will employ and a house no one can sell? That sounds more like hell to me,' he said, but he was unable to stop himself from laughing. She was bright, intelligent and, under other circumstances—the uncomplicated, no strings, hot sex circumstances—would no doubt be a lot of fun. Unfortunately, this was getting more complicated by the moment.

'I'm not promising heaven,' she protested, 'but it won't be hell. Honestly.'

That he could believe... 'I bet you say that to all the poor saps trying to sell a house in a recession.'

'I do my best to give it to them straight,' she replied. 'And I do everything I can to help them to make the best of the property they're selling. That's my job.'

'Paint it magnolia and hide the clutter in the cupboards?' he suggested.

'Getting rid of the clutter so that you can open the cupboards is better. Storage space is a big selling point.' She looked at him over the mug. 'Giving the place a good clean helps. Brushing out the dead leaves. Fixing broken windows.'

He frowned. 'Are you telling me that there's a broken window at the Chase?'

'You didn't know? I did point it out to your caretaker. He said he'd mention it to the executors.'

And they hadn't bothered to mention it to him. Well, he'd made his position clear enough. Not interested...

'Look, I'm not pretending that it's going to be easy,' she said. 'You're not selling a well-kept four-bed detached house in an area with good schools.'

'I wouldn't need you if I was.'

It was an admission that he did need her and they both knew it.

'What I'm promising, Darius, is that you won't have to be personally involved in any way.' She reached out a sympathetic hand, but curled her fingers back before it touched his arm. Even so, his skin tightened at the imperceptible movement of air and the shiver of it went right through him. 'I do understand how difficult this must be for you.'

'I doubt it.' Nobody could ever begin to understand how he felt about the Chase. The complex mix of memories, emotions it evoked.

'No, of course not, but Hadley Chase has been in your family for centuries. I can see how it must hurt to be the one who has to let it go.'

'Is that what you think?' he asked, looking up from those curled-up fingers, challenging her. 'That I'm ashamed because I've failed to hold on to it?'

'No! Of course not.' The blush flooded back to her cheeks. 'Why should you be? This is the fault of preceding generations.' The possibility that by criticising his recent ancestors she might be digging an even bigger hole for herself must have crossed her mind and she moved swiftly on. 'I'll do everything possible to make this as painless as possible,' she promised. 'All you have to do is let the caretaker and your lawyer know that I'll be handling things on your behalf, then you needn't give it another thought.'

This time his laugh was forced, painful. 'If you could guarantee that you'd have a deal.'

'I can guarantee that I won't disturb you again without a very good reason,' she assured him.

Too late. Natasha Gordon was the most disturbing woman he'd ever met, but the Chase was a millstone around his neck, a darkness at the heart of his family, his grandfather's last-ditch attempt to regain control of a world he'd once dominated, ruled. To control the future. To control him. The sooner he was rid of it, the burden lifted, the better.

'Suppose I agree to let you loose on it,' he said, as if it wasn't already a done deal, 'do you have a plan?'

'A plan?'

'You don't have an advertising budget,' he pointed out, 'or a shop window for passers-by to browse in, or even a listing in the *Yellow Pages*.'

'No, but I do have the Internet, social media.'

Oh, shit…

'Did you say something?'

Not out loud, he was almost certain, but his reaction had been so strong that she had undoubtedly read his mind. 'You can't use my name,' he warned, gesturing around the studio, 'or any of this to generate publicity.' This was his world. He had created it. No one else. He wouldn't have it touched by his family or the Chase.

'It'll be a low-key approach,' she assured him, far too easily. 'Nothing flashy, nothing to embarrass you. You have my word.'

'Your word, in this instance, is worthless. Once it's on the Net you'll lose control.'

'Only if I get it right.'

'Is that supposed to reassure me?'

She frowned, obviously confused by his attitude. 'It's just a house, Darius.'

She was wrong, but he couldn't expect her to understand his love/hate relationship with the place. With his family. 'You've got all the answers,' he said dismissively.

She shook her head. 'If I had all the answers, I wouldn't be here,' she said, 'I'd be at Morgan and Black, lining up viewings with the property managers of the kind of men and women who can afford to buy and maintain an English country house to use for two or three weeks in the year. During the shooting season,' she added, in case he didn't get the point, 'or maybe for Christmas and the New Year, before they move on to Gstaad or Aspen for the skiing.'

'That's...'

'Yes?'

'Nothing.'

He shouldn't care who bought it, or how little they used it... He didn't. And he had no reason to trust her, or to believe that she'd lost her job for anything other than sheer incompetence. Only the fact that Miles Morgan had lied about a breakdown, publicly humiliating her in a way that even if she had been grossly negligent would still have been unforgivable. And that he'd disliked the man on sight.

What Natasha Gordon had done to him on sight was something else. The fact that he wasn't thinking with his brain was reason enough to stay well clear of any harebrained idea she came up with, but the Revenue would not wait forever for the inheritance tax he would have to pay on the estate. The truth of the matter was that he couldn't afford to wait until the fuss died down.

'Okay.'

Tash was used to being looked at. She had no illusions about being any kind of a beauty, but—cosseted and nurtured on all that was good and nourishing by a mother who'd nearly lost her—she'd developed from a skin-and-bones kid into an unfashionably curved lushness that men seemed to find irresistible.

She'd quickly learned to keep both flirtatious vendors and buyers at a distance, but Darius Hadley had not flirted with her. The connection was something else, something visceral, and now he was looking at her with an intensity that heated her to the bone.

With each stroke of his pencil on the paper she became increasingly conscious of her body. Every line he drew felt like a fingertip stroked across her skin. It was as if she was coming undone; not just her top button, but every part of her was unravelling as she became exposed to him.

Far from keeping her distance, she'd barely stopped herself from reaching out, laying her hand on the solid muscle of his arm, sliding a finger along the dark hair gathered in a line along his forearm. But one touch would never be enough; it would be lighting the blue touchpaper, setting off a chain reaction that nothing could stop. And the problem with that was...?

'Did you hear me? I said okay.'

'Okay?' The breath hitched in her throat as she repeated the word. He'd agreed? 'Is that okay as in yes?' she asked. 'You'll give me a chance?'

There was a seemingly endless pause and for a moment he seemed to be somewhere else. Possibly thinking of all the reasons why it was a bad idea. What his lawyer would say. It would undoubtedly compromise his case against Morgan and Black...

'A conditional yes.'

Uh-oh...

'I'll give you a chance to sell Hadley Chase on one condition.'

'Anything,' she said.

'You're that desperate?' he asked, with a look that warned her she should have asked what condition.

'Anything that's legal, decent and honest,' she said, scarcely daring to breathe. Make that legal and honest. She was prepared to negotiate on decent...

'Desperate, but not stupid.'

Probably... 'What is it?'

'I want you to sit for me.'

'Sit?' For a moment she couldn't think what he meant but, as he continued to look at her, hold her fixed to the spot with no more than the power of his gaze, she knew exactly what he meant.

Her mouth dried and her hand fluttered from her shoulder to somewhere around her thigh in a gesture that took in all the important bits in between.

'As in *sit*?' she asked. 'Pose? Model for you?'

'If you're asking whether I'd want you naked, the answer is yes,' he said bluntly. 'It's your body that I want to draw, not your clothes.'

'Oh...' She blinked as a rush of blood heated her skin, her lips, and something deep within her liquefied. Appalled by how much she wanted to do it, she curled her fingers into her palms to stop herself from reaching for her buttons right then and there.

Misunderstanding her silence, he said, 'You're asking me to take you on trust, Natasha. That's a two-way deal.'

'Trust is important,' she agreed, 'but the thing is, I'm not asking you to take your clothes off.'

'I will if it will make it easier for you,' he said.

'Yes... No!' What on earth was she thinking? It was outrageous. She should be outraged, not tingling with excitement at the thought of exposing her ample curves to his molten gaze. So much for keeping this professional... 'Would you have asked if I was a man?'

He shrugged. 'Possibly. The right man, one with more than good muscle definition to commend him, and, like you, Natasha, he would have assumed I wanted more than a model.'

'I'm assuming nothing,' she declared, despite the betraying heat lighting up her cheeks that an artist, a man who saw more than most, would pick up in an instant, 'but I've just been handed a very painful lesson about mixing business with pleasure.' He said nothing so she continued. 'My fault. I broke the work/life balance golden rule.'

'With Morgan?' he asked.

'Miles? Good grief, no!'

'Then it has to be Toby Denton, the guy who's occupying your desk, driving your car. Did he get a hat-trick?'

'I'm sorry?'

'Did he break your heart, too?'

'Oh... No...' She shook her head. 'We didn't have that kind of a relationship.'

'What was it like?'

'A bit like a starter home,' she said. 'Something you know you're going to grow out of sooner rather than later. I was too busy for anything serious and, while he might look like perfect boyfriend material, there aren't many women who will play second fiddle to a rugby ball. The occasional night out, plus one do, sleepover suited us both.'

'Colleagues with benefits? It was still a betrayal.'

'Yes.' Worse, she would never know whether it had been a spur-of-the-moment thing or planned from the start and she had been duped, taken for a fool.

'Well, thanks for the vote of confidence,' he said after a moment, 'but sitting isn't a pleasure. It's uncomfortable, tedious, muscle-aching work. And you're right. Business and pleasure is a bad combination. Good models are hard to find, which is why I don't complicate the relationship with sex.'

'Does that mean...' She stopped. Of course it did. He'd just said so. Which was good. Really good. 'Can I see?' she asked, holding out her hand for the sketch pad, no longer so knicker-wettingly eager to get her kit off. 'What you've drawn?'

He handed it over without a word and she studied the small details he'd put down with little more than the stroke of a pencil.

Her mouth, fuller, sexier than she'd ever seen in the mirror when she'd grabbed a second to slide lipstick over it. The curve of her neck emerging from her collar, the line of her leg, her skirt stretched across her backside as she'd bent to search the fridge for milk—it was definitely time to get on the treadmill. Her eyes, giving away the feelings that vibrated through her whenever she looked at him.

'I understand why some primitive people thought the

camera stole away their soul,' she said, shaken by what he'd seen in those few moments, fixed on paper with so few lines. How much more would he see if he was being serious? She would be utterly exposed—and not just because she'd be stripped to her skin. 'It's not what I was expecting.'

Darius leaned back against the stepladder, folding his arms. 'Did you imagine I was drawing your internal organs?'

She swallowed, managed a wry smile. 'Well, that is more your style. This is just me.'

'What's on the surface. The image you show the world. I'll go deeper.'

'You won't find much muscle definition,' she warned him.

'You have a lot of everything, Natasha.'

'I was sick as a kid,' she said. 'My mother spent my childhood trying to fatten me up. I ran away from home to escape the egg custard.' She glanced up at the skeletal horse, then at the sketch pad, flipping back through the pages to see what else was there—anything to avoid looking at him, betray her eagerness for him to draw her, sculpt her—and discovered that every page was filled with drawings of her. Far more than he could have done in a few minutes. 'I don't understand. You couldn't have done all this today.'

'No.' His face was expressionless.

'But the other day... You only saw me for a minute or two and this is—'

'I've only scratched the surface.'

The room seemed to darken as their gazes locked, acknowledging the raw, subliminal connection in that moment when they'd faced one another across Morgan's office.

A shiver ran through her and she closed her eyes. When she opened them again, the sun was pouring in through the skylights and Darius was still waiting for her answer. He knew it would be yes...

'Will I be a limited edition bronze?' she asked. 'On display in a gallery window? Like the horse.'

'It's possible. If your interior lives up to the promise of the packaging.'

'My packaging!'

'It's very attractive packaging.'

'An excessive amount of packaging, I think you just said. Will you give me a couple of months to shed ten pounds?'

'Don't even think about it,' he said, taking the pad from her. 'Are you concerned that you'll be recognised?'

'Recognised?' The tension evaporated as she laughed at the idea of any of his subjects being recognised in the finished sculpture. 'Unlikely, I'd have thought.' She hoped. If anyone found out, she knew what interpretation they'd put on it. 'I might have to make it a condition.'

'It's all about trust,' he said, not joining in, and for a moment she was afraid that she'd offended him. 'So? Do you have any more problems?'

Problems?

Only one. The fact that she was more interested in the man than his house. She'd forgotten why she was here, that her future depended on getting this right. That problem.

'How about the fact that you'll be making money out of your side of the bargain while I'll be working for nothing?' she suggested in an attempt to bring them both back to the reason she was here.

'We might both be wasting our time, Natasha,' he said, pushing away from the stepladder, suddenly much too close. 'But if I discover depths in you that are worth exploring I'll...' His eyes suggested that his thoughts were a long way from art.

'Yes?' The word was thick in her throat. Not just his thoughts—her own were on a much lower plane...

'I'll give you a first casting.'

'So that I can put my "depths" on the sideboard for everyone I know to look at?'

'You'll love every minute of it,' he said. 'All those horny men running their hands over cold bronze, imagining the warm, living flesh.'

'No…' There was only one man she wanted running his hands over her flesh and he was right there, in front of her.

'Every woman longs for something in her past with which to scandalise her grandchildren,' he said. His face was all shadows, his eyes leaden, his voice so soft that it was barely audible.

'How would you know that?' she whispered.

He lifted his hand in what felt like slow motion and grazed her cheek with the roughened tips of his fingers and, as he drew them down the line of her jaw, a jolt went through her body as if it had been jump-started.

Her nipples tightened, puckering visibly beneath the heavy silk of her shirt, sending twin arrows of heat to the apex of her thighs, a bead of sweat trickled down her back and Darius, his thumb teasing the corner of her mouth, smiled darkly.

Question asked and answered.

She was finding it difficult to breathe, speech was beyond her; they both knew that she couldn't wait to have her depths thoroughly explored in every conceivable way, so she did the only thing left to her.

He didn't take his eyes from her face as she slipped the tiny pearl buttons of her shirt one by one until the silk parted and then, her eyes never leaving his, her parted lips swollen, burning, she turned her head to suck his thumb into her mouth.

Her tongue swirled around it, licking it, tasting clay and cake, sugar and something spicy that hadn't come out of a jar. She whimpered when he took it from her. Whimpered again when he dragged its moist, broad pad across her lips.

'Shush…' he murmured and there was a moment of perfect stillness when the world centred on that small contact, balanced on a knife-edge. Then he slowly lowered his mouth to hers, retraced the path of his thumb with his tongue and she nearly fainted from the hot burst of pleasure that flooded through her. It was only his arm supporting her that kept her on her feet as her lips parted and his tongue embarked on a meltingly slow dance of exploration.

She reached for him, cradling his head as the kiss deepened and her senses were bombarded from all directions. His hair tangled in her fingers, stubble tickled her palms. The scent of metal and clay and the oiled wooden handles of the tools he used clung to him, earthy and elemental. His hands tugged her shirt from her waistband and slid up her back, his thumbs nudged her breasts. The hard bulge of his erection butted into her hip.

He leaned back to look at her as he swept aside silk and lace, his calloused fingers lifting her breasts free of her bra, grazing the tender skin. And then his tongue swept over the rock-hard tip of her breast and her knees buckled.

There was a crash as he swept bones, tools aside and, without apparent effort, lifted her bodily onto the bench.

Yes…

The word spiralled through her, triumphant, exhilarating, liberating. She might have shouted it, but all she could hear was the sound of blood pounding in her ears as her pulse went off the scale. All she could feel was the heat of his mouth trailing moist kisses down her throat, his teeth, razor stubble grazing the swollen, sensitive skin of her breast, his suckling tongue sending a lightning bolt to her throbbing, swollen core.

'Darius…' It was a breathless, desperate plea and his hand was between her thighs, pushing aside the flimsy barrier to greet the liquid fire that flashed to meet first one and then two of those deliciously long fingers driving into her.

She reared to meet them, wanting more, demanding more as the furnace, lit in the very first moment she'd set eyes on him, hit meltdown. She'd wanted it then, wanted it as she'd beaten butter and sugar into submission, wanted him inside her...

She clutched at hard shoulders, her nails digging into his flesh through the soft cloth of his shirt as his knuckle hit the sweet, screaming spot. She had no breath to scream, urge him on; all she could do was make small desperate sounds as she arched upwards, demanding more, as he made her wait, taking his time, stroking, tormenting, teasing her throat, her breasts, her stomach with his teeth, his tongue, keeping her on the limit of endurance with his fingers, the subtle pressure of his thumb until her body, lost in bliss, slipped from her control and became entirely his. Only then did he release her in a shattering orgasm that went through her like a tornado, lifting, spinning, dumping her dazed, slicked with sweat and clinging to him like a life raft.

Her head was a dead weight against his shoulder, her limbs like sun-warmed putty, and if he hadn't been holding her she would have slithered to the floor in a boneless heap.

CHAPTER FIVE

FOR A LONG moment the only things moving in the room were dust motes dancing in the sunlight streaming in from above. Then Darius eased back a little.

'Are you okay?' he asked.

Okay? *Okay*?

'Give me a minute to locate my bones and I'll let you know.'

'Hang on...' He slid an arm beneath her knees and, lifting her clear of the bench, carried her to the sofa.

'Mmm...' She let out a contented sigh as she stretched out on the cushions, looking up at him from beneath lids too heavy to lift. She reached for his belt, planning to hook her fingers under it and pull him closer so that she could get at that deliciously flat belly beneath the baggy T-shirt, do a little nibbling on her own account. Ease the pressure of what had to be a very painful bulge against the zip of his jeans.

He caught her, wrapping his hand around her wrist, keeping her from her goal.

His eyes were burning her up and he held her tightly for a moment before, with a visible effort, he released her and then, taking care not to let his fingers touch her skin, lifted the lace of her bra and carefully replaced it over her breasts.

'Darius?'

He didn't answer but began to refasten her shirt buttons

with all the concentration of a bomb disposal officer defusing an unexploded bomb. One wrong move, one touch…

'What are you doing?' she demanded. Then, as the reality began to sink in, 'No…'

'I work here, Natasha, and I meant it when I said I don't have sex with my models.'

'I'm not a model…'

'No.' A faint smile tugged at the corner of his mouth. 'A professional model would never undress in front of an artist but, unless you're carrying a stash of condoms in that bag, we're done.'

The implication that she went to work armed and ready for action was like a bucket of cold water. Did he think she did that with everyone who needed a little encouragement to use her services?

Well, why wouldn't he? He knew she was desperate— desperate enough to sit naked so that he could draw her.

She'd completely lost the plot, forgotten that this was just business…

'Sorry,' she said, swinging her legs to the floor and forcing him to step back. 'You're not the only one who doesn't get down and dirty on the job,' she said, frustration making her snippy. 'Sex with a client is definitely off the agenda.'

'Just as well I'm not a client, then. Unless you've changed your mind about waiving your fee for selling the Chase?'

'No,' she said. 'A deal's a deal. I'll settle for the perks.'

'Perks?'

'The chunk of bronze to go on the mantelpiece, the hand job. Thanks for that, by the way; it's been too long…' The words were out before her brain was engaged… 'Give me a call when you want me to strip naked for you,' she added, putting some stiffeners in her legs so that she could stand up. Get out of there. 'You'll find my number inside the lid of the cakebox.'

'Most people find a business card more convenient,' he

said, flipping it open and glancing at the label on which she'd printed her name, telephone number and email address as he searched for a phone amongst the scattered tools and bones on his workbench and programmed in the number. 'You can carry more than one at a time.'

'Unfortunately, my card is out of date and since I had no way of knowing if you'd listen to me...' She swallowed. He'd done a lot more than listen and she'd done a lot more than talk. 'In my experience, men don't throw away homemade cake, no matter where it's come from.'

'You were confident that once I'd tasted it I'd want more?'

The scent of sex hung in the air as thick as paint and they both knew that the taste he was referring to had nothing to do with confectionery.

No, no, no... 'Oh, please!' she said. 'When I have all those horny men queuing up at my front door for my lemon drizzle.'

Take that, Mr Hadley...

'Really?' He sucked on the tip of his thumb. 'Personally, I prefer my sugar light on the lemon, heavy on the spice.' A hot flush raced from her navel to her scalp as she realised that he was tasting her. 'Sticky ginger...' he said, volley intercepted and returned. Point won... 'I've sent you my number. In case you run into any problems.'

'Problems. Right.' There wouldn't be any problems. She'd make sure of that. But first she had to get out of here before she spontaneously combusted.

Jacket...

Where was it?

She looked around, knowing that she should be grateful that she wasn't crawling around on her hands and knees looking for her underwear.

She should.

Really.

Darius spotted her jacket lying on the floor beside the sofa and, beating Natasha to it, scooped it up. She took a nervous step back, keeping him at arm's length. She was mad at him. The condom remark had been crass, deliberately so—a bucket of cold water on an overheated situation that had got out of hand. Unfortunately, all it had done was create steam. They were both still on a hair trigger and playing Russian roulette which was why, instead of following her excellent example and tossing it to her, he shook her jacket out and held it up, inviting her to turn around and slide her arms into the sleeves.

She could have ignored him, said she'd carry it, but after the slightest hesitation she turned, holding her arms towards him so that he could ease it on. She smelled of spice and sex and, with a groan he couldn't stifle, he slid his hands down from her shoulders to cup her lovely breasts, pulling her against him while he breathed a kiss against her neck. She leaned back into him with a whimper that was half despair, half bliss and for a moment he just held her, before summoning the willpower to give her a gentle push towards the door.

'Go,' he said.

She turned in his arms and looked up at him, her eyes liquid, appealing.

'Now,' he said, his forehead touching hers, her breasts brushing against his chest. He was wood and there was nothing he could do about it. 'Please.'

She took a breath. 'Right. Yes… This was so not what I intended.' She took a step back, picked up her bag, made it as far as the door, then paused. 'I won't bother you again until I have some news.'

'I won't be holding my breath.'

Wrong on both counts.

He'd been bothered the minute he'd set eyes on her. Unable to get her out of his mind. And breathless ever since she'd walked into his studio with that mesmerising sway of her hips.

'How will you get there?' he asked. A tiny frown puckered her smooth forehead. 'The Chase. Now that the devious Denton is driving your Beemer?'

'Oh…' She shook her head, as if clearing it. 'I'll hire something.'

'A waste of money. You'd be better off putting a deposit on a van,' he said. 'That way you can put your name on the side and use it as free advertising. Sell the house and I'll design you a logo.'

Things were safer than feelings…

'If I sell the house,' she pointed out, 'I won't need one.'

'If you sell the house, Natasha, you won't need to work for anyone else. It won't only be eager estate agents, and horny men pining for you, but desperate vendors who'll be beating a path to your door.'

'Thanks, but self-employment doesn't figure in my five-year career plan.'

'I think we've established that right now you don't have a career or a plan.'

'The career is temporarily on hold. The plan is a work in progress,' she said and, as if to underline the fact that—perks notwithstanding—this was strictly business, she offered him her hand.

Despite the danger to his simmering libido, he was unable to resist taking it. Small, soft, with perfectly groomed nails, it lay like a touch of velvet against his clay-roughened palm evoking X-rated thoughts and he needed to get her out of his studio before common sense went to hell in a hand basket.

'Please go,' he said.

Her lips parted as if she was going to say something. Clearly she thought better of it and, having opened the door, she stepped through into the street and closed it behind her without another word.

He slipped the latch before Patsy decided to pop in and give him the third degree, leaning his forehead against it while he called the estate executor to update him on the situation.

Brian Ramsey spluttered and protested at the inappropriateness of allowing Natasha access to the house, but Darius cut him short.

'You chose Morgan and Black to handle the sale. They messed up,' he said. 'Now we'll do it my way. Please make sure that Gary Webb is available tomorrow to let her in.'

'Mr Webb is on sick leave and really, in the light of recent events, I have to insist that Miss Gordon is accompanied by someone responsible. Tell her that if she comes in the office later this week I'll check the diary and see when someone is available.'

Oh, right. Next month some time. Maybe. This was the man who'd conspired with his grandfather to ensure that a Hadley remained at the Chase for another generation.

'What's the matter with Gary?' he asked.

'He had a fall.'

Tash walked away on legs that were all over the place, her stomach churning with every kind of emotion imaginable.

She needed to sit down. Needed coffee. Ice cream...

For heaven's sake, she was a grown-up and smart enough to know that leaping on a man you barely knew was never going to end well, especially when it was supposed to be strictly business. *Especially* when her entire life plan depended on it being strictly business.

What on earth had she been thinking?

Scratch that. No one had been thinking, least of all her. Apparently she still wasn't because she couldn't wait for the return match and next time she'd have more than cake in her bag...

She was grinning, helplessly, at the thought when her phone began to ring. She checked the number, ultra cautious since her name had been plastered all over the evening papers. Journalists might believe that she was safely tucked up out of harm's way in the Fairview where they couldn't get at her, but it hadn't stopped them trying her number, leaving sympathetic messages, wanting her side of the story. As if she was going to fall for that.

It wasn't a journalist. It was Darius.

'Text me your address,' he said, before her brain could unscramble itself and deliver a simple hello.

'Excuse me?'

'The caretaker is in hospital and the legal lot insist that you're accompanied by a responsible adult.'

'That's very, um, responsible of them.' She'd bet the house that wasn't all they'd said. They would have had a dozen good reasons why he should pull out of their deal. Given a minute, she could probably come up with at least that many herself. But he hadn't... 'What's the matter with Mr Grumpy?'

'He fell off a ladder. Broken leg, broken wrist, bruises.'

'Oh...' How to go from feeling great to feeling about two inches high in ten seconds. 'I'm so sorry.' And she was. He'd been a grouch but he didn't deserve that. 'Is he going to be okay?' Then, as an awful thought struck her, she said, 'He wasn't trying to fix that window, was he?'

'Is that a guilty conscience I can hear, Miss Gordon?' Darius asked. 'Maybe you should take him some of your cake.'

'Darius!'

He laughed. 'Relax, Sugarlips. This is not your fault—he was clearing a blocked gutter at the village hall, but you're right, it needs fixing. I'll get it sorted.'

Sugarlips? Oh, cripes…

'I could arrange that for you,' she offered, doing her best not to think about what had made him pick on that particular endearment. She should definitely not think about him sucking the tip of his thumb. She could still taste him, smell him on her… 'I have a first-class honours degree in estate management.'

'Well, bully for you. Call the National Trust; maybe they'll give you a job.'

'They did,' she said. 'I turned it down.'

There was a brief silence which told her that she'd finally managed to surprise him, then he said, 'I'll pick you up at eight tomorrow morning.'

'You?'

'I'm the only responsible adult available at short notice.'

'Oh…' Her heart, already going like the clappers, hit warp speed.

'Of course you could wait for Brian Ramsey to find some free time in his diary but he isn't particularly happy with my choice of sales agent so he won't be in any hurry.'

'No, thanks. I talked to Brian Ramsey about cleaning up the house. He was barely polite when I was representing an agency he had engaged.'

'Then I'll see you tomorrow. You can bring lunch.'

'Blokes do windows, women do food?'

'You could take me to the pub if you'd prefer, but I was thinking of your budget.'

'A picnic it is. Any allergies?' she asked. 'Anything you won't eat?'

'Just save the wussy lemon cake for your legions of admirers. You know what I like.'

He disconnected before she could reply and Tash had to fight the insane urge to run back to the studio and write her address in lipstick on his sketch pad. On his chest. Across his stomach…

'Are you all right, dear?' A woman waiting for the bus was looking up at her with concern.

'Um… Yes… Thank you.' She sat down on the bench beside her, flapped her shirt collar to create a bit of breeze around her face. 'I've just, um… It's a bit warm, isn't it?'

Darius was at the door on the dot of eight and despite a sleepless night—or maybe because of it—Tash was waiting for him. No short skirt, no dangerous buttons with a mind of their own, no sexy high heels. Today she was kitted out in a pair of comfortable jeans, a baggy T-shirt and a pair of running shoes, bought when she'd decided to get a grip on her weight and decided to go running with Toby. Once had been enough and any wear on the soles was down to the occasional dash to the corner shop for emergency baking supplies.

Her laptop bag was ready for business, lunch was packed; she hadn't left herself with a single excuse to delay so that she would have to invite him up while she gathered her stuff. No excuse to offer him coffee, or invite him to try the spiced cookies she'd been baking at three that morning.

There was work to do, her career to save, Hadley Chase to sell and when he buzzed from the front entrance she was ready to go.

Strictly business.

She ran down the stairs, swung through the door…

Oh, good grief.

He didn't say anything when she skidded to a stop on the pavement and the casual *hi* that she'd been mentally rehearsing died on her lips at the sight of him leaning back against the door of an elderly Land Rover.

If the vehicle was well past its prime, Darius, in a black polo shirt and faded denims that clung to his thighs, was looking like every kind of sin she'd ever wanted to commit.

He was just so damned beautiful that every one of her

nerve endings sent out a 'touch me' tingle and she was seriously wishing she'd gone for a shirt with unreliable buttons and a bra that pushed her boobs up to her chin. He might keep a poker face when he was looking down her cleavage but she knew exactly what he was thinking. Right now she hadn't a clue.

She'd run through this moment over and over as she was taking a shower, picking out what to wear for exploring a dusty old house, cutting sandwiches. Imagining what he'd say, what he'd do. Rehearsing every possible combination of responses.

Would it be a curt let's-forget-what-happened nod? Eminently sensible...

Her heart had skipped a little beat at the prospect of a let's-think-about-this kiss on the cheek. Sensible but with possibilities...

Or please, please, please, a let's-do-it kiss that would buckle her knees and have her melting on the pavement.

None of the above.

He kept his distance, one eyebrow slightly raised as he took in her passion-damping clothes, her hair fastened in a single plait that was held together with nothing sexier than an elastic band. Then, just when she thought it was safe to breathe, he reached out, ran his thumb over her mouth and said, 'Good morning, Sugarlips.'

His low, sexy voice vibrated against her breastbone and the carrier containing their lunch slipped through her fingers and hit the pavement.

An annoying little smile lifted the corner of his mouth as he straightened and opened the passenger door. 'I hope there was nothing breakable in there.'

'The flask is well padded, but I don't suppose it will have done the cake much good,' she replied before, blushing like an idiot, she scrambled up into the passenger seat, leaving him to pick it up.

She concentrated on fastening her seat belt as he climbed in beside her, filling the space with his presence, his earthy scent mingling with the smell of hot oil.

Her fingers were shaking so much that he took her hand, unpeeled her fingers from it and clicked it home.

'It was a bit stiff…'

'I know how it feels.'

She tried not to look, but was unable to help herself. Oh, cripes…

'I'm sorry the transport doesn't meet your usual standard of comfort,' he said, leaning forward to start the engine, ignoring the tension twanging the air between them; presumably a man who spent his life around naked women posing on a pedestal would have had plenty of practice.

She made an effort to focus her thoughts elsewhere. On the house with the puce living room that had been on the market for months and the owner's outrage when she'd suggested that a quick coat of magnolia might help…

Her breathing slowed, the pulse pounding in her throat became a gentle thud.

Better.

'No problem,' she said. 'As you pointed out, I'm working this job economy class.'

'You've got it,' he said, a wry smile creating a crease in his cheek and undoing all that effort. Fortunately the Land Rover, vibrating noisily, covered the shiver that rippled through her.

'So, what's the plan?' he said.

'Plan?'

'I assumed you'd been up half the night working on your plan to find a buyer for the Chase.'

'It shows, huh?' The expensive stuff that was supposed to conceal dark shadows round the eyes clearly wasn't doing the job.

'Just guessing,' he said, ratcheting up the smile, and

the swarm of butterflies in her stomach, which until then had at least been flying in close formation, went haywire.

Think about that hideous purple and yellow bathroom...

'Nearly right,' she managed. 'I was up half the night creating a media presence for Hadley Chase on Facebook and Twitter.'

Nearly right. Nearly true. She'd done that within half an hour of getting home. The major time had been spent finding and following media types—and the people they followed—journalists, the local Berkshire newspapers and county magazine. Anyone who had an interest in country houses, property, local history, social history. Anyone who might conceivably be interested in following Hadley Chase.

She'd spent the rest of the night trying to come up with a really convincing reason why she should call him and cancel. She needed to keep her distance, keep it professional.

She also needed to get to Hadley Chase this week, rather than at the convenience of a lawyer who thought she was poison, so here she was, on the dot of eight o'clock, her brain out to lunch and her stomach throwing a butterfly party while she drooled over the man.

Forget strictly business. She should have lured him up to her flat and invited him to shag her brains out. Maybe then she'd be able to concentrate on the job in hand.

He glanced back over his shoulder, giving his attention to the traffic. Giving her a moment to catch her breath.

She focused on the memory of a house with an orange front door. And that had been the best bit. A kitchen with every tile on both walls and floor a different colour. Heard herself saying, 'So jolly...'

Maybe he wasn't as cool as he looked either and needed a moment of his own because he didn't press her on the plan. Which was just as well. She wasn't getting paid so she couldn't afford to throw money at the problem; she was going to have to be inventive.

'How's Mr Gr...er...Gary?' she said, raising her voice above the noise of the engine when the silence had gone on too long.

'Comfortable, according to the nurse I spoke to.'

'I'm really sorry.'

'Not half as sorry as he is, I suspect.'

'I meant I'm sorry that you have to do this. You didn't want to be involved. In the sale.'

They were stopped in traffic and he looked across at her as if unsure how to answer her. His eyes were liquid silver in the morning sunlight, with a hint of steely blue. Then someone hooted impatiently from behind and once they were rattling along the motorway the noise of the engine, the tyres, the trucks rushing past, made anything but the most urgent conversation impossible.

Tash made an effort to focus on the problem ahead—she had no illusions about the Chase being an easy sell—but she was sitting within inches of Darius Hadley. Sunlight was glinting over the steel wristband of his watch, drawing attention to the hand wrapped lightly around the steering wheel, the fingers that had been inside her, driving her wild with pleasure less than twenty-four hours ago.

Who could focus on anything but the mesmerising flex of the muscles in his forearm, his thigh as he changed gear, switched lanes?

Swamped by lust, heated by the sun beating in through the windscreen on her breasts, thighs, she closed her eyes to shut out temptation. When she opened them again, her cheek was pressed against his shoulder, she was breathing in the scent of warm male and her first inclination was to close them and stay exactly where she was.

She felt, rather than saw, Darius glance down at her. 'It must have been a late night. Not many people can sleep in a Land Rover.'

Humbled, she reluctantly straightened. 'I was just resting

my eyes,' she said, using a yawn to surreptitiously check her chin for dribble. 'While I focused on the plan.'

'Sure you were,' he said, grinning.

'The brain does its best work while the subconscious is switched off,' she said, realising that they'd left the motorway. How long had she slept?

Her satnav had kept her on the main roads but Darius, on home ground, had ignored the dual carriageway that bypassed the village of Hadley and as she looked around, trying to figure out where they were, he slowed and turned down a track half hidden by the rampant growth of early summer spilling from the verges.

'I hope we don't meet anyone coming the other way,' she said as they bounced, very slowly, through a tunnel of fresh new summer leaves along a dirt track so narrow that the frothy billow of cow parsley brushed both the sides of the Land Rover.

'If we do, they'd better have a good reason for being here,' he said. 'This is estate land.'

'This is the back way in?' she asked, trying to recall a map she'd seen, orientate herself. A chalk stream, low after an unusually dry spring, was curling quietly around shingle banks just below them on the right, which put them at the lower end of the estate and, as she turned and looked up, she caught a glimpse of tall chimneys through a gap in the trees.

'The main road goes round in a long loop to bypass the village,' he said. 'This entrance is known only to estate residents, who have more respect for their suspension than to use it, and locals doing a little rough shooting for the pot.'

She looked at him. 'Do you mean poachers?'

'My grandfather would have called them that,' he said. 'I don't have a problem with the neighbours keeping the pigeon and rabbit population under control in return for the odd trout.'

'Well, that's very neighbourly, but people who buy this kind of property tend to be nervous of unidentified gun-fire,' she said, trying to pin down what exactly was wrong with the way he said 'grandfather'. 'If...when...I find you a buyer, someone had better warn the locals that they'll have to find their small game somewhere else.'

His jaw tightened, but all he said was, 'I'll make sure Gary passes the word. When...*if*...you find a buyer. Having burned the midnight oil and spent the drive down here leaving the work to your subconscious,' he said, 'have you got any further than creating a Facebook page?'

'It's a work in progress,' she admitted. Between reliving their close encounter in his studio and wondering how soon they could manage a replay, she hadn't been giving nearly enough thought to saving her career. 'What I need is a story.'

'A story?' He slowed almost to a stop, looking at her instead of the track.

'Relax, Darius, I've got the message. Your name is off limits. Cross my heart,' she added and then, as his eyes darkened, she drew her finger, very slowly, across her left breast in a large X.

His foot slipped from the accelerator, the engine stalled and only the ticking of the engine disturbed a silence so thick that it filled her ears.

'You are in so much trouble, Natasha Gordon,' he said, his face all dark shadows, his eyes shimmering with heat.

'Is that a promise?' she asked, her breath catching in her throat. 'Or are you all talk?'

The click of their seat belts being released was like a shotgun in the silence and then his hands were on her waist and, without quite knowing how she'd got there, she was straddling his thighs, her mouth a breath away from lips that had haunted her since the moment she'd first seen him.

She wiggled a little, snuggling her backside closer to the

impressive bulge in his jeans, and he groaned. 'Correction. *I'm* in so much trouble...'

'Talk, talk, talk...' she murmured against his mouth, cutting off any attempt at a response with a swirl of her tongue over his lower lip. There was a satisfying buck from his hips and, giving no quarter, she sucked it into her mouth.

Darius leaned back to give her more room.

There had been a bulge in his pants ever since she'd appeared on her doorstep in curve-disguising clothes, her hair in restraints, minimal make-up. She'd been doing her best to appear cool but she hadn't needed lipstick to draw attention to a mouth that had been hot, swollen, screaming *kiss me* at a hundred decibels.

He just about managed to restrain himself—if he'd kissed her they would never have left London and he wanted this over. He'd done a good job of keeping his mind on the road while he was driving along the motorway, but then she'd fallen asleep with her head against his shoulder, her lips slightly parted, wisps of escaping hair brushing his neck. Now the scent of hot woman was filling his lungs.

'You want action, Sugarlips?' he said. 'Help yourself.'

Needing no second invitation, she slid her hands through his hair, tangling it in her fingers, a little cat smile tugging at her lips as she made him her captive, teased him with her mouth, sucking, nipping, inviting him to come out and play.

He was in no hurry. Right now her breasts were snuggled against his chest, her backside was tormenting his erection, her mouth trailing moist kisses under his chin.

There was nothing more arousing than a woman intent on pleasure and, resting his hands on her hips, he did no more than support her, holding her steady so that she could concentrate on driving him wild.

It didn't take long. Her top, barely skimming her waistband, rode up as she leaned forward and he closed his eyes, memorising each curve of her lovely body as his hands, with a will of their own, slid up to graze the silk of her skin. Her waist dipped above the flare of her hips; there was nothing straight about her, he discovered, as his thumbs teased the edges of her stomach and she squirmed on his lap.

For a moment he was the one holding his breath but then he reached her ribcage and he felt the hitch of her breath under his hands as his fingers took a slow walk up her spinal column, kneading each vertebrae in turn, pausing only to release the catch on her bra, so that his thumbs were free to imprint the soft swell of her breasts in his memory. They had just reached her nipples when her tongue found the pulse throbbing in his neck.

With a roar, he pulled her top, bra over her head and tossed them behind him, then forgot to breathe as she leaned back against the steering wheel, eyes smoky, slumberous, only the tiniest rim of blue circling satin-black pupils.

'Perfect,' he said, filling his hand with her full, ripe breasts, thumbing her rock-hard nipples, stroking them with his tongue, sucking on them. Just perfect…

'Darius…' There was an urgency in her voice now and he popped the button at her waist, slid down the zip and eased his hands down inside the back of her jeans, a scrap of lace, easing them down as he cupped her peachy backside in his hands and lifted her towards his mouth.

He swirled his tongue around the dimple of her navel, mouthed soft kisses in the hollow of her pelvis, blew against the blonde fluff of her sex and she whimpered, wanting more. She was right—this wasn't enough. He wanted her naked. He wanted her out of here, lying on a bank of soft grass down by the stream with sunlight, filtered through the leaves, playing on her skin. He wanted to touch every inch of her, memorise her body. Be inside her…

'Let's get out of here,' he said, pushing open the door

and half falling with her into the verge, where they lay laughing, catching their breath amongst long grass, red campion, a few late bluebells that were a perfect match for her eyes. 'Come on,' he said, hauling her up, holding her close, not wanting to let her go even for the short scramble down the bank.

She clutched at jeans that were heading for her knees. 'Where are we going?'

'You're not going anywhere.'

'What the...?' He swung round and Natasha gave a little shriek as they were confronted by a helmeted, visored security guard. 'Where the hell did you come from?' he demanded.

Ignoring his question, the guard said, 'This is private property. You're going to have to leave.'

'What? No...' Then cursed himself for every kind of fool—Ramsey had told him that he'd employed a security firm to keep an eye on the place. Cursed again as he realised that Natasha was standing there without a stitch above her waist and not much below it and putting himself between them. 'Show a little respect,' he said, boiling with anger that the man hadn't had the decency to look away. More likely couldn't take his eyes off her.

Despite his helmet and a uniform designed to make him look as much like a policeman as possible without breaking the law, the man took a nervous step back, looked away.

'There's no need for that,' he said defensively. 'I'm just doing my job.'

'Hanging about like some Peeping Tom. You're the trespasser,' he said, wrenching off his polo shirt and handing it to Natasha, bundling her back into the seat they'd just fallen out of before turning furiously on the man. 'This is my land.' The words were out of his mouth before he realised what he was saying. 'I am Darius Hadley and I own this estate.'

'Good try, but Mr Hadley is dead,' he replied, 'and the house is being sold, so if you'd just get back in the vehicle. You can turn around about fifty yards ahead—'

'I know where I can turn. I know every inch of this estate,' he said, cutting him off, but clearly words weren't going to do it. Taking his wallet from his back pocket, he opened it and held it out so that the man could see his driver's licence. 'Darius Hadley,' he repeated, while the man checked the name and photograph. 'The previous owner was my grandfather.'

'Even so, sir, I'll have to check with the office.'

'Check with who you like. How did you know we were here?' It seemed unlikely that a patrol just happened to be passing at the exact moment he'd stalled his engine.

'There's CCTV on all the entrances, Mr Hadley. Apparently this one is something of a lovers'...'

'Get rid of it.'

'I'm sorry...'

'I want the cameras down now. Every one of them, is that clear?'

'I can't—'

Darius didn't wait for the excuses, but reached into the Land Rover for his mobile phone and called Brian Ramsey.

'Ramsey,' he said, before the man could do more than say his name, 'I understand that you've had security cameras installed at the Chase. Get rid of them. And the security company.'

'Darius...' he said, in what he no doubt thought was a soothing voice. 'The house is empty and this is the most economic...'

'It's intrusive. The tenants have a right to privacy.'

'I'm sure if you asked them they would tell you that there have been problems with trespassers, poachers. The trout stream is a selling point and the insurance company...'

'There's a public footpath across the estate and those

poachers are not just keeping down the rabbit population, they're local people and they do a better job of keeping an eye on the place than any security firm. No arguments. I own this estate and I want the cameras gone. Today.'

He ended the call without waiting to hear more and turned to the man. 'You heard me. You're fired.'

CHAPTER SIX

'ARE YOU OKAY?'

'There's nothing wrong with me,' Natasha said as Darius climbed in beside her. 'You could do with a few lessons in reality, though.'

'What?' About to reach for the ignition, he sat back, dragged his fingers through his hair. Far from okay, she was furious. 'I'm sorry. That was—'

'Don't apologise to me,' she snapped. 'What on earth were you thinking?'

He glanced at her, aware that he was missing something but not sure what. 'I was thinking that perhaps you might just be a little bit upset at being seen half-naked by a total stranger,' he said.

'Really? And how would that be different from you making a bronze of my entirely naked body for the entire world to stare at?' He wasn't deceived by the mildness of her tone. She was mad and actually he didn't blame her. On a stupid scale of one to ten that had to be a nine. She might have been up there with him, reaching for ten, but he'd started it. Clearly some serious grovelling was in order, but she wasn't done. 'I am not made of porcelain, Darius; I won't break if some bloke gets an eyeful of my tits, but that man probably has a wife and family to support.'

What? He was apologising to her, but apparently her only concern was some lout who'd leered at her breasts.

'How do you suppose his employers will react when they're told they've lost their contract because someone— a man who was just doing his job keeping Hadley Chase safe from intruders—hacked off the high and mighty Darius Hadley?'

High and mighty?

'I'm not—'

'No? You should have *heard* yourself. *"This is my land!"* Really? Because I got the strong impression that you don't give a tuppenny damn about the place.'

'I give a damn,' he said.

'About selling it as quickly as possible with the least possible inconvenience to yourself.'

'No...'

'When was the last time you actually set foot on the place?'

'You have no idea—'

'So tell me.'

Tell her? What? That his father had sold him? Share the shrivelling knowledge that his value had been counted in sterling. That his grandfather had forced his own son to choose between the woman he loved beyond reason and his infant son.

He was still holding his cell phone and, instead of answering her, he hit redial.

'Ramsey...I'm sorry,' he began before the man had a chance to say more than his name. 'You're right, the house must have a security presence and the company are doing an excellent job. Please ask them to pass on my apologies to the guard I met this morning. He took me by surprise but he was simply doing his job and it has been pointed out to me that I behaved like a jerk.'

He didn't wait for an answer, but disconnected, tossed the phone back on the shelf and reached for the ignition.

Natasha cleared her throat. 'Do you want your shirt back?'

'Keep it,' he said. 'I'll wear your top. Now you've cut me down to size, it'll be a perfect fit.'

'Oh, I think you fill this one pretty well,' she said, pulling it over her head and handing it to him, before turning behind to recover her top and bra from the back seat. By the time she was straight he had pulled up in front of the house.

To the right the parkland fell away to the river; then, beyond it, the Downs offered a breathtaking view for miles around.

Tash sighed. Beside her, Darius had that same locked-away look that he'd had when she'd first set eyes on him, except now she knew that it was not simply about the advertisement. For a moment, before he'd called Brian Ramsey, told him to apologise to the security guard, she'd seen the darkness, a pain like a knife in his heart.

There was something about this house, what had happened here, that hurt bone-deep, and yet he'd brought her here. She'd like to think it was because he wanted to spend the day with her, maybe fool around a little—fool around a lot if the last few minutes were anything to go by. Now she realised that she had simply provided him with a hook, that her need had given him an excuse, a way back.

The minute he came to a halt, she climbed down, grabbed her bags from the back seat but, instead of going straight to the door, she walked to the edge of the lawn where there was a strategically placed bench, giving him breathing space to come to terms with being here before he had to go inside.

Meanwhile, she had a job to do and she'd better jolly well stop lusting after Darius; she took out her mini camcorder and began to create a panorama to post on Facebook.

The crunch of his boots on the gravel warned her that he had followed her. 'The house might have a few shortcomings, but the setting is perfect,' she said, not looking up until the view was blocked by his broad chest. She didn't stop filming but, instead of panning from left to right, she lifted the lens until his face filled the screen.

'Here are the keys. The alarm code is 2605.'

'You're leaving me to it?' she asked, letting the camera fall to her side, a little hollow spot of disappointment somewhere below her waist that he was ducking out. 'I thought you'd been appointed responsible adult?'

'Apparently I failed at the first hurdle. Don't worry. I'll ask that security guard to frisk you for the family silver before you leave,' he said.

'You were wrong, Darius.'

'Totally.' He met her gaze head-on. 'I lashed out because I felt guilty.'

'I realise that, but I'm an adult; I knew where I was, what I was doing. The responsibility was equally mine.'

'But you didn't know what I knew.'

'Oh? And what was that?'

'Ramsey told me he'd employed a security company; it just never occurred to me that they would be monitoring the place so closely.' He shrugged, summoned up the ghost of a smile. 'Forget that; I wasn't thinking about anything except getting you naked.'

She resisted the urge to fling herself at him again and, keeping her own smile low-key, said, 'Ditto.'

His own smile deepened a fraction, but he shook his head.

'Shall I tell you why I liked being with Toby?' she asked.

'No—'

'He never patronised me,' she said. 'He never doubted that I knew what I was doing.' Okay, he wasn't that bright. If she knew what she was doing, she wouldn't be this close to a man who made her self-preservation hard drive crash whenever she thought about touching him. About him touching her. 'He never felt the need to protect me.'

'He stole your job!'

'He was paying me the ultimate compliment, Darius. He knew that I was strong enough, smart enough, to survive.'

'Maybe, but I wasn't patronising you. I was just doing that macho shit...'

'I know.' About to reach out, touch him, reassure him, she tucked the house keys in her pocket, sat down on the bench, took a flask out of her bag, keeping her hands busy.

She'd wanted him to share his pain. Maybe, while she had him on her hook, she could show him how.

'I spent the first twenty-one years of my life being protected, Darius. It gets old.' She unscrewed the cups from the top of the flask, looked up. 'Have you got time for coffee?'

Darius recognised his moment to make his excuses and walk away. It was what he always did when things became complicated, involved—walking away from emotional entanglement. Something he'd been signally failing to do ever since he'd set eyes on Natasha Gordon in Morgan's office.

He'd walked, but he'd hardly made it across the road before he was looking back, hooked on that luscious body, those eyes. Now, layered on that first explosive impact, was her sweet, spicy, delicious scent, the taste of her skin, her mouth entwining itself around him, binding him to her.

He should be running, not walking away, but he'd been running since he was seventeen years old. Running from the house behind him and yet here he was, because Natasha had needed him. Or maybe he'd needed the excuse she gave him to return, face it. Whichever it was, he barely hesitated before joining her on the bench, taking the coffee she'd poured for him.

'Thanks.'

'You're welcome,' she said, but didn't follow it up with an offer of something sweet to go with it. Just as well—

'cake' would, in his mind, forever be a euphemism for sex and even he balked at a garden bench with half an acre of lawn in front of them.

'Okay,' he said, 'I'm hooked. Tell me about the first twenty-one years of your life.'

'All of them?' she asked. 'I thought you had to be somewhere.'

He leaned an elbow on the back of the bench, making it clear he was going nowhere. 'Hospital visiting.' Another hurdle to face. 'Gary isn't going anywhere.'

She took a sip of her coffee.

'Come on,' he said, waggling his eyebrows at her. 'You know you want to tell me.'

'But do you really want to hear?'

He was beginning to get a bad feeling about this, wishing he'd gone with his first thought and walked away. 'How about a quick rundown of the highlights?' he suggested.

'Lowlights would be more accurate,' she said.

'Were they that bad?'

'No...' She reached out as if to reassure him and for a moment her fingers brushed his arm. 'But highlights are all sparkle and excitement. Champagne and strawberries.'

'And lowlights are egg custard?'

She laughed. 'Give the man a coconut. My first twenty-one years were all wholesome, nourishing, good-for-you egg custard when I longed for spicy, lemony, chocolatey, covered-in-frosting, bad-for-you, sugar-on-the-lips cake,' she said.

'Thanks for the coconut, but I don't deserve it,' he said. 'I have absolutely no idea what you're talking about.'

'Of course not. No one ever does.'

'Try me.'

She looked at him over the rim of her cup, then put it down. 'Okay. It's taking quiet beach holidays in the same cottage with my family in Cornwall every year, when I dreamed of being in a hot-air balloon floating across the Serengeti, bungee jumping in New Zealand, white water rafting in Colorado like my brothers.'

'Why?'

'Given the choice, wouldn't you have preferred hot-air ballooning?'

He thought about it for a moment then said, 'Actually they both have a lot to commend them and Cornwall does have surfing.'

Tash, who was finding this a lot harder than she imagined, grabbed the distraction. 'You surf? In one of those clinging wetsuits?' She flapped a hand to wave cooling air over her face. 'Be still my beating heart.'

'You don't?' he asked, refusing to be distracted.

'Surf? I can't even swim. The most dangerous thing I do at the seaside is paddle up to my ankles with my nephews and nieces. Build sandcastles. Play shove ha'penny down the pub.'

'And again, why? You mentioned that you were sick as a kid, but you look pretty robust now.'

'Robust?' She rolled the word round her mouth, testing it. 'Thanks for that. It makes me feel so much better.'

'No need to get on your high horse; you have a great body—one that I guarantee would cause a riot in a wetsuit—but that wasn't the "why" I was asking. Why were your parents so protective?'

And suddenly there it was. She'd lived a lifetime with everyone knowing what had happened to her, looking at her with a touch of uncertainty, of pity.

She'd left all that behind when she'd left home. She hadn't told anyone in London, not even Toby, but when Miles had introduced a private health scheme for the staff late last year, the insurance company had put so many restrictions on her that he'd called her into his office, convinced she was a walking time bomb. She'd told him everything and now the bastard had used it against her.

Had it played on his mind when he was thinking of promoting her? Because it stayed with you, stuck like dog muck on a shoe. Telling Darius was harder than she'd imagined when she'd blithely set out to show him how to trust someone so totally that you exposed yourself in ways that had nothing to do with getting naked.

Their relationship was purely physical and she never saw it being anything else. He had 'loner' stamped all over him, but she didn't want to alter the image he had of her. To have the 'attractive packaging' undermined by that darkness he would find in her inner depths and exposed in bronze. But he'd given her his trust when not many men in his situation would have given her the time of day and if she could get him to open up she would have repaid him whether she sold Hadley Chase or not.

'I had cancer—' There it was, the great big nasty C-word. 'Leukaemia—'

'Leukaemia?' Well, that put a dent in his smile. 'Oh, God, I'm sorry. I thought…'

'What?'

'From what you said about being force-fed egg custard…'

'What?'

'The newspaper hinted at some psychological problem…' He looked distinctly uncomfortable. 'Patsy wondered if you might have had some kind of eating disorder.'

'You've got to be kidding!' The tension erupted in a burst of laughter. 'Look at me!'

Darius looked and he wanted to laugh, too. 'I told her she was way off beam,' he said. 'I'm beginning to have a very warm regard for egg custard.' His fingers lightly traced the outline of her face from temple to chin. 'That is a very healthy glow.'

'I think the word you're looking for is pink and over-weight,' she said, 'which actually is pretty ironic.'

'Pretty' was too bland a word for Natasha. She was no pretty milkmaid... 'It is?'

'I'm told that people suffering from anorexia look at themselves in the mirror and see fat even when they're skin and bones. Well, my parents look at me and see skin and bones despite the fact that I'm—'

'Luscious.'

'Nicely fielded,' she said, turning away, but he hooked his finger around her chin, forcing her to look him in the eyes.

'I know what I mean, Natasha.'

'Do you?'

'Believe me. I can usually wait to get a room.'

'Are you saying that you don't usually toss women into the nearest verge?' she teased, laughing now as the tension of telling her story left her and he added a whole raft of other words to describe Natasha Gordon. Ripe, earthy, soft, warm and unbelievably sexy... 'That you'd rather have a safe double bed?'

'Safe?' There was nothing safe or comfortable about this relationship. He had no idea what Natasha would say or do next. What he would do. His fingers seemed to burn when he touched her. He had no control over his responses... 'You will live to regret that.'

'Promises, promises...' For a moment they just looked at one another, then she turned away from the intensity of it and he allowed her to break the contact between them. 'Actually, robust is good. My family still treat me as if I've been stuck back together with some very dodgy glue and might fall apart at any moment.'

'No swimming, because pools are a germ factory and who knows what's in the sea?' he suggested.

'That's pretty much how it went.'

'It must have been difficult for them to truly believe that you've made a full recovery,' he said. 'I imagine you never quite trust the fates once you've been through something like that.'

'It wasn't just my parents. I've got three older brothers and they lived through it, too. Tom, the eldest, became a doctor because of what happened to me.'

'What about the other two?'

'James is a vet; Harry is a sports teacher. He's nearest in age to me and appointed himself my personal bodyguard when I started school. If anyone got too close, too rough, watch out.'

He knew he'd have been the same, but he could see it wouldn't be much fun to be on the receiving end of that kind of protection. 'How did you cope with that?'

'I regret to say that I loved it. I was a proper little princess,' she admitted ruefully, 'and, with three gorgeous brothers, everyone wanted to be my friend. It was only when I was fifteen and Harry discovered that I had a crush on a boy in the lower sixth that it all got out of hand.'

He grinned. 'I suppose he warned him off his little sister?'

'Oh, it was worse, far worse than that. The poor guy obviously didn't have a clue that he was the object of my desire. He always smiled at me in the corridor—probably because I *was* Harry's sister—and I'd just built up this huge fantasy. As you do…' He glanced at her and she rolled her eyes. 'Teenage girls.'

'An alien species,' he agreed. 'And?'

'And my sweet brother asked him, as a personal favour, to take me as his date to a school disco.'

'You're kidding?'

'I wish,' she said, 'but Harry was captain of sport and played under-eighteen rugby for the county. A request from him was in the nature of a decree from Mount Olympus.'

'So you had your dream date?'

'Bliss city.'

'But?'

She sighed. 'There is always a "but",' she agreed. 'I discovered what Harry had done, which was a total nightmare, but worse, much worse, I discovered that everyone else knew.'

'Before? After? During?'

'During. The classic overheard gossip in the loo... The girl he would have taken if Harry hadn't stuck his oar in was giving vent to her feelings about the spoiled, fat little cow who'd got her brother to twist her boyfriend's arm.'

'Ouch,' he said, flippantly enough, but deep down he was imagining what that must have been like for an over-protected fifteen-year-old girl. The embarrassment, the shame... 'What did you do?'

'I waited in the cubicle until they'd gone, then I slipped out of school and walked home.'

'Of course you did. How far was it?'

'A couple of miles. It wouldn't have been a problem, but I'd abandoned my coat because I didn't want anyone to see me leave.'

'Coat? What time of year was this?'

'It was the Christmas disco,' she said, and he let slip a word that he immediately apologised for.

'No, you're okay.' She held up her hand and began to count off the reasons why that word was just about perfect. First finger... 'There was the no-coat thing, which on any level was pretty dumb.' Second finger... 'There were the sparkly new shoes which weren't made for long-distance walking and fell apart after half a mile.' Third finger... 'Then it began to rain.'

'Your date didn't miss you?'

'Not for a while. When a girl disappears into a cloak-room who knows how long she'll be and I don't suppose he was in any hurry...' She shrugged. 'Anyway, my feet hurt, my dress was ruined and my life was over. Worse, I knew my parents would be waiting up for me, wanting to hear about my date. I couldn't face all that concern, all that sympathy, so I hid in the garden shed.'

'Oh, I can see where this is going. No one knew where you were. They organised a search party, called the police, dragged the river?'

'All of the above.'

'You're kidding?'

She laughed at his horrified reaction. 'Okay, not the river. Tom came looking for a torch and found me before it got that far. I was given a severe talking to by the local constabulary on the subject of responsibility and Dad grounded me for the whole of the Christmas holidays. No parties or holiday outings for me. Not much of a punishment, to be honest. I wanted to hibernate.'

'He knew that. He was making it easy for you.'

'Oh... Of course he was.' She shook her head. 'I never realised.'

'You were upset.'

'It got worse. School insisted that I had "counselling",' she said, making quote marks with her fingers, 'because obviously anyone who behaved so irrationally, so irresponsibly, had problems and needed help.'

Hardly irrational, he thought. More like a wounded animal going to ground. Something he knew all about.

'Not a Christmas to remember, I'm guessing.'

'White-faced parents, Harry in the doghouse with everyone. A total lack of ho-ho-ho. On the upside, by the time the holidays were over there were other scandals to talk about.'

'And the downside?'

'I'm still trying to prove that I can put one foot in front of the other without one of them holding my hand. Proving to my brothers that their broken little sister is all mended.'

Darius, thinking that if they'd seen her laying into him they might be convinced, said, 'Any luck?'

'The nearest I came was last Christmas when I drove home in the BMW.'

'Ho-ho-ho!'

She dug him in the ribs with her elbow. 'Men are so shallow. If I'd known how easy it was to impress them I'd have saved my bonuses for a flash car instead of putting down a deposit on my flat.'

'The fact that you didn't proves how smart you are.'

She sighed. 'Not smart enough to see this coming. Every morning I wake up and, just for a moment, everything is normal.'

Ten seconds, he thought. You had about ten seconds when you thought life still made sense before that jolt as you remembered and it was like the first moment all over again.

'I just feel so stupid.'

'Only someone you trust, someone you love can betray you, Natasha. It always comes out of left field.' He felt, rather than saw her turn to look at him. There would be a question mark rippling the creamy skin between her brows and he held his breath, waiting for the questions.

How did he know? When had his world come crashing down? Who had betrayed him? For what seemed an age the only sound was a blackbird perched high in the cedar tree. It was one of those long silences that the unwary rushed to fill and, even though he recognised the danger, he found himself tempted to tell her anyway.

She stirred before he could gather the words. Begin...

'The real downside was the guilt,' she said. 'I was old enough then to see what it did to my mother, to understand what she must have been through when I was little, so when Dad suggested I take my degree at Melchester University...'

Conflicting emotions twisted his gut. Relief that she'd let him off the hook, regret that he'd missed his chance.

'You wanted to make it up to them,' he said.

'It was okay, actually. Melchester has one of the best estate management courses in the country and, with all those lads living away from home for the first time, I was never short of a date.'

He doubted her mother's cooking was the only lure but he didn't want to think about that. 'So what made you toss away the dream job with the National Trust and run away to London to work for Miles Morgan?'

'I live in a small town. I was the little girl who'd had leukaemia. My sickness defined me. No one could see past it, not even my family.'

'So you finally made the break.'

'No... I lied to them, Darius.'

'Lied?'

'I knew that if I took the National Trust job, just down the road, I'd never leave. Never do anything. I'd marry someone I'd known all my life, who knew everything I'd ever done...'

'You told them you didn't get it?'

She nodded. 'It felt like breaking out of jail.' She tossed away the dregs of her coffee, staring out over the neglected lawn. 'I'll be honest. This isn't where I saw myself five years on from my degree, but I've worked harder than anyone so that I wouldn't have to go home and prove them all right.' She turned to look at him. 'You think I'm terrible, don't you? That I don't know how lucky I am to have a family who cares about me.'

Close. Very close. Apparently he wasn't the only one reading body language, studying inner depths. She must have learned a thing or two watching the men and women trying to hide their reactions to the houses she showed them, playing their cards close to their chest.

'I have no family,' he said, 'so I'm in no position to judge.'

'None?' And in a moment her expression turned from inward reproach to concern. 'I'm so sorry, Darius. That's really tough. What happened to your parents?'

Yes, well, that was the thing about trusting someone with your secrets; it was supposed to be a two-way deal but his moment of weakness had passed and he was already regretting this excursion into her past. Why complicate something as simple as sex?

'I have no parents.' He drained his coffee, screwed the top back on the flask and put it back in her bag. 'Did you ever tell them the truth?' he asked before she could push him for details. 'About the job?'

She shook her head.

'Maybe you should,' he advised. Clearly she was harbouring the guilt.

'They'd be devastated. And now, after all that horrible stuff in the paper, all those between-the-lines insinuations that I'm mentally unstable, they're out of their minds worried again.'

Her eyes were shining, but the tears were more of anger than anything else, he was certain. Was that how it was? Love? This complicated mishmash of guilt, anxiety, the desperate need not to hurt, to protect? Add in passion, sacrifice, the world well lost and you were well and truly stuffed... Or maybe blessed beyond measure.

Natasha blinked back the threatening tears and he put his arm around her, drew her close. There was a moment of stiffness, resistance and then she melted against him. 'My mother is desperate for me to go with them on the annual trek to Cornwall so that she can look after me,' she said. 'Heal me with sea air, walks on the beach, evening games of Scrabble.'

'Instead, you're playing hide the sausage in the woods with a disreputable sculptor who's going to put your naked body on display for the entire world to see,' he said.

She snorted, buried her face into his shoulder and suddenly, sitting there, his arm around her, both of them shaking with laughter, felt like a perfect moment.

Above them the swallows swooped just above head height, the scent of roses was drifting on a warm breeze and the temptation to stay there, looking out over the heat-hazed valley, almost overwhelmed him.

CHAPTER SEVEN

'DARIUS?'

He stirred and Natasha lifted her head, looked up at him.
'I'm sorry I shouted at you.'

'I'm not.' Tears of pain and laughter had clumped her
eyelashes together. He used the pad of his thumb to wipe
away one that had spilled over, kissed lips that were raised
in what felt like an invitation. 'You can tell your family
from me that they don't have a thing to worry about. You
are strong in every way and I'm really glad you're on my
side.'

Really glad as he kissed her again and, lost in the sweetness of her mouth, for once in his life not thinking about an
exit strategy. It should be scaring the wits out of him, but
the connection between them had an honesty that overrode
any fear of commitment. Natasha needed him on her side
to re-establish her career, didn't know that security guard
from Adam and yet she had instantly empathised with him
and she hadn't hesitated to give it to him with both barrels
when she thought he was wrong. How many women in her
situation would have done that?

When he was with her, he had no sense of losing himself, but of becoming something greater.

Blessed.

It was Natasha who moved.

'Enough of this maudlin self-pity,' she said. 'I've got work to do.'

He looked back at the house. Huge, empty… 'Are you going to be all right on your own?'

She gave him a warning look and he held up his hands. 'Sorry…'

'No… I shouldn't be so defensive.' Then, as he made a reluctant move, 'Actually, there is one thing.'

'Yes?'

Tash had felt the exact moment that Darius had wanted to move. For a blissful few minutes he'd been still, utterly relaxed and his kiss had been so tender that tears had once again threatened to overwhelm her.

After such an emotional exchange most men would have said *anything* but that shuttered 'yes' was warning enough, if she'd needed it, not to get too deeply involved with Darius Hadley. He wasn't a keeper and no one could protect her from that kind of pain.

'If I find any diaries, can I borrow them?'

'Diaries?'

'I imagine there are diaries, letters?' she prompted. 'Something interesting must have happened in three and a half centuries. You've got a ballroom, so presumably there were country balls? The occasional drama over a little inappropriate flirting? Maybe a duel?' she added, just to get a response.

'I have no idea,' he said stiffly, all his defences back up.

'Oh, for goodness' sake, Darius, lighten up,' she said crossly. 'If there had been any scandal to be dug up, the newspapers would have been all over it when that blasted ad became a news item.'

It didn't mean there wasn't a family skeleton rattling around in the cupboard because it was obvious that something wasn't right. He'd changed the subject faster than greased lightning when she'd asked him about his parents.

She lifted an eyebrow, inviting him to come clean, but even yesterday, with a bulge in his pants that had to have hurt, he'd been unreadable, hiding whatever he was thinking, feeling. What had it taken to build that mask?

What would it take, she wondered, to shatter it?

No, no, no…

'A house that grand, that old, must have hosted some interesting people over the centuries?' she persisted. It was all very well to casually toss out the words 'social media', but posting pictures of the house on Facebook and flinging 'buy this' Tweets around like confetti wasn't going to do the job.

'Not interesting in your sense of the word. The Hadleys were riding, shooting, fishing country squires with no pretensions to high society.'

'More Jane Austen than Georgette Heyer,' she said with a sigh. 'I don't suppose she ever came to tea? Jane Austen,' she added. Much as she loved Georgette Heyer's books, a visit from her wouldn't arouse the same kind of interest. 'I need a way in, something to grab the attention, create interest, start a buzz going.'

'Why don't you make up a story?'

'Excuse me?'

'Most family history is based on Chinese whispers—expanded and decorated with every retelling. Our story is that James Hadley was given the estate by Charles II for services rendered during his exile. How much more likely is it that he bought it cheap for a quick sale from one of Cromwell's confederates who, come the Restoration, decided the climate in the New World might be better for his health?'

'You're such a cynic, Darius Hadley.'

Off the dangerous territory of recent history, he grinned. 'A realist. Who's going to challenge you if you say Jane Austen stayed one wet week in April and, confined to the house, spun a story to keep everyone amused?'

'I have no doubt that some obsessive Janeite would know exactly where she was during that particular week.'

'Really?'

'I'm afraid so. They didn't have email or Skype or television to keep them amused so they wrote long detailed letters to their family and friends telling them where they were, what they were doing. And instead of blogging, they kept *diaries*...' She lifted her hands in a *ta-da* gesture.

'Being caught out in a blatant lie might grab the house another headline. *Mad Estate Agent Lies About Austen Connection*?' he offered. 'You did say any publicity would be good publicity.'

'I think you've had all that kind of "good" publicity you can handle and I'm trying to restore my reputation, not sink it without a trace so, unless you can point me to an entry in one your ancestors' diaries along the lines that "Mrs Austen visited with her daughters, Cassandra and Jane. It rained all week, but Jane kept the children amused acting out scenes from a little history of England she has written..." we'll save that as a last resort.'

'You're the expert,' he said. 'You'll find the diaries in my grandmother's room. She was writing a history of the house. I don't know if she ever finished it.'

'A history?' She was practically speechless. 'There's a history! For heaven's sake, Darius, talk about pulling hen's teeth!'

He grinned. 'I've made the woman happy. If there's nothing else?'

'No... Yes...' She fished in the picnic bag and produced a small plastic box. 'Take Gary these cookies from me. They're not as healthy as grapes, but they'll help a cup of hospital tea go down.'

Tash let herself into the house, dealt with the alarm and then, as the Land Rover rattled into life, she turned and watched it disappear as the drive dipped and curved through the woods. It seemed a little early for hospital visiting, but he'd shown no interest in going inside the house and she suspected that it served as a useful excuse to avoid whatever it was that he didn't want to talk about.

Despite her airy assurance that she would be fine, it was a huge old place, undoubtedly full of ghosts and, as she opened the glazed doors that led from the entrance lobby into the main reception hall, what struck her first was the stillness, the silence.

Out of the corner of her eye she saw something move, but when she swung round she realised that it was only her reflection in a dusty mirror.

Heart beating in her throat, she looked around but nothing stirred except the dust motes she'd set dancing in the sunlight pouring down from the lantern fifty feet above her and, just for a moment, she was back in the studio with Darius holding her, limp, sated in his arms. Reliving the desperate frustration when that wretched guard had turned up.

They were so not done.

No, no, no... Concentrate...

Beneath the mirror, an ornate clock on the hall table had long since stopped. Dead leaves had drifted into the corner of each tread of that dratted staircase. All it needed was a liveried footman asleep against the newel post and she would have stepped into the *Sleeping Beauty* picture book she'd had as a child.

As the germ of an idea began to form, she began to film the scene in front of her, panning slowly around the grand entrance hall with its shadowy portraits, an ormolu clock sitting on an elegant serpentine table thickly layered with dust, paused on the room reflected in soft focus through the hazy surface of the gilded mirror.

She opened doors to shuttered rooms where filtered light gave glimpses of ghostly furniture swathed in dust sheets, climbed the magnificent Tudor staircase—not a woodworm in sight—and explored bedrooms in varying stages of grandeur.

There was a four-poster bed that looked as if Queen Elizabeth I might have slept in it in the master suite. Next door was a suite for the mistress of the house—a comfortable, less daunting bedroom, a dressing room and bathroom and a small sitting room with a chaise longue, a writing desk and a bookshelf filled with leather-bound journals. Research material for his grandmother's history.

The desk had just one wide drawer and nestling inside it was a heavy card folder tied together with black ribbon and bearing the title *A History of Hadley Chase by Emma Hadley.* She had just untied the ribbon and laid back the cover to reveal a drawing of the Tudor house that had been added to and 'improved' over the years when her phone pinged, warning her of an incoming text.

It was from Darius.

Darius stopped twenty yards from the main gate and the gatehouse cottage that Gary shared with his grandmother.

Mary Webb had been his grandmother's cook and the nearest thing to a mother he'd ever had. She'd given him the spoons to lick when she was making cakes, stuck on the plasters when he'd scraped a knee, given him a hug when his dog died. And, like everyone else in this place, had known his history and kept it from him.

When he'd learned the truth he'd walked away from the house and everyone connected with it and never looked back. That had been his choice, but while he had a home, a career, there was no guarantee that Gary, a few years older, who'd made him a catapult, lain in the dark with him watching for badgers, taught him to ride a motorbike, would have either when the estate was sold.

This is my land...

The words had come so easily. But they were hollow without the responsibilities that went with it. *Noblesse oblige*. Natasha hadn't used those words, but when she'd rounded on him that was the subtext.

She'd asked him how long it had been since he'd set foot on this estate. Almost as long as he'd lived here. An age. A lifetime. He would never have come back if he'd had his way and yet, because of her, he was here. Not for the land, but for a woman. The irony was not lost on him.

He took out his phone, sent her a two-word text and when he looked up Mary Webb was standing on the doorstep. Seventeen years older and so much smaller than he remembered.

Sixteen years.

The text was unsigned, but it came from Darius and could only mean one thing. She'd asked him how long it was since he'd last set foot on Hadley Chase. He hadn't answered, but he had been listening.

Sixteen years...

The article she'd read about his commission for the sculpture of the horse had mentioned that he'd been at the Royal College of Art and from the date she'd been able to work out that he had to be thirty-one, maybe thirty-two. That meant he'd have been sixteen or seventeen when he left the Chase, long before his grandfather became sick or he'd left for art school. It suggested a family row of epic proportions. A breach that had never been healed. Scarcely any wonder he hadn't wanted her digging around, poking in the corners stirring up ghosts.

But this was a tiny crack and through it other questions flooded in. Not just what had caused the rift, but where could a hurting teenage boy with no family have gone?

She tried to imagine herself in that situation. Imagine

that instead of hiding out in the shed, she'd run away. It happened every day. Teenagers running away from situations they couldn't handle.

Where would she have run to? How would she have lived?

How would she have felt returning home after sixteen years, a stranger, changed beyond recognition from the cossetted girl who'd painted her nails, pinned up her hair, put on a new dress and sparkly shoes to go to a school disco?

He'd shown no interest, no emotional attachment to the property until that security guard had ordered him to leave but then the claim had been instinctive. Possessive.

'This is my land...'

She looked around her. Darius had lived here while he was growing up, going to school. All his formative years had been spent roaming the estate. In this house. It had made him who he was, given him the strength to survive on his own. She would have expected a photograph on the desk, on the bedside table. There was nothing, but there had to be traces of him here. His room...

When she'd visited the Chase in order to prepare the details for the kind of glossy sales brochure a house of this importance demanded, there had been a team of them from Morgan and Black, walking the land, detailing the outbuildings, the cottages, the boathouse. Inside, she had concentrated on the main reception and bedrooms while junior staff had gone through the minor rooms, the attics.

She arranged the desk to look as if the writer had just left it for a moment, took photographs of that and the view from the window, then picked up the folder and went in search of the room which had been Darius Hadley's private space.

She found it at the far end of the first floor corridor. Grander than most bedrooms, with a high ceiling, tall windows looking out over the park and furnished with pieces that had obviously been in the house for centuries. And yet it was still recognisable for what it was. A boy's bedroom. Unchanged since he'd abandoned it.

Her brother Tom was about the same age and he'd had the same poster above his bed, the same books on his shelves.

The similarity ended with the books and posters. Tom had always known what he wanted to do and by the time he was seventeen he'd had a skeleton in his room, medical diagrams on the walls.

Darius, too, had been focused on the future. There were wall-to-wall drawings, tacked up with pins, curling at the edges.

One of them, the drawing of a laughing retriever, each curl of his coat, each feather of his tail so full of life that he looked as if he was about to bound off the paper after a rabbit.

On a worktable lay a folder filled with watercolours. Distant views of the house, the hills, the birds and animals that roamed the estate. The faint scent of linseed oil still clung to an easel leaning against a far wall. She opened a wooden box stacked beside it. Brushes, dried up tubes of paint. He'd moved on from sketches and watercolours to oil, but none of those were here.

She turned to the wardrobe and a lump formed in her throat as she saw his clothes. A pair of riding boots, walking shoes, battered old trainers bearing the shape of his youthful foot lined up beneath shirts, a school uniform, jackets, a suit and, in a suit bag from a Savile Row tailor, what must have been his first tux, never worn.

What kind of a life had he had here? Privileged, without a doubt, and yet he'd apparently walked away from it, leaving everything behind. His clothes, his art, his life.

She'd been seven or eight when Tom was that age and he'd seemed like a god to her then, but when she'd been sixteen, seventeen, the boys in her year had seemed so im-

mature, so useless. She couldn't imagine any of them cop-
ing without their mother to do their washing, put food in
front of them, provide a taxi service.

She sat on the narrow bed, rubbed her hand over the
old Welsh quilt that he'd slept under, then kicked off her
shoes, leaned back against an impressive headboard, putting herself in his place, looking out of the window at the
view he'd grown up with, trying to imagine what had been
so bad that it had driven him away. And failing. It was so
beautiful here, so tranquil.

She sighed. No doubt her home life would have looked
enviable to an outsider and in many ways it was. But she'd
been older, an adult when she'd left. He'd been a boy.

She let it go and, propping the folder against her thighs,
began to read his grandmother's history of Hadley Chase.

Darius was right—nothing important had happened,
no one of great significance was mentioned—and yet his
grandmother had edited the journals, adding her own com-
mentary and illustrations on events, providing an insight
into the lives of those living and working in the house, on
the estate and in the village since the seventeenth century.
The births, marriages, deaths. The celebrations. The trag-
edies, changes that affected them all. Tash had reached the
late eighteenth century when her phone rang.

'Hi...' she said, hunting for a tissue.

Darius, pacing Mary's living room while she packed a
bag, heard the kind of sniff that only went with tears.

'Natasha? What's happened? Are you hurt?'

'No...' Another sniff. 'It's nothing.'

'You're crying.'

'I was just reading about an outbreak of smallpox in
the village in 1793. Seven children died, Darius. One of
them was the three-year-old son of Joshua Hadley. He wrote
about him, about the funeral. It's heartbreaking...'

She'd found the history. It had figured heavily in his

education as the heir to the estate and the death of small children had been a fact of life before antibiotics.

'It was over two hundred years ago,' he reminded her.

'I know. I'm totally pathetic, but your grandmother drew a picture of his grave. It's so small. This isn't just a history; it's a work of art.'

'And full of smallpox, floods, crop failure.'

'Full of the lives of the people who've lived here. Not just the bad bits, but the joys, the celebrations. Your grandmother's illustrations are exquisite. Clearly it's in the genes,' she prompted.

He ignored the invitation to talk about his grandmother. 'You'll find Joshua's portrait in the dining room.'

'Actually, I'm looking at some of your early work right now,' she said, not giving up. 'Watercolours.'

'Chocolate-box stuff,' he said dismissively.

'That's a bit harsh. I love the drawing of your dog. What was his name?'

What was it about this woman? Every time he spoke to her, she churned up memories he'd spent years trying to wipe out. The only reason he was even here, being dragged back into the past, was because of her.

He should have just signed the whole lot over to the Revenue and let it go. It wasn't too late... Except there were things he had to do. People he had to protect.

'Darius?'

'Flynn,' he said. 'His name was Flynn.'

'He looks real enough to stroke.'

Even now, all these years later, he could feel the springy curls beneath his fingers. Smell the warm dog scent. Leaving him behind had been the hardest thing, but he'd been old—too old to leave the certainty of a warm hearth and a good dinner.

He'd mocked her sentimentality over a child who'd died

two hundred years ago but now he was the one with tears stinging at the back of his eyes.

'Darius, are you okay?'

He cleared his throat. 'Yes...'

'So, can I use all this stuff?'

'Will a smallpox outbreak help to the sell the house, do you think?' he asked.

'I'll probably miss out that bit.'

'Good decision.'

'So that's yes?'

'That's a yes with all the usual conditions.'

'You've already got me naked,' she reminded him.

He'd meant the ones about keeping his name out of it but, just as easily as she could dredge up the sentimental wasteland buried deep in his psyche, she could turn him on, make him laugh. 'You're naked?' he asked.

'Give me thirty seconds.'

He gripped the phone a little tighter. The temptation was there, but the thought of walking back into that house was like a finger of ice driving into him. 'Not even thirty minutes, I'm afraid. I've hit a complication.'

'Where are you?' she asked, as quick to read a shift in tone as body language.

'I stopped at the gatehouse to visit Mary Webb, Gary's grandmother,' he explained. 'He lives with her.'

'Oh... That was kind.'

'It was a duty call. She used to be my grandparents' cook. I couldn't just drive past.' He'd thought he could. He'd spent the last seventeen years mentally driving past.

'Kindness, duty, it doesn't matter, Darius, as long as you do it.'

'I'm glad you think so. She's five-foot-nothing and frail as a bird these days but it hasn't stopped her from reading me the riot act.'

'Give her a cookie,' she said, not asking why she was

angry. No doubt she understood how a woman would feel who'd lost—been abandoned by—a child she'd cared for, loved since infancy. Who, as a result of what happened that day, had lost her own grandson. His grandfather had not been a man to cross… 'People from the village are keeping an eye on her, doing her shopping, but she needs more than that so I'm taking her to see Gary, then driving her down to stay with her daughter in Brighton.'

'That should be a fun drive.'

'I'll blame you every mile of the way.'

'If it helps,' she said.

No, but thinking about her might. 'I'll survive,' he assured her. Probably. 'But I have no idea how long I'll be.'

'Don't worry about it. You take care of Mrs Webb. I can sort out some transport for myself. There's a bus to Swindon and I can catch a train from there. Don't give it a second thought. It's not a problem. Piece of cake—'

Her mouth was running away with her as she tried to hide her disappointment. It should have been an ego boost but all he wanted was to reach down the phone and hold her. Helpless, he waited until she began to repeat herself, finally ground to a halt, before he said, 'I'm taking her in Gary's car. I'll leave the Landie keys under a flowerpot in the porch for you.'

'Oh.'

'That's it?' he asked. 'You're finally lost for words?'

'No. I was just thinking that if you're bringing Gary's car back, I might as well stay here and wait for you.'

'It'll be late.'

'We might have to stay the night,' she agreed.

Not in a million years… 'I've got a better idea. Let's meet halfway at your place. We can have that picnic you promised me.'

'Oh? And what will you bring to the party?'

'A bottle of something chilled and a packet of three?' he offered.

'Three? That's a bit ambitious, isn't it?'

'One for yesterday, one for this morning, one for fun?' he suggested.

Her laugh was rich and warm. 'Talk, talk, talk...' she said, and ended the call.

He was grinning when he looked up and saw Mary watching him.

'My suitcase is on the bed,' she said primly. Then, as he passed her, she put her hand on his arm. 'It was the motorbike, Darius. That's why he told you about your Dad. Gary never cared about any of the other stuff you had, but that motorbike...'

'I know...'

It was Gary, with a battered old machine that he was renovating, who'd taught him to ride on the estate roads, so when he'd come down and found a brand-new silver motorbike waiting for him on his seventeenth birthday, the first thing he'd done was fire it up and drive it down to show him.

Cock-of-the-walk full of himself, too immature to understand how the one who'd always been the leader might feel when he saw him astride a machine so far out of his own reach. The understanding, in that split second, of the reality of their friendship; how, from that moment on, every step would take them further apart. For him there would be sixth form, university, the eventual ownership of this estate. For Gary, who'd left school at sixteen with no qualifications, there would be only a life of manual labour on little more than the minimum wage. And he'd used the only weapon he had to put himself back on top.

'He didn't do anything wrong. He told the truth, what he knew of it, that's all.'

'He was a stiff, proud man, your grandfather. He broke

your grandmother's heart, barring your father from the house while he stayed with your mother. The poor lady was never the same after. It wasn't that she didn't want to love you, Darius, just that she'd lost so much that she couldn't bear the risk.'

'Everyone lost, Mary. My grandfather most of all.'

Tash rolled off his bed and crossed to the window to look out across the park in the direction of the gates, rubbing her arms briskly to rid herself of the tingle of excitement that, just hearing the sound of his voice, riffled her skin into goose bumps.

Silly. She couldn't see the gatehouse cottage for the trees, but she was still grinning. She'd taken their relationship a step beyond a place Darius was comfortable with, hoping it would help him open up. Maybe it had. He'd stopped to talk to Gary's grandmother and the fact that she was angry with him suggested a strong emotional bond.

You only got angry with people you cared about. The fact that he'd mentioned it suggested that it mattered; he hadn't just called in, done the minimum, but had seen a need and acted on it. The journey might not be a comfortable one, but she doubted it would be silent; Mary Webb knew his secrets and he would be able to talk to her.

The fact that he'd felt able to tell her that she'd been angry suggested...

Stop it. Right there. The last thing she needed right now was a load of emotional complications messing with her head. Keep it simple.

Darius pressed the bell and Natasha's voice, distorted by static, said, 'Who's there?'

'You'd better not be expecting anyone else.'

'My cake is in great demand,' she said.

'Sugarlips!'

'First floor, the door on the right,' she said, and buzzed him up.

'I'm in the kitchen,' she called as he opened the door, and he kicked off his shoes alongside hers and followed her voice.

Her top, something silky in a rich chocolate, slid from her shoulder, a short pink skirt in some floaty material rose up, drawing attention to her long legs, bare feet, as she reached for a couple of wine glasses and, without saying a word, he put his arms around her and buried his mouth in the delicious curve between her shoulder and neck, sucking in her flesh, nipping at the sweet spot at the base of her neck.

A shiver of pleasure went through her as his hands found her breasts and she relaxed into him. It was the thought of this moment that had sustained him through an emotionally fraught day. The thought of holding her, breathing in the scent of her hair, her skin...

'Hello, you,' she said, laughing as she turned in his arms, reaching up to put her arms around his neck. Her hands didn't quite make it, her smile fading as her eyes searched his face and instead she cradled his cheeks in her palms, her thumbs wiping the hollows beneath his eyes as if to brush away dark shadows that only she could see. 'You've had a rough day...'

'No talking,' he said roughly. His ears were ringing with sixteen years of history as they'd talked about about everything, about every*one* but his mother. And now when Natasha would have answered him he cut her off with an abrupt, hungry kiss. For a heartbeat she was shocked into stillness and then she wrapped her arms around his neck, one of those long legs against his thigh and melted against him, her hot silk mouth the entrance to paradise.

He kissed her slow and deep while his hands reacquainted themselves with the feel of her skin, the already familiar shape of her curves, spreading wide around her waist, pushing up her top as his thumbs caressed the hollows of her stomach, his fingers teasing out all the little hotspots in her ribs.

Her fingers tangled in his hair, hanging on to him as she responded with little moans against his tongue and he fed on her sweet, spicy nectar that blotted out memory, blotted out everything but this moment, this need.

She uttered a soft cry as he broke off to get rid of her top, her bra and then leaned back with a sigh of contentment as he took his mouth, his tongue on a slow exploration of her body.

Definitely no talking...

CHAPTER EIGHT

TASH WAS INCAPABLE of coherent speech as Darius, his hands cradling her backside, sucked on the sensitive spot beneath her chin, curled his tongue around the horseshoe bone at the base of her throat, trailed hot, moist kisses between her breasts.

She whimpered as he ignored them and kept on going down, down, then he hit her navel and his tongue did things that had her gasping, breathless, climbing up him with her legs.

He propped her on the counter without missing a beat, then, with his hands free, he pushed up her skirt and slid his hand beneath the scrap of lace, pressing his thumb against the hot, swollen little button screaming for attention, then slowly circled it, in time with his tongue.

'Unngh...' she said, grabbing the collar of his polo shirt and hauling it, hand over hand, until it was over his head, then swallowed as she got the full impact of his powerful shoulders, arms moulded by the heaving of tons of clay, stone, metal, his broad chest arrowing to a narrow waist, hips, a mouth-watering bulge...

'Want to do it here?' he asked, his eyes burnished coal, teasing her with the tip of his finger before plunging it deep inside her.

'Unngh uuuunngh,' she urged, tightening around it, wanting more, wanting everything.

'Or would you rather move this to a nice safe bed?'

Safe…

There was nothing safe about this except the leaving-nothing-to-chance protection she'd stowed in the tiny seam pocket of her skirt and she answered him by taking it out, holding it between her teeth as, never taking her eyes from his, she tugged on his belt, flipped the button…

She looked up and, taking the condom from between her lips, he lowered his mouth to within a breath of hers and said, 'Don't stop now.'

He closed the gap, taking the word 'kiss' to a whole new meaning as, fingers shaking, she lowered his zip with the utmost care, eased her hands inside his jeans and pushed them down, releasing him. Clung to his hips as he disposed of her underwear, sheathed himself.

Then he looked up, straight into her eyes. 'Ready?' he asked.

'No talking,' she whispered and he was inside her with a thrust that went to her toes, held it while she caught her breath, opened her eyes. 'Don't stop now,' she murmured, wrapping her arms around his neck, her legs around his waist, taking in everything he had to give.

He gave it slowly, totally focused on her, reading her response to every thrust, every touch, taking this most basic of all acts and, instead of snatching for swift satisfaction, raising it into something new, something extraordinary, only taking his own release when he'd brought her to the point of incoherent howling meltdown.

Tash, shaking, shattered, wasn't sure which of them was supporting the other, only that they were holding each other, her cheek pressed into the hollow of his shoulder, listening to his heart return to a slow steady thud, breathing in the arousing scent of fresh sweat. All she knew was that she was glad she'd shut the kitchen window. That it was double-glazed…

* * *

Darius was the first to recover, straightening, lifting Natasha to the floor, holding her until he was certain that she could support herself. Or maybe holding on to her so that she could support him.

That was so not how it was meant to be.

Wound up by a day that had been filled with memories he'd spent half a lifetime trying to eradicate, he'd come looking for a hot, fast, cleansing release. Basic sex. What had just happened was something else...

He cleared his throat. 'I don't know about you, but I could do with a drink.'

She lifted her head, kissed his cheek. 'Sounds perfect.' She spotted the bottle he'd put on the kitchen table, picked up the glasses and handed them to him. 'Bring them through to the bathroom.'

There was no way they could both cram into her tiny shower cubicle so Tash filled the tub, added some bubbles, lit scented candles. He brought two glasses half filled with a pale chilled wine, set the bottle on the ledge and climbed in. She settled between his legs, leaning back against his chest, sipping the wine in restful silence as she relived each moment, each touch.

So much for the keep-it-simple sex. That had been as far removed from the simple gratification of a basic need as she'd ever experienced. No one had ever concentrated so completely on her in that way. Given so much...

His skin, golden in the candlelight, was too tempting and she turned her head, found the tender spot behind his knee with her tongue. He rescued her glass as, spurred on by his instant reaction, she half turned to take her mouth on an exploration of the smooth silk of his inner thigh, then turned to face him.

'Here or in a nice safe bed?' she asked.

'No bed is ever going to be safe with you in it but I'll

risk it,' he said, drawing her up his body so that he could kiss her. 'And this time I'm going to lie back and let you do all the work.'

Not work... All pleasure.

Tash woke to the early-morning sun, her body all delicious aches, and the night came flooding back. How she had made him the centre of their lovemaking, focusing on him so intently that she could read his response to every touch, giving herself in a way that she had never imagined and discovering a whole new level of pleasure in doing so.

She turned to reach for him but she was alone but for a sheet a paper on the pillow beside her. He'd drawn her as she'd slept—her breasts exposed, the curve of her buttock visible above the sheet tangled around her thighs, her hand extended towards him as if calling him back to bed.

Anyone looking at it would know that she had spent the night making love to the artist. If it had been anyone else, she'd have said that it was beautiful, but looking at herself, so vulnerable, so exposed, was disturbing. And why had he left it? Did he leave a picture for all his lovers? Something for the scrapbook? Something to scandalise the grandchildren?

Coffee. She needed coffee. Peeling herself off the bed, she tucked the drawing away in a drawer, pulled on a wrap and went through to the kitchen.

There was a note propped up against the kettle.

Sorry to kiss and run, but the horse is booked in at the foundry next week. Keep the Land Rover and the house keys for as long as you need them. D.

Next week? The horse had looked a long way from finished when she'd seen it and yet he'd taken a precious day to drive her to Hadley Chase. Of course this was a Darius

Hadley sculpture. What she thought was finished and what he considered finished...

She reached for her phone to text him...what? Thanks for the keys? For his time? For everything? There had been a lot of 'everything' to thank him for.

Keep it simple, she reminded herself, keying in the words:

Thanks for yesterday. N.

That covered it. Then she realised that she'd used N instead of T, which made it a lot more complicated. He was not a keeper and she was Tash, not Natasha. This was no more than a bit of a fling while she sorted herself out, she reminded herself.

So why did it feel like so much more?

Because she was all over the place. Because her life had been turned upside down. Because he was so much more...

She hit send before her brain fried tying itself in knots avoiding the truth.

Tash spent the next few days building up a media presence for Hadley Chase. She scanned some of the watercolours and used one that Darius had painted of the house as the header for the Facebook page, the ready-made web page she'd invested in and the Twitter account. It was very similar to the photograph she'd taken. No wonder he'd said she had a good eye.

Once it was all in place, she scheduled one-hundred-and-forty-character 'bites' from the history on the Twitter feed, adding his grandmother's exquisite illustrations, and then she did the same thing with the rest of his paintings. She linked it to the Facebook page and to the webpage where she'd laid out the house details.

She recorded a voice-over for the 'Sleeping Beauty'

video that she'd made inside the house and posted that on YouTube, linking each room to something from the history.

By the following week, she was gathering quite a following, getting lots of shares and re-Tweets, but most of the people who commented were less interested in the house than the artist and the history.

Who had painted the watercolours? Where could they buy them? Were prints available? Was the house open to the public? Where could they buy the book?

So far, no one had connected the paintings with Darius Hadley—hardly surprising considering the sculptures that had made his name. She considered sending a link to the Facebook page to Freddie Glover. She knew he'd get it, and no doubt wet himself in his rush to get his hands on the pictures. But Darius had dismissed the pictures as chocolate-box stuff and, besides, she'd given him her word.

There was no word from Darius—well, he was busy—but whenever the doorbell rang she rushed to see who it was.

'Tash?'

'Hi, Mum,' she said, buzzing her up, quashing her disappointment as she reached for the kettle. 'This is a surprise. I thought you'd be busy cooking and packing for the holiday.'

'Cooking,' she said, taking a casserole dish from a basket and popping it into the fridge. 'I ran out of room in the freezer.'

As you do…

'And you came all the way to London to give it to me?' she teased.

'Not just that. I thought, since you aren't working, we could spend the day together. We could go shopping… maybe have afternoon tea at Claibournes? Dad offered to treat us.'

Oh, right. This wasn't just food, it was the entire take-your-mind-off-it scenario.

'Actually, Mum, I'm a bit busy.'

'You're working? Has Miles Morgan—?'

'No. I'm handling a private sale for a client,' she said quickly, ignoring the fact that the definition of a client was someone who paid for your services. After all, a first casting Darius Hadley bronze would be worth a bob or two. Assuming he was still interested. 'So, what are you shopping for? You've left it a bit late for holiday stuff.' And her mother never left anything until the last minute. Obviously, she'd decided on a little face-to-face persuasion to join them.

'The holiday is off.'

'Off?'

Her mother sighed, laid out a couple of cups and saucers, heated the teapot. 'We had a call last night. Apparently the water tank overflowed, a ceiling came down and the cottage is uninhabitable for the foreseeable future. The kids are devastated.'

'Oh…I'm sorry.'

She cracked a wry smile. 'Really?'

'Absolutely. I know how much you enjoy it.' It might not be her idea of a good time, but Cornwall was a spring half-term tradition that went way back, rain or shine, and as a child she'd loved it. When she had children of her own she would love it again. 'Can't you find somewhere else?'

'For nine adults and seven children at half-term? And it's the bank holiday.'

'Eight adults,' Tash reminded her, getting down the cake tin. 'Lemon drizzle?' she offered, putting it on a plate. 'What will you do?'

'Organise some day trips, I suppose. We'll manage.' She took a piece of cake, rolled her eyes in appreciation. 'You could open a cake shop,' she said. 'Or maybe an Internet home delivery service? Lots of demand for good home-made cake.'

'I could, but I won't.'

'Just a thought. Tell me about this private sale.'

'Actually, it's Hadley Chase.'

Her mother frowned. 'Isn't that the house—?'

'Yes. I've promised the owner that I'll find him a buyer.'

'And he agreed?'

'Why wouldn't he? I have a terrific track record.'

'With an agency behind you,' she said. 'Glossy brochures, ads in the *Country Chronicle*…' She stopped, realising that wasn't the most tactful thing to say. 'Advertising costs the earth.'

'Not necessarily.'

She showed her mother the Facebook page and got an unimpressed *humph*. 'People who buy stately homes aren't going to see this,' she said.

'It's all about getting a buzz going. Getting noticed by the media.' Getting them to follow you was the hardest part. They apparently took the view that they were there to be followed.

Her mother took another look. 'Well, you do seem to have a lot of comments.'

'Most of them asking who painted the picture of the house.' The one thing she couldn't tell anyone. 'Or if the history has been published and where can they buy it.' Maybe she should be following publishers. Art dealers.

'It is a lovely picture. Who did paint it?'

Yes, well, there was the rub.

'I found it in the house. It wasn't signed.'

'Well, someone who lived there was very talented.' She took another forkful of cake, then said, 'What you need is a plan.'

'This is the plan,' she admitted. 'Well, one of them. I've made a sort of *Sleeping Beauty* story. Pictures of the stairs covered in leaves, furniture shrouded in dust sheets, cobwebby attics, glimpses of the view through dusty windows, matching the room with sound bites from the history, and put it on YouTube.' She played it through.

'It's very…atmospheric.'

'Thanks. That's exactly what I was going for,' she said.

Her mother sighed. 'This is all very arty and interesting but what would you have done if Miles Morgan hadn't…' She made a vague gesture, clearly not wanting to say the words. 'To recover the situation?'

'Well, I would have suggested…' She stopped. Keep it simple… Okay, she couldn't afford to hire a firm of contract cleaners but maybe, just maybe… 'Mum, can I offer you a proposition?'

'You can offer me another piece of that cake,' she said, pouring out the tea, adding a splash of milk. 'What kind of proposition?'

'Well, you can see for yourself that Hadley Chase is a beautiful country house set in amazing grounds. It has a chalk stream with trout fishing for Dad and the boys, rods included,' she added. She'd seen them hung on racks in one of the storerooms. 'There are views to die for, and Hadley is a classic English village with thatched cottages, a centuries-old pub and a village green. I know it's not Cornwall,' she said quickly, 'but it will be free.'

'Well, that sounds delightful and incredibly generous of you, considering it's not your house,' her mother replied, suspicious rather than enthusiastic, 'but you seem to have glossed over the delightfully atmospheric cobwebs. And didn't it say in the paper that the staircase was about to fall down?'

'There is nothing wrong with the staircase that a vacuum, a duster and a little elbow grease won't fix.' She waited for the penny to drop. It didn't take long.

'So when you say "free", what you actually mean is that we'll be spending our holiday dealing with the dust and the leaves and whatever else is lingering in the corners. In other words, giving the place a thorough scrub?'

'Not all of it,' she protested. 'Just the main rooms.'

'And the bedrooms, unless we're going to camp on the lawn. And the bathrooms. And the kitchen.'

'I'll do the kitchen before you get there. Really, it's not that bad.'

Her mother sipped her tea.

'Seven days, eight adults,' she prompted. 'All I'm asking is an hour a day from each of you and in return you get to stay in an ancient and historic manor house. I promise,' she continued before her mother could raise any other objections, 'that no one at the WI will have holiday pictures to beat yours. Not some pokey little cottage, not even an apartment in a stately home, but the whole place, four-poster beds and a ballroom included, to yourselves.'

'I don't know, Tash—'

'You should read Emma Hadley's history. I've scanned it and printed it so you can take a copy with you. The illustrations are beautiful,' she said. 'You could give a talk. I'll make a PowerPoint presentation for you.' A tiny giveaway muscle in the corner of her mother's mouth twitched and, confident that she was hooked, Tash sat back. 'Of course, if it's too much for you, I could give Harry a call. If he and Lily have got nowhere booked for half-term I'm sure he would love to help...'

'You will be staying with us?' her mother asked, matching her guilt play and trumping it. 'Not just cleaning up the kitchen and then running away back to London?'

That was the thing with mothers. They could see through you, right down to the bone. A bit like a sculptor she knew...

'Oh, I'll have to be there,' she said. 'I'll be holding an open day on the last Saturday. With afternoon tea. Is there any chance of a few of your scones?'

'Is there any chance that you will be coming to Cornwall next year?'

She was a mere amateur compared to her mother.

'You can count on it. I've decided to take up surfing.'

Her mother, ignoring that, stood up. 'I suppose I'd better go home and get everyone organised. We'll bring our own bedding. And towels,' she added. 'Mice will almost certainly have made nests in the linen cupboards.'

Oh, joy…

'I'll ask one of the boys to pick you up on Saturday morning.'

'No need. Darius…Mr Hadley has loaned me his Land Rover.'

'*Darius* Hadley?' Her mother frowned. 'That name rings a bell. Would I have seen him in *Celebrity*?'

'I couldn't say,' she said truthfully.

Tash still had the keys and she had Darius's permission to do whatever it took to sell the house. No need to disturb him when he was so busy. Except, of course, someone would have to inform the security people that he would be having house guests.

And an open day on the Saturday.

What should she do? Text, phone and leave a message or go and see him? Her mother would not be amused if the police arrived mob-handed to evict them. She had to be sure he'd got the message and if he was working flat-out he might not check his phone.

She would just have to go and see him.

It was quicker to take the Underground than drive across London or take the bus and, since there was a truck completely blocking his street, she'd clearly made the right decision.

There was quite a crowd watching the drama and she spotted Patsy among them. 'What's going on?'

'They're loading up the horse. Darius!' she called. 'You've got company.'

He appeared from behind the truck, sweaty, dusty. There was clay in his hair and smeared across his cheek where he'd wiped away sweat with the back of his hand and a week's worth of beard only added to the piratical look.

'Hang on,' he said, 'I just need to see this on its way.'

'Take your time.'

His face split in a wide grin. 'I always do.'

Oh, yes...

She caught Patsy's eye and hoped she hadn't said that out loud. Judging by the eye-roll, she didn't need to. 'Have you sold the house yet?' she asked.

'No, but I'm working on it.'

'If there's anything I can do—' she produced a business card '—give me a call.'

'I can't afford help,' she said. 'That's why I'm here. I've offered my family a week in the country in return for their help cleaning the place up.'

'Well, now, I can't afford to take my boy away this half-term. If you need more hands, I'll work for board and country air.'

'Well, thanks. The more the merrier.'

'Clear it with Darius and give me a ring,' she said, glancing at her watch. 'See you later.'

Tash pressed herself against the wall as the truck started up and Darius joined her as it slowly pulled away, the crated horse lashed down in the back. They watched it pull out into the main road and disappear, then he looked down at her.

'You look like ice cream. I'd kiss you,' he said, 'but I stink.'

'It's a good stink.' Earthy clay, freshly sawn pine mingled with the sharp scent of honest sweat and, lifting a hand to his face, she rubbed her palm against his beard. 'And I want to try this.'

He lifted her hand, touched it to his lips. 'That's all I've got,' he said, tucking her arm around his waist and, with his arm around her shoulder, headed up the street. 'I haven't been to bed since I got out of yours.'

She stopped. 'You took time out to take me to Hadley Chase when you were that pushed?'

'Don't...' He touched the space between her brows. 'Don't frown. I was already struggling. The house, a whole lot of mess being dragged up from the past... You fired me up.' He unlocked the door to a small mews cottage at the end of the street. 'How do you feel about being my muse?'

His muse? For just a moment the image of herself as his inspiration sparkled in her imagination. She forced herself back to earth. 'It sounds a bit Pre-Raphaelite to me. I'm getting images of scantily dressed women lounging around a cold and draughty studio while louche men discuss their vision. I think I'll pass.'

'I didn't say becoming my muse, I said being her.'

'I don't get a choice?'

'Neither of us do, apparently.'

'Oh... Well, I'm glad to have helped,' she said, leaning against him briefly. 'Have you eaten?'

'Patsy kept me fuelled up. Have you been trying to get hold of me?' he asked, taking a phone out of his back pocket. 'The battery on this is flatter than a pancake.'

'I did leave a message, but I thought if you were working you wouldn't pick it up.'

'It's that important?'

'I haven't sold the house,' she said quickly, 'but it was too important to leave to chance.'

'Scrub my back and you'll have my full attention,' he assured her, kicking off his boots in the tiny lobby, peeling off his T-shirt and letting it lie where it fell.

On the outside, the cottage fitted with the rest of the

street. Inside, it was bare polished wood floors, white walls, spare steel lamp fittings and old rubbed leather chairs.

He slipped the buckle of his belt, let his jeans fall, stepped out of them and, naked, walked up the open staircase that led to a sleeping loft, not stopping until he reached a granite and steel wet room.

'If you're going to scrub my back you'd better lose the clothes or they'll get soaked,' he warned as he flipped the tap. His eyes gleamed wickedly. 'Or you could leave them on. Either way works for me.'

'Behave yourself.' She hadn't come dressed down. She'd wanted to make an impact, wanted him to notice her and even before she reached for the hem of the clinging crossover top she was wearing she could see that she had. 'I have to go home on the Tube.'

She unhooked the swirl of printed chiffon that stopped six inches above her knee, kicked it away and stepped out of her shoes.

'Stop right there,' he said when she was down to the champagne lace bra and panties that she'd bought with birthday money and even in the sale had cost twice anything else she wore next to her skin. 'I really want to see those wet.'

'When you can do more than kiss my hand,' she said, but took her time over removing them since he appeared to like them so much. 'Turn round.'

His eyes were focused on her breasts. 'Do I have to?'

Oh, boy. That was a tough one. His thick dark curls, the streaks of clay on his cheeks, his chest, water sluicing over his skin gave him the elemental look of some tribal chieftain who'd battled the elements and won through.

Every primitive instinct was urging her to take a step forward, press her body against his and go for it but the dark hollows in his temples, beneath his eyes warned her that it was the last thing he needed.

She picked a gel off the shelf, made a circular gesture with her finger and after a moment he turned, placed his hands flat against the granite, bracing himself, or more likely propping himself up.

His finely muscled back, narrow waist, taut buttocks were, if anything, even more distracting.

Get a grip, Tash. You can do this…

She applied the gel to his hair, stretching up on her toes to ease out the dried-in clay with her fingers, leaning into him to massage his scalp—her body, breasts sliding against him as the soap cascaded down his back.

He groaned as she repeated the process. 'Dear God, woman, what are you doing?'

'Torturing myself,' she said as she applied gel to a sponge and began working it into his shoulders.

'That makes two of us. If you have something important to tell me you'd better get on with it, while I can still think.'

'I've organised a cleaning party for the house. We'll be staying there from Saturday for the entire week.'

'Staying?' He half turned to look at her.

'Relax. It's just my family.' She worked the soap down his back, into the hollow above those gorgeous tight buttocks.

'No…' he began, then caught his breath as she used her hands to work the soap between his thighs.

'The Cornwall holiday fell through so I offered them a week in the country in return for a little light housework.'

'I can't ask your family to clean my house,' he said.

'You didn't—I did,' she said, getting down on her knees and working the foam behind his knees, over his totally gorgeous calves. 'Patsy's volunteered, too.'

'Patsy?'

'I saw her in the street. She said I should run that by you.'

'The whole damn street will know every detail within an hour of her coming home.'

'It's just an old house,' she reminded him. 'A lot of dull portraits, a couple of four-poster beds and a kitchen out of the Ark. I just need you to tell Ramsey and the security people that we'll be there,' she said. 'Now you can turn around.'

He turned and for a moment the breath stopped in her throat. He might not have been to bed in a week, but one part was still wide awake and ready for action.

Everything slowed down as she dropped the sponge and used her fingers between his toes, his ankles, the tender spot behind his knees, the smooth skin inside his thighs. Then she stood up and soaped his chest, his stomach.

At one point he reached for her but she tutted. 'No touching...'

His legs were trembling by the time she reached the parts that did not know when to lie down and quit.

'Sweet heaven,' he said, leaning back, clutching at a rack holding a pile of towels, his eyes closed as she took him in her palm, stroking him until, with a shuddering sigh, he spilled into her hand. And then she flipped off the water, put her arms around his neck and kissed him very gently. 'Now, go to bed.'

Darius, dazed, barely able to speak, reached up and pulled a towel down from the rack, wrapped it around her and pulled her warm, wet body against him. 'Stay with me,' he begged.

'Is that what a muse would do?' she asked, looking at him, her eyes dark, intense, searching. A smallest of frowns defeating her smile. 'Be there so that when you wake up you can draw her sated, replete, every desire satisfied?'

'I left a note,' he said. 'I left the picture...'

'Why?'

'You were sleeping. Taking it would have been as if I was stealing something intimate from you.'

'Oh.' She leaned her forehead against his chest so that

he shouldn't see her eyes. See what she had been thinking. 'If you want it, Darius, take it. It's yours.'

He took a step back, lifted her chin, reading her as easily as most people read headlines. 'You thought it was a kiss off?' he asked. 'A Darius Hadley sketch in return for some hot sex?'

'No! Maybe.' Her shoulders dropped. 'I don't know you, Darius.'

'No, you don't,' he said, pulling another towel from the rack, wrapped it around his waist. 'If I ever did anything that skanky I would sign and date it so that it would be worth something. A realisable asset.'

'Darius…'

He didn't wait for her mumbled apology. She hadn't trusted him and that was a deal-breaker. He picked up the receiver of the landline beside the bed, punched in a fast-dial number.

'Ramsey? Darius Hadley.' He didn't bother with the courtesies. 'My agent has organised a clean-up of the house. Please inform the security people that they will be resident on site from…' He looked across at Natasha, hovering in the doorway of the wet room, a towel clutched to her breast.

'Today,' she said on a gasp. 'I'm going down there today to turn on the water, clean up the—'

'From today,' he said, despite everything, unable to take his eyes off her as Ramsey droned on about the inadvisability of letting a group of strangers into the house. The damp strands of hair clinging to pink cheeks, creamy shoulders and it was all he could do to stop himself from going to her. Begging forgiveness…

This was the madness. The same madness that had seized his father. Wanting a woman beyond sense, beyond reason.

'Your objections are noted but, to tell you the truth, Ramsey,' he said, cutting him off, 'I don't actually care what you think. The only reason I don't just sign the whole lot over to the Treasury is because someone has to protect the tenants and I know that won't be you.' He cut off Ramsey's protest. 'Is there anything else?' he asked, returning the receiver to the cradle, but leaving his hand on it, anchoring him to the spot.

Tash swallowed. His face was shuttered and the apology bubbling up in her throat died unspoken.

Shouting at him when he'd behaved like a jerk had been a momentary bump in the road, no more than a shake-up. Doubting his honour was, apparently, a damned great rock. She'd crossed some invisible line and the damage was terminal.

'There's just one more thing,' she said, clutching the towel to her breast. Being naked had, in an eye blink, gone from the most natural, most perfect thing in the world to the most awkward.

This definitely came under the 'never mix business with pleasure' rule but, despite the lack of encouragement to continue, there was still business to be done.

'Unlike Morgan and Black, I can't afford to put on a three-course lunch at the Hadley Arms, so I'm holding an open day on Saturday week,' she said. 'I'll be serving afternoon tea. On the lawn if the weather holds, in the ballroom if it doesn't.' There was still no response. Not even a sarcastic comment about cake. He just kept his hand on the phone as if waiting for her to go so that he could make another call. 'While I have no doubt that potential buyers and the property press would like to meet you, it's not essential.' Not one word. 'That's all.'

She gathered her clothes, made it downstairs on rubber legs, pulling them on over still damp skin as she headed for the door, banging it hard shut behind her. So that he'd know she'd gone. So that she couldn't go back.

Damn, damn, damn… How could she have got it so wrong? How could she have got herself so involved?

Involved was for the future, when she was established, with a man who was ready to settle down, raise a family. It wasn't for now and it certainly wasn't with a man who had heartbreak stamped all over him. She'd known from the first moment she'd set eyes on him that he wasn't a man made for happy ever after. This was supposed to be a fling. Hot, fast, furious and, like the bronze of an anonymous nude figure, something to rub your fingers over in passing when you were old and remember with a smile.

Okay. The bronze wasn't going to happen. Her career, on the other hand, still needed to be rescued. That deal was still on. It was back to strictly business.

Which was what she'd wanted in the first place. Until she didn't.

'Natasha?' She'd reached the corner of the street without being aware how she'd got there and practically bumped into Patsy as she came out of the corner shop carrying a bundle of files. 'Are you okay?'

'Oh, um, yes… Just in a hurry,' she said, suddenly aware of damp strands of hair clinging to her cheek and neck, that her top, pulled on over damp skin, was twisted, telegraphing what had just happened as loudly as if she'd posted his drawing on Facebook. 'There's so much to do. I, um, told Darius you had volunteered to join the clean-up party.'

'Let me guess. He said no.'

'No.' He hadn't. He'd muttered about gossip but he hadn't actually said no. Why would he? She'd been posting pictures of Hadley Chase all over the Net and there was nothing Patsy could tell the neighbours that they couldn't see for themselves. 'I'll be glad to have you if you're still up for it.'

'I'll be there, rubber gloves and dusters at the ready.'

'It won't all be work,' she assured her. 'Does your boy like fishing?'

She grinned. 'I guess we'll find out.'

Tash opened her bag and took out one of the new business cards she'd ordered off the Net—*Natasha Gordon, Property Consultant*—and offered it to Patsy. 'Email me if you have any special food requirements. And everyone is bringing their own bedding. Is that okay?'

'None and no problem. I'll come tomorrow afternoon straight after school if you like? Help you get the bedrooms ready.'

'You are such a star!'

'We'll be there at about six.'

'Great.' She was halfway around the corner when Patsy called, 'Natasha…' She half turned. 'Your skirt is caught up in your knickers.'

CHAPTER NINE

THE FIRST THING Tash did when she arrived at Hadley Chase was hunt down the stopcock in the scullery and turn the water on. It was, of course, stuck fast, so her next task was to brave the cobwebs and spiders in the toolshed to find a wrench so that she could shift it.

Someone had left all the taps open, which was obviously the right thing to do, but meant that once the tank had filled and the water was flowing she had to tour the house, turning them all off, mopping up leaks and making a note of where they were so that they could be fixed. A job for her dad, and she fired off a text to him, asking him to bring some plumber's mait.

She paused on the first floor landing, aware that something had changed but for a moment unable to think what it was. Then she realised that it was the window.

Despite working day and night to finish his sculpture, Darius had remembered his promise to get it fixed and for a moment she leaned her forehead against the cool surface of the glass. She had wanted him to trust her with the darkness that lay at his heart but she'd been so quick to leap to the conclusion that he was about as deep as an August puddle. And if he was, wasn't that what she'd expected? Gone into with her eyes wide open? Except he'd been angry, because… Well, because didn't matter.

Without trust there was nothing. And that was what she had. Nothing.

With a throat full of dust and desperate for a cup of tea, she plugged in the electric kettle. It blew a fuse. She mended it with the wire and screwdriver she'd brought with her. Next job, lighting the ancient solid fuel range cooker...

By the time she'd got it going, she was coated in smoke and black dust and more cobwebs from the fuel store, her knuckles were sore and she was seriously considering her mother's suggestion of an alternative career in the confectionery business.

Unfortunately, having spent the previous night emailing individual invitations to the open house and afternoon tea—spiced with the painting of the house and extracts from the history as attachments—to everyone she could think of, partners and children included since it was the weekend, any career change would have to be put on hold until she'd shifted two years' worth of dust.

The first job was the fridge. She washed it down, then switched it on. Another fuse blew, tripping all the electrics for the second time.

This time she went through them all, changing the wire in three that looked a bit dodgy. That done, she toured the house again, checking every light switch. The last thing she needed was to have them go pop when it was dark.

It was dark by the time she'd wiped down the last surface in the scullery. She picked up the bowl of water to tip down the sink and then screamed as she caught sight of a face in the window, slopping water down her filthy jeans and over her shoes in the process. Belatedly realising that it was her own face, smudged with coal dust, she laughed a little shakily. Then a second face appeared beside it.

This time the scream wouldn't come.

She opened her mouth, but her throat was stuffed with rocks and no sound emerged, even when the back door opened and a black-clad figure put his head around the door.

'Sorry, miss, I didn't mean to startle you.'

It was the security guard who'd tried to move them on.

'Mr Hadley called the office to tell us you'd be here and asked if I would look in on you and check that you were all right. He thought you'd be easier if it was someone you knew by sight.'

Since the rocks were taking their time to budge, she tipped the remaining water down the sink.

He shrugged awkwardly. 'I'm sorry about the other day.'

'No problem… Just doing your job… I'm fine,' she said, sounding unconvincing even to herself. 'Would you like a cup of tea?' she offered, peeling off her rubber gloves and squelching her way into the now gleaming kitchen.

'I can do better than that,' he said, placing a carrier on the table from which emerged the mouth-watering scent of hot fried food and the sharpness of vinegar.

Until that moment she hadn't thought of food but, suddenly assailed by sharp pangs of hunger, she said, 'Please tell me that's fish and chips.'

He grinned. 'Mr Hadley thought you might be glad of something hot to eat.'

Darius… Her heart, just about back to normal, missed a beat. She'd said she didn't know him, but it seemed that he knew her.

'There appear to be two lots,' she said, peering into the carrier.

'Well, I haven't had my supper yet. I was going to have it in the van, but why don't I put the kettle on while you dry off?'

It was barely light when Darius woke, fully aroused—he'd been dreaming about Natasha. One moment she'd been a vision in something floaty, looking and smelling like a summer garden, the next she'd been pressed up against him, naked, soapy wet, her fingers kneading his scalp, her breasts against his back. And when he'd turned round and she'd taken him in her hand...

He closed his eyes, wanting that moment back. Wanting her to be there with him. He'd asked her to stay, but then...

Then he'd done what he always did with any woman who got too close, who he wanted too much; he'd used the first excuse that offered itself to make it impossible for her to stay.

She was so easy to read. Every thought, every idea was right there in her lovely face and she knew it. The fact that she'd buried her face in his chest was enough to warn him that she was hiding something and damn it, of course he was mad that she could think such a thing of him. But why wouldn't she?

She'd just been betrayed in the worst possible way. Her confidence had to be shaky. And he'd made all kinds of excuses not to wake her because she could read him, too. Would have seen what he could not hide. That it had been a panic run.

What he'd felt, what he'd drawn, had terrified him. He'd had to leave her a note so that she knew about the Land Rover and keys, but it had been bare of emotion. He'd left mixed messages and she'd interpreted them just as he'd hoped she would. Until he'd walked around that truck and his heart had practically leapt out of his chest with joy.

He knew what he felt was senseless. And he'd acted senselessly.

He took a cup of coffee out into the tiny yard he shared with a couple of randy pigeons and a pot of dead daffodils, watching the sun turn the sky from a pale grey to blue, stirring only when there was a long peal on the doorbell.

It was Patsy with a large cardboard envelope. It was addressed to him c/o Patsy and when he turned it over, saw it was from Natasha, he didn't have to open it to know what it was.

'*I don't know you...*'

Of course she didn't. He'd never let anyone close enough to know him. He didn't know himself.

'Why did she send it to you?' he asked. 'How did she know your address?'

'I don't keep it a secret,' she said, looking pointedly at his door. The cottage, like the studio, bore no number. 'She's a nice woman, Darius.'

'No...' There were a dozen words rushing into his head to describe Natasha, but 'nice' wasn't one of them. Vivid, fun, kind, thoughtful, vulnerable, hot, glorious, spicy sweet... He realised that Patsy was looking at him a little oddly. 'Sorry, yes, of course you're right.'

'I'm going to Hadley Chase as soon as school is out this afternoon. When will you be coming down?'

'I have to go to the foundry today,' he said. 'Take the horse apart so that they can start making the moulds.' Dozens of intricate parts, every one of which had to be checked for imperfections through each stage of the process.

'And tomorrow?' she asked.

'It's going to take weeks,' he said, but she knew that. That wasn't what she was asking.

She didn't press it. 'Any message?'

He shook his head. 'No, wait.' He took a card out of his wallet and handed it to her. 'Pay for the food. And whatever's needed for the open house party. Tell them to help themselves to whatever wine is left in the cellar.'

'Is that it?'

'Michael will find it very different,' he said, reluctant to let her go, disapproval in every line. She knew how he was. That he never got involved.

'That's the point of a holiday,' she said and—for the first time since he'd known her—she refused the opportunity to talk at length about her son, about anything and left him standing on his doorstep.

He closed the door, opened the envelope, took out the drawing and traced every line of Natasha's spicy sweet sleeping body with his finger.

Sated, replete, every desire satisfied...

'Not just you, Sugarlips,' he murmured. 'Not just you.'

Natasha opened her eyes and lay quite still, not sure for a moment where she was. Then, as everything came into focus and she saw the distant hills through a tall window, she remembered. She was at Hadley Chase, lying in the bed that Darius Hadley had slept in as a boy.

She'd crawled into it some time after midnight, every limb aching, too exhausted to bother with the curtains—nothing but a passing owl would see her—and curled into his pillow, wishing he was there with her.

No chance.

For a while she'd been warmed by the fact that he'd asked the security people to check on her, bring her something hot to eat—he must have known that the old range cooker wouldn't deliver on day one—and she had sent a text, thanking him. Nothing fancy.

Thanks for supper. Most welcome. T

No more, no less than any well brought-up woman would do.

There was no response. Of course not. You didn't expect a reply to a bread-and-butter thank-you note. The food, she reminded herself, had been no more than a courtesy. She might have mortally offended his sense of honour, but she had organised a freebie clean-up of his house: *noblesse oblige* and all that.

She reached for her phone, kidding herself she was

checking the time—hoping that he might have unbent sufficiently to ask if she was okay in the empty silence of the night.

Nothing. No texts. No missed calls.

She sighed, rolled out of bed, winced a little as she stood up. Her knees creaked and her shoulder hurt from all the stretching and bending and scrubbing, but at least there was hot water for a shower.

She stoked up the oven, took a cup of tea out into the garden and sat on a bench beneath a climbing rose massed with creamy buds. A small muntjac doe with a tiny fawn wandered across the lawn within feet of her. She took a photograph with her phone and Tweeted it—there was nothing like cute animals to get a response—not forgetting to add the website URL.

Her mother and sisters-in-law would arrive with a ton of food, she knew, but ten adults and eight children were going to take a lot of feeding so she headed to the village to make the day of the butcher and the couple who ran the village store and farm shop. Orders placed, she treated herself to coffee and a muffin at the pub while she took advantage of their free Wi-Fi to check her Facebook and Twitter pages.

There were a couple of messages on Facebook asking her to get in touch, one from a publisher, the other from the features editor of a magazine, both asking her to ring them.

They were both interested in Emma Hadley's history of Hadley Chase so she invited them to the open house on Saturday. Maybe she should invite Freddie, the art dealer, too. If she could sell the book, the paintings and the house in one day she would become a legend.

Meanwhile, acceptances to the open house were coming in; even the regional television news magazine were hoping to send a team. No response yet from the *Country Chronicle* despite personal notes to both the editor and the advertising manager who, in her opinion, owed Darius a two-page feature at the very least.

She checked a missed call from her mother, a response to the text to her Dad. She'd left a voicemail expressing disbelief that her daughter had spent the night alone in a house that was miles from anywhere. If she'd known, if she'd *told* her, she stressed, she would have come on ahead of her father.

Normally the suggestion that she couldn't cope would have infuriated her. Instead, she found herself in total agreement. Last night, she would have totally welcomed her mother's company. She was smiling at that thought when she realised that someone was standing on the far side of the table.

Expecting it to be the girl wanting to clear her coffee, she said, 'I'm done.' Then, when she didn't begin to clear she looked up and her heart stopped.

'Darius...' Her vocal cords seemed to be in some disarray, too. 'I...um... How did you get here?'

'I took a train to Swindon,' he said, 'and then caught the bus. Piece of cake.'

He should have smiled then, but he didn't.

'You've still got Gary's car,' she said as her brain, buffering the emotion dump, the rush of sensations, images of him racing through her memory like a speeded-up film, finally caught up.

'It needed servicing.'

'Don't tell me,' she said, 'you're not just Darius Hadley, sculptor. You moonlight as Mike, the man who repairs cars while you wait.'

Smile now. Smile, pull out a chair, sit down, tell me why you're here. Please...

'I spotted the Land Rover as I drove through the village.' No smile. Still standing.

'I've been organising supplies for the week and stopped

to use the Wi-Fi.' She gestured vaguely at the open laptop. 'If you're stopping, will you sit down? I'm getting a crick in my neck.'

He pulled out the chair opposite and one of his knees brushed against hers as he sat down but he moved it before she could catch her breath and shift hers.

'Would you like some coffee?' she asked.

He shook his head.

Could this be any more awkward?

'I've…um…got a publisher interested in your grandmother's history,' she said, her legs trembling with the strain as she tucked her feet back as far as they would go so that she didn't accidentally touch him.

'Then my troubles are over.'

Sarcasm she could do without. This she could do without.

'Why are you here, Darius?'

'Why did you send the drawing back?'

Oh, shoot. That was so complicated, so mixed up, such an emotional reaction…

'Why didn't you just tear it up?' he insisted, looking straight into her eyes. 'Throw it in the trash with the teabags and potato peelings.'

She blew out her cheeks, tucked a strand of hair behind her ear. 'It was a beautiful drawing, Darius. There was no way I could have destroyed it.'

The truth, plain and simple.

'You could have taken it to your friendly art dealer,' he said.

'Unsigned?'

'With a letter from you as provenance, he would have snatched your hand off.'

'No!' Her protest was instinctive. She could never share such an intimate moment with Freddie, or any other art dealer.

'You could have simply kept it,' he persisted.

'Something to shock the grandchildren?'

It was the second time she'd offered him a chance to smile at the memory of an earlier, happier moment. For the second time he did not take it, but simply waited, demanding total honesty, the exposure of feelings she'd been unwilling to even think because once you'd thought them...

'You left me something of yourself, Darius. A memory to treasure.' Explaining this was like tearing away layers of flesh. Total exposure of the inner depths he talked about. But infinitely safer than thoughts that even now were rushing in. 'I lost the right to anything so precious when I destroyed that with my lack of trust.'

'Trust is a two-way thing, Natasha.'

'You took me on trust, no questions asked.'

'That was business. This...'

She'd asked herself what it had taken to build that impenetrable façade. What it would take to shatter it. Suddenly, in that hesitation, she had a glimpse into the darkness. Trust. It was all about trust.

'This?'

He shook his head. 'You shared your past with me, Natasha, offered me the chance to open up to you, but I didn't have your courage.'

'No...' She instinctively reached out a hand to him, grasped his fingers. 'It's hard. It wasn't the moment. I understood.'

'And I understand about the drawing. If it hadn't mattered, you'd have either kept it as a souvenir of a hot night, or you'd have been checking out the value with Freddie Glover.'

'If it hadn't mattered,' she replied, 'you wouldn't have been so angry.'

And for a moment they both just sat there, looking at each other, aware that they had just crossed some line.

Then he turned his hand beneath hers so that their fingers were interlocked.

'I've been walking away from people since I was seventeen years old,' he said. 'I keep trying to walk away from you.'

'Why?'

'Is there anything in the Land Rover that will spoil if it's left for an hour or two?' he asked, ignoring the question. She shook her head. He stood up, closed up her laptop and took it across to the bar. 'Will you look after this, Peter?'

He nodded. 'It's been a while, Darius.'

'Too long,' he said, heading for the door. 'We'll catch up later.'

'Darius…' she protested. 'My entire life depends on my laptop!'

'It'll be safer there than left in the car. I'll come back for them both later.'

'Yes, but…'

'I walked away from Hadley Chase. I have to walk back.' He'd reached the doorway, looked back, held out his hand to her. 'Will you walk with me?'

'Why me, Darius?' she asked, taking it.

'I don't know,' he said, and finally there was the hint of a smile. 'Only that no one else will do.'

He said nothing more until they were through the open gates of Hadley Chase and walking down the path that led to the river.

'The Clarendon family used to live over there,' he said, pausing at a gap between the trees and looking across the river to where a four-square Georgian house nestled beneath a rise in the Downs. 'The families were very close. My father and Christabel Clarendon were practically betrothed in their prams.'

His father… 'The house is the headquarters of an IT firm now,' she said. 'Steve told me.'

'Steve?'

'The security guy. They had a false alarm there last night.' She turned to look up at him. 'Betrothed?'

'They were both only children,' he said, moving on. 'There was land and money on both sides and it was the perfect match.'

'It takes a bit more than that.'

'Does it? Arranged marriages are the norm in other cultures and they'd known one another since they were children. There would be no surprises.'

'There are always surprises.'

'Yes...' They were climbing now through the woods and he stopped before an ancient beech tree that had once been coppiced and had four thick trunks twisting from its base. He looked up. 'It's still here. The tree house.'

He put a foot on a trunk that had been cut to form steps and, catching a low branch, pulled himself up to take a look, then disappeared inside.

'Is it safe?' she asked, following him. 'Wow... This is some tree house.'

'Gary built it for me,' he said.

'Gary?' The floor was solid planks of timber, the roof a thick thatch where swallows had once nested, the sides made from canvas that rolled up. There was a rug and a pile of cushions, faded, torn, chewed or pecked. 'Why?'

'His dad worked on the estate. Gamekeeper, gardener, whatever needed to be done. When Gary left school, he became his dad's assistant and did odd jobs around the estate. One of those odd jobs was to keep me amused during the school holidays. One summer he amused me by building this.'

'He did a great job.'

'It was more than a job. He was like an older brother,' he said. 'The kind that teaches you all the good stuff. The stuff that adults tell you is bad for you.'

'Drinking, lads' mags, smoking the occasional spliff? I've got brothers,' she reminded him when his eyebrows rose. 'You can't know how much I wished I was a boy.'

'Can I say, just for the record, that I'm glad you're not?'

'Oh, me too,' she assured him. 'Men wear such boring shoes.'

He looked down at the purple ballet pumps she was wearing. 'Pretty.'

For a moment she had a vision of him bending down, taking one off, kissing her instep... She cleared her throat. 'What did you do up here?'

'When I was younger I used it the way any kid would. Hideout, den, a place to keep secret stash. We used to sit up here watching badgers at dusk.'

'Brilliant.'

'It was... Of course, Gary never put that much effort into anything without an ulterior motive. When I was away at school, he brought girls here.' He shrugged. 'I did too, when I was older.'

'The young master seducing the village maidens?' she teased.

'Rather the opposite,' he said and his sudden grin sent a lump to her throat for a magical youth that had been somehow blighted. 'I'll check it out, clean it up for your nephews and nieces.'

'Does that mean you're staying?'

'I've put off the foundry until Monday but they can't start without me. Is there room?' he said, sliding his arms around her waist, drawing her close, and the down on her cheeks stood up as if she were a magnet and he was the North Pole.

'No problem. I'll share. Your room is pretty much as you left it, give or take a few things. I borrowed some of the chocolate-box pictures for the blog. I've had a lot of interest,' she rushed on, to cover just how important his answer was. 'There's a greeting card manufacturer...'

'That's the take,' he said, ignoring the throwaway distraction. 'What's the give?'

'Me,' she said. 'If there's still a vacancy for a muse?'

'So when you said share...?'

'I could bunk in with Patsy, but I barely know her, while we're—'

He groaned, pulling her into his arms, kissing her with a hot, sweet, haunting tenderness that could rip the heart out of you. It was the perfect kiss you saw in the movies, the kiss a girl dreamed about before life gave you a reality check, the kiss you'd remember when every other memory had slipped away into the dark. When he finally drew back, rested his forehead against the top of her head, he was trembling.

'Darius...' She cradled his face in her hands, wanting to reassure him, to tell him... 'You kept the beard,' she said shakily.

She felt him smile against her palms. 'You said you liked it.'

'As I was saying, we're compatible in practically every way.'

'I doubt your parents would be impressed with our, um, compatibility,' he said, climbing down the tree, lifting her after him. 'And then there are those three over-protective brothers of yours. I'm seriously outnumbered.'

'That's ridiculous, Darius. It's your house.'

'No. I'll get a room at the pub.' He took her hand and began to walk up the path towards the house. 'I thought we might go back to the beginning, slow things down a little. Maybe date?'

'Date?'

'An old-fashioned concept, involving the back seat of the movies, Sunday lunch in a country pub, dancing.'

'You dance?'

'I can learn.'

'Well, perfect, but what about the muse thing?'

'Getting naked? Inspirational sex?' He grinned. 'We can do that too.' They had reached the edge of the lawn and they both turned to look at the house. 'We appear to have company,' he said as they spotted the small red car at the same moment that the woman leaning against it spotted them.

'Brace up, Darius. It's my mother.'

CHAPTER TEN

'MUM!' TASH GAVE her a hug. 'How lovely! Can I introduce Darius Hadley, the owner of Hadley Chase?'

'Mr Hadley.' Her mother's eyebrows remained exactly where they were. It just felt as if they'd done an imitation of Tower Bridge.

'Darius,' he said, offering his hand with a smile Tash recognised from the pages of the *Country Chronicle*. Protective camouflage that he wore in public, but never with her. 'I can't tell you how grateful I am to you for pitching in and helping like this.'

'I'm helping my daughter,' she said. 'I thought you were on your own, Tash, or I wouldn't have been so concerned.'

'I was and, believe me, if you'd had any idea you would have been a lot more concerned. Three electrical blowouts, a gazillion spiders and the fright of my life when the security guard peered in through the window.'

'Well, really! How thoughtless.'

'No…thoughtful. Darius was concerned about me, too, so he called their office and asked if Steve could bring me some fish and chips. He was perfectly sweet. He made up the Aga, made sure I knew how to set the alarm and checked all the outbuildings before he left.'

'I'm really glad you're here, Mrs Gordon,' Darius said before she could comment. 'I didn't think I'd be able to get away, but I've put back the project I'm working on until Monday. I met Natasha in the village just now when I stopped to book a room at the pub.'

'He's just shown me the most amazing tree house, Mum,' she said, taking out the keys and unlocking the front door and, just like that, they were through it and in the hall; no drama about the big moment when he stepped back into the house. 'The kids are going to love it. I'll make some coffee. Why don't you show my mother the portrait of Emma Hadley, Darius?' she suggested, pushing him in a little deeper. He glanced at her, the only sign of tension a touch of white around his mouth. 'She's going to give a talk to the Women's Institute on the history of this place.'

'Of course. It's in the library, Mrs Gordon,' he said.

'Laura,' she said. 'I don't understand. Why are you staying in the village?'

'Well, obviously I'll be here, doing as much as I can, but this is your holiday. You won't want a stranger—'

'Nonsense! Of course you must stay here.'

Tash grinned. *Bazinga…*

'Mum, Mum, we've found a boathouse! There's a single scull!'

Patsy rolled her eyes. 'I told you not to go near the river without an adult, Michael.'

'Tom and Harry and James are down there, river dipping with the little kids.'

'Are you interested in rowing, Michael?' Darius, who was cutting the lawn, had stopped for a drink of the fresh lemonade Patsy had brought out.

'He's been desperate to try it ever since the Games,' she said.

'Well, let's go and take a look at it. I'll need a hand to get it down. Any volunteers?' He glanced around at the women stretched out on the grass, soaking up the sun, studiously avoiding looking at Natasha, who took the view that the one-hour rule didn't apply to her and was busy washing down the external doors and windowsills.

'Take Tash,' Patsy suggested. 'Please. She's making us feel guilty.'

'Natasha?' he prompted. 'Do you want to give these women a break?'

'They're on holiday, I'm not.' But she peeled off her rubber gloves and joined him.

'Did you sleep well?' he asked as they followed Michael down to the river.

'Not especially,' she admitted. 'You'd think in a house of this size we might manage a few minutes on our own. If the kids had been ordered to chaperone us, they couldn't have done a better job of it.'

'Your mother knew what she was doing when she insisted I stay,' he said. 'If it's any consolation, I'm not getting much sleep, either.'

'Memories?' she asked.

'More the fact that my childhood bed no longer smells of dog, but of you. Which is very disturbing, especially when I've spent the last twenty-four hours under the close-eyed scrutiny of your three very large brothers who, let me tell you, are nowhere as easy to charm as your mother.'

'Maybe you should stop being so charming to their wives,' she suggested, a little tetchily, he thought.

'You want me to be charming to you?'

'No! That is so not what I want and you know it.'

He knew but they'd reached the boathouse and Michael was dancing with impatience, waiting for the slowcoach adults to catch up.

'Anticipation only increases the gratification,' he said.

'That had better be a promise.'

'Cross my heart,' he said, drawing a cross over his chest, just as she had, and she groaned.

'Come on!'

'Okay, let's see.'

The buckles on the straps were rusted but they finally managed to free them and lower the scull into the water and then watch as it filled with water.

'I'm sorry, Mike; the hull is cracked.'

'Can it be fixed?' he asked once they hauled it out of the water and Darius had located the damage.

'Maybe, but it's a fibreglass hull and will have to go to a special workshop.' Seeing his disappointment, he said, 'You know, if you're really keen on trying this, Michael, I'll find you a club in London where you can get some proper training.'

The boy's mouth dropped open. 'Wicked!'

'You'd better go and ask your mother. Tell her that it's my contribution to the medal tally in 2020,' he called after him.

Natasha was grinning. 'He's a great kid.'

'Patsy worries about him. I think that's why she volunteered for your work party. She can't watch him twenty-four-seven and he's getting to the age for trouble.'

'Sport is a good alternative.' She looked at the scull. 'Was this yours?'

'It belonged to my father. He was a rowing blue. When I was a kid like Michael, I used to sit in that seat, put my feet and hands where his had been and try to feel him.'

'You never knew him?' she asked.

He shook his head. 'He was a lecturer at the School of Oriental and African Studies. He lived there during the week and came home to the estate cottage where he and Christabel had set up home for the weekends and during the holiday.'

'That doesn't sound like a great way to start a marriage.'

'It was her choice, apparently. She didn't like London.'

'What happened?'

'Not a what—a who. An Iranian student of such shimmering beauty that one look was all it took for my father to lose his head, his reason, his sanity.'

'Your mother.' And, when he glanced at her, 'The name is the giveaway.'

He nodded. 'My father abandoned Christabel and his unborn child without a backward glance and went to live in France with Soraya.'

Unable to bear the musty boathouse, the memory of that boy trying to reach out to a father he'd never known, he walked out into the clean air, kicked off his shoes and sat on the crumbling dock. These days his feet trailed in the water, soaked into the bottom of his jeans.

Natasha picked her way carefully over the boards and sat down beside him, her toes trailing in the water, waiting for him to continue or not as he wished.

'My grandfather cut him off without a penny, hoping it would bring him to his senses,' he said. 'But he was senseless.'

'And Christabel? What did she do?'

'She took it badly, lost the baby she was carrying. A boy who would have been the heir to all this.'

'Poor woman…'

'Her parents sold the house across the river and moved away. Gary told me that she'd killed herself.'

'No!'

'My grandfather denied it but I was never sure so I did a search a few years back.' He plucked a piece of rotten wood from the plank beside him, shredded it, dropping the pieces in the water. 'She lives in Spain with her husband, three children.'

'Did you get in touch with her?'

'I wanted to. I wanted to talk to someone who'd known my father so I went to the house, hoping to see her. They were just going out…' He shook his head. 'Rumour always has a grain of truth. She might have tried something desperate and she didn't need me descending like a black crow in the midst of her lovely family, raking up the past.'

Tash felt tears sting the back of her eyes and the lump in her throat was so big that she couldn't say anything. Instead, she squeezed his hand.

He glanced at her. 'Is that approval? I got something right?'

'Absolutely.' She slid her arm around his waist and he put his arm around her shoulders so that her head was resting against his shoulder. 'What happened to your parents?' Something bad must have happened or he wouldn't have been living with his grandparents.

'When I was a few months old, Soraya's mother became desperately ill and she had to go home. She left me with my father, which seems a little odd, but they weren't married and maybe she was afraid to tell her family that she was living with a married man. That they had a child.'

'I think I'd find that pretty difficult, to be honest.'

'It seems they already knew. Two days after she left, my father received a message from her father. He wanted to bring his family to Europe and, to get exit visas, they needed money to bribe officials. A lot of money. The bottom line was that if he wanted to see Soraya again he would have to pay.'

'But…that's appalling!'

'My father, beside himself, went to my grandfather, begged him for help and the old bastard gave it to him, but at a price.'

'You…' She'd known there was something, but could never have guessed anything so desperate. So cruel.

'He'd lost his heir. His son was unfit in his eyes. I wasn't the golden child of the perfect marriage, but I was all he had left.'

'You were the price he had to pay to rescue your mother.'

'Ramsey drew up a legally binding document surrendering all parental rights to them. I was to live with my grandparents, they would have full control of my education and upbringing and I would be my grandfather's heir on the condition that my parents understood that they would be dead to me. And my father signed it.'

'Of course he signed. How could he do anything else? He loved your mother, Darius; he couldn't abandon her.'

'No. I was safe and she needed him.'

A kingfisher flashed from a post into the water. A duck rounded up her fluffy brood. Somewhere along the riverbank a child shrieked with excitement. All bright, wonderful things, but what had been a charmed day now had a dark edge to it.

'What happened?' she asked.

'My grandfather handed over the cash, my father left for the airport and that's the last anyone ever heard of him or my mother. Not that anyone was looking.'

'I'm so sorry.'

'When he died, I insisted that Ramsey carry out a proper search for them before the house was put on the market. If either of them were alive this belonged to them.'

'Was there nothing in the house you could sell?'

'Unfortunately, the Hadleys weren't great art collectors. No one had the foresight to commission Gainsborough to paint the family portraits, buy Impressionists when they were cheap, snap up a Picasso or two.'

'Ancestors can be so short-sighted. What about land? Or the cottages?'

'The land is green belt and can't be built on. The cottages are occupied by former members of staff. I'll use what's left from the sale to rehouse them.'

'And the London flat?'

'When he was diagnosed with Alzheimer's, Ramsey insisted my grandfather sign a power of enduring attorney in my name. I sold the flat to finance his nursing care. There's some money left, but not enough to pay the inheritance tax.'

'Your grandfather might have raised you, Darius Hadley, but you are nothing like him.'

'At seventeen I was halfway there. Arrogant, spoilt, thought I owned the world. If I'd stayed here, I would have been exactly like him.'

She wanted to tell him he was wrong. She just tightened her hold around his waist and for a moment he buried his face in her hair. After a while, he said, 'My grandmother came to my first exhibition. She was dying by then, but she defied him that once. I went to her funeral but when my grandfather saw me he thought I was my father and began ranting at me...'

'Did Ramsey discover any more about what happened to your parents?' she said, desperate to distract him from the horror of that image.

'Only rumours. That the family had been caught trying to leave the country and they were all either rotting in jail or dead. That my father had made the whole story up just to get his hands on the money and he and Soraya were living somewhere in the sun. That my father was the victim of a honeypot trap and once he'd handed over the money he was disposed of. Take your pick.'

'No. Not the last one.'

And for the first time the smallest hint of a smile softened his face. 'You know that for a fact, do you?'

'One hundred per cent,' she said. 'Maybe, for a passion so intense that nothing else mattered they might have surrendered their son. Considered it their penance. But if it had been a con, Soraya would have got rid of you the second she realised she was pregnant.'

Totally focused on him, on his pain, she saw the gone-in-a-moment swirl of emotion deep in his eyes; scudding clouds of joy, sorrow, dark and light, every shade of grey.

'You didn't know any of this? Growing up?' He shook his head. 'Gary. Gary told you.' Who else? 'Was it one too many beers on one of your owl-or badger-watching adventures?'

'It wasn't beer that loosened his tongue. It was a motorbike. He had an old bike that he'd rebuilt from scrap and he taught me to ride when I was barely tall enough to reach the pedals. When I got a brand-new bike for my seventeenth birthday he was the first person I wanted to share it with.'

'Oh…' She could see what was coming.

'Young, brash, spoilt, it never occurred to me how he would feel. Obviously, I'd always had more than him, but this was grown-up stuff, stuff he wanted and could never afford on the pittance my grandfather paid him. Stuff I didn't have to work for, but would come to me just because my name was Hadley. It was like a chasm had opened up between us and he lashed out with the only weapon he had to put himself back on top. It just came out. How my father had sold me so that he could be with his whore.'

'Chinese whispers,' she said, perfectly able to imagine how gossip whispered in the village had been distorted, twisted with every retelling. Garbled, warped…

'He was already back-pedalling, trying to take it back before I'd fired up the bike to go and confront my grandfather, but nothing could unsay those words. I demanded to know the truth and the old man didn't spare me. He said I was old enough to know the truth and he laid it out in black and white. My father had betrayed his wife, abandoned his unborn child for a—'

'Darius…'

She'd cut in, not wanting him to repeat the word, but he raised his hand to touch her cheek, looked down at her. 'Let me finish. Get it out in the light.' He made a gesture that took in the sagging boathouse, the house out of sight behind the trees. 'This is all he really cared about. Preserv-

ing the house, preserving the name. Nothing that was real.'
He took his wallet from his back pocket, opened it, handed
her a photograph. 'This is what my father cared about.'

'She's beautiful, Darius.' The snapshot was of a young
woman laughing at something the photographer had said,
her eyes filled with so much love that it took her breath
away. To be looked at like that... 'Where did you get this?'

'It arrived in an envelope after my grandmother came
to the exhibition. No note.'

'A smile like that against four hundred years of history. No contest.' She looked up at Darius, at the same
dark eyes... 'She would have come for you. Crawled over
broken glass. No piece of paper would have stopped her.'

'Yes. I've always known, deep down, that they're dead
but I hoped...'

'Where did you go? How did you live?' she asked.
'When you left?'

'Not in a cardboard box under Waterloo Bridge,' he said,
apparently reading her mind. 'I went to Bristol, sold the
bike, rented a room, signed on at a sixth form college and
got a job stacking supermarket shelves.'

'The *bike*?' she said. 'You told me you walked out!'

'Metaphorically,' he said, but the darkness had been replaced with the beginnings of a smile. 'I wanted...I needed
you to walk with me.'

'All you had to do was ask.' For a moment they just
looked at one another until it was too intense, too full of
the unspoken words in her head and she scrambled for another thought. 'What happened to Gary?' she asked, her
voice catching in her throat.

'You always go straight to the heart of what's important, Natasha. I'm banging on about ancient history and
you bring me crashing back to earth with what's real. The
human element.'

'I wasn't dismissing what happened to you. But you said

it, Darius. You had everything going for you while he had nothing and I can't imagine your grandfather was a man to overlook such an indiscretion.'

'You're right, of course. I didn't betray Gary but it couldn't have been anyone else. Mary told me that my grandfather gave him a choice—he left the estate and never returned, or his father and grandmother would lose their jobs and the cottages that went with them.'

'Hurting, angry, lashing out... He made them all pay.'

'If I'd stayed I could have stopped that.'

'How? By bargaining with him? What would you have surrendered to save him?' He had no answer to that. 'He would have had you at his mercy, Darius. You were both better off away from here.'

'Right again. My mistake was not stopping to pick up Gary on the way out. I'll always regret that.'

'I don't imagine you were thinking very clearly,' she said, untangling herself from his arms. 'Come on,' she said, standing up, picking up her shoes. 'There's grass to cut, doors to be washed...'

Darius caught her hand. 'Thank you.'

There was nothing she could think of to say, so she stood on her toes and kissed him. It was supposed to be brief, sweet, over in a moment, but neither of them wanted it to stop. Even when the kiss was over they didn't want to let go.

'If we don't go back soon, they'll wonder where we are.'

'You wanted to take a good look at the boathouse, check if it will have to be pulled down or whether it can be restored,' he offered.

'Right,' she said, leaning her forehead against his chest before forcing herself to step away, get back to washing down paintwork. When she turned around her brother James was leaning on the wall of the boathouse, arms folded over the fishing rod he was holding. He'd clearly been there for some time.

CHAPTER ELEVEN

DARIUS WAS THE first to recover. 'Did you manage to catch supper?' he asked.

'With half a dozen children screaming and splashing about? They've scared away every fish within five miles so we thought we'd leave the women to sort out lunch while we walk down to the village and test the local ale. It's a Sunday holiday tradition. There'll be a pint waiting when you've finished checking out the structural integrity of the boathouse.'

He didn't wait for an answer.

'Did that sound like a friendly invitation,' Darius asked, 'or am I going to be pinned to the dartboard?'

'The pre-Sunday lunch trip to the pub is a mysterious male tradition,' she replied, 'from which mothers, wives and sisters are excluded. All I can tell you with any certainty is that you're the first man I've kissed who's ever been invited by my brothers to join them.'

'So that's good?'

'Probably, but if they do pin you to the dartboard by your ears I'll give them all particularly noxious jobs tomorrow.'

'I'll want pictures,' he said.

'I'll post them on Facebook,' she promised. 'When are you leaving?'

'After lunch. I've got to do what I should have done on Friday before the foundry starts up on Monday morning.

I can't promise to be here on Saturday. Once we start, we don't stop until it's done.'

'I didn't expect you to come this weekend. It's been…'

'Fun, Natasha. It's been fun.'

'Even getting beaten by my mother at Scrabble?' He said nothing. 'You let her win? Go!' she said, laughing, pushing him away. 'Before your beer gets warm.'

Before she dragged him under the nearest bush.

Darius, pausing for a break, checked his phone. There was a text from Natasha.

Needs full structural survey. Xxx

She'd attached a photograph of the boathouse.

Grinning, he took a selfie and sent it back with a text.

Needs total scrub down. Xxx

Natasha had kept in touch, sending pictures of the house emerging from its cocoon, but it was her suggestive little texts that made him smile. He'd replied with pictures of bones emerging from moulds. No comment needed.

Tash sighed with pleasure. Hadley Chase was gleaming, as perfect as she could have hoped, brought back to life, not just by sunlight and polish, but the laughter of children, the smell of baking, the armfuls of flowers from the long neglected cutting garden supplemented by cow parsley, willow herb gathered by her sisters-in-law to create huge free-form flower arrangements.

Tables had been laid in the conservatory for tea, the hired water boiler and teapots lined up and ready, the doors thrown open to the lawn, where the children were playing croquet with a set Harry had found in one of the outbuildings as the first cars began to arrive.

'It looks magical, Tash. If Darius were here he wouldn't be able to let this go,' Patsy said.

'Maybe that's why he's staying away.'

'Or not. Isn't that his Land Rover?' Patsy had offered to drive her home so that he could take the Land Rover back to London. 'Go and say hello,' she said as he drove straight round to the back of the house.

'Too late,' she said as the editor of the *Country Chronicle* advanced towards her, hand outstretched.

'Tash! I'm so glad to see you looking so well.'

'As you can see, Kevin, rumours of my breakdown were not just exaggerated but completely untrue.' She took his hand. 'Thank you for coming today. It means a great deal to me.'

'You have Peter Black to thank for that. He is so angry with you that he threatened to withdraw all Morgan and Black advertising if I covered the Hadley Chase open day.'

'A bit of a hollow threat, I'd have thought. There is nowhere else for this kind of property.'

'Hollow or not, I can't allow advertisers to dictate what we print.' He looked around. 'I have to congratulate you, my dear; your campaign has caused quite a stir. The children are a nice touch, by the way. Can we photograph them with the house in the background for our feature?'

'Feature?'

He smiled. 'Two pages? Maybe more if Darius Hadley will talk to me. I don't like being threatened.'

Darius stood back, watching Natasha greet visitors, delegate various members of her family to show them around the house, confident, professional, totally focused on the task she'd set herself. She'd told him she was the best and she was right. For a while she'd been entirely his but after this her world would reclaim her.

It was what he'd wanted, he reminded himself. It was the way he always wanted things. A hot flirtation and then move on. No emotional engagement.

Too late. It had been too late the moment he'd set eyes

on her, too late the minute he'd allowed her to stay. Kissed her. He'd let down his guard, done what he'd sworn he'd never do. He'd fallen hopelessly, ridiculously in love and where once he would have thought that made him a fool, he now knew that it made him a better man.

The thought made him smile and he was just going to her, to tell her that, when Morgan appeared on the doorstep. He instinctively took a step forward to protect her, but she had it covered, her voice clear, calm, composed.

'Miles? This is unexpected.'

'I'm here to apologise, Tash. I've been made a fool of.'

'Really?' She didn't step back to let him inside.

'That idiot Toby has gone.'

'Gone?' That rattled the cool.

'He's signed a contract to play professional rugby in Italy. It seems that's where he was last month. Not on a tour, but having trials, medicals, negotiating a deal. When his parents found out they were furious so they cooked up this scheme to cause a crisis, get rid of you and force him to forget the sports nonsense and put the company, his family first. He arrived at the reception not knowing what the hell was going on, but his mother cried and he was cornered.'

'Why on earth couldn't they just let him be happy?'

'Families, inheritance…' He shrugged. 'You know how it is.'

'Yes…' she said. 'Yes, I know.' She cleared her throat. 'Was Janine involved?'

'She and Peter were always…close. Let's just say that she's currently seeking alternative career opportunities.'

'And what about Morgan and Black?' she asked.

'There is no Black. That is the second reason I'm here. I'm looking for a new partner, Tash. I would like it to be you.'

Darius didn't wait for her answer. He'd just heard the

sound of hell freezing over and he'd felt the chill to his bones.

He hoped to escape unnoticed but Laura was in the kitchen, loading up a trolley with sandwiches, cakes, scones.

'Darius! How lovely to see you. Does Tash know you're here?'

He shook his head. 'She's busy.'

'Is it going well out there?'

'There seem to be a lot of people. Can I give you a hand?'

'I've got it covered. Why don't you take a last look around while the house is looking at its best? The way it must have been when you lived here.'

'It might have looked like this, Laura. Polished within an inch of its life, flowers everywhere, but it never felt like this. It had no heart. You and Derrick, your family, Natasha...'

He stuck his hands in his pockets, stared up at the ceiling, struggling to find words that would convey how they'd transformed this place. Made it somewhere he wanted to come, could walk in and not feel that he was somehow wanting. A want he'd understood when he'd learned the truth. He was a second-best replacement for the boy who'd died in the womb.

There was only one word... 'Love... Love has done this. Your family came together to do this for Natasha because you love her. That's the difference.'

Laura put a sympathetic hand on his arm.

'You're tired, Darius. Working all hours at the foundry and selling a house is as stressful as death or divorce, even when you've only lived there a few years. Four hundred years...' She shook her head. 'I can't begin to imagine how you must be feeling.'

'No...'

He'd had a window, a few hours, and he'd grabbed it,

wanting to be here, to stand by Natasha, but she didn't need him. This was what she'd been working for. The prize. She had everything she wanted.

'Sit down. I'll get you a cup of tea and something to eat. Something to keep up your blood sugar levels. There are cucumber sandwiches, scones, or I've made some Bakewell tarts?'

'Try spiced ginger.'

Natasha was standing in the doorway, flushed, laughing, and his heart leapt as it always did when he saw her. And each time it was different. That first time it had been purely physical, like a rocket going off. The rocket was still there, but now there was so much more. She was so much more. But her laughter, her joy was for something else.

'Well, I'm sure you could do with a break, too,' her mother said, 'so why don't you get it for him while I take the trolley through to the conservatory?'

Natasha walked across the kitchen, sat on his lap, put her arms around his neck and kissed him. 'How are your blood sugar levels now?' she asked, her eyes sparkling, the pulse in her throat thrumming with excitement.

'Up. Definitely up…' he said. 'In fact, this might be a very good time to check out the structural integrity of the boathouse.'

'Tash…' She slid off his lap, tucked a stray strand of hair behind her ear and was four feet away by the time her father appeared in the doorway. 'There's a Mr Darwish asking for you. I've put him in the library.'

'Yikes! Major property buyer.' She stopped at the door, leaned back. 'By the way, we're getting a double page spread in the *Country Chronicle*. Kevin Rose, the editor, knows you are *the* Darius Hadley. I'm afraid you're busted.'

'It was only a matter of time before someone made the connection,' he said. 'Will it help if I talk to him?' he asked, as if he hadn't heard their conversation.

'Darling, if you talk to him we'll be on the front cover.'

'Great,' he said as she flew out of the door. 'I'll do that, then.'

They both watched the space where she'd been for a moment. 'Her career is her world, Darius. She had a bad start in life and maybe we overprotected her.'

'She told me. All of it.'

'She threw up a job that had been her dream to get away. Be independent. Prove something to us.'

'To herself, I think.' That she wasn't that kid lying in a cancer ward, or a basket-case teenager. And she'd done it, becoming the top-selling agent for her company with a bright red BMW sports coupé to prove it. And when she'd been knocked back she'd proved it all over again. 'You knew she turned down the National Trust job?'

He smiled. 'She told you about that too.' He crossed to the fridge. 'I play golf with the man she would have worked for. He asked me why she'd turned the job down—a first, apparently. I never told her mother. Beer?'

'No… Once I've talked to Kevin Rose, I have to get back to London.' She'd given him so much; the least he could do for her was deliver the front page of the *Country Chronicle*. With that very public demonstration of her ability to turn disaster into triumph, she would be able to name her price when she was negotiating terms with Miles Morgan. 'This was just a flying visit. I'm installing a sculpture in Lambourn in a week or two and I had to come down to look at the site.' It was a pathetic excuse by any standards, but Derrick accepted it at face value. 'If I don't manage to catch Natasha before I go, tell her…' What? What could he say? 'Tell her she's better than the best.'

'Darius? Can you talk?'

'If you're quick.'

Tash frowned. Nothing had seemed quite the same between them since the open day. Okay, she'd been busy, he had to be somewhere else, but he'd left without saying goodbye and something was missing. The sex—snatched in brief moments when he wasn't working—was still stunningly hot, but the perfect focus that made her believe that she was the only woman in the world had gone. And those fun 'dates' had been forgotten. It was as if the shutters had come down and she was afraid that the reality of the sale had cut deeper than he'd anticipated. In which case he wasn't going to want to hear this.

Or he was ready to move on. In which case he would.

'I'm working,' he prompted impatiently.

'Yes... Sorry... I just wanted you to know that I've got two firm offers for the house on the table.'

'Two? Are we going to have a bidding war?' He sounded bored rather than excited by the prospect.

'Behave yourself. One is from an overseas buyer who's looking for a small country house to complement his London apartment. He's offering the guide price.'

'Take it.'

'The second offer is lower. I've negotiated them up from their opening bid but it's still half a million below the guide price.'

'So why are we talking about it?'

'Because it's a better package.'

'Can you keep this short? They're waiting to weld the heart in place.'

'Really? You're that close?'

'Natasha, please...'

'Sorry. The second offer is from the IT company across the river. They're expanding and need more space but there are planning restrictions on their own site. The thing is, most of the staff live locally and their children go to the village school so they don't want to move.'

'Then maybe they should up their offer.'

'It's lower, but it's actually worth more. I've managed to exclude the estate cottages, which means you won't have to rehouse the tenants and you'll have more disposable income from the sale. Sitting tenants will also affect the resale value of the properties so it will help reduce the inheritance tax bill. Repairs and maintenance can be offset against tax and the cottages will be realisable assets in the future. Finally—'

'There's more?'

'Finally,' she said, 'they know Gary; he's done jobs for them in the past and they will keep him on as caretaker and odd job man with a salary and company benefits that he could never have hoped to achieve from your grandfather's estate.'

She could have simply presented Darius with the easy offer, job done. They both had what they wanted. House sold, reputation restored and she'd always known that there was no future in this relationship. It wasn't his fault that she'd got four-letter-word involved and she wasn't about to drag it out to the bitter end. Better let go while they were still friends.

But when the first bid had come in from the IT company she'd immediately seen the possibilities—the value to the village, to the people Darius felt responsible for—and she'd hammered out the best deal she'd ever put together. One she would always be proud of. Not only did it ensure that Hadley continued to thrive, but it would keep a link for Darius with the village that bore his name.

'Their surveyor has just left,' she said. 'Say yes and the money will be in the bank by the end of the month.' She waited. 'Hello? Am I talking to myself here?'

'No...' He sounded bemused. 'I'm simply speechless. You are an extraordinary woman, Natasha Gordon. Nothing left to prove. To anyone.'

'Thanks…' Her voice caught in her throat. 'I'll, um, let Ramsey have the details, then, shall I?'

'I suppose so.'

'Darius? Is this what you want? Only if you've changed your mind about selling, tell me now.'

'Why would I do that? Hadley Chase is the last place on earth I'd ever live.'

'I don't know. It's just that you seem a little scratchy.'

'Do I? Why don't you come over and smooth me out?'

Smoothing him out was something she'd taken great pleasure in doing on numerous occasions while he'd been working twelve-hour days, but there was something decidedly off in that invitation. As if he wanted her, but hated himself for it. Or maybe he wanted her to hate him. Whatever it was, all the pleasure drained out of her day.

'I thought you were working,' she said. An alternative to the flat *no* that she knew was the right response. That she couldn't quite bring herself to say.

'You've got me,' he said. And that had sounded like relief.

'I'll call Ramsey now,' she said. 'Get things underway.' He didn't answer. 'Darius? Is this it?'

'Yes,' he said. Abrupt. To the point. 'Job done. Time to think about your fee.'

'The bronze…'

Tash swallowed. No. He'd said it. Job done. And they both knew that they weren't talking about the sale of a house but, after all they'd been through, shared, there was no way she could sit for him like a model being paid by the hour.

'You've done enough. Your interview with Kevin Rose was above and beyond. Do you need any help clearing the house?' she asked. 'There are some lovely pieces of furniture here.' She was sitting at his grandmother's desk and if she could have afforded it she'd have made an offer.

'No. There's nothing there I want. Ramsey will deal with it.'

Nothing? Really? She sat back. Where had the photograph of his mother come from? It could only have been his grandmother. She stroked her hands across the lovely desk. She'd seen one very like it on an antiques programme on the television. That one had had a secret drawer.

Darius stared at the phone for a long time before he hit end call. He'd lied about working. The horse was finished, delivered to the man who'd commissioned it and awaiting positioning in the place where it would forever be leaping over an unseen fence.

He tossed the phone on the sofa where Natasha had sat on the day she'd come to see him, promising him a whole lot more than the sale of his house when she'd looked at him with those big blue eyes and invited him to try her cake.

Senseless. Except that he hadn't lost his senses. He'd found them. Found something he'd never truly known as a boy. Found whatever it was his father had found, because family history suggested that the 'perfect marriage' had been his grandfather's idea. His way of controlling the future.

It was something he'd been running away from as a man, afraid that, like his father, he'd lose himself to something he couldn't control. But he'd been so wrong. You didn't lose yourself; you found yourself in love. Became whole.

He walked across to the clay sculpture that he'd begun the day he drove back from Hadley Chase, knowing that it was over. He'd worked in the foundry in the day, worked on this at night, capturing for ever that moment when she'd reached out to him in her sleep.

He hadn't needed the drawing. His hands had worked the clay, formed the well-known curves, her shoulders, the bend of her knee, her hair tumbled against the pillow.

His fingers curled around the hand extended towards him, that he couldn't see for the tears blinding him.

'Darius...'
   'Natasha?'
   'I need to see you. Can you spare me half an hour?'
   'I'm at the studio. Come over.'
   Tash ended the brief call. One last time, she promised herself. One last time.
   It was late by the time she arrived at the studio. The studio door stood open and she looked through but the sun was low and the interior was dim. 'Darius?'
   He was taking down the photographs of the horse, clearing the decks and, as she hesitated in the doorway, he half turned and it was all still there and more. The heart-leap, the joy, only a hundred times more powerful, underscored by every touch, every kiss, every memory they had made together.
   'No cake?' he asked.
   'No time,' she said. 'I've been rushed off my feet with work. It's dark in here.'
   He flicked a light switch and illuminated the area by his desk, sofa, and she walked across, put down the thick envelope she was carrying.
   'More paperwork?' he asked.
   'No. I...' This was going to be the last time she saw him and she didn't want it to be like this... 'I was looking at your grandmother's desk and it occurred to me that I'd seen one very like it on an antiques programme. On the television.'
   'You're here to tell me that it's worth a fortune?'
   'No. I'm here to tell you that it had a secret drawer.'
   He became very still. 'That was in it?'
   'No, it was empty, but it's what got me looking through the rest of the house. I knew there had to be more than that one photograph. I found this in the attic.'

She opened the envelope, tipped out the contents. Photographs, letters that had come from his parents' flat in Paris. The report of the car accident where they'd died, fleeing across the border with her family. Their death certificates. A letter his father had left for him in case anything went wrong. He'd known the danger...

'I'll leave you to look at them.'

'No!' His hand gripped her arm, holding her there beside him, and he picked up a photograph of his mother holding him in her arms, his father standing beside him with such a look of love on his face that it had brought tears to her eyes when she'd seen it.

And suddenly the stiffness, the self-protective armour melted and she was in his arms, holding him, wiping the tears from his cheeks, murmuring hush sounds as he thanked her.

'Did you ever see your grandfather again?' Tash asked a long time later, after he'd read the letter, looked at the photographs. 'After your grandmother's funeral?'

'That was when Ramsey realised how sick he was. He wouldn't have it, of course, and it was only after a fall and a stay in hospital that we were able to move him into a nursing home for his own safety. I used to go and visit him. Mostly he had no idea who I was; occasionally he thought I was my father and asked me how Christabel was. How long before the baby was due.'

'It's a terrible thing, Alzheimer's,' she said. 'It robs you of the chance to end things properly. Tell people that you love them.'

'Say the words while you can?'

'I...' How could she say yes and not tell him that she loved him? How could she load him with that emotional burden? 'It's complicated.'

'That's what I thought, but I'm going to make it simple.'

He stood up, took her hand and led her across the studio and switched on the floodlights above his work plinth, lighting up a sculpted figure, a scene that was imprinted on her heart.

She took a step closer, looked at herself as Darius had seen her. The figure lying semi-prone amongst a tangle of sheets was sensuous, beautiful, and he hadn't had to reveal her ribs or her organs to show her inner depths. Every thought, every feeling was exposed. Anyone who looked at it would know that this was a woman in love.

The detail was astonishing. In the modelling of the hands, the tiny creases behind the knee, the dimples above her buttocks. They hadn't been in the drawing. He'd done this from memory.

When she turned he was there, watching her.

'She's beautiful, Darius,' she said a little shakily, 'but she's going to be a bit of a tight fit on the mantelpiece.'

'She won't leave here. She's not for display in a gallery window. This was personal, Natasha, for me, an attempt to hold on to something rare, something special. But once it was done I realised that only the real flesh-and-blood woman will do. Tomorrow it will be nothing but a lump of clay.'

'You're going to destroy this?'

'Why would I keep it? Every time I looked at it I'd know what kind of fool I was for sitting back and making a sketch instead of responding to that invitation and getting back into bed with you. For not saying the words. A statue won't laugh with me, cry with me, knock itself out making the world right for me.'

'No.' It could never do that. 'But it will always be perfect. Never grow old. Never demand anything of you—'

'Never give anything back,' he said. 'Never...'

'Never?' she prompted.

'Never love me back.'

He'd said the words as if he was tearing lumps off his flesh.

Not just hot, gorgeous sex but something bigger, something deeper. The one thing that in his privileged youth he'd never known. The one thing that in his successful career he'd never allowed himself.

'Love?'

'The biggest four-letter word in the dictionary,' he said. 'You're right; you should say the words rather than live with regret. I love you, Natasha Gordon, with all my heart. That's it. No claim, no expectation and absolutely no regret.'

Now she was the one with tears stinging her eyes. 'I told myself I didn't want you to feel guilt, Darius, that I wanted you to remember me with pleasure, but I was afraid to put myself on the line... Your courage shames me, you deserve more but I love you, Darius Hadley. With all my heart.' His expression was so intense that for a moment she couldn't speak. Then, never taking her eyes from his, she made a gesture in the direction of the sculpture. 'It's there, on display, for all the world to see.'

For a moment neither of them moved, breathed, and then he kissed her so tenderly, holding her as if she were made of glass. It was a shatteringly beautiful moment, nothing to do with sex, but a promise...

When he drew back, resting his forehead against hers, he said, 'There are a couple of other things I have to say. I need a plus one at the unveiling of the horse next week. The Queen is doing the honours so you'll need a hat.'

She blinked back the stupid tears and began to smile. 'A hat? Right.'

'I've looked up dancing classes but I need a partner. And how do you fancy seeing the new James Bond movie?'

'That's three things.'

'Is that too demanding? Only the thing is, Natasha, I'm looking for more than high-octane no-commitment sex. I'm looking for a grown-up full-time relationship with a woman who knows what she wants—a woman who will have time for me and a family as well as a career. So I'm asking—is that something you can fit around your new job?'

'New job?'

'Didn't hell just freeze over?' he asked. 'I overheard Morgan offer you a partnership.'

And suddenly everything fell into place. 'Is that why you've gone all moody on me?' she asked.

'Moody?'

'Moody, shuttered, closed-up, just like you were when we first met.'

'It's what you wanted.'

'Absolutely.'

'So why didn't you tell me?'

'Maybe because you got all moody, shuttered, closed up,' she said, turning to him on legs that were shaking as she realised how close she'd come to losing this. 'No time for anything but a quickie. Running away. If you'd been talking to me I'd have told you all about it. And that I turned him down.'

'But...' His frown was total confusion. 'You weren't even tempted?'

'I told you, Darius, I could never trust a man who treated me the way Miles did, but it wasn't just that. I like being my own boss. Tailoring my sales pitch to meet individual needs. Looking for the right house for a client who appreciates good service. I like doing things my own way.'

'I like doing things your way, too,' he replied as she began slipping her buttons one by one.

'I have to get up,' Tash protested, making an effort to wriggle out of Darius's warm embrace. 'I've got an appointment at eleven.'

'Where are you going?' he asked, his hand on her belly

spooning her against him as he nuzzled the tender spot behind her ear.

'Sussex. I've found the perfect house for a client and she's flying in from Hong Kong to see it.' She bit her lip as his hand moved lower.

'Is this the one you've been raving about?'

'Mmmm… Can I tempt you to a day out in the country?' she asked in an attempt to distract him. Distract herself. She really, really had to get going… 'Once the viewing is over we could take a walk on the Downs, have lunch at a country pub. Can you spare the time?'

'No,' he said, moving so that she flopped over onto her back and was looking up at him. 'Can you?'

No! The answer was definitely, almost certainly, maybe *nooooo*, but his lips were teasing hers, his hand was much lower and the word never made it beyond a thought.

Damn it, he always did that! She woke in plenty of time to get where she had to be and then he ambushed her. She grinned as her little van pulled out of the mews and she headed south towards the Sussex Downs. It was just as well that she'd started putting the alarm forward half an hour or she'd be permanently late.

As it was, she needn't have worried. She picked up the keys from the selling agent in good time but when she pulled up outside the gates there was no sign of her client, only a voicemail message on her phone saying that she'd been held up, but would she go ahead and take photographs for her of the garden and especially of the grotto.

Terrific. She just hoped it wasn't a wind-up. Over the last few months there had been a few of those—wasted journeys to see non-existent clients, non-existent houses. Rivals who resented the splash of publicity following her sale of Hadley Chase. The feature on her new consultancy in the *Country Chronicle*. She'd got smarter about checking before she wasted time or money on them, but this one had checked out.

She took her camera and her camcorder, filming the walk up the drive to the sprawling house, smothered in an ancient wisteria that would look so pretty in the spring.

It was absolutely perfect—and not just for her client.

There was room for an office, a cottage in the grounds for Patsy—who was working for her now—and Michael. And a small barn tucked away at the rear.

It was a house where two people could grow their lives, their family, and there was no use kidding herself. The only reason she'd wanted Darius to come with her was so that he would see it and fall in love with it too.

The mews cottage was great, but there was no room for an office for her, no room for anything except the two of them indulging in a lot of that high-octane sex. She swallowed. He was the one who'd said he wanted more—commitment, a family.

She didn't need to tour the house to take photographs. She'd done that, leaving them where Darius could see them, hoping... She'd taken a few of the garden but, with a sigh, she set off to take more.

The low sun was gleaming through grasses, scarlet dahlias that were making the most of a lingering autumn. The leaves in the hidden woodland dell that housed a grotto created in the bole of what had once been a huge tree.

She'd seen photographs but hadn't been down there. Today, though, she followed a narrow rill that fell in steps before dropping into a natural stream that trickled into a pool within the grotto. Light was filtering from above and more than just water gleamed in the darkness.

None of this had been in the agent's photographs and, curious, she stepped down. For a moment she couldn't believe what she was seeing and then, as she did, she caught her breath.

It was a bronze of the figure Darius had made, that he'd said he was going to destroy. She was here, lying on a bed, surrounded by a pool—a woodland nymph reaching out for her lover.

She didn't need the tingle at the base of her spine, didn't have to turn around, to know Darius was there with her.

'It's beautiful,' she said.

'Yes.'

She turned. 'How did you know?'

'I didn't. I gave you a description of the house that would be perfect for us. Five bedrooms, room for a home office, an outbuilding of some sort, a staff cottage, and I waited for you to find it.'

'But what about Mrs Harper?'

'There is no Mrs Harper. I'm your client.'

'You? But…' She shook her head. 'But how did you organise this?' she demanded, flinging out a hand in the direction of the sculpture.

'The owner indulged me. Unfortunately, the downside to that was his insistence that it stay, whether we buy or not.'

'But…but…but…' she spluttered. And then she knew. 'You've already bought it, haven't you?'

'It seemed wise, just in case he got a better offer. I've leased out the studio. You decide whether we keep the mews or your flat for our London bolthole; you can find a tenant for the other, which leaves only two questions.'

'Two?'

'The first is: will you marry me?'

She swallowed.

'What's the second question?' she asked.

'I think you'll find that your mother is hoping for a Christmas wedding. Are you happy with that?' He waited as she struggled with a throat that was Sahara-dry. 'If you need a hint, yes and yes are the correct answers.'

She flung herself into his arms, laughing and crying a

little at the same time. 'Yes, and yes, and yes, and yes...'
And then she threw a punch at him. 'You discussed it with
my mother!'

'Let's just say there was some heavy hinting going on
the last time we went for Sunday lunch.'

'Oh, good grief. It's not compulsory, you know!'

'Too late. We've booked the church.' And then he was
kissing her and she said nothing more for a very long time.

Wedding bells, fairy lights glistening over a white frost.
Red berries and ivy twisted around pew ends and around
the Christmas roses in her bouquet. White velvet and her
grandmother's pearls. And Darius.

Darius waiting for her at the altar. Darius holding out
his hand to her, folding it in his and holding on tight, then
smiling as if this was the best day in his life. And Natasha
smiling back because it was the best day of hers. So far.

* * * * *

MILLS & BOON

MODERN

Power and Passion

Prepare to be swept off your feet by sophisticated, sexy and seductive heroes, in some of the world's most glamourous and romantic locations, where power and passion collide.

JOIN THE
MILLS & BOON
BOOKCLUB

* **FREE** delivery direct to your door

* **EXCLUSIVE** offers every month

* **EXCITING** rewards programme

50% OFF
YOUR FIRST
PARCEL

Join today at
Millsandboon.co.uk/Bookclub